PENGUIN

SKETCHES FROM A HUNTER'S ALBUM

IVAN TURGENEV, Russian novelist, was born in Oryol in 1818, and was the first Russian writer to enjoy an international reputation. Born into the gentry himself, and dominated in his boyhood by a tyrannical mother, he swore a 'Hannibal's oath' against serfdom. After studying in Moscow, St Petersburg and Berlin (1838–41), where he was influenced by German Idealism, he returned to Russia an ardent liberal and Westernist. He gained fame as an author with a series of brilliant, sensitive pictures of peasant life. Although he had also written poetry, plays and short stories, it was as a novelist that his greatest work was to be done. His novels are noted for the poetic 'atmosphere' of their country settings, the contrast between hero and heroine, and for the objective portrayal of heroes representative of stages in the development of the Russian intelligentsia during the period 1840–70. Exiled to his estate of Spasskoye (1852–5) because of his *Sketches*, he later wrote *Rudin* (1856), *Home of the Gentry* (1859), *On the Eve* (1860) and *Fathers and Sons* (1862), but was so disillusioned by the obtuse criticism which greeted this last work that he spent the rest of his life abroad at Baden-Baden (1862–70) and in Paris (1871–83). His last novels, *Smoke* (1867) and *Virgin Soil* (1877), lacked the balance and topicality of his earlier work. He died in Bougival, near Paris, in 1883.

RICHARD FREEBORN, Emeritus Professor of Russian Literature at the University of London, was previously Professor of Russian Studies at Manchester University, a visiting Professor at the University of California at Los Angeles, and for ten years Hulme Lecturer in Russian at Brasenose College, Oxford, where he graduated. He has published widely on Russian literature including *Turgenev, A Study*, *The Rise of the Russian Novel* and *The Russian Revolutionary Novel*, and was awarded a D.Lit. in 1984 by the University of London for his scholarly contributions to his subject. More recently he has completed a study of the famous Russian critic, Vissarion Belinskii. His other translations of Turgenev include *Home of the Gentry* (Penguin Classics), *Rudin* (Penguin Classics), *First Love and Other Stories*, *A Month in the Country* and *Fathers and Sons*. He has also translated Dostoevsky's *An Accidental Family (Podrostok)*.

IVAN TURGENEV

SKETCHES
FROM A
HUNTER'S ALBUM

TRANSLATED WITH AN
INTRODUCTION AND NOTES BY
RICHARD FREEBORN

PENGUIN BOOKS

PENGUIN BOOKS

Published by the Penguin Group
Penguin Books Ltd, 80 Strand, London WC2R 0RL, England
Penguin Putnam Inc., 375 Hudson Street, New York, New York 10014, USA
Penguin Books Australia Ltd, 250 Camberwell Road, Camberwell, Victoria 3124, Australia
Penguin Books Canada Ltd, 10 Alcorn Avenue, Toronto, Ontario, Canada M4V 3B2
Penguin Books India (P) Ltd, 11 Community Centre, Panchsheel Park, New Delhi – 110 017, India
Penguin Books (NZ) Ltd, Cnr Rosedale and Airborne Roads, Albany, Auckland, New Zealand
Penguin Books (South Africa) (Pty) Ltd, 24 Sturdee Avenue, Rosebank 2196, South Africa

Penguin Books Ltd, Registered Offices: 80 Strand, London WC2R 0RL, England

www.penguin.com

The following stories were first published, in this translation, in
1967, under the same title: 'Khor and Kalinych', 'Yermolay and the
Miller's Wife', 'Bezhin Lea', 'Kasyan from the Beautiful Lands',
'Bailiff', 'Two Landowners', 'Death', 'Singers', 'Meeting', 'Hamlet
of the Shchigrovsky District', 'Living Relic', 'Clatter of Wheels',
'Forest and Steppe', 'The Russian German' and 'The Reformer and the
Russian German'.
Translation, Introduction and Notes copyright © Richard Freeborn, 1967

The following stories are first published in this translation, 1990:
'Raspberry Water', 'District Doctor', 'My Neighbour Radilov', 'Farmer
Ovsyanikov', 'Lgov', 'The Office', 'Loner', 'Lebedyan', 'Tatyana
Borisovna and her Nephew', 'Pyotr Petrovich Karataev', 'Chertopkhanov
and Nedopyuskin' and 'The End of Chertopkhanov'.
Translation, Introduction and Notes copyright © Richard Freeborn, 1990

036

Printed and bound in Great Britain by Clays Ltd, Elcograf S.p.A.

ISBN-13: 978–0–14–044522–0

www.greenpenguin.co.uk

CONTENTS

INTRODUCTION

———————— ❧ ————————

Turgenev's *Sketches* were originally published in the Russian journal *The Contemporary* between 1847 and 1851. In 1852 they were published for the first time in a separate edition – a circumstance that led to Turgenev's arrest, followed by exile to his estate of Spasskoye. Much later, during the last decade of his life, he added further *Sketches* to those already published, with the result that the total number of such *Sketches* reached twenty-five.

This full translation has been given the title *Sketches from a Hunter's Album*, rather than the slightly more usual – and perhaps slightly less accurate – title *A Sportsman's Sketches* or *A Sportsman's Notebook*, etc., because Turgenev's work, although usually transliterated as *Zapiski okhotnika* and literally meaning *Notes of a Hunter*, is not so much about hunting as about the rural world of Russia that he knew so well. It is essentially an album of pictures drawn from Russian country life in the period prior to the Emancipation of the serfs in 1861. The manner and spirit of the original work are, to my mind, most appropriately conveyed by emphasizing the compact, pictorial quality which the word 'Album' can suggest. This translation has aimed at completeness, both by including all the *Sketches* omitted from the first edition published under this title (Penguin Classics, 1967) and by including in an Appendix the fragments which are now generally regarded as forming part of the work as a whole.

Ivan Sergeyevich Turgenev was born in Oryol, some two hundred or so miles south of Moscow, in 1818. He spent his boyhood on his mother's estate of Spasskoye. Here he naturally learned about the injustices of the serf system as well as experiencing its brutalities through the frequent beatings meted out to him by his mother. He survived such domestic tyranny, concealed though it may have been behind a façade of civilized values, but the experience taught him to detest all tyrannies, especially the tyranny of serfdom and the political tyranny of Tsarist absolutism. Apart from some indifferent home teaching and schooling, he received a higher education at the universities of Moscow and St Petersburg and then went abroad, to Berlin University, at the end of the 1830s. The experience of western Europe turned him into a convinced advocate of European civilization. He returned to Russia in 1841 as a Westernizer or Westernist (*zapadnik*) and remained true to that conviction for the rest of his life. Westernists, it should be explained, were those members of the Russian intelligentsia who were committed to the belief that Russia should be westernized, following the initiative already taken in this respect by Peter the Great at the beginning of the eighteenth century. They were opposed by the Slavophiles, who wished to reject western influences and based their hopes for Russia on the Orthodox Church and the presumed spiritual and social superiority of things Russian.

Although Turgenev had been writing poems and articles since the middle of the 1830s, it was not until 1843 that he published his first successful work, a long narrative poem entitled *Parasha*. He was praised for this work by the critic Vissarion Belinsky, and it was partly due to Belinsky's influence that Turgenev began to devote himself to realistic depiction of the inadequacies in Russian society. Thus he became not only a chronicler of his own generation and his own society, but also a critic of his own generation's Hamletism and of the fundamental injustice of serfdom on which Russian society was based. In some respects, Turgenev's assumption of such roles was accidental. Intending to be a poet, he had by the latter part of the 1840s begun to demonstrate that he had remarkable talents as a writer of prose; intending to write a series of 'physiological' sketches of urban life on the lines of Gogol's *St Petersburg Stories* or Dostoevsky's *Poor Folk*, he found himself writing about the Russian countryside in which he had grown up; intending, in a moment of despair, to abandon literature for good, he left a short work entitled 'Khor and Kalinych' in the editorial offices of the newly resuscitated journal *The Contemporary*, and the success of the work when it was first published early in 1847 (with an editorial subtitle describing it as 'from the Notes of a Hunter') persuaded Turgenev to return to literature and marked the beginning of the *Sketches*, which were to bring him lasting fame.

A representative of the new Russian intelligentsia, as much at home in Paris or Berlin as in Moscow or St Petersburg, of noble birth, liberal political inclinations and cosmopolitan culture, extraordinarily gifted and well-read, Turgenev possessed an urbane charm that made him excellent company in any society. Though he admired women, he never married. His emotional life was dominated by the attachment which he formed for the famous singer Pauline Viardot, whom he met during her first visit to St Petersburg in the 1843-4 opera season and with whom he was to remain on terms of close intimacy until his death in 1883. Whether or not he was her lover has led to a great deal of speculation, but it is characteristic of a certain contrariness in his nature that he should also have been on very amicable terms with Pauline's husband, Louis Viardot. For the provenance of the *Sketches* this second relationship is more important, because Louis Viardot and Turgenev were not only in love with the same woman, but they were also in love with hunting, and it is very likely that a little collection of hunting memoirs entitled *Souvenirs de chasses* which Louis Viardot published in 1846 gave Turgenev the idea for his own work.

Other Russian writers had, of course, written about the peasantry – Radishchev, Pushkin, Gogol – and there were also such European writers as George Sand and Maria Edgeworth whom Turgenev could have taken as models. Strictly speaking, however, his *Sketches* are not modelled on anything save his own experience. He wrote most of them while he was outside Russia between 1847 and 1851, either while travelling in Europe or during a period spent on the Viardot estate of Courtavenel in the French countryside. The fact that he was drawing on memory may account for the brilliant lustre, so evocative and even nostalgic, that surrounds the best of them. Equally, perhaps, it may be that some of the luxuriance of the countryside about Courtavenel shines through the richness of the nature descriptions. In any case, a degree of trial and error accompanied their composition. They grew out of the success of 'Khor and Kalinych' and the fact that his mother failed to provide him with adequate means. While writing them he was also busy pursuing a career as a dramatist – a career that culminated in 1850 with the writing of his only important play, the five-act comedy *A Month in the Country*, after which he abandoned the theatre for good. These

Sketches, therefore, are not all of a piece. In some respects they are occasional pieces, experiments in a particular kind of portraiture, tracts for the times cast in the mould of literature, trial sketches for his future work as a novelist. The order that he finally chose for them (the order followed in this translation) does not observe a strict chronology and can be considered evidence for supposing that he never regarded them as truly completed. Despite this, they have a certain stylistic cohesion as well as common ground for their content and they acquired soon after their first appearance their reputation as masterpieces which occupy a very special place in Russian literature.

'Khor and Kalinych' illustrates many of their most characteristic features. It introduces the author in the role that he is to assume throughout his work – the role, that is, of intelligent, interested but uncommitted observer. The observation has two discernible aspects to it: there is the lucid, clear-cut, pictorial aspect contributed by Turgenev the writer and artist; and there is what might be called the sociological aspect, which involves a Turgenev who cannot help being a member of the nobility, of the landowning class, and who to that extent is both a stranger in the world of the peasants and a frankly curious observer anxious to describe this world to his readers. For fear of censorship and no doubt for reasons of taste Turgenev does not attempt to lay undue emphasis on the fact of serfdom, but the propagandist element in his portraits of the two peasants, Khor (the polecat) and Kalinych, is clearly discernible. They can be said to represent differing types both of personality and, loosely speaking, of literary portraiture. Such differentiation serves not only to emphasize the individual human qualities in the two peasants but also anticipates Turgenev's later interest in the division of human beings into those who are by nature predominantly Hamlet-like and those who are predominantly Quixotic (in his lecture of 1860). Apart, though, from laying stress on the intelligence of both the peasants, on their individuality as well as their 'typical' differences, this first *Sketch* also illustrates what is, in general, Turgenev's common attitude – so far, at least, as these *Sketches* are concerned – towards the nobility. On these grounds alone there is good reason for supposing that the tendentiousness in these *Sketches* is rather more anti-establishment than overtly pro-peasantry.

'Khor and Kalinych' also sheds light on such common features of peasant life as the 'eagles' who exploit the peasant women, the itinerant scythe traders and the strict hierarchy that governs the relationship between Khor and his family, despite the good-natured bantering between Khor and his son Fedya. Naturally Turgenev's interest in Khor's character and family life is matched by an equivalent curiosity on Khor's part; their mutual ignorance is sufficient comment in itself on the division which exists between master and peasant. Such comments as Turgenev's about the conviction, derived from his talk with Khor, 'that Peter the Great was predominantly Russian in his national characteristics', or Khor's caginess when Turgenev taxes him on the subject of purchasing his freedom are further reminders of the divisive half-truths, even illusions, which make communication and understanding between the classes so difficult. In other words, Turgenev's conviction that the Russian peasantry can be used as an argument in favour of Westernism seems to be as much special pleading based on ignorance or first impressions as is Khor's apprehension that he would tend to lose his individuality when he became free. It is rare, in fact, for Turgenev to attempt to argue or, in a strict sense, converse with the peasants; he is content to prompt them into speaking about themselves, framing the encounter and recorded speech with passages of commentary or nature description. The fact that most of the *Sketches* are offered as brief, summery episodes tends to set in relief the ephemeral, not to say fleeting, manner of Turgenev's encounter with the peasants and to make of them creations of a particular moment, with little identity beyond a nickname; their patronymics, like their parentage, have been obliterated in the anonymity of their servile condition. The framework of the peasant encounters, then, tends to objectivize and simultaneously to distance. It is a distancing, of course, which usually has the effect of making the encounter doubly significant, as though a lyric poem had been born of an anecdote, a work of art from a snapshot. But the difference, let it not be forgotten, is really due to ignorance.

The simple, almost anecdotal charm of the first *Sketch* is followed by the more explicitly condemnatory tone of 'Yermolay and the Miller's Wife' (*The Contemporary*, No. 5, 1847). Zverkov's attitude towards the peasantry, especially in regard to Arina, is the nub of this episode. The reader is not explicitly asked to contrast Turgenev's attitude to Yermolay with Zverkov's treatment of Arina, but this is the most likely moral to be drawn: it lays bare at one stroke the inhumanity of the system. Arina seems to have been based on fact, for Turgenev's mother apparently treated one of her maidservants in a similar fashion. Yermolay, Turgenev's frequent hunting companion, is also drawn from life – a serf, Afanasy Alifanov, belonging to one of Turgenev's neighbours. Turgenev purchased his freedom and later gave material help to his family (though Yermolay is not endowed with a family in this *Sketch*). Descendants of Alifanov were reported as still living at Spasskoye in 1955.

'Raspberry Water' (*The Contemporary*, No. 2, 1848) is a fine example of the distancing manner which Turgenev as observer-narrator employs in describing his encounters with the peasantry. An episode, no more, it illustrates through the story of Stepushka, the reminiscences of Foggy and the fragmentary dialogue passages devoted to Vlas, the extremes of deprivation and extravagance co-existing in the serf system. In the end, of course, the tragedy of such injustice is what reverberates throughout the heat of the afternoon as well as in the laconic shorthand of the exchanges between Foggy and the luckless Vlas. The silence of the wretched Stepushka is the most terrible of mute reproaches to serfdom's inhumanity. But 'District Doctor' (*The Contemporary*, No. 2, 1848), albeit so different in its extended internal narrative and sentimental manner, can be said to articulate just as strongly the inherent injustice of the social divide. As an essay in first-person narration, it introduces the reader, if only tentatively, into the milieu of the genteel, impoverished nobility which is to figure quite prominently in later *Sketches*. Here the character of the district doctor with the improbably awful name is too thin and close to caricature for the story to have any of the tragicomic impact of the Shchigrovsky Hamlet's tale.

Radilov's dilemma, though similarly emotional, has in 'My Neighbour Radilov' (*The Contemporary*, No. 5, 1847) a more complex ethical meaning. Inexplicit as an issue in the story but essential for its understanding is the fact that the Orthodox Church proscribed marriage between a husband and his sister-in-law, which in Radilov's case meant that he was not permitted to marry Olga. The complication of her supposed envy towards her sister and Radilov's secretive, if outwardly, bland character (totally devoid of the trivial passions that commonly beset Russian landowners, as Turgenev amusingly enumerates them) suggests some of the hidden tensions and tragedies present in the life of the poorer nobility. They scarcely compare, however, with the more explicit problems raised by Farmer Ovsyanikov (*The Contemporary*, No. 5, 1847), a figure who by social standing and inclination has a role roughly similar to Turgenev's in his observation of the life around him. Pithy, strong-minded and wise, Ovsyanikov is an ideal channel for conveying critical attitudes towards serfdom without courting the danger of censorship. An eighteenth-century personality who admires the past while remaining clear-eyed about the beneficial and negative aspects of the present, he is, in terms of characterization, among the most fully drawn and vivid of the types depicted in the *Sketches*, even though he does no more than sit and talk. 'Lgov' (*The Contemporary*, No. 5, 1847) offers two equally vivid portraits, those of the pretentious hunter Vladimir with his injured chin and forefinger and Old Knot (Suchok), the peasant who had been given a range of fatuous employments and names at the whims of his various masters and mistresses. As a whole, this story is a brilliant account of a disastrous duck-shooting expedition that simultaneously exposes the disastrous effects of arbitrary power, whether of man over man or man over nature.

The realism of Turgenev's manner, in the sense that it respects the observed fact or in the more special sense that it so focuses the lens of the writer's eye that it endows the subject with a dramatic immediacy, is splendidly illustrated by 'Bezhin Lea' (*The Contemporary*, No. 2, 1851). The opening description of a July day is an example of Turgenev at his most brilliant. A special magic haunts the picture that Turgenev offers us and suggests that such beautiful July days are a part of innocence, of boyhood, clothed in the magic of recollection. The reality, then, is the night in which Turgenev encounters the peasant boys around their fires, hears their stories of hauntings and darkenings of the sun. Serfdom here is not represented as a problem of social relationships; it is a presence, like the darkness, surrounding and enclosing the boys' lives. The drama of flickering firelight and darkness has a quality of sorcery that illuminates the darkness and light in the boys' minds, dramatically holds them in the writer's eye, photographs them for ever for the reader's gaze. Then, after the mystery of the night's experience, comes the splendour of the morning and Turgenev's always clear-minded insistence on the ephemerality of life with the announcement that Pavlusha had been killed in falling from a horse. The colour words, the visual richness, the simplicity of the encounter so magnificently recreated and the finely etched characterizations of the boys leave a residue of wonder.

Equally rich in descriptive detail is the story of Turgenev's meeting with 'Kasyan from the Beautiful Lands' (*The Contemporary*, No. 3, 1851). Kasyan, supposedly an adherent of some unnamed religious sect, is one of the most remarkable peasant portraits in these *Sketches*. His quasi-biblical speech is the vehicle not only for a protest against the shedding of blood; it is also a means of expressing his own repudiation of established society in the name of that dream-world of folklore 'where no leaves fall from the trees in winter, nor in the autumn neither, and golden apples do grow on silver branches and each man lives in contentment and justice with another'. But this *Sketch*, composed at a time when Turgenev's proselytizing Western-ism had been somewhat modified as a result of the Paris revolution in 1848, is not as explicit a plea for justice as is 'Bailiff' (*The Con-temporary*, No. 10, 1847). 'Bailiff' was written in May and June of 1847, though the final place and date which Turgenev gave to it (Salzbrunn, in Silesia, July 1847) was his way of acknowledging agreement with the sentiments expressed by Belinsky in his famous 'Letter to Gogol'. Belinsky, convalescing at Salzbrunn, wrote his letter in violent reaction against the obscurantist Slavophile ideas that Gogol had professed in a curious work entitled *Selected Passages from a Correspondence with Friends*. Turgenev was in Salzbrunn during part of Belinsky's convalescence, and the latter's plea for justice in Russian social and political life, as expressed in the 'Letter to Gogol', later became Turgenev's sole religious and political credo. Of all the *Sketches* 'Bailiff', with its exquisitely savage portrait of the foppish tyrant Penochkin and its equally acute study of his bailiff, con-tains by far the most outspoken attack on the exploitation of the peasantry.

The following three *Sketches* provide further examples of such exploitation through exposing the disguises used by landowners to conceal their tyranny. The creation of 'offices' of the kind described in 'The Office' (*The Contemporary*, No. 10, 1847) proved popular with Russian landowners as a means of controlling their peasantry through a bureaucratic hierarchy of clerks and petty officials. The opportunity for bribery and corruption in such circumstances is amply demonstrated by this *Sketch*, in which the narrator's role is made so neutral by his eavesdropping that the whole story has a dramatic, documentary realism to it. This is not the only example of the narrator as eavesdropper, but in this case the non-participant role clearly involves a withdrawal of sympathy. In 'Loner' (*The Contemporary*, No. 2, 1848), by contrast, the portrait of the giant peasant forester with the superb physique and fearsome reputation is projected with the greatest sympathy. This is a rare instance of Turgenev as narrator actually being admitted into the home-life of the peasantry. The scene of poverty he encounters in the peasant's hut, as well as in the suppressed but, for all that, very real distress of the motherless daughter and baby, has a poignant and vivid strength to it. The fact that the powerful peasant should be single-mindedly pursuing his guardianship of the forest to the detriment of other peasants, though no doubt in the interests of true conservationism, is tragically ironic. The actual beneficiary of the Loner's zeal is absent from the picture. Not so in the case of 'Two Landowners', which provides more evidence of the sickeningly callous treatment meted out by landowners to their serfs. Possibly because this *Sketch* was so critical, Turgenev did not publish it originally in *The Contemporary* but included it among his collection of *Sketches* when they were first published as a separate edition in 1852.

The crudities of Russian provincial society figure prominently in the next *Sketches* (both published first in *The Contemporary*, No. 2, 1848). Here the tone, particularly in 'Lebedyan', yields to a mocking, sardonic manner which highlights the rumbustious, if colourful, coarseness and double-dealing of the provincial horse fair. Khlopakov's reiteration of his supposedly funny nonsense words compares ironically with the unctuous pieties of the unscrupulous horse-dealer Chernobay: Turgenev's observant, tight-lipped description of both types is masterly in its sarcasm. As for 'Tatyana Borisovna and her Nephew' this light-hearted *Sketch* may confound the reader by the gradual reversal of sympathies which occurs when the boorish, insensitive nephew returns to his aunt's house. Turgenev uses the work as much as anything as a vehicle for pouring scorn on the artistic standards and tastes of his day.

Despite the sardonic tone of some of them, the value of these

Sketches as socio-political tracts for the times hardly needs to be emphasized. Their effect was such that they made a very real contribution to the movement for emancipating the serfs after the Crimean War. Yet they are probably better understood nowadays as one of the stages in Turgenev's development as a writer, revealing some of the themes and motifs which recur so frequently in his work and imbue it with a significance as much philosophical as social or political. 'Death' (*The Contemporary*, No. 2, 1848), for example, implies clearly enough that there is another kind of injustice apart from the injustice of social inequality. The isolation of the human personality in relation to nature and eternity exercised Turgenev more deeply, in the final analysis, than did the social or political issues of his time. 'Death' illustrates his concern for the way peasants die, with no particular emphasis laid on the morbid aspects of such a subject. It illustrates even more clearly the compassion that he feels for the wretched Avenir, the 'eternal student', whose sensitive, enthusiastic nature proves to be as superfluous in life as it is in the context of Russian society. Viewed in relation to its essentially ephemeral character, as Turgenev undoubtedly viewed it, the human personality becomes valuable for the beauty which it exhibits in life.

Beauty is the theme of 'Singers' (*The Contemporary*, No. 11, 1850) in the sense that it is the beauty of Yakov's singing that so touches the hearts of his listeners that he is universally acknowledged to be the winner of the competition. It is, of course, a fleeting beauty. Turgenev chanced upon it in taking refuge from the heat of the day and refused to idealize the episode by omitting the drunken scene at the end. Apart from depicting the peasants as endowed with a culture of their own, this *Sketch* seizes upon a moment of epiphany in which Yakov's singing and the tearful desperation of the boy's final cries seem to embrace the full range of peasant heartache.

Heartache, along with a gradual deepening of the emotional content of the *Sketches*, characterizes both 'Pyotr Petrovich Karataev' (*The Contemporary*, No. 2, 1847) and 'Meeting', if from wholly different social points of view. Karataev's ruinous love for the peasant girl Matryona, offered as an internal narrative, echoes Radilov's dilemma and anticipates in some ways Chertopkhanov's, though Karataev is in every respect the most deeply affected and the most articulate of those members of the landowning class who fall victim to serfdom's rigid division between the classes. An ordinary but companionable fellow, he finds that his hopeless love for Matryona turns him into both heartbroken flotsam and deceived lover whose feelings of protest and revenge have echoes in the soliloquies of Hamlet. 'Meeting' (*The Contemporary*, No. 11, 1850) deals explicitly with peasant emotion, observed from outside, as it were, and is the only attempt Turgenev made in his *Sketches* to describe such emotions among the peasantry. The glitter of the natural scene at the beginning reflects and sets in relief the expectations of the peasant girl awaiting her lover, just as the final breath of autumn is an orchestration of her tears, but for once the touch is a shade too sentimental, the artlessness betrays a shade too much of the artifice that contributed to its making.

'Hamlet of the Shchigrovsky District' (*The Contemporary*, No. 2, 1849) is a study in the Hamletism of Turgenev's generation. As an anatomy of provincial society, the opening description of the dignitary's arrival and the ensuing dinner is one of the most uproariously sardonic descriptions to be found in Turgenev's work. The anonymous Hamlet's subsequent recital of misfortunes and misalliances mixes the tragic and the comic in a narrative that explores what he refers to as 'the extreme limit of unhappiness'. By the time he sticks his tongue out at himself in the mirror it is clear that the tragedy of his superfluity reflects the tragic loss of illusions and fond hopes experienced by Turgenev's generation as a whole. The Hamlet's preoccupation with self has comic aspects to it, but his final reconciliation is in its own way as bitter an acceptance of social inequality and complete obliteration of individuality as is the peasant's subservience to his master.

The independence of the 'loner', of the man, no matter what his social status or role, who opts for such freedom as he can obtain within the limits of the system evidently appealed to Turgenev and no figure in the *Sketches* exemplifies such independence better than Chertopkhanov. He made his first appearance in 'Chertopkhanov and Nedopyuskin' (*The Contemporary*, No. 2, 1849). His dashing, colourful personality, so naturally inclined to protect the weak and vulnerable, as he shows in the patronage which he extends to the unfortunate Nedopyuskin, has an eccentric side to it that may antagonize as much as it can endear. In general the issue of serfdom here slips into the background and is replaced by a study of bachelor-hood. The curious little ménage cultivated by the two bachelors, Chertopkhanov and Nedopyuskin, has an idyllic appeal. It seems, among these *Sketches*, as nearly ideal a condition as can be imagined. But the story of Chertopkhanov was not destined to end there. In 1872 Turgenev published a sequel 'The End of Chertopkhanov' (*The Herald of Europe*, No. 11) in which he not only dispensed with the device of narrator but he also adopted a looser, chronicle manner in telling the story of Chertopkhanov's last years and death. In style and content, therefore, this work scarcely seems to form an organic part of the *Sketches*. It is the longest of them and among the most pessimistic. Divided into short chapters, it traces the slow decline of Chertopkhanov after his abandonment by Masha and the death of his bosom friend. Though the wonder horse Malek Adel be-comes the treasured companion of his bachelorhood, the doubts in Chertopkhanov's mind surrounding the 'second' Malek Adel seem to reinforce a sense that his eccentricity, like his fanatical pride, has a self-destructive edge to it. The story is noteworthy for its sympathetic portrayal of the Jewish horse-dealer Moshel Leiba, a second ben-eficiary of Chertopkhanov's love of justice, yet the portrayal of the central figure himself as doomed by his own self-delusion and doubts fails on the whole to sustain his tragic image to a successful conclusion.

No *Sketch* is more poignant or beautiful than 'Living Relic'. It first appeared in 1874 in a collection of stories published to raise funds for famine victims in the Samara Province. The lucidly simple portrait of the peasant woman Lukeria who religiously endures the long travail of her illness evokes the image of a saint enduring a solitary martyrdom. The comparison with Joan of Arc does not aggrandize her fate. Lukeria's humble, philosophical acceptance of misfortune reflects Turgenev's pessimistic view, increasingly marked in his later years, that life must involve such submission to fate. This readiness to submit forms the crux of another *Sketch* first published in 1874, 'Clatter of Wheels'. Though the narrator's fears prove to be unfounded at the moment of crisis, the *Sketch* has a nice blend of humour and tension interlaced with characteristic passages of nature description. Finally, 'Forest and Steppe' (*The Contemporary*, No. 2, 1849), which was always the concluding piece in the several editions of the *Sketches* that appeared during Turgenev's lifetime, reminds us that the hunter's milieu was the forest regions, not the 'limitless, enormous steppe no eye can encompass'.

The Appendix contains two fragments first published in 1964 which in their finished form would probably have proved to be as outspokenly critical as any of the completed *Sketches*. In their existing form the fragments are interesting for their terse and pungent thumbnail portraits of two different types of despotic landowner. 'The Russian German' perhaps also helps to explain something that may seem puzzling to a twentieth-century reader – namely the ease with which Turgenev was able to range far and wide on his hunting trips. That he had so little fear of trespassing is one mark of the time-span that separates his age from ours. It is also, of course, the hallmark of these hunting memoirs of his in which he, the footloose, supposedly free-ranging hunter, chooses for the greater part to depict the equally footloose, supposedly unattached peasantry, 'superfluous' after their fashion within the serf system. They are his hunter's 'prey'; but they are not the 'sitting ducks' that the landowners are once they come within range of Turgenev's hunter's eye. The latter, immured in their homes as in their internal narratives, are picked off more easily and more wickedly and with greater understanding than are the fleeting portrayals of the peasantry, so often caught casually but brilliantly on the wing.

Although these *Sketches* belong to an age that is now quite remote, the wryly humorous detachment, visual honesty and poetic sensibility with which Turgenev endowed them have served to maintain the freshness and distinction of their literary appeal. In his novels, especially *Fathers and Sons*, he was no doubt to achieve greater things, but his *Sketches* were his first major achievement. He was aware both of their value and their imperfections, as we know from a letter that he wrote to his friend Annenkov in 1852:

I am glad that this book has come out; it seems to me that it will remain my mite cast into the treasure-chest of Russian literature, to use the phraseology of the schoolbook . . . Much has come out pale and scrappy, much is only just hinted at, some of it's not right, oversalted or undercooked – but there are other notes pitched exactly right and not out of tune, and it is these notes that will save the whole book.

Turgenev's verdict, though understandably erring on the critical side, has proved to be a just one. A translator can only hope that he has been able to reveal the justice of it in his translation, despite the many temptations placed in his way to oversalt or undercook the poetry, simplicity, irony and beauty of the original Russian.

KHOR AND KALINYCH

———————— ❦ ————————

WHOEVER has happened to travel from Bolkhov County into the Zhizdra[1] region will no doubt have been struck by the sharp differences between the nature of the people in the Oryol Province and those in Kaluga. The Oryol peasant is a man of little stature, round-shouldered, gloomy, given to looking at you from under his brows and used to living in miserable huts of aspen wood, working on the *corvée*[2] principle, taking no part in trade, eating poorly and wearing bast shoes; whereas the Kaluga peasant, who pays quit-rent, is used to living in spacious fir huts, has a tall build, looks at you boldly and merrily with a clean, clear complexion, trades in grease and tar and wears boots on feast days. An Oryol village (I am talking about the eastern part of the Oryol Province) is usually situated among ploughed fields and close to a ravine which has somehow or other been transformed into a muddy pond. Apart from some wild broom, which is always ready to hand, and a couple of emaciated birches, there won't be a tree visible for miles and hut will nestle against hut, the roofs strewn with rotten straw. A Kaluga village, on the other hand, will be surrounded for the most part by woodland; the huts, more independent of each other and straighter, are roofed with boards; the gates can be tightly closed, the wattle-fencing round the yard has not collapsed and fallen inwards to offer an open door to any passing pig. And for the hunter the Kaluga Province provides more in the way of game. In the Oryol Province the last areas of woodland and 'plazas'* will disappear in five years or so, and there is no marshland whatever; while in the Kaluga Province wooded areas stretch for hundreds, and marshland for dozens, of

---

* In the Oryol Province large solid masses of bush are known as 'plazas'; the local Oryol dialect is noted for a wide variety of original, sometimes very apt, sometimes rather ugly, words and turns of phrase.

miles, and that noble bird, the grouse, still thrives, the great-hearted snipe is plenteous and the noisy partridge both delights and frightens the hunter and his dog with its explosive flight from cover.

While out hunting in the Zhizdra region I became acquainted with a small Kaluga landowner, Polutykin, also a passionate hunter and, consequently, an excellent fellow. Admittedly, he had acquired one or two weaknesses: for instance, he paid court to all the rich young ladies of marriageable age in the province and, being refused both their hands and admission to their homes, confessed his grief heartbrokenly to all his friends and acquaintances while continuing to send the young ladies' parents gifts of sour peaches and other raw produce from his garden; he was fond of repeating one and the same anecdote which, despite Polutykin's high opinion of its merits, simply failed to make anyone laugh; he was full of praise for the works of Akim Nakhimov[3] and the story *Pinna*;[4] he had a stammer; he called his dog Astronomer; instead of *however* he used to say *howsoever*, and he introduced in his own house a French cuisine, the secret of which, according to his cook's ideas, consisted in completely altering the natural taste of each dish: in the hands of this culinary master meat turned out to be fish, fish became mushrooms, and macaroni ended up dry as powder; moreover, no carrot would be permitted in a soup that had not first assumed a rhomboidal or trapezoidal shape. But apart from these minor and insignificant failings Polutykin was, as I've said, an excellent fellow.

On the day of our meeting Polutykin invited me to spend the night with him.

'It'll be about five miles to my place,' he added, 'a long way on foot, so let's drop in on Khor first of all.' (The reader will permit me to overlook his stammer.)

'And who is this Khor?'

'One of my peasants. He lives not far from here.'

We set off for his place. Khor's isolated settlement stood amid woodland in a clearing that had been given over to cultivation. It consisted of several frame dwellings of fir linked by fences. An overhanging roof, supported by thin pillars, ran along the front of the main hut. We entered and were met by a tall, handsome young man of about twenty.

'Hello, Fedya! Is Khor at home?' Polutykin asked him.

'No, Khor's gone off to the town,' the young man answered, smiling and displaying a row of snow-white teeth. 'Would you like the cart got ready?'

'Yes, my good fellow, harness the cart. And bring us some *kvas*.'[5]

We entered the hut. No cheap pictures, such as are made in Suzdal, were stuck on the clean, beamed walls; in one corner, before a heavy icon in its silver frame, a small lamp was kept burning; the table, constructed of lime-wood, had recently been scrubbed and wiped clean; and among the beams and the window-frames there were neither scurrying cockroaches nor lurking, contemplative beetles. The young man soon appeared with a large white jug full of good-tasting *kvas*, a large portion of good wheat loaf and a dozen salted cucumbers in a wooden bowl. He placed these refreshments on the table, leaned against the door and proceeded to watch us smilingly as we ate. We had barely finished when the cart drove up to the porch. We went out to find a curly-haired, red-cheeked boy of about fifteen sitting in the driver's seat and restraining with difficulty a frisky, piebald stallion. Around the cart there stood six or so young giants, all very similar to each other and to Fedya.

'They're all Khor's boys,' Polutykin remarked.

'We're the Khor lads,' echoed Fedya, who had followed us out on to the porch, 'and there aren't all of us here – Potap's in the forest and Sidor's gone to the town with the old man. Now watch out, Vasya,' he continued, turning to the young driver, 'remember you're driving the master! See you go quietly over the bumps or you'll smash the carriage and upset the master's stomach!'

The remaining Khor brothers grinned broadly at Fedya's witticism.

'Let Astronomer be seated!' exclaimed Polutykin pompously.

Fedya, not without a show of pleasure, lifted the uneasily smiling dog into the air and deposited it on the floor of the cart. Vasya gave rein to the horses and we set off.

'And that's my office,' Polutykin said suddenly, pointing to a tiny, low-walled house. 'Would you like to see inside?'

'Certainly.'

'It's not used now,' he said, climbing down, 'but it's still worth looking at.'

The office consisted of two empty rooms. The caretaker, a bent old man, ran in from the yard at the back.

'Good day, Minyaich,' said Polutykin, 'and have you any of that water?'

The ancient caretaker made off and at once returned with a bottle and two glasses.

'You try it,' Polutykin said to me. 'It's some of my good spring water.'

We each drank a glassful, while the old man regaled us with low bows to the waist.

'Well, it's time now, it seems, for us to be off,' my new friend remarked. 'In this office I got a good price from the merchant Alliluyev for ten acres of woodland I once sold him.'

We took our seats again in the carriage and in half an hour were entering the forecourt of Polutykin's mansion.

'Tell me, please,' I asked him at dinner, 'why is it that Khor lives apart from your other peasants?'

'He lives apart because he's one of my clever ones. About fifteen years ago his hut burned down and he came to my late father and said: "If you please, Nikolay Kuzmich, allow me to settle on some of the marshland in your forest. I'll pay you a good rent for it." "And what do you want to settle in a marsh for?" "That's my business, sir; all I ask, Nikolay Kuzmich, sir, is that you don't use me for any kind of work, but name whatever rent you think is right." "Fifty roubles a year!" "Thank you, sir." "No falling down on the rent payments, mind you!" "Of course, sir, no falling down . . ." And so he settled in the marshland. And from that time he's become known as Khor the Polecat.'

'I suppose he's got rich?' I asked.

'He's got rich. He now pays me a hundred silver roubles a year in rent, and I'll probably raise that a bit before long. Many times I've said to him: "Buy yourself off, Khor, buy your freedom!" But he, wily polecat that he is, always assures me he's got nothing to do it with, no money, nothing. He's a sly one!'

On the next day, directly after morning tea, we set off on a hunting expedition. On our way through the village Polutykin ordered the driver to stop at a squat little hut and called out loudly:

'Kalinych!'

'At once, sir, at once!' a voice cried from the yard. 'I'm just doing up my shoe.'

We went on at a walking pace and just beyond the village we were caught up by a man of about forty, of tall, thin build, with a small head bent well back on his shoulders. This was Kalinych. At the very first glance I took a liking to his warm-hearted, ruddy and slightly pock-marked face. Kalinych (as I learned subsequently) was accustomed to go out on a daily hunting trip with his master, would carry his bag, sometimes also his gun, note where a bird had fallen, act as water-carrier, gather wild strawberries, build shelters and run behind the buggy; indeed, without him Polutykin was helpless. Kalinych was a man of the happiest and most amenable disposition. He hummed endless tunes to himself, glancing around him on all sides in a carefree way and talking slightly through his nose, smiling, screwing up his light-blue eyes and giving frequent tugs at his scanty, wedge-shaped beard. He had a habit of walking slowly but with long strides, leaning a little on a long, thin stick. In the course of the day he more than once chatted with me and showed no servility towards me, but he looked after his master like a child. When the intolerable midday heat forced us to seek shelter, he led us into the depths of the wood to the place where he kept bees. Here he invited us into his little hut, adorned with tufts of dry, sweet-scented herbs, prepared fresh hay for us to lie on and then placed a kind of net sacking over his head, picked up a knife, a pot and a lighted brand and went out to his bees to cut out a honeycomb for us. We drank down the warm transparent mead like spring water and fell asleep to the monotone humming of the bees and the leaves' talkative rustling.

I was awakened by a gentle gust of breeze. I opened my eyes and saw Kalinych. He was sitting in the half-open doorway whittling a spoon. For a long while I looked admiringly at his patient face, as unclouded as an evening sky. Polutykin also awoke, but we did not get up at once. After a long walk and a deep sleep it is very enjoyable to lie quietly in the hay while one's body relaxes and dreams, one's face burns with a slight flush and a sweet drowsiness presses on the eyes. Finally we arose and again set off on our wanderings until evening.

Over supper I again turned the conversation to Khor and Kalinych.

'Kalinych is a good man,' Polutykin told me, 'diligent, obliging, a good peasant. Howsoever, he can't keep his holding in proper order because I'm always taking him off with me. He goes hunting with me every day. You can judge for yourself what happens to his holding.'

I agreed with him, and we went to bed.

Next day Polutykin had to go into town on business connected with his neighbour, Pichukov. Pichukov had ploughed up some of Polutykin's land and on this ploughed land he had also administered a beating to one of Polutykin's female serfs. I went out hunting alone and just before evening turned into Khor's place. On the threshold of his hut I was met by an old man – bald, small in stature, thick-set and broad-shouldered; it was Khor himself. The sight of this polecat aroused in me considerable curiosity. The cast of his features reminded me of Socrates: the same high, protuberant forehead, the same small eyes, the same snub nose. Together we entered the hut. Once again Fedya brought me some milk and brown bread. Khor sat down on a bench and, stroking his curly beard with the utmost calmness, proceeded to converse with me. He was evidently a man aware of his standing in the world, for his speech and his movements were of a measured slowness and he gave occasional chuckles through his long whiskers.

We touched on such subjects as the sowing, the harvesting and the life of the peasantry. He seemed to be in agreement with me on most things, but after a while I began to have apprehensions of my own, feeling that I wasn't saying the right thing, since everything I said began to sound so strange. Khor sometimes expressed himself in a rather puzzling fashion out of caution, I assumed. Here is an example of our conversation:

'Listen, Khor,' I was saying to him, 'why don't you buy yourself off from your master?'

'But why should I? Now I know my master and I know the rent I must pay. Our master's a good man.'

'But surely it's better to be free,' I remarked.

Khor gave me a sideways glance.

'That's for sure,' he muttered.

'Then why not buy yourself off?'

Khor gave a little turn of the head.

'What, sir, am I to use to buy myself off with?'

'Surely, old man, you've got . . .'

'If Khor was among free people,' he continued in a low mutter, as though speaking to himself, 'then everyone without a beard would be a bigger fish than Khor.'

'Then cut off your beard.'

'What's a beard good for? It's just like grass, you can cut it if you want to.'

'Well, then?'

'It's like this – Khor'll straightaway find himself among merchants. They live a good life, that's for sure, and they wear beards.'

'Don't you also do some trading?' I asked him.

'We do a wee bit o' trading, a bit of oil here, some tar there . . . What about it, sir, can I order them to harness up the cart?'

You're one who knows his own mind and keeps a strong rein on his tongue, I said to myself. 'No,' I said out loud. 'I don't need the cart. I'll be going hunting in this region tomorrow and, if you'll allow me, I'd like to spend the night in your barn.'

'With pleasure, sir. Are you sure you'll be all right in the barn? I'll get the women to lay down a sheet for you and a pillow. Hey, women, come along!' he shouted, getting up. 'And you, Fedya, you go along with them. Women are a stupid lot by themselves.'

A quarter of an hour later Fedya showed me the way to the barn with his lantern. I flung myself down into the fragrant hay and my dog curled up at my feet. Fedya wished me good night; the door creaked and banged to behind him. I was unable to go to sleep for a long time. A cow came up to the door and breathed loudly once or twice; the dog gave it a dignified growl; a pig strolled by, grunting in its preoccupied way; a horse somewhere close by began to chew the hay and snort . . . Finally I fell asleep.

Fedya awoke me at first light. I had grown to like this gay, lively young fellow very much, and so far as I could tell he was also Khor's favourite. They made very good-natured fun of each other. The old man came out to meet me. Whether it was because I had spent the night under his roof, or for some other reason, he treated me now in a much more kindly fashion than on the previous day.

'The samovar's ready for you,' he said with a smile. 'Let's go and have some tea.'

We took our places round the table. A buxom girl, one of his daughters-in-law, brought in a bowl of milk. One by one his sons came into the hut.

'What a fine, grown-up crowd you have!' I remarked to the old man.

'Yes,' he murmured, biting off a tiny piece of sugar, 'it doesn't seem like they've got much complaint to make against me and the old woman.'

'And do they all live with you?'

'They do. That's how they want it.'

'And they're all married?'

'There's one of 'em not married yet,' he answered, indicating Fedya who was as usual leaning against the door. 'Vaska's young yet, and he can wait a bit.'

'What do I want with marriage?' Fedya protested. 'I'm all right as I am. What good's a wife? To have howling matches with, eh?'

'There you go again ... I know what you're up to! You've got those silver rings on your fingers and you're all the time sniffing round the girls out in the yard. "Give over, you ought to be ashamed!"' the old man continued, mimicking the servant girls. 'I know your sort, you'll never do a hand's turn you won't!'

'What good is there in a woman, I ask you?'

'A woman is a worker about the house,' Khor remarked importantly. 'A woman looks after a man.'

'And why do I need a worker about the house?'

'You're one for having other people pull the chestnuts out of the fire, that's why. I know your sort.'

'If that's so, then marry me off, eh? Come on now, say something!'

'Enough now, enough! You're a joker, you are. Just look how we're upsetting our guest. I'll marry you off, never you worry ... Now, sir, please don't be annoyed: as you can see, he's just a child and he hasn't had time to pick up a lot of sense yet.'

Fedya just shook his head.

'Is Khor at home?' a familiar voice called from beyond the door, and Kalinych entered the hut carrying a bunch of wild strawberries which he had collected for his friend, Khor the polecat. The old man greeted him warmly. I looked at Kalinych in astonishment because I confess I had not expected such 'niceties' from a peasant.

That day I went out hunting four hours later than usual, and I spent the next three days at Khor's place. I became preoccupied with my new acquaintances. I don't know how I had won their confidence, but they talked to me without any constraint. It was with pleasure that I listened to them and watched them. The two friends were not a bit like each other. Khor was an emphatic sort of man, practical, an administrator, hard-headed; Kalinych, on the other hand, belonged in the company of idealists, romantics, men of lofty enthusiasms and lofty dreams. Khor understood the realities of life – that is to say, he had built a home for himself, saved up some money, arranged things satisfactorily with his master and other responsible authorities; whereas Kalinych walked about in bast sandals and got by somehow or other. Khor had raised a large, obedient and united family; whereas Kalinych had at one time had a wife, of whom he was terrified, and no children. Khor could see through my friend Polutykin; whereas Kalinych simply worshipped his master. Khor loved Kalinych and would always give him protection; Kalinych loved and respected Khor. Khor spoke little, gave only occasional chuckles and kept his thoughts to himself; whereas Kalinych would express himself heatedly, although he never sang like a nightingale as the lively factory man is liable to . . . But he possessed certain innate talents which Khor himself was willing to recognize; he could charm away bleeding, terror and rages, and he could cure worms; bees obeyed him because of his light touch. While I was there Khor asked him to lead a newly purchased horse into the stables, and Kalinych fulfilled the old sceptic's request conscientiously and with pride. Kalinych was closer to nature, whereas Khor was closer to people and society; Kalinych never liked thinking things out for himself and believed everything blindly, whereas Khor had reached a high pitch of irony in his attitude to life. He had seen much, knew much, and I learned a lot from him.

For instance, from the stories he had to tell I learned that each summer, before the harvesting, a small cart of a particular kind appears in the villages. A man in a caftan sits in the cart and sells scythes. If the payment is in cash, he asks a rouble and twenty-five copecks in silver coinage or a rouble and fifty copecks in paper money; if it's to be on credit, he asks three paper roubles and one silver rouble. All the peasants, of course, buy on credit. Two or three weeks later he reappears and demands his money. By this time the peasant has just harvested his oats and has the necessary with which to pay. He accompanies the trader to a tavern and there they complete their business. Some of the landowners took it into their heads to buy their own scythes for cash and distribute them on credit to their peasants for the same price. But the peasants seemed dissatisfied with this, and even succumbed to melancholy over it; they were deprived of the pleasure of giving each scythe a twanging flick, of putting their ear to it and turning it about in their hands and asking the rascally salesman twenty times over: 'Well, now, that's a bit of a wrong'un, isn't it?'

Much the same sort of trickery occurs during the buying of sickles with the sole difference that in this case the women also become involved and sometimes force the trader to give them restraining slaps for their own good. But the womenfolk suffer most grievously of all in the following instance. Those responsible for supplying material to the paper factories entrust the buying of rags to a particular species of person, known in certain districts as 'eagles'. Such an 'eagle' is given two hundred paper roubles by a merchant and then sets out to find his prey. But, in contrast to the noble bird after which he is named, he does not fall boldly and openly upon his victim; on the contrary, this 'eagle' uses cunning, underhand means. He leaves his cart somewhere in the bushes on the outskirts of the village and then, just as if he were some casual passer-by or bum on the loose, makes his way through the back alleys and backyards of the huts. The women can sense his approach and creep out to meet him. The business between them is quickly completed. For a few copper coins a woman will hand over to the 'eagle' not only the meanest cast-off rag but frequently even her husband's shirt and her own day skirt. Recently the womenfolk have found it worth while to steal from each other and to unload their ill-gotten hemp or homemade sacking on the 'eagles' – an important augmentation and consummation of their business! The peasants, for their part, have pricked up their ears and at the least sign, at the merest hint of the approach of an 'eagle', they resort briskly and vigorously to remedial and preventive measures. In fact, it's downright insulting, isn't it? It's their business to sell the hemp, and they do indeed sell it, though not in the town – they would have to drag themselves to the town for that – but to itinerant traders who, for want of a proper measure, consider that forty handfuls are equal to thirty-six pounds in weight – and you know the size a Russian can give to his handful or his palm when he's in real earnest!

I, inexperienced as I am and not a 'countryman' (as we say in the Oryol district), had had my fill of such stories. But Khor did not do all the talking; he also asked me a great deal. He knew that I had been abroad, and his curiosity was aroused. Kalinych betrayed no less interest, but he was chiefly affected by descriptions of natural scenery, mountains, waterfalls, unusual buildings and large cities. Khor was concerned with questions of administration and government. He took things one at a time: 'Are things there like they are here, or not the same? Well, sir, what's you got to say about that?' Whereas during the course of my recital Kalinych would exclaim – 'Ah, dear Lord, Thy will be done!' Khor would be quiet, knitting his thick brows and only occasionally remarking: 'That wouldn't likely be the thing for us, but t'other – that's the proper way, that's good.' I cannot convey all his queries, and, besides, there's no need. But from our talks I derived one conviction which my readers probably cannot have expected – the conviction that Peter the Great was predominantly Russian in his national characteristics and Russian specifically in his reforms. A Russian is so sure of his strength and robustness that he is not averse to overtaxing himself: he is little concerned with his past and looks boldly towards the future. If a thing's good, he'll like it; if a thing's sensible, he'll not reject it, but he couldn't care a jot where it came from. His sane common sense will gladly make fun of the thin-as-a-stick rationalism of the Germans; but the Germans, in Khor's words, were interesting enough folk and he was ready to learn from them. Owing to the peculiar nature of his social station, his virtual independence, Khor mentioned many things in talking with me that even a crowbar wouldn't have dislodged in someone else or, as the peasants say, you couldn't grind out with a millstone. He took a realistic view of his position. During my talks with Khor I heard for the first time the simple, intelligent speech of the Russian peasant. His knowledge was fairly broad, after his own fashion, but he could not read; whereas Kalinych could.

'That rascal's been able to pick up readin' and writin',' Khor remarked, 'an' 'e's never had a single bee die on 'im since he was born.'

'And have your children learned to read and write?'

After a pause Khor said: 'Fedya knows.'

'And the others?'

'The others don't.'

'Why not?'

The old man did not answer and changed the subject. As a matter of fact, despite all his intelligence, he clung to many prejudices and preconceived notions. Women, for example, he despised from the depths of his soul, and when in a jovial mood derived amusement from them and made fun of them. His wife, an aged and shrewish woman, spent the whole day over the stove and was the source of persistent complaints and abuse; her sons paid no attention to her, but she put the fear of God into her daughters-in-law. It's not surprising that in the Russian song the mother-in-law sings:

> O, you're no son o' mine,
> You're not a family man!
> 'Cos you don't beat your wife,
> You don't beat your young one . . .

Once I thought of standing up for the daughters-in-law and attempted to solicit Khor's sympathy; but he calmly retorted that 'Maybe you like to bother yourself with such nonsense . . . Let the women quarrel . . . You'll only be worse off if you try to part them, and it isn't even worth dirtying your hands with it.' Sometimes the bad-tempered old woman crawled down from the stove and called in the dog from the yard, enticing it with: 'Come on, come on, nice dog!' – only to belabour its scraggy spine with a poker, or she would stand under the awning out front and 'bark insults' at whoever passed by, as Khor expressed it. Her husband, however, she feared and, at his command, would climb back on to her perch on the stove.

But it was particularly curious to hear how Kalinych and Khor disagreed when talking about Polutykin. 'Now, look here, Khor, don't you say anything against him while I'm here,' Kalinych would say. 'Then why doesn't he see that you've got a proper pair of boots to wear?' the other would object. 'To hell with boots! Why do I need boots? I'm a peasant . . .' 'And I'm also a peasant, but just look . . .' Saying this, Khor would raise his leg and show Kalinych a boot

that looked as if it had been cobbled from the skin of a mammoth.
'Oh, you're not an ordinary peasant!' Kalinych would answer. 'Well,
surely he ought to give you something to buy them sandals with?
After all, you go out hunting with him and everyday you'll need
new ones.' 'He gives me something to get bast sandals with.' 'That's
right, last year he grandly gave you ten copecks.' At this Kalinych
would turn away in annoyance and Khor would burst out laughing,
his tiny little eyes almost vanishing completely.

Kalinych had quite a pleasant singing voice and could strum a little
on the balalaika. Khor would listen and listen, and then he would
bend his head to one side and begin to accompany in a plaintive
voice. He particularly liked the song: 'O, mine's a hard lot, a hard
life!'

Fedya never let pass an opportunity to poke fun at his father,
saying, 'Well, old man, what've you got to complain about?'

But Khor would rest his cheek on his hand, close his eyes and
continue complaining about his hard lot. Yet at other times no one
was more active than he: he would always be busying himself with
something – repairing the cart, making new fence supports or taking
a look at the harness. He did not, however, insist on exceptional
cleanliness, and in answer to my comments once remarked that 'a
hut ought to have a lived-in smell'.

'But,' I remarked in return, 'look how clean it is out at Kalinych's
where he keeps bees.'

'Bees wouldn't live there, see, sir, unless it was clean,' he said with
a sigh.

On another occasion he asked me:

'Do you have your own estate, sir?'

'I do.'

'Is it far from here?'

'Sixty or seventy miles.'

'Well, sir, do you live on your estate?'

'I do.'

'But mostly, I reckon, you're out enjoying yourself with that
gun?'

'Yes, I must admit that.'

'And that's a good thing you're doing, sir. Shoot them black grouse
as much as you like, but be sure and see you change your bailiff often.'

On the evening of the fourth day Polutykin sent for me. I was sorry to have to say goodbye to the old man. Together with Kalinych I took my place in the cart.

'Well, goodbye, Khor, and keep well,' I said. 'Goodbye, Fedya.'

'Goodbye, sir, goodbye, and don't forget us.'

We drove off. Dawn had just set fire to the sky.

'It's going to be beautiful weather tomorrow,' I said, looking at the bright sky.

'No, there'll be rain,' Kalinych contradicted. 'Look how the ducks are splashing about, and the grass has got a strong smell.'

We drove through bushy undergrowth. Kalinych began to sing in a low voice, bouncing up and down on the driver's seat and gazing all the while at the dawn.

The next day I was gone from under Polutykin's hospitable roof.

YERMOLAY AND THE MILLER'S WIFE

I N the evening the hunter Yermolay and I set off for 'cover'. But perhaps not all my readers know what 'cover' means. Pray listen, gentlemen.

In the springtime, a quarter of an hour before sundown, you go into a wood with your gun but without your dog. You seek out a place for yourself somewhere close by a thicket, look around you, inspect the firing mechanism on your gun and exchange winks with your companion. A quarter of an hour passes. The sun sinks below the horizon, but it is still light in the wood; the air is fresh and translucent; there is the spirited chatter of birds; the young grass glows with a happy emerald brilliance. You wait. The interior of the wood gradually darkens; the crimson rays of an evening sunset slowly slide across the roots and trunks of the trees, rise higher and higher, moving from the lower, still almost bare, branches to the motionless tips of the sleep-enfolded trees. Then the very tips grow faint; the pink sky becomes a dark blue. The woodland scent increases, accompanied by slight wafts of a warm dampness; the breeze that has flown into the wood around you begins to die down. The birds fall asleep – not all at once, but by types: first the finches fall silent, a few instants later the robins, after them the yellow buntings. The wood grows darker and darker. The trees fuse into large blackening masses; the first small stars emerge diffidently in the blue sky. The birds are all asleep. Only the redstarts and little woodpeckers continue to make an occasional sleepy whistling . . . Then they are quiet as well. Once again the ringing voice of the chiff-chaff resounds overhead; somewhere or other an oriole gives a sad cry and a nightingale offers the first trills of its song. Your heart is heavy with anticipation, and suddenly – but only hunters will know what I mean – suddenly the deep quiet is broken by a special kind of croaking and hissing, there is a measured beat of rapidly flapping wings – and a woodcock, beautifully inclining its long beak, flies out from behind a dark birch into your line of fire.

That is what is meant by 'standing in cover'.

In such a fashion, Yermolay and I set off for 'cover'; but forgive me, gentlemen: I must first of all acquaint you with Yermolay.

Imagine to yourself a man of about forty-five, tall and lean, with a long delicate nose, a narrow forehead, little grey eyes, dishevelled hair and wide, scornful lips. This man used to go about winter and summer in a yellowish nankeen coat of German cut, but belted with a sash; he wore wide blue trousers and a cap edged with astrakhan which had been given him, on a jovial occasion, by a bankrupt landowner. Two bags were fixed to the sash, one in front, which had been artfully twisted into two halves for powder and bird-shot, and the other behind – for game; his cotton wadding Yermolay used to extract from his own, seemingly inexhaustible cap. With the money earned by him from selling his game he could easily have purchased a cartridge belt and pouch, but the thought of making such a purchase never even so much as entered his head, and he continued to load his gun in his customary fashion, arousing astonishment in onlookers by the skill with which he avoided the danger of overpouring or mixing the shot and the powder. His gun had a single barrel, with a flintlock, endowed, moreover, with the awful habit of 'kicking' brutally, as a result of which Yermolay's right cheek was always more swollen than his left. How he managed to hit anything with this gun even a wiseacre might be at a loss to explain, but hit he did.

He also had a setter, a most remarkable creature named Valetka. Yermolay never fed him. 'Likely I'd start feeding a dog,' he would argue, 'since a dog's a clever animal and'll find his food on his own.' And so it was, in fact: although Valetka astonished even indifferent passers-by with his unusual thinness, he lived and lived a long time; despite his miserable condition, he never even once got lost and displayed no desire to abandon his master. Once, when he was young, he disappeared for a day or two, carried away by love; but that foolishness soon took leave of him. Valetka's most remarkable characteristic was an incomprehensible indifference to everything under the sun. If I had not been talking about a dog, I would have used the word 'disillusionment'. He usually sat with his short tail tucked underneath him, frowning, shuddering from time to time and never smiling. (It is well known that dogs are capable of smiling, and even of smiling very charmingly.) He was extremely ugly, and there was not a single idle house-serf who let pass an opportunity of laughing venomously at his appearance; but Valetka endured all these taunts, and even blows, with astonishing composure. He provided particular satisfaction for cooks, who immediately dropped whatever they were doing and dashed after him with shouts and swearing whenever through a weakness common not only to dogs, he used to stick his famished muzzle through the half-open door of the enticingly warm and sweet-smelling kitchen. Out hunting, he distinguished himself by his tirelessness and possessed a good scent; but if he happened to catch up with a wounded hare, he at once gobbled the whole lot down with pleasure, right to the last little bone, in some cool, shady place under a leafy bush and at a respectful distance from Yermolay who swore at him in any and every dialect, known and unknown.

Yermolay belonged to one of my neighbours, a landowner of the old school. Landowners of the old school dislike 'wildfowl' and stick to domestic poultry. It is only on unusual occasions, such as birthdays, name-days and elections, that the cooks of old-time landowners embark on preparing long-beaked birds and, succumbing to a high state of excitement, as do all Russians when they have no clear idea of what they are doing, they invent such fancy accompaniments for the birds that guests for the most part study the dishes set in front of them with attentiveness and curiosity, but can in no wise resolve to taste them. Yermolay was under orders to supply the master's kitchen once a month with a couple of brace of grouse and partridge, but he was otherwise permitted to live where and how he wanted. He had been rejected as a man unfit for any kind of real work – a 'no-good', as we say in the Oryol region. Naturally, he was given no powder and shot, following precisely the same principles as he adopted in not feeding his dog. Yermolay was a man of the most unusual kind: free and easy as a bird, garrulous to a fair extent, to all appearances scatter-brained and awkward; he had a strong liking for drink, could never settle in one place, when on the move he ambled and swayed from side to side – and, ambling and swaying, he would polish off between thirty and forty miles a day. He had

been involved in a most extraordinary variety of adventures,
spending nights in marshes, up trees, on roofs, beneath bridges,
more than once under lock and key in attics, cellars and barns,
relieved of his gun, his dog, his most essential clothing, receiving
forceful and prolonged beatings – and yet after a short time he
would return home clothed, with his gun and with his dog.
One could not call him a happy man, although he was almost
always in a reasonably good humour; generally, he looked a trifle
eccentric.

Yermolay enjoyed passing the time of day with any congenial
character, especially over a drink, but never for very long: he would
soon get up and be on his way. 'And where are you off to, you devil?
It's night outside.' 'I'm for Chaplino.' 'What's the good of you
traipsin' off to Chaplino, more'n seven miles away?' 'I'm for spending
the night there with the peasant Sofron.' 'Spend the night here.' 'No,
that's impossible.' And Yermolay would be off with his Valetka into
the dark night, through bushes and ditches, and the peasant Sofron
would most likely not let him into his yard – what's more, might
bash him one on the neck 'for being such a disturbance to honest
folk'.

Yet no one could compare with Yermolay in skill at catching fish
in the springtime flood-water or in grabbing crayfish with his bare
hands, in scenting out game, luring quail, training hawks, capturing
nightingales with 'woodsprite pipe' song or 'cuckoo's fly-by'.* Of
one thing he was incapable: training dogs. He lacked the patience for
it.

He also had a wife. He would visit her once a week. She lived in a
scrappy, partly collapsed little hut, managed somehow or other,
never knew from one day to the next whether she would have
enough to eat and, in general, endured a bitter fate. Yermolay, that
carefree and good-natured fellow, treated her roughly and coarsely,
assumed a threatening and severe air in his own home – and his poor
wife had no idea of how to indulge him, shuddered at his glance,
bought drink for him with her last copeck and dutifully covered him
with her own sheepskin coat when he, collapsing majestically on the

---

* These terms are familiar to nightingale lovers: they denote the best 'figures' in a
nightingale's singing.

stove, fell into a Herculean sleep. I myself had occasion more than once to notice in him involuntary signs of a certain morose ferocity. I disliked the expression on his face when he used to kill a winged bird by biting into it. But Yermolay never remained at home longer than a day: and once outside his home territory he again turned into 'Yermolka', as he was known by nickname for a good sixty odd miles around and as he used to call himself on occasion. The meanest house-serf felt himself superior to this tramp – and perhaps precisely for this reason always treated him in a friendly fashion; while peasants at first took pleasure in driving him away and trapping him like a hare in the field, but later they let him go with a blessing and, once they were acquainted with this eccentric fellow, kept their hands off him, even giving him bread and striking up a conversation with him . . . This was the fellow I chose as my hunting companion, and it was with him that I set off for 'cover' in a large birch wood on the bank of the Ista.

Many Russian rivers, after the pattern of the Volga, have one hilly bank and the other of meadowland; the Ista also. This small river winds in an exceedingly capricious fashion, crawling like a snake, never flowing straight for five hundred yards at a time, and in certain places, from the top of a steep hill, one can see six or seven miles of dams, ponds, watermills and kitchen gardens surrounded by willows and flocks of geese. There is a multitude of fish in the Ista, especially bullyheads (in hot weather peasants lift them out by hand from beneath the overhanging bushes). Little sandpipers whistle and flit to and fro along the stony banks which are dotted with outlets for cold, sparkling spring water; wild ducks swim out into the centre of ponds and look guardedly about them; herons stand up stiffly in the shade, in the inlets and below the river's steep sides.

We stood in cover for about an hour, shot a couple of brace of woodcock and, wishing to try our luck again before sunrise (one can go out for cover in the morning as well), decided to spend the night at the nearest mill. We made our way out of the wood and went down the hill. The river was rolling along, its surface dark-blue waves; the air thickened under the pressure of the night-time moisture. We knocked at the mill gates. Dogs began to yelp in the yard.

'Who's there?' called a husky and sleepy voice.

'Hunters. Let us in for the night.'

There was no answer.

'We'll pay.'

'I'll go and tell the master ... Aw, damn you dogs! Nothing awful's happenin' to you!'

We heard the workman enter the hut; soon he returned to the gates.

'No, the master says, he won't give orders to let you in.'

'Why won't he?'

'He's frightened. You're hunters – soon as you're in here you'll likely set fire to the mill. Just look at them firing-pieces you got there!'

'What nonsense!'

'The year afore last this mill of ours burned down. Cattle-dealers spent the night here and some way or another, you know, they set fire to it.'

'Anyway, friend, we're not spending the night outside!'

'Spend it anyway you know ...' He went off with a clattering of boots.

Yermolay dispatched after him a variety of unpleasant expressions. 'Let's go into the village,' he said, finally, with a sigh. But it was more than a mile to the village.

'We'll spend the night here,' I said. 'It's warm outside, and the miller'll let us have some straw if we pay him.'

Yermolay tacitly agreed. We began knocking on the gates again.

'What d'you need now?' the workman's voice called again. 'I've told you – you can't come in.'

We explained to him what we wanted. He went off to consult his master and came back with him. The wicket-gate creaked. The miller appeared, a tall man with a plump face, bull-necked, and large and round of stomach. He agreed to my suggestion.

A hundred paces from the mill stood a structure with a roof, but open on all four sides. Straw and hay were brought out to us there; the workman set up a samovar on the grass beside the river and, squatting on his haunches, began blowing busily up the samovar's chimney. The charcoal flared up and brightly illumined his youthful face. The miller ran off to waken his wife and eventually proposed that I should spend the night in the hut; but I preferred to remain out in the open air. The miller's wife brought us some milk, eggs, potatoes and bread. Soon the samovar was bubbling and we set about having some tea. It was windless and mists were rising from the river; corncrakes were crying in the vicinity; from the direction of the mill-wheels came such faint noises as the drip-drip of water from the paddles and the seepage of water through the cross-beams of the dam. We built a small fire. While Yermolay baked potatoes in the ashes, I managed to doze off.

A light-voiced, suppressed whispering awoke me. I raised my head: before the fire, on an upturned tub, the miller's wife was sitting and conversing with my hunting companion. Earlier I had recognized, by her dress, movements and way of speaking, that she was a former house-serf – not from among the peasantry or the bourgeoisie; but it was only now that I could take a good look at her features. She appeared to be about thirty; her thin, pale face still contained traces of a remarkable beauty; I was particularly taken by her eyes, so large and melancholy. She leaned her elbows on her knees and placed her face in her hands. Yermolay sat with his back to me and was engaged in laying sticks on the fire.

'There's sickness again among the cattle in Zheltukhina,' the miller's wife was saying. 'Both of father Ivan's cows have died ... Lord have mercy on us!'

'And what about your pigs?' asked Yermolay after a short silence.

'They're alive.'

'You ought to give me a little porker, you ought.'

The miller's wife said nothing and after a while gave a sigh.

'Who are you with?' she asked.

'With the squire – the Kostomarov squire.'

Yermolay threw a few fir fronds on the fire; at once they broke into a universal crackling and thick white smoke poured straight into his face.

'Why didn't your husband let us into the hut?'

'He was frightened.'

'There's a fat old pot-belly for you ... Arina Timofeyevna, be a dear and bring me a wee glass of some of the good stuff!'

The miller's wife rose and disappeared into the gloom. Yermolay began singing softly:

> A-walking to my sweetheart
> Wore the shoes off of my feet . . .

Arina returned with a small carafe and a glass. Yermolay straightened up, crossed himself and gulped down the drink at one go. 'That's lovely!' he added.

The miller's wife again seated herself on the tub.

'So, Arina Timofeyevna, tell me, are you still feeling poorly?'

'I'm still poorly.'

'How so?'

'The coughing at night hurts me so.'

'It seems the master's gone to sleep,' said Yermolay after a brief silence. 'Don't you go to no doctor, Arina, or it'll get worse.'

'I won't be going in any case.'

'You come and be my guest.'

Arina lowered her head.

'I'll drive my own – my wife, that's to say – I'll drive her away for that occasion,' Yermolay continued. 'Sure an' all I will!'

'You'd do better to wake up your master, Yermolay Petrovich. See, the potatoes are done.'

'Let him go on snoozing,' my faithful servant remarked with indifference. 'He's run about so much it's right he should sleep.'

I turned over in the hay. Yermolay rose and approached me.

'Come and eat, sir – the potatoes are ready.'

I emerged from beneath my roofed structure and the miller's wife got up from her place on the tub, wishing to leave us. I started talking to her.

'Have you been at this mill long?'

'Two years come Whitsun.'

'And where is your husband from?'

Arina did not catch the drift of my question.

'Whereabouts is your husband from?' Yermolay repeated, raising his voice.

'From Belev. He's a townsman from Belev.'

'And you're also from Belev?'

'No, I'm a serf . . . I was one, that is.'

'Whose?'

'Mr Zverkov's. Now I'm free.'

'What Zverkov?'

'Alexander Silych.'

'Were you by any chance his wife's chambermaid?'

'How d'you know that? Yes, I was.'

I looked now with renewed curiosity and sympathy at Arina.

'I know your master,' I continued.

'You do?' she answered softly, and lowered her eyes.

It is fitting that I should tell the reader why I looked at Arina with such sympathy. During my period of residence in St Petersburg I happened to become acquainted with Mr Zverkov. He occupied a fairly important position and passed as a capable and well-informed man. He had a wife, plump, emotional, given to floods of tears and bad temper – a vulgar and burdensome creature; there was also a runt of a son, a real little milord, spoiled and witless. Mr Zverkov's own appearance did little in his favour: out of a broad, almost square face, mousey little eyes peered cunningly and his nose protruded, large and sharp, with wide-open nostrils; grey close-cropped hair rose in bristles above his wrinkled forehead and his thin lips were ceaselessly quivering and shaping themselves into sickly smiles. Mr Zverkov's habitual stance was with his little legs set wide apart and his fat little hands thrust in his pockets. On one occasion it somehow came about that I shared a carriage with him on a trip out of town. We struck up a conversation. As a man of experience and business acumen, Mr Zverkov began to instruct me concerning 'the path of truth'.

'Permit me to remark to you,' he squeaked eventually, 'that all of you, you young people, judge and explain every single matter in a random fashion; you know little about your own country; Russia, my good sirs, is a closed book to you, that's what! All you read are German books. For example, you've just been saying this and that to me on this question of – well, that's to say, on this question of house-serfs . . . Fine, I don't dispute it, that's all very fine; but you don't know them, you don't know what sort of people they are.'

Mr Zverkov loudly blew his nose and took a pinch of snuff.

'Permit me to tell, for example, one little tiny anecdote, which could be of interest to you.' Mr Zverkov cleared his throat with a cough. 'You certainly know what kind of a wife I have; it would seem hard to find anyone kinder than her, you will yourself agree. Her chambermaids don't just have food and lodging, but a veritable paradise on earth is created before their very eyes ... But my wife has laid down a rule for herself: that she will not employ married chambermaids. That sort of thing just will not do. Children come along and so on – well, a chambermaid in that case can't look after her mistress as she should, can't see to all her habits: she's not up to it, she's got something else on her mind. You must judge such things according to human nature.

'Well, sir, one day we were driving through our village, it'd be about – how can I say exactly? – about fifteen years ago. We saw that the elder had a little girl, a daughter, extremely pretty; there was even something, you know, deferential in her manner. My wife says to me: "Coco ..." You understand me, that's what she – er – calls me "... we'll take this little girl to St Petersburg; I like her, Coco ..." "Take her with pleasure," I say. The elder, naturally, falls at our feet; such happiness, you understand, has been too much for him to expect ... Well, of course, the girl burst into tears like an idiot. It really is awful for them to start with – I mean, leaving the house where they were born; but there's nothing to be surprised at in that. Soon, however, she had grown used to us. To start with she was put in the maids' room, where they taught her what to do, of course. And what d'you think? The girl made astonishing progress; my wife simply fawned on her, and finally, passing over others, promoted her to be one of her own chambermaids. Take note of that! And one has to do her justice: my wife never had such a chambermaid, absolutely never had one like her: helpful, modest, obedient – simply everything one could ask for. As a result, I must admit, my wife even took to spoiling her a bit too much: dressed her superbly, gave her the same food as she had, gave her tea to drink – well, you just can't imagine how it was!

'So she spent about ten years in my wife's service. Suddenly, one fine morning, just think of it, Arina – Arina was her name – came unannounced into my study and flopped down at my feet. I will tell you frankly that I can't abide that sort of thing. A man should never forget his dignity, isn't that true? "What's it you want?" "Good master, Alexander Silych, I beg your indulgence." "In what?" "Allow me to get married." I confess to you I was astonished. "Don't you know, you silly girl, that the mistress hasn't got another chambermaid?" "I'll go on serving the mistress as I have done."

"Nonsense! Nonsense! the mistress does not employ married chambermaids." "Malanya can take my place." "I beg you to keep your ideas to yourself." "As you wish . . ."'

'I confess I was simply stunned. I will let you know that I'm the sort of man who finds nothing so insulting – I dare say even strongly insulting – as ingratitude. There's no need for me to tell you – you already know what my wife is: an angel in the very flesh, inexplicably good-natured. The blackest scoundrel, it seems, would take pity on her. I sent Arina away. I thought she'd probably come to her senses; I'm not one, you know, who likes to believe in man's black ingratitude and evil nature. Then what d'you think? Six months later she again honours me with a visit and makes the very same request. This time, I admit, I drove her away in real earnest and gave her due warning and promised to tell my wife. I was flabbergasted . . . But imagine my astonishment when a short while later my wife came to me in tears and in such an excited state that I was even alarmed for her. "What on earth's happened?" "It's Arina . . ." You'll appreciate that I'm ashamed to say it out loud. "It simply can't be! Who was it?" "The lackey Petrushka."

'I exploded. I'm that sort of man – I just don't like half-measures! Petrushka wasn't to blame. He could be punished, but he wasn't to blame, in my opinion. Arina . . . well, what, well, I mean, what need to say anything more? It goes without saying that I at once ordered her hair to be cut off, had her dressed in her shabbiest clothes and packed off to the country. My wife was deprived of an excellent chambermaid, but I had no choice: one just cannot tolerate bad behaviour in one's own house. Better that a rotten limb should be cut off at once . . . Well, now you judge for yourself – well, I mean, you know my wife, she's, she's, she's – she's an angel, when all's said and done! After all, she was attached to Arina – and Arina knew that and yet behaved shamelessly . . . Eh? No, say what you like – eh? There's no point in discussing it! In any case, I had no choice. The ingratitude of this girl annoyed and hurt me personally – yes, me, myself – for a long time. I don't care what you say, but you'll not find any heart, any feeling, in these people! No matter how much you feed a wolf, it's still got its heart set on the forest . . . Science to the fore! But I simply wanted to demonstrate to you . . .'

And Mr Zverkov, without finishing, turned his head away and

buried himself more snugly in his coat, manfully suppressing an unwanted agitation.

The reader no doubt understands now why I looked at Arina with sympathy.

'Have you been married long to the miller?' I asked her at last.

'Two years.'

'Do you mean that your master actually allowed you?'

'Someone bought me off.'

'Who?'

'Savely Alekseyevich.'

'Who's he?'

'My husband.' (Yermolay smiled to himself.)

'But did my master talk to you about me?' Arina added after a short pause.

I had no idea how to answer the question.

'Arina!' the miller shouted from a distance. She rose and walked away.

'Is her husband a good man?' I asked Yermolay.

'Not bad.'

'Do they have any children?'

'There was one, but it died.'

'The miller must've liked her, didn't he? Did he give a lot of money to buy her off?'

'I don't know. She knows how to read and write. In their business that's worth . . . that's a good thing. Reckon he must've liked her.'

'Have you known her long?'

'A good while. Formerly I used to go to her master's. Their estate's round about these parts.'

'And did you know the lackey Petrushka?'

'Pyotr Vasilyevich? Sure I did.'

'Where is he now?'

'Went off to be a soldier.'

We fell silent.

'It seems she's not well, is that so?' I asked Yermolay finally.

'Some health she has! . . . Tomorrow, you'll see, they'll be flying well from cover. It'd be a good idea for you to get some sleep now.'

A flock of wild ducks raced whistling over our heads and we heard them alight on the river not far away. It was already quite dark and beginning to grow cold; in the wood a nightingale was resonantly pouring out its song. We burrowed down in the hay and went to sleep.

RASPBERRY WATER

AT the beginning of August the heatwaves are frequently intolerable. At that time, from midday until three, the most determined and single-minded man is in no condition to go hunting and
the most devoted dog starts 'licking the hunter's spurs', meaning he
follows at his heels, squeezing up his eyes in pain and exaggeratedly
sticking out his tongue, and in response to his master's reproaches
despondently hangs his tail and assumes a confused expression but
won't venture forward at any cost. It was on just such a day that I
happened to be out hunting. I had long resisted the temptation to lie
down somewhere in the shade, if only for a moment. My tireless
bitch had gone on roving about among the bushes for a long time,
although she evidently expected nothing worthwhile to come of her
feverish activity. The stifling heat forced me at last to think about
conserving the last of our energies and faculties. I dragged my way
somehow or other to the river Ista, already familiar to my tolerant
readers, went down the steep bank and walked across the damp
yellow sand in the direction of the spring which is famous throughout
the region for its name, 'Raspberry Water'.[1] The spring has its
source in a fissure on the river bank which has turned gradually into
a small but deep creek, and twenty or so paces from there it falls with
a happy, prattling noise into the river. Oak trees have spread down
the sides of the creek and about the source of the spring itself there is
a green area of short, velvety grass. The rays of the sun never
penetrate its cold, silvery moistness. I reached the spring and found
lying on the grass a birchwood scoop which had been left by a
passing peasant for general use. I drank, lay down in the shade and
glanced round me. By the inlet formed by the flowing of the spring
into the river and therefore always covered with shallow ripples two
old men were sitting with their backs to me. One, fairly thickset and

tall, in a neat, dark-green caftan and a fluffy peaked cap, was fishing. The other, thin and small, in a wretched little patched frock-coat of mixed material and without a hat, held on his knees a jug of worms and occasionally, as though he were trying to protect himself from the sun, ran his hand over his bald head. I studied him a bit more closely and recognized him as Stepushka from Shumikhino. I beg the reader's permission to introduce this man.

A few miles from my village is the large village of Shumikhino, with a stone church erected to Saints Cosmas and Damian.[2] Opposite this church there used to be extensive manorial buildings surrounded by various structures such as outbuildings, workshops, stables, greenhouses and outhouses for carriages, baths and temporary kitchens, accommodation for guests and estate managers, conservatories, swings for the peasantry to enjoy and other more or less useful buildings. In the manorial buildings themselves wealthy landowners used to live, and everything went well for them until suddenly, one fine morning, the whole blessed place was burned to the ground. The gentlefolk took themselves off to another nest; the estate fell into disuse. The extensive burnt-out area became a kitchen garden which was here and there surrounded by piles of bricks left over from the former foundations. Such of the woodwork as survived was used to knock together a small peasant hut covered with ship's planking which had been bought ten years or so before for the purpose of building a pavilion in the Gothic manner. A gardener, Mitrofan, his wife Aksinya and their seven children were housed in this hut. Mitrofan was ordered to supply greens and vegetables for the manorial table, which was 150 miles away, while Aksinya was given charge of a Tyrolean cow purchased in Moscow for a considerable sum but, unfortunately, deprived of any means of reproduction and therefore barren of milk from the day of purchase. She was also entrusted with a crested, smoke-grey drake, the only surviving 'manorial' bird. The children, due to their tender years, were given no tasks to perform, which, however, in no way prevented them from becoming complete layabouts. On a couple of occasions I'd happened to spend the night at this gardener's hut and in the course of doing so I'd had from him cucumbers which, God knows why, even at the height of summer were outstanding for their size, rubbishy watery taste and thick yellow skins. It was there I'd first

seen Stepushka. Apart from Mitrofan and his family and a deaf old
churchwarden Gerasim, who lived out of Christian charity in a tiny
room in the house of a one-eyed soldier's widow, not a single real
servant remained in Shumikhino, since Stepushka, with whom I'm
intending to acquaint the reader, couldn't be regarded as a man in
a general sense, nor as a manorial servant in particular.

Every man has at least some position or other in society, or at least
some connections. Every manorial servant receives, if not pay, then
'support', but Stepushka received absolutely no financial help at all,
had no relations and no one knew of his existence. He didn't even
have a past; no one spoke about him; he'd never been included in the
census. There were dark rumours abroad that he'd at one time been
employed as a valet, but who he was, where he came from, whose
son he was, how he came to be a resident of Shumikhino, in what
fashion he came by the frock coat of mixed material which he'd
worn from times immemorial, where he lived and what he lived on
– about all these things positively no one had the slightest idea and,
truth to tell, such questions didn't concern them. Grandpa Trofimych, who knew the family tree of all manorial servants in an
ascending line to the fourth generation, even he had said only once
that he thought, so it was said, Stepan'd been related to a Turkish
woman whom the late master, Brigadier Aleksey Romanych, had
brought back in a cart from the wars. Even on holidays and days of
general celebration when there were abundant free handouts of
buckwheat pies and green wine in the good old Russian tradition,
even on such occasions Stepushka didn't make his way to the laden
tables and full barrels, didn't bow down, didn't kiss the master's
hand, didn't drink back at one go a whole glass in his master's
presence and to his master's health, a glass filled by the fat hand of an
estate steward; but there was always some kind soul or other who, in
passing, would hand the poor wretch a partly eaten piece of pie. On
Easter Sunday he was greeted in Christ's name but he never turned
back his greasy sleeve and fetched from his back pocket his painted
egg and handed it, sighing and winking, to the young master and
mistress or even to the mistress herself. In summer he lived in a store-
room behind the henhouse and in winter in the entrance to the bath-
house; in severe frosts he spent the night in the hayloft. People were
used to having him about, sometimes even hit him, but no one used

to talk to him and he, it seems, had grown used to keeping his mouth shut from birth onwards. After the fire this abandoned man found refuge in – or, as the Oryol peasants say, 'got his foot into' – Mitrofan the gardener's place. The gardener didn't lay a finger on him, nor did he invite him to stay, nor drive him away. Stepushka didn't in fact live in the gardener's hut. He lived in, or hung about, the kitchen garden. He'd move and walk about without a sound, and sneeze and cough into his hand, not without fear, and eternally fussed and bothered on the quiet, just like an ant, always looking for food, just for food. And if he hadn't spent from morning to evening worrying about food, my Stepushka'd have died of hunger! It's a bad business if you don't know in the morning what you'll have to fill yourself with by the evening! So Stepushka'd spend his time sitting under the fence eating a radish or sucking a carrot or crumbling in his lap a dirty head of cabbage; or he'd be groaning under the weight of carrying a bucket of water somewhere; or he'd get a little fire going under a pot and throw some black bits and bobs into it from out of his breast pouch; or in his own little hidey-hole he'd be wielding a piece of wood, knocking in a nail, making a little shelf for some crust or other. And he'd do it all without a word, just as if he were all the time on the lookout and about to hide. And then he'd be gone for a couple of days and no one'd notice his absence . . . You'd take a second look and he'd be there again, sitting under the fence and surreptitiously feeding kindling under a little three-legged pot. He had a small face, yellowish little eyes, hair down to his eyebrows, a sharp little nose, enormous, transparent ears, like a bat's, and a beard shaved literally two weeks ago, never any longer or shorter. This was the Stepushka I met on the bank of the Ista in the company of the other old man.

I approached them, exchanged greetings and sat down beside them. In Stepushka's companion I recognized another acquaintance. It was one of Count Pyotr Ilyich —'s freed serfs, Mikhaylo Savelyev, known as Foggy. He lived in the house of a consumptive townsman of Bolkhov, the proprietor of an inn where I'd stayed fairly often. Young officials and other idle folk (merchants piled high with striped feather coverlets are indifferent to it) who travel on the Oryol high road can see even to this day, a short way beyond the village of Troitsky, an enormous wooden house on two floors, stuck right beside the road, completely abandoned, its roof collapsed and its windows stove in. At midday in clear sunny weather it's hard to imagine anything sadder than this ruin. Here Count Pyotr Ilyich used to live, famous for his lavish hospitality, a rich magnate of the last century. The whole province used to visit him and would dance and make merry in fine fashion, to the deafening accompaniment of homegrown music and the crackling of fireworks and Roman candles. And probably there's more than one old lady who nowadays passes by that abandoned manorial residence and sighs and recalls long-vanished times and long-vanished youth. The Count spent much time in feasting, spent long strolling with welcoming smiles among the crowds of obsequious guests; but his estate, sad to say, did not last out his lifetime. Having ruined himself thoroughly, he went off to St Petersburg to seek an official niche for himself and died in a hotel room before anything had been decided. Foggy'd been employed as a butler in his house and had achieved his freedom in the Count's lifetime. He was a man of seventy or so, with pleasant, regular features. Almost the whole time he smiled, as nowadays only those from the epoch of Catherine the Great are used to smiling, in a kindly and dignified manner. In conversation, he would slowly protrude and compress his lips as he sweetly squeezed up his eyes and pronounced his words with a slight nasal intonation. He would blow his nose and sniff tobacco also without any haste, as if he were engaged in doing something very serious.

'Well, Mikhaylo Savelyich,' I began, 'have you caught anything?'

'Take a look in the basket. A couple of perch and five or so sculpin. Show 'em, Steve.'

Stepushka held out the basket to me.

'How are you, Stepan?' I asked him.

'I . . . I . . . I . . . I get by, sir,' answered Stepan, stammering as though his tongue was moving heavy weights.

'Is Mitrofan well?'

'Well, yes-s-sir.'

The poor wretch turned away.

'Not biting, they're not biting,' said Foggy. 'It's too hot. Fish're all hidin' under the bushes, all asleep . . . Give us 'nother worm, Steve.' (Stepushka got out a worm, placed it on his palm, hit it once or twice, stuck it on the hook, spat on it and handed it to Foggy.)

'Thanks, Steve . . . And you, sir,' he went on, turning to me, 'you're out huntin', sir, are you?'

'As you can see.'

'I see, sir . . . And what's that dog you got, sir, an Inglish or Furland?'

The old man liked to take the opportunity to show he'd been about the world and knew a thing or two.

'I don't know what breed it is, but it's a good one.'

'I see, sir . . . D'you go out ridin' with dogs?'

'I've got a couple of packs.'

Foggy smiled and shook his head.

'That's the way of it — one's a great dog-lover, t'other's not interested like. What I think is, accordin' to my simple way o' thinkin', dogs oughter be kept more for show, so to speak . . . And so as everythin' was in proper order, the horses in proper order, and the men lookin' after the dogs, and everythin'. The dead Count – the Lord bless 'im! – weren't a great one for huntin', truth to tell, but he kept dogs and once or twice a year he'd ride out with 'em. The huntsmen'd gather out in the courtyard in red caftans with gold braid and they'd blow the horn. Then his excellency'd come out and they'd lead the horse to him. Then his excellency'd mount the horse and the master of hounds, he'd help with the stirrups and then take his hat off his head and hand up the reins in his hat. Then his excellency'd crack his whip and the huntsmen'd start hallooin' and off they'd all go out of the yard. A groom'd be ridin' just behind the Count and keepin' two o' the Count's favourite hounds on a silk leash and lookin' round, keepin' an eye on everythin', you know . . . And this groom, he'd be sittin' high, high up, on a Cossack saddle, red-cheeked like, keepin' his eyes on everythin' like . . . Well, there'd be guests, you see, at a thing like that. Entertainin' to see, but you got to observe decorum . . . Oh, it's got away, dammit!' he added suddenly, jerking his fishing rod.

'They do say, don't they, the Count lived it up in his time?' I asked.

The old man spat on a worm and cast his line again.

'A grandee he were, and that's the truth. The top-rank important persons, one can say, used to visit 'im from St Petersburg. In their sky-blue ribbons like they'd sit at table and eat. And he was a great one for hospitality. He'd summon me and say: "Foggy, for tomorrow we must have live sterlets. Order 'em, understand?" "Yes, your excellency." He'd order right from Paris embroidered caftans and wigs and sticks and scents and eau-de-cologne, the very best, and snuff boxes and pictures, big ones like. And if he'd give a banquet – oh, my Lord, oh, my God! – what fireworks, like, what outings! There'd even be cannons firin'! He kept forty or so musicians. He kept a music master, a German, and that German, he gave 'imself such airs, he did, wantin' to eat at table with the guests. So his excellency ordered 'im out of 'is house, sayin': "In my house musicians must know their place." That was 'is right as a master, and that's the truth. They'd start dancin' and they'd dance right through till dawn, mostly the schottische, like, the matradura and such . . . Ah, I've got one, I've got one!' (The old man pulled a small perch out of the water.) 'Take it, Steve. The master was a master as should be,' the old man continued, casting again, 'and he was a good kind soul. He'd give you a blow – in a moment he'd have forgotten. One thing, though: he kept fancy women. Oh, good Lord, those fancy women! They're what ruined 'im. And mostly he took 'em from the lowest class o' people. You'd wonder what more they'd want? Oh, they'd want the very best in the whole of Europe, that's what they'd want! You might say, why not live to your heart's content, that's what masters're for . . . But to be ruined for it, that's not right. There was one in particular, called Akulina, she's dead now, God bless 'er! She was ordinary enough, policeman's daughter from Sitov, but what a bitch she was! She'd beat the Count about the cheeks. Utterly bewitched him. She got a relative of mine shaved and sent off to the army for droppin' choc'late on 'er dress – and he wasn't the only one, mind. Still, those were good times, they were!' the old man added with a deep sigh, bowed his head and fell silent.

'Your master, so far as I can see, was a severe man, wasn't he?' I began after a short silence.

'Then it was in fashion, sir,' the old man replied, shaking his head.

'Now they don't do that sort of thing,' I remarked, not taking my eyes off him.

He looked at me sideways.

'Now things are better, so they say,' he muttered and cast his line far out.

We were sitting in the shade, but even in the shade it was stifling. The heavy, heat-laden wind had literally fallen to nothing and one's burning face sought any kind of breeze, but there was no breeze at all. The sun literally beat down from a blue, darkened sky. Directly opposite us, on the other bank, a field of oats glowed yellow, with wormwood growing in it here and there, and yet not a single stalk so much as quivered. A little lower down a peasant's horse stood in the river up to its knees and lazily waved about its wet tail. Occasionally a large fish swam to the surface beneath an overhanging bush, emitted bubbles and then slowly sank to the bottom, leaving behind it a slight ripple. Grasshoppers sawed away in the sun-browned grass. Quail cried out as if despite themselves. Hawks floated smoothly above the fields and frequently stopped in one spot, rapidly beating their wings and fanning out their tails. We sat motionless, oppressed by the heat. Suddenly, behind us, there came a noise from the creek as someone descended towards the spring. I looked round and saw a peasant of about fifty, covered in dust, in a peasant shirt and bast shoes, with a woven bag and coarse coat flung over his shoulder. He approached the spring, drank thirstily and then stood up.

'Eh, is it Vlas?' cried out Foggy, peering at him. 'Good to see you, brother. Where's God brought you from?'

'Good to see you, too, Mikhaylo Savelyich,' said the peasant, coming up to us. 'A long way off.'

'Where's that?' Foggy asked him.

'I been off to Moscow to see the master.'

'Why's that?'

'To ask 'im somethin'.'

'Ask 'im what?'

'Ask 'im so as I'd pay less rent or did unpaid labour, you know, or got resettled . . . My boy died, see. So it's hard for me on my own to get by.'

'Your son's dead?'

'Dead. My dead boy,' the peasant added after a pause, 'was a cabbie in Moscow. He used to pay my rent, see.'

'Are you really on quit-rent now?'

'I am.'

'What did your master say?'

'What did he say? He drove me away, he did. He said, how'd you dare come straight to me? I've got a bailiff, you gotta see 'im first, he says. And where'd I resettle you anyhow? You gotta pay off what you owes me first, he says. Blew up, he did.'

'Well, so you came back here?'

'Back here. I wanted to know, you know, whether my dead boy'd left any things behind 'im, but I couldn't get no sense out of 'em. I said to 'is boss: "I'm Philip's father," and he says to me: "How'm I to know that? Anyhow your son didn't leave nothin'. He was owin' me money." So I came back here.'

The peasant recounted all this with a slight tone of mockery, as if none of it applied to himself, but tears stood in his small, shrunken eyes and his lips quivered.

'So you're off home now, are you?'

'Where else? 'Course I'm goin' home. The wife'll be blowing in 'er fist from hunger, she will.'

'You oughter . . .' Stepushka suddenly started to say, got mixed up, fell silent and began poking around in the jug of worms.

'You'll be seein' the bailiff then?' Foggy went on, glancing at Steve with some surprise.

'What'd I go to 'im for? I'm owin', it's true. Before he died my boy'd been sick for a year and didn't pay no quit-rent for 'imself . . . I'm not worryin' about that, 'cos I got nothin' myself anyhow . . . It won't matter how clever you are, brother, you'll waste your time 'cos I got nothin', not a hair on my head!' The peasant roared with laughter. 'No matter what he thinks up, that Kintilyan Semyonych . . .' And Vlas burst out laughing again.

'What's that? That's real bad, brother Vlas,' Foggy announced, pausing between the words.

'What's real bad about it? It's not . . .' But Vlas's voice broke at that point. 'Oh, it's bloody hot,' he went on, wiping his face with his sleeve.

'Who's your master?' I asked.

'Count —, Valerian Petrovich.'

'Pyotr Ilyich's son?'

'Pyotr Ilyich's son,' said Foggy. 'Pyotr Ilyich, the late Count, gave 'im Vlas's village while he was still alive.'

'Is he well?'

'He's well, thank God,' Vlas answered. 'Gone all red, fat-faced, he has.'

'You see, sir,' Foggy continued, turning to me, 'it'd be all right like if it were outside Moscow, but it's right here he's on quit-rent.'

'How much?'

'Ninety-five roubles,' mumbled Vlas.

'Well, you can see for yourself, can't you – just a little bit o' land and all the rest's the master's woodland.'

'And that's been sold, they say,' remarked the peasant.

'Well, you can see for yourself ... Give us a worm, Steve ... Hey, Steve, what's up? Gone to sleep, 'ave you?'

Stepushka shook himself. The peasant sat down beside us. We fell silent again. On the opposite bank a voice struck up a song, but it was protracted and sad ... My poor Vlas gave way to his grief ...

Half an hour later we all went our separate ways.

DISTRICT DOCTOR

———————— ❦ ————————

ONE time in the autumn, on coming back from a long trip, I caught a cold and had to go to bed. Luckily the fever struck me in a provincial town, in a hotel, and I sent for a doctor. In half an hour the district doctor appeared, a man of small stature, thinnish and black-haired. He wrote out the usual prescription for something to make me sweat, ordered the application of a mustard plaster and very skilfully slipped his five-rouble payment into his coat cuff, all the while drily coughing and glancing to one side, and was just on the point of leaving when a conversation was struck up and he remained. The fever tormented me. I foresaw a sleepless night and was glad to chatter with the good fellow. Tea was served. My good doctor started talking. He was no fool and expressed himself vivaciously and rather entertainingly. Strange things happen on this earth: you can live a long while with someone and be on the friendliest of terms, and yet you'll never once talk openly with him, from the depths of your soul; while with someone else you may scarcely have met, at one glance, whether you to him or he to you, just as in a confessional, you'll blurt out the story of your life. I don't know what made me deserve the confidence of my new friend, save that, on the spur of the moment, he 'took to me', as they say, and recounted to me a fairly remarkable episode, and it is his story I now wish to relate to the well-disposed reader. I will try to express myself in the doctor's own words.

'You don't happen to know, do you,' he began in a weak and quavering voice (the result of unadulterated birch snuff), 'you don't happen to know the local judge, Mylov, Pavel Lukich? . . . You don't? . . . Well, it doesn't matter.' (He coughed and wiped his eyes.) 'So you see it was like this, as you might say, so as not to tell a lie – during Lent, just when everything was thawing. I was sitting with him, at our judge's house, and I was playing whist. Our judge was a good chap and very fond of playing whist. Suddenly' (my doctor friend frequently used the word 'suddenly') 'they tell me someone's asking for me. I ask what he wants. He's brought a note – it must be from a patient. Let me see it, I say. Yes, it's from a patient . . . Well, that's all right, it's our bread and butter, you know . . . It's like this: the note's from a lady, a landowner and widow, who says her daughter's dying, come for God's sake, horses've been sent to fetch you. Well, that's not so bad so far, except that she's twenty miles away and it's dark outside and the roads are bloody awful! What's more, she herself's poorly off, there's no more'n couple of silver coins in it for me, and that's doubtful, probably I'll have to make do with a bit of cloth and a few crumbs of this and that. But duty comes first, you know, when someone's dying. Suddenly I transfer my cards to an inveterate member of our group, Kalliopin, and set off home. I see a little cart standing by my porch harnessed with peasant horses – big-bellied, huge-bellied, and woolly coats on 'em thick as felt – and a coachman's sitting there without his hat, as a mark of respect. Well, I think, it's clear as daylight, my good fellow, that your lords and masters don't eat off gold plate . . . You may laugh at that, but I'll tell you one thing, those of us who're poor, we notice these things . . . If a coachman sits there like a prince, for instance, and doesn't take his cap off and even grins to himself under his beard and twirls his whip, you can bet you'll get a couple of real big banknotes! But I see there's not a whiff of that in this case. However, I tell myself, you can't do a thing about it – duty comes first. I grab hold of the most obvious medicines and set off. Believe it or not, I scarcely manage to get there. The road's absolutely hellish – streams, snow, mud, gullies, and then suddenly it turns out a dam's burst – one disaster after another! Still, I get there. The house is small, with a straw roof. There's light in the windows, meaning that they're waiting. I go in. I'm met by an old woman, very dignified, in a bonnet. "Please help," she says, "she's dying." I tell her: "Don't worry. Where's the patient?" "This way please." I find myself in a small, clean room, with a lamp burning in the corner and a girl of about twenty lying on the bed unconscious. She's literally blazing hot and breathing heavily in a fever. There are two other girls there, her sisters, frightened and tearful. "Yesterday evening," they tell me, "she was in perfect health and had a hearty appetite. This morning she complained of having a headache, but towards evening she suddenly became like this . . ." I tell them again: "Don't worry" – a doctor's obligation, you know – and I set to work. I bled her, ordered mustard plasters to be applied and wrote out a prescription. Meantime I'm looking at her, can't take my eyes off her, you know – well, my God, I've never seen such a face before – in a word, she's beautiful! Pity for her literally tears me apart. Such delightful features, such eyes . . . Then, thank God, she got a bit better, started sweating and realized where she was, looked around her, smiled, ran her hand across her face . . . Her sisters bent over her and asked her how she was. "All right," she says and turns over. I see she's gone to sleep. Well, I say, we must let her rest now. So we all go out of the room on tiptoe. Only a maid remains behind to watch over her. In the sitting-room the samovar's ready, along with a bottle of Jamaican – in my business, you know, you can't get by without a tot of rum. They offer me some tea and beg me to stay overnight. I say yes – after all, where could I go at that time of night? The old woman goes on groaning and sighing. "What for?" I ask. "She'll live, don't you worry. It'd be better if you got some rest yourself. It's two o'clock in the morning." "You'll be sure and rouse me if anything happens?" "I'll do that, I'll do that." The old lady went off to her room and the sisters went off to theirs. A bed was set up for me in the sitting-room. So I lay down, but I couldn't sleep. Hardly surprising, though you'd have thought I'd be worn out. I simply couldn't get the sick girl off my mind. Finally I couldn't stand it any more and suddenly got up, thinking I'd go and see what was happening to my patient. Her bedroom was just off the sitting-room. Well, I rose and opened her door softly, my heart beating like mad. I see the maid's asleep, her mouth wide open and snoring, the wretch! But the sick girl's lying with her face towards me and moving her arms about, poor thing. I'd no sooner approached than she suddenly opens her eyes and stares at me. "Who is it? Who's there?" I got confused. "All right, don't be frightened, my dear," I say. "I'm the doctor and I've come to see how you are." "You're the doctor?" "Yes. Your mother sent into the town for me. I've bled you, my dear, and now you must rest and in a couple of days, God grant, we'll have you on your feet again." "Oh, yes, doctor, you mustn't let me die . . . please, please." "Don't say such things, God be with you!" But her fever'd returned, I thought. I felt her pulse and found her feverish. She looked at me and then suddenly seized me by the hand. "I'll tell you why I don't want to die, I'll tell you, I'll tell you ... now we're alone. Only, please, don't tell anyone else. Just listen." I bent down to her and she strained her lips toward my ear and her hair touched my cheek – I can tell you, my head was spinning from being so close to her – and she started whispering ... I couldn't understand a word ... Of course, she was delirious ... She went on whispering and whispering, so fast it didn't sound like Russian, and then she stopped, shuddered, dropped her head on the pillow and shook her finger at me. "See you don't tell anyone, doctor." I calmed her somehow or other, gave her a drink, roused the maid and left.'

At this point, sighing bitterly once again, the district doctor took some snuff and paused for a moment.

'However,' he went on, 'the next day the sick girl, contrary to my expectations, was no better. I thought and thought about her and suddenly decided to stay, although other patients were waiting for me ... And, you know, you mustn't neglect your patients: a practice can suffer from that sort of thing. But, in the first place, the sick girl was in a desperate state; and, secondly, to tell the truth, I had a strong personal attachment to her. What's more, I liked the whole family. Although they didn't have much in the way of possessions, they were extraordinarily well educated, one might say. Their father'd been a man of learning, a writer. He'd died, of course, in poverty, but he'd succeeded in giving his children an excellent education and he'd also left many books behind. Because I looked after the sick girl so zealously, or for some other reason, I have to say that they grew very fond of me in that household and treated me as one of the family ... Meantime, the state of the roads became frightful. All communications, so to speak, were completely severed. Even medicine was only obtainable from the town with difficulty ... The sick girl didn't get any better ... Day after day, day after day ... Well, you see, sir, you see ...' (The doctor fell silent.) '... I don't rightly know how to put it, sir ...' (He again took some snuff, wheezed and drank some tea.) 'I'll tell you straight out, my sick patient ... how can I put it? ... well, fell in love with me ... or no, she didn't so much fall in love as ... well, besides ... I can't rightly say, sir ...' (The doctor hung his head and went red.)

'No,' he went on vivaciously, 'it wasn't love! When all's said and done, you've got to know your own worth. She was an educated girl, intelligent, well-read, while I'd completely forgotten, one might say, all the Latin I'd ever learned. As for my figure' (the doctor glanced at himself with a smile) 'I didn't have all that much to boast about. But the Lord God hadn't made a complete fool out of me – I can tell black from white, you know, and I can make sense of things as well. For instance, I understood very well that Alexandra Andreyevna – she was called Alexandra Andreyevna – felt for me not love so much as what might be called a friendly disposition and a kind of respect. Although she may perhaps have been mistaken in her attitude, her state was, well, you can judge for yourself . . . Besides,' added the doctor, who'd spoken so brokenly and scarcely without drawing breath, in evident confusion, 'I've probably let my tongue run away with me, so you won't understand a thing . . . So, look, if you don't mind, I'll tell it all just as it happened.'

He finished his glass of tea and started speaking in a quieter voice.

'So it was like this. My patient grew worse – worse and worse. You're not a medical man, my good sir, so you can't understand what happens in the soul of someone like me, particularly at the beginning, when he starts to realize that the illness is getting the better of him. Your self-confidence flies out the window! You suddenly feel so small it's hard to describe. It seems to you you've forgotten everything you've ever learned, and your patient no longer trusts you, and others round you start noticing you're at a loss and start telling you the symptoms and looking at you from under their brows and whispering . . . oh, it's bloody awful! Surely, you think, there's got to be a medicine for this illness, it's just a case of finding it. Is this it? You try it – no, it's not that! You don't give the medicine time to work but try another, then another. You pick up your book of prescriptions and study it – ah, that's the one! Sometimes you just open the book at random and think, what the hell . . . But all the time the patient's dying, while another doctor might've saved him. You say you need a second opinion, because you can't take all the responsibility on yourself. And what a fool you look in such circumstances! Well, as time goes by you get used to it, it's nothing. Your patient's died, but it's not your fault, you followed the rules. But what's much worse is when you can see the blind trust they place in you, yet you feel you're not in any position to help. It was precisely such trust that Alexandra Andreyevna's family placed in me, while forgetting that their daughter was in danger. I was also, for my own part, assuring them it was all right, while my heart was right down in my boots. To cap all my misfortunes, the weather got so bad that the coachman couldn't go for the medicines for whole days at a time. And I never left the sick girl's room, couldn't tear myself away, told her silly jokes and played cards with her. At nights I sat beside her bed. The old lady thanked me with tears in her eyes and I thought to myself: "I don't deserve your thanks." I confess to you quite openly – there's nothing left to hide now – I fell in love with my patient. And Alexandra Andreyevna grew very fond of me and wouldn't allow anyone else into her room. She began talking to me, asking me where I'd done my training, what my life was like, who my parents were, who'd I go visiting? I felt I shouldn't let her talk, but I couldn't really stop her, definitely stop her, you know. I'd seize myself by the head and tell myself, "What're you doing, you blackguard?" But she'd take my hand and hold it, look at me, gaze at me, gaze and gaze at me and turn away and sigh and say, "How good you are!" Her hands were so hot, her eyes so round and longing. She'd say: "Yes, you're good, you're a good man, you're not like our neighbours . . . No, you're not like them at all, not at all . . . How is it we haven't met before?" And I'd say: "Alexandra Andreyevna, don't fret . . . Believe me, I don't feel, I've no idea why I should deserve this, only just don't fret, for God's sake, don't fret . . . everything'll be all right, you'll get well." But I ought to tell you, by the way,' the doctor added, bending forward and raising his eyebrows, 'that they didn't have much to do with the neighbours, because the small fry weren't really up to them and they were too proud to curry favour with the rich. I'm telling you they were an extremely well-educated family, so for me, you know, it was a privilege to be there. She'd only accept medicine from me . . . she'd raise herself, the poor girl, with my help, and have the medicine and look at me and my heart'd literally beat faster and faster. But all the while she was getting worse, worse and worse, and I thought she's bound to die, bound to. Believe me, I was ready to lie down in the coffin myself, what with the mother and the sisters seeing it all and looking me straight in the eyes, their confidence gradually slipping away: "What's wrong?

How is she?" "Oh, it's nothing, nothing at all!" And how could it be nothing at all when her mind was already being affected? So there I am one night, sitting once again beside the sick girl. The maid's also there, snoring her head off . . . you couldn't blame her really, she'd been chivvied from pillar to post. Alexandra Andreyevna'd felt bad all evening; the fever'd tormented her. Right up until midnight she'd been tossing and turning and then she'd finally gone to sleep; or at least she lay there quietly. The lamp in the corner was burning before the icon and I sat there, you know, bent up, also snoozing. Suddenly, as if someone'd given me a shove in the side, I turned round and there – good God! – was Alexandra Andreyevna looking me straight in the eyes, with her lips apart and her cheeks literally on fire. "What's wrong?" "Doctor, I'm going to die, aren't I?" "God forbid!" "No, doctor, no, please, don't tell me I'll live . . . don't say that . . . Oh, if only you knew! . . . Listen, for God's sake don't hide from me what my condition is really!" She spoke, taking such quick breaths. "If I know for sure I'm going to die, then I'll tell you everything, everything!" "Please, Alexandra Andreyevna, please!" "Listen, I've not slept at all and I've been watching you . . . for God's sake . . . I trust you, you're a good man, you're an honest man, I beg you in the name of all that's holy, tell me the truth! If only you knew how important it is for me . . . Doctor, for God's sake tell me, am I in danger?" "What can I tell you, Alexandra Andreyevna? Please don't . . ." "For God's sake I implore you!" "I can't hide from you, Alexandra Andreyevna, that you *are* in danger, but God is merciful . . ." "I'll die, I'll die . . ." And she was literally overjoyed. Her face became so happy I was frightened. "Don't be frightened, don't be frightened, death doesn't worry me at all." She suddenly raised herself and leant on one elbow. "Now . . . well, now I can tell you that I'm grateful to you from the bottom of my heart, that you're a good, kind man and I love you . . ." I stared at her like an idiot and I felt real fright, you know . . . "Do you hear what I'm saying, I love you . . ." "Alexandra Andreyevna, I'm not worth it!" "No, no, you don't understand me, you don't understand . . ." And suddenly she stretched out her arms and seized me by the head and kissed me. Believe you me, I almost cried out. I flung myself on to my knees and buried my head in the pillows. She fell silent, her fingers quivering in my hair. I could hear her crying. I began comforting her, trying to assure her – oh, I don't know what it was I said to her! I said: "You'll wake up the maid, Alexandra Andreyevna . . . Thank you, thank you, believe me . . . now be quiet." "That's enough of that, enough," she went on saying. "God be with them, let them all wake up, let them all come in here, I don't care, after all I'm going to die . . . What's wrong with you, why d'you look so scared? Lift your head up . . . Or maybe you don't love me, maybe I've made a mistake? . . . In that case forgive me." "Alexandra Andreyevna, what're you saying? . . . I love you, Alexandra Andreyevna." She looked me straight in the eyes and opened her arms. "Hold me, then." I'll tell you in all honesty I don't know how I didn't go mad that night. I felt that my sick girl was driving herself crazy. I could see she wasn't in her right mind and I realized that if she hadn't thought herself about to die she wouldn't have given me a single thought. You know, like it or not, it's horrible to be dying at twenty-five years of age without ever having loved someone – and that's what was driving her crazy, that's why, out of desperation, she'd chosen me . . . Do you see now what I mean? Well, she wouldn't let me out of her arms. "Have pity on me, Alexandra Andreyevna, and have pity on yourself," I said. "Why?" she said. "What's pity got to do with it? After all I'm going to die." She repeated this again and again. "If I knew I'd be alive and again be a proper young lady, I'd be ashamed, really ashamed . . . but it's not like that, is it?" "But who said you're going to die?" "Oh, no, enough's enough, you can't fool me, you're a poor liar, you've only got to look at yourself to see that." "You will live, Alexandra Andreyevna, I'll cure you. We'll ask your mother's permission . . . and we'll get married and live happily ever after." "No, no, I've got your word for it, I've got to die . . . you promised me . . . you told me . . ." It was a bitter thing for me, bitter for many reasons. You know how it is, sometimes little things happen which seem nothing at all, but they hurt. It occurred to her to ask me my name, not my surname but my forename. As bad luck would have it, I'd been given the name Tripthong. Yes, yes, Tripthong, Tripthong Ivanych. In that household they all called me "doctor". There was nothing to be done about it, so I said: "Tripthong, milady." She screwed up her eyes, shook her head and whispered something in French – oh, something impolite – and then laughed, which was also bad. So that's how I spent practically the whole night with her. In the morning I left her room half out of my mind. I went back to her room in the afternoon, after tea. Oh, my God, oh, my God! I couldn't recognize her. I've seen better looking corpses. In all honesty I swear to you I don't understand now, I really don't understand how I survived that torture. Three days and three nights my sick girl scraped by . . . and what nights! The things she said to me! And on the last night, just imagine, there I sat beside her and prayed to God that she'd be taken quickly, and me as well. Suddenly the old lady, her mother, came rushing in. I'd already told her, the mother, the day before that there was little hope, things were bad and it might be an idea to fetch the priest. The sick girl, on seeing her mother, said: "Oh, what a good thing you've come . . . Look at us, we love each other, we've given each other our word . . ." "Doctor, what's wrong, what's she saying?" I was stunned. "She's delirious," I said. "It's the fever." But she said: "Enough's enough, you were saying something quite different just now, and you accepted the ring from me . . . Why pretend now? My mother's kind, she'll forgive, she'll understand, and I'm dying, why should I tell a lie? Give me your hand . . ." I jumped up and ran out. The old lady, of course, guessed what'd happened.

'I won't weary you any longer, and in any case I find it painful to remember. My sick patient died the following day. The Kingdom of Heaven be hers!' (The doctor added this rapidly and with a sigh.) 'Before she died she asked that the rest of the family should go and I should stay with her alone. "Forgive me," she said. "Perhaps I'm to blame in your eyes . . . it's the illness . . . but believe me, I never loved anyone more than you . . . don't forget me . . . take care of my ring . . ."'

The district doctor turned away. I took his hand.

'Oh,' he cried, 'let's talk about something else! Or perhaps you'd like a little game of whist? Chaps like us, you know, shouldn't give way to such highfalutin' feelings. Chaps like us should only bother with things like stopping the children crying or the wife scolding. Since then I've contracted a legal marriage, as they say . . . Well, you know . . . I found a merchant's daughter. Dowry of seven thousand roubles. She's called Akulina, which is about right for a Tripthong. She's a woman with a fierce tongue, but thankfully she's asleep all day . . . What d'you say to some whist?'

We sat down to whist for copeck stakes. Tripthong Ivanych won two and a half roubles off me and went home late, very content with his victory.

MY NEIGHBOUR RADILOV

———————— ❧ ————————

IN the autumn woodcocks are frequently to be found in the ancient lime groves. There are a good many such lime groves in Oryol province. Our forebears, in choosing a place to live, always set aside half-a-dozen acres of good land for orchards along with avenues of limes. After fifty years, at most seventy, these estates, these 'nests of the gentry', have vanished one by one from the face of the earth, the houses have decayed or been sold off for their timber, the stone-built service areas have been turned into mounds of rubble, the apple trees have dried and been used for firewood, the hedges and fences have all gone. Only the limes have grown up, as before, in their splendour and now, surrounded by ploughed fields, speak to our present flighty generation of 'all fathers and brothers now dead and buried'. An old lime is a beautiful tree. It is spared even by the merciless axe of the Russian peasant. With its small leaf and mighty branches spread wide on all sides, it creates eternal shade beneath it.

One time, wandering with Yermolay through the fields in search of partridges, I noticed a neglected orchard and went off in that direction. I'd hardly entered it when woodcock rose with beating wings from a bush. I fired and at that moment, a few feet from me, there was a cry and the frightened face of a young girl looked out from behind the trees and instantly vanished. Yermolay ran up to me, shouting: 'Why're you shooting? A landowner lives here!'

I'd hardly had time to answer him, and my dog'd scarcely had time to bring me a dead bird with dignified self-importance, when there was a sound of rapid footsteps and a tall, bewhiskered man emerged from a thicket and stopped in front of me looking very dissatisfied. I apologized as best I could, gave him my name and offered him the bird which I'd shot on his property.

'As you wish,' he said with a smile. 'I'll accept the bird, only on the condition that you stay and have dinner with me.'

I confess I wasn't overjoyed at his offer, but it was impossible to refuse.

'I'm a local landowner and your neighbour, Radilov. You may have heard of me,' my new acquaintance continued. 'It's Sunday today and the dinner should be a good one, otherwise I wouldn't have invited you.'

I answered as one should answer in such circumstances and set off to follow him. A recently cleared path quickly led us out of the lime grove and we entered a vegetable garden. Amid old apple trees and overgrown gooseberry bushes there grew innumerable round pale-green heads of cabbage with hop tendrils winding round their tall stems; sticking up in the beds were close-set rows of brown sticks all entwined with dried-up peas; large flat pumpkins literally lay about on the ground; cucumbers hung yellowing under dusty angular leaves; tall nettles swayed above the fence; in two or three places there grew masses of wild honeysuckle, elder and dogrose, the remains of what had formerly been well-kept flowerbeds. Beside a small fish pool, filled with reddish, slimy water, was a well surrounded by puddles. Ducks busily splashed and waddled about in these puddles; a dog, shivering and screwing up its eyes, gnawed at a bone on a patch of grass; a piebald cow also lazily nibbled the grass there, occasionally casting its tail over its scrawny back. The path turned to one side and beyond tall willows and birches there glanced at us a small, antiquated, grey house with a shingle roof and crooked porch. Radilov stopped.

'Of course,' he said, looking at me warmly and directly in the face, 'the thought has just occurred to me that perhaps you've no wish to come to me at all. In which case . . .'

I didn't let him finish and assured him that, on the contrary, it would be very pleasant to have dinner with him.

'Well, you know what I mean . . .'

We went into the house. A young fellow in a long caftan of thick blue cloth met us on the porch. Radilov at once ordered him to give Yermolay some vodka, at which my hunting companion bowed respectfully towards the back of the benevolent donor. From the hallway, which was papered with various colourful pictures and hung with birdcages, we entered a small room – Radilov's study. I took off my hunting togs and put my gun in one corner. The young fellow in his long frock-coat busily brushed me down.

'Well, let's go into the drawing-room,' said Radilov courteously. 'I'll introduce you to my mother.'

I followed behind him. In the drawing-room, sitting on a divan in the centre of the room, was a tiny old woman in a brown dress and white bonnet, with a kindly, shrunken face and a modest, sad expression.

'Mother, I'd like to introduce our neighbour Mr —'

The old woman rose and bowed to me without releasing from her bony hands a worsted handbag as fat as a sack.

'Have you been long in our parts?' she asked in a weak, quiet voice, blinking her eyes.

'No, ma'am, not long.'

'Are you intending to stay long?'

'Until the winter, I think.'

The old woman fell silent.

'And here,' chimed in Radilov, pointing out to me a tall, thin man I'd not noticed on first entering the drawing-room, 'is Fyodor Mikheich . . . Come on, Fedya, give our guest a taste of your art. What are you hiding in the corner for?'

Fyodor Mikheich instantly jumped out of his chair, took from the window ledge a cheap-looking fiddle, picked up a bow – not by the end, as is normal, but by the middle – leaned the fiddle against his chest, closed his eyes and launched into a dance, singing a ditty and sawing away at the strings. In appearance he was about seventy. A long nankeen frock-coat bounced about sadly on his dry bony limbs. He danced, either boldly giving himself a shake, or, as if on the point of collapse, swayed his small bald head, stretched his veiny neck, tapped his feet and sometimes, with evident difficulty, bent his knees. From his toothless mouth came his frail voice. Radilov must have guessed from the expression on my face that Fedya's 'art' gave little pleasure.

'Well, old chap, that's enough,' he said. 'You can go off and receive your reward.'

Fyodor Mikheich at once replaced the fiddle on the window ledge, bowed first to me as a guest, then to the old woman, then to Radilov and then left the room.

'He was also once a landowner,' continued my friend, 'and a rich one, but he went bankrupt and now he lives with me . . . But in his time he wàs considered the foremost Casanova in the province. He stole two wives from their husbands, used to keep singers, sang himself and was a masterly dancer . . . Perhaps you'd like some vodka? Dinner's already on the table.'

A young girl, the very one I'd caught sight of in the garden, came into the room.

'Ah, here's Olya!' noted Radilov, slightly turning his head. 'I beg you to love and leave her . . . Well, let's go and have dinner.'

We went into the dining-room and sat down. While we were doing this, Fyodor Mikheich, whose eyes glistened and nose had reddened from his 'reward', sang out 'Victory, thy trumpets sound!'[1] He had a special place laid for him at a small table without a table-napkin. The poor old man could hardly boast of his neatness and he was therefore always kept at some distance from polite society. He crossed himself, sighed and began eating like a shark. The dinner was actually not bad and, since it was Sunday, would not have been passable without some quivering jellies and Spanish vol-au-vents (like small pies). In the course of the dinner Radilov, who'd done ten years' army service in a foot regiment and been in Turkey, launched into various stories. I listened attentively to him and meanwhile observed Olga on the quiet. She wasn't very pretty, but the resolute and calm expression of her face, her broad white forehead, thick hair and, in particular, her hazel eyes, small but intelligent, clear and vivacious, would have struck anyone, no matter who, in my place. She seemed to follow closely Radilov's every word and not sympathy so much as passionate attention was displayed on her face. In years Radilov could've been her father. He used an intimate form of address to her, but I guessed at once she couldn't be his daughter. In the course of our conversation he mentioned his late wife – 'her sister,' he added, indicating Olga. She quickly blushed and lowered her eyes. Radilov paused and changed the conversation. The old woman didn't say a word throughout the meal, ate practically nothing herself and did not play hostess to me. Her features emanated a kind of timid and hopeless expectancy and the sort of elderly sadness which can squeeze the heart of an onlooker so painfully. Towards the end of the meal Fyodor Mikheich showed signs of wanting to sing the praises of his hosts and their guest, but Radilov glanced at me and told him to stop. The old man drew his hand across his lips, blinked, bowed and sat down again, but this time on the very edge of his chair. After dinner Radilov and I repaired to his study.

In people who are constantly and strongly preoccupied by one thought or by a single passion there is always some common feature noticeable, some common likeness in behaviour, no matter how different their qualities, their abilities, their position in society and their education. The longer I observed Radilov, the more it seemed to me that he belonged to such a category of person. He would talk about running his estate, about the harvest, about the haymaking, about the war, about the provincial gossip and forthcoming elections, he would talk quite freely, even with a sense of involvement, but suddenly he'd give a sigh and sink into an armchair, drywashing his face like a man worn out by hard work. It seemed his entire spirit, kindly and warm though it was, was penetrated, permeated through and through, by a single feeling. I was struck by the fact that I couldn't find in him any passion for food or wine or hunting or Kursk nightingales or epileptic pigeons or Russian literature or trotting horses or Hungarian jackets or cards or billiards or going dancing in the evening or paying visits to the local town or the capital or paper and sugar-beet factories or brightly decorated gazebos or tea parties or trace-horses driven into bad ways or even fat coachmen with belts right up to their armpits, those magnificent coachmen whose every movement of their necks, God knows why, makes their eyes literally pop out of their heads ... 'What sort of a landowner *is* this?' I thought. Besides he gave no impression whatever of being gloomy or dissatisfied with his fate. On the contrary, he literally radiated indiscriminate goodwill, cordiality and an almost shameful readiness to make friends with all and sundry. It's true you had the feeling at the same time that he couldn't really be friends, couldn't really be on close terms with anyone, and he couldn't not because he didn't really need other people but because his whole life had been turned inwards. Studying Radilov closely I couldn't ever imagine him happy, either now or at any time. He was also not endowed with good looks, but secreted in his eyes, in his smile and in his whole being there was something extraordinarily attractive – and yet it was secreted. So it seemed you wanted to know him better and really be friends with him. Of course, from time to time he showed signs of being the landowner and steppe-dweller he was, but as a man he was nevertheless a splendid chap.

We'd just begun talking about the new provincial marshal of nobility when suddenly Olga's voice on the other side of the door announced: 'Tea's ready.' We went into the drawing-room. Fyodor Mikheich sat as usual in his corner, between the window and the door, his legs modestly pressed together. Radilov's mother was knitting a sock. Through the open windows came autumnal freshness and a fragrance of apples. Olga busily poured tea. I watched her now with greater attention than I had during dinner. She spoke very little, as was common among provincial girls, but in her, at least, I saw no inclination to make some fancy remark accompanied by an appalling sense of emptiness and feebleness; nor did she sigh, as if from an excess of inexplicable feelings, nor roll up her eyes, nor smile dreamily and vaguely. She had a calm, cool look about her, as of someone resting after a great happiness or a great distress. Her walk and her gestures were assured and unconstrained. I took a great liking to her.

Radilov and I started talking again. I don't remember how we reached the point of agreeing that it's often the most insignificant things that produce the greatest impression on people, rather than the most important ones.

'Yes,' said Radilov, 'I experienced this myself once. I was married, you know. Not for long ... just three years. My wife died in childbirth. I thought I'd never get over it. I was appallingly grief-stricken, knocked flat by it, but I couldn't shed a tear and went about the place crazy with it all. They dressed her in suitable clothes and laid her on the table – right here, in this room. The priest came. The deacons came, they started singing, praying, wafting incense. I made all the obeisances, bowed right down to the ground, and yet I couldn't manage a single tear. My heart'd literally turned to stone, my head as well. I couldn't feel a thing. That was how the first day passed. Can you credit it! I even slept that night. The next morning I went in to see her. It was summertime and the sun shone on her from head to toe, and so brightly. Suddenly I saw ...' (At this point Radilov shuddered.) 'What d'you think? One of her eyes wasn't completely shut and over this eye a fly was walking ... I collapsed like scythed corn and when I came to I cried and cried and simply couldn't stop myself . . .'

Radilov stopped. I looked at him and then at Olga and I'll never forget the expression on her face. The old woman laid the sock on her knees, took a handkerchief from her handbag and stealthily wiped away a tear. Fyodor Mikheich suddenly stood up, seized his fiddle and in his untutored, quavering voice started singing. He very likely wanted to cheer us all up, but we all gave a shudder from the first sound he made and Radilov asked him to stop.

'Besides,' he went on, 'it's over and done with. You can't bring back the past and, in the end, you know, all's for the best in the best of all possible worlds . . . As Voltaire once said, I think,' he added hurriedly.[2]

'Yes, of course,' I agreed. 'What's more, one can put up with unhappiness, and there's no situation so awful you can't get out of it somehow.'

'You really think so?' Radilov asked. 'Well, perhaps you're right. I remember once in Turkey I was lying in a hospital half-dead.[3] I had marsh fever. We couldn't exactly boast of our hospital buildings – after all, it was wartime and a case of God help us! Suddenly more sick ones were brought in, but where could they go? The doctor rushed about here and there, but there wasn't any space. Then he came up to me and asked the orderly if I was still alive. The orderly answered: "He was alive this morning." The doctor bent down and heard I was breathing. The friendly chap couldn't resist saying: "Nature's a bloody fool. Here's a man dying, absolutely certain to die, but he's just scraping by, just hanging on, and all he's doing is occupying a space and stopping others from coming in." "Well," I thought, "you're in a really bad way, Mikhaylo Mikhaylich . . ." But I got better, you know, and I'm alive to this day, as you can see. So it seems you're right.'

'Oh, I'm right whatever the situation,' I answered. 'Even if you'd died, you'd still have got out of your bad situation.'

'OK, OK,' he added, suddenly and powerfully striking the table with his hand, 'you must just make up your mind! Why put up with a bad situation, eh? What's the point of scraping by, hanging on . . .'

Olga stood up quickly and went out into the garden.

'Well, Fedya, give us a tune!' shouted Radilov.

Fedya jumped up and walked about the room with that show-off special walk of a boy mincing about in front of a tame bear, beginning to sing:

'Once a-walking past our gates . . .'

The noise of a carriage resounded at the porch steps and in a moment or so a tall old man entered the room, broad-shouldered and solidly built, Farmer Ovsyanikov by name . . . But Ovsyanikov is such a remarkable and unusual person that, with the reader's permission, we will talk about him in the next Sketch. As for the present story I'll simply add that the next day Yermolay and I set off hunting as soon as it was light and after hunting we went home and a week later I went once again to see Radilov, but I found neither him nor Olga at home, and a couple of weeks later I learnt he'd suddenly vanished, abandoning his mother and going off somewhere with his sister-in-law. The entire province was stirred by the event and started talking about it, and it was only then that I finally fathomed the look that had been on Olga's face during Radilov's story. It hadn't just been a look of compassion; it had been a look burning with envy.

Before leaving the country I visited Radilov's old mother. I found her in the drawing-room playing a game of 'donkey' with Fyodor Mikheich.

'Have you any news of your son?' I asked her eventually.

The old woman burst into tears. I didn't ask her any more about Radilov.

FARMER OVSYANIKOV

❧

IMAGINE, dear readers, a full, tall man of about seventy, with a face a little reminiscent of Krylov's,[1] with clear and intelligent eyes looking at you from under overhanging brows, with dignified bearing, measured speech and a slow walk: that was Ovsyanikov for you. He wore a capacious blue frock-coat with long sleeves, buttoned right up to the top, a lilac silk neckerchief, brightly polished boots with tassels and looked in general like a well-to-do merchant. He had beautiful hands, soft and white, and often in the course of conversation he would finger the buttons of his frock-coat. Ovsyanikov, in his dignity and statuesqueness, with his shrewdness and indolence, his directness and obstinacy reminded me of the Russian boyars of pre-Petrine times . . .[2] Their old-style Russian dress would have suited him. He was one of the last representatives of that former age. All his neighbours held him in the greatest esteem and considered it an honour to know him. His own people, homesteading farmers like him,[3] practically worshipped him, doffed their hats to him even from a distance and were proud of him. Generally speaking, it's been difficult so far among us to tell a homesteading farmer from a peasant. Their farms are scarcely better than a peasant's, their calves feed on buckwheat, their horses are barely alive and their harnesses are made of rope. Ovsyanikov was an exception to the general rule, though he couldn't pass for rich. He lived alone with his wife in a comfortable, neat little house and kept only a few servants, whom he dressed in traditional Russian dress and described as workers. They were the ones who worked his land for him. He didn't make himself out to be one of the gentry, never pretended to be a landowner, never 'forgot himself' to the point of sitting down at the first invitation and at the appearance of a new guest always rose to his feet, but with such dignity, such a grand display of welcome, that the guest would invariably bow lower despite himself. Ovsyanikov observed the customs of old not out of superstition (he had a reasonably free-thinking character), but out of habit. For example, he didn't like carriages with springs because he didn't find them restful, so he travelled about either in a racing droshky or in a small red cart with a leather cushion and drove his good bay trotter himself. (He only kept bays.) The coachman, a young red-cheeked lad with a fringed haircut, dressed in a bluish, belted sheepskin jacket and a flat woollen cap, would sit respectfully beside him. Ovsyanikov always slept after dinner, visited the bath-house on Saturdays, read only religious books (for which purpose he importantly placed on his nose round silver spectacles), rose and went to bed early. However, he always shaved and wore his hair cropped in the German style. He would receive his guests very courteously and affably, but he never used to bow low to the waist, never made a fuss, never regaled them with fancy dried or salted things. 'Wife!' he would say slowly, without rising and slightly turning his head towards her. 'Bring the gentlemen something nice to eat!' He considered it sinful to sell wheat, since it was God's gift to man, and in 1840, at a time of general famine and appalling inflation, he distributed all his reserves among the local landowners and peasants; the following year they gratefully repaid their debts in kind. Neighbours frequently ran to Ovsyanikov with pleas to arbitrate and settle their differences and they practically always submitted to his judgement and took his advice. Many reached ultimate redivisions of their land through his good offices . . . But after two or three brushes with female land-owners he announced that he would refuse to arbitrate between members of the female sex. He couldn't stand fuss and bother and panicky hastiness and a lot of female chatter and 'vanity'. One day his house caught fire. One of his workers rushed in to him shouting: 'Fire! Fire!' 'What're you shouting for?' asked Ovsyanikov calmly. 'Fetch me my hat and stick . . .' He was personally very fond of training horses. On one occasion a frisky Bityuk horse* rushed him downhill and into a ravine. 'Hey, hey, you underage colt, you, you'll kill yourself,' Ovsyanikov reproved him kindly and a moment later he

---

* 'Bityuks', or 'of Bityuk stock', were a special breed of horses that came from Voronezh province, in the famous 'Khrenov' region (the former stud belonging to Countess Orlova) – *Author's note.*

flew into the ravine along with the racing drozhky, the boy sitting behind him and the horse. Fortunately, there were mounds of sand at the bottom of the ravine. No one was hurt and the horse simply dislocated its leg. 'Well, you see,' continued Ovsyanikov in a calm voice, getting up from the ground, 'I told you so.' And the wife he'd chosen suited him. Tatyana Ilyinichna Ovsyanikov was a tall woman, dignified and taciturn, with a brown silk kerchief always tied round her head. She conveyed a feeling of coldness, although it wasn't that anyone complained of her severity but, on the contrary, many poor people called her their very own mother and benefactress. Her regular features, large dark eyes and fine lips remained evidence of her once famous beauty. The Ovsyanikovs had no children.

I met him at Radilov's, as the reader already knows, and a couple of days later I called on him. I found him at home. He was sitting in a large leather armchair and he was reading from the monthly calendar of saints' lives. A grey cat purred on his shoulder. He received me, as was his custom, courteously and somewhat grandly. We struck up a conversation.

'Tell me the truth, Luka Petrovich,' I said by the by. 'Surely, in your time, things were better?'

'Some things were truly better, I can tell you,' Ovsyanikov replied. 'We lived quieter lives, and it's true there was more of everything . . . But it's better now. And for your children it'll be better still, God grant.'

'Luka Petrovich, I'd expected you to start praising the old days.'

'No, I've no reason to praise them old days especially. I'll give you one example. Take yourself, you're a landowner, just as much a landowner as your late grandad, but you'll never have as much authority as he had! What's more, you're not the same kind of man. Nowadays there's other gentlemen putting pressure on us, but it seems you'll never get rid of that. The corn's gotta be ground, you know, that's the only way you'll get flour. No, I won't be seeing nowadays what I saw so much of in my youth.'

'What, for instance?'

'Take, for example, what I gotta say about your grandad. A man of authority, he was! He'd squash the likes of us. You very likely know – well, of course, you know your own land – the wedge of land stretching from Chaplygino to Malinin? You've got it under oats now. Well, that's ours — our land as ever is. Your grandad took it off us. He rode up, pointed, said: "That's my property," and took it. My father — he's dead now (God rest his soul!) — he was a just man, but hot-tempered, too, and didn't stand for that — who wants to lose his property anyway? — and he went to court. He went to court, mind, but the others didn't — they were too frightened. So your grandad was told that Pyotr Ovsyanikov'd lodged a complaint against him, to the effect that his land'd been taken away ... Your grandad at once sent his master of hounds Baush to us, along with some men. They seized my father and took him to your estate. I was a small boy and I ran after him barefoot. So what d'you think, eh? They took him to your house and there they gave him a beating right under the windows. And your grandad stood on the balcony and watched, he did. And your grandma sat at the window watching too. My father called out: "Dear lady, Marya Vasilyevna, help me, have mercy on me!" But all she did was raise herself a little and glance down at him. So they got father to promise he'd give up the land and they ordered him to thank them for letting him go with his life. So it's remained yours. Go and ask your peasants what that piece of land's called. "Cudgel's Piece" they call it, because it was taken away with a cudgel. That's why there's nothing much for us, us small folk, to regret about the old order of things.'

I didn't know what to say to Ovsyanikov and didn't dare look him in the face.

'And there was another neighbour of ours in those times, Komov, Stepan Niktopolionych. He was a real pain to my father, if not with one thing, then another. He was a drunkard and he liked to play host, and as soon as he'd had a drop to drink he'd be saying in French "*Se bon*" and he'd lick his lips — then there'd be all hell let loose! He'd send round to all his neighbours asking them to visit. His troikas literally stood ready, and if you didn't go he'd be down on you at once! ... What a strange fellow he was! In a "soberous" state he'd never tell a lie, but as soon as he'd had a drop he'd begin telling how in St Petersburg he'd got three houses on the Fontanka — one red with one chimney, another yellow with two chimneys and a third blue without chimneys — and three sons (he'd never been married, mind), one in the infantry, one in the cavalry and one just ordinary

... And he'd say that a son lived in each of the houses, and the eldest
entertained admirals, the second one generals and the third one
nothing but Englishmen! Then he'd stand up and he'd say: "To the
health of my eldest son, he's the most respected!" – and then he'd
burst into tears. And woe to anyone who tried to refuse the toast!
"I'll shoot you!" he'd shout. "And I won't let you have a Christian
burial!" Or he'd jump up and shout: "Dance, all God's people, dance
– to your heart's content and my delight!" Well, you'd gotta dance,
though you might die, dance you must. He was a right pain to his
peasant girls. All night long, as ever was, till morning they'd be
singing in chorus and whichever reached the highest note got a prize.
And as soon as they'd get tired he'd rest his head on his hand and
start wailing: "Oh, what a poor orphan girl I am! They're leaving
me all forlorn!" Then the stable-lads'd rightaway start encouraging
them. My father became a favourite of his, but he couldn't help that,
could he? He nearly drove my father into the grave and would've
done, if he'd not died himself, thank God, by falling off a dovecote
when drunk ... That's the kind of neighbours we had in those days!'

'How times have changed,' I remarked.

'Yes, yes,' Ovsyanikov agreed. 'Still, it's gotta be said that in the
old days the gentry lived more sumptuously. Which is to say nothing
about the grandees, I had my fill of seeing them in Moscow. They
say there aren't any of them left there.'

'You've been to Moscow?'

'Yes – long, long ago. I'm going on seventy-three now an' I went
to Moscow in my sixteenth year.'

Ovsyanikov sighed.

'Who did you see there?'

'Many grand personages I saw and each one I saw lived openly,
for everyone to admire and wonder at. Only not one of them
matched Count Aleksey Grigoryevich Orlov-Chesmensky.[4] I used
to see Aleksey Grigoryevich often 'cos my uncle was his butler. The
Count used to live out by the Kaluga Gate, on Shabalovka. Now he
was a real grandee! Such bearing, such gracious words of welcome –
unimaginable, indescribable. His height alone was worth something
and as for his strength, his look! ... So long as you didn't know him,
hadn't met him face to face, you'd be really frightened and shy, but
as soon as you met him he'd bring the sun's warmth into your life

and you'd be full of joy. He'd let anyone into his presence and be interested in everything. In the races he drove himself and he'd race with each one, never overtaking right away, never humiliating, never breaking away, but only going ahead at the very end. And he was so nice about it, consoling his opponent and praising his horse. He used to keep the very best sort of tumbling pigeons. He'd go out into his courtyard, seat himself in an armchair and order the pigeons to be released. And all round about, on the roofs, his men'd be standing with guns to protect against hawks. A large silver bowl with water in it would be put at the Count's feet and he'd watch the pigeons reflected in the water. Hundreds of paupers and beggars lived off his bread – and the amount of money he handed out! But when he was angry, it was like a roar of thunder! You'd be frightened, but there'd be nothing to cry about. A moment later you'd look at him and he'd be smiling. He'd give a feast and the whole of Moscow'd be drunk! And what a clever chap he was! After all, he beat the Turks. He loved wrestling, too. He'd have strong fellows brought to him from Tula and Kharkov and Tambov and all over. If he outwrestled someone, he'd give him a prize, but if he got beaten he'd give lavish rewards and kiss the winner on the lips . . . During my time in Moscow he organized such a hunt as had never before been seen in all Russia. He invited all the hunters as ever were from all parts of the kingdom to be his guests and named the day three months ahead. So they all gathered. They brought dogs and huntsmen – a whole army of them there were! First they all feasted as was right and proper and then they all set off for the town gate. Such a crowd of people there were, all pushing and shoving! And what d'you think? It was your grandad's dog outran all of them.'

'You mean Pretty Lady?' I asked.

'Pretty Lady, Pretty Lady, that's right . . . The Count, he started saying: "Sell me your dog. Take whatever you like for her." "No, Count," your grandad said, "I'm not a merchant, I don't go round selling worthless rubbish, but as a matter of honour I'd be prepared to give up my wife, only I'll not give up Pretty Lady . . . I'd rather go to prison." And Aleksey Grigoryevich praised him. "That's what I like to hear," he said. Your grandad brought her back in his carriage. And when Pretty Lady died, he buried her in the garden with musical accompaniment, buried the bitch and erected a stone with an inscription over her grave.'

'So Aleksey Grigoryevich never did anyone down, then,' I remarked.

'That's always the way it is: it's the petty ones that see the pettiness in others.'

'What sort of a chap was this Baush?' I asked after some moments' silence.

'How is it you've heard about Pretty Lady but you haven't heard about Baush? He was your grandad's chief huntsman in charge of the hounds. Your grandad was as fond of him as he was of Pretty Lady. He was fiercely loyal, and whatever your grandad ordered him to do he'd do it in a flash, even if it meant getting knifed for it ... And when he set the hounds on some scent he'd fill the whole forest with his shouts. And then he might suddenly straighten up, slip off his horse and lie down flat. When the hounds couldn't hear his voice any more, that'd be that – finished! They'd give up the scent and wouldn't go on no matter what. Heck, wouldn't your grandad be angry! "Life," he'd say, "it's not worth living, unless I string up that good-for-nothing! I'll tear that Antichrist inside out! I'll pull his heels right through his throat, I will!" And it'd end by him sending to know what was wrong, why weren't the hounds being set on. And Baush in such circumstances used usually to ask for something to drink, have a drink, then climb to his feet and start his view-halloo all over again.'

'It seems you're also fond of hunting, Luka Petrovich?'

'I'd love hunting, yes ... but not now. Now my time's passed, but when I was young ... I felt awkward, you know, on account of my being a farmer. It's not for the likes of us to start trying to be gentry. Mind, there've been those of us farmers, drinkers and incompetents, who've sucked up to our lords and masters – and a lot o' good it's done them! They've just brought shame on themselves. They'd be given some trashy, stumbling horse and have their hats knocked off their heads again and again or get swiped with a horse-whip supposedly meant for the horse and they'd have to pretend to laugh at it and make others laugh. No, I tell you, the lower down the social scale you are, the stricter you've got to behave, otherwise you'll be in the dirt.

'Yes,' Ovsyanikov continued with a sigh, 'much water's flowed under the bridge since I was born and now times are different. In particular I've noticed a great change in the gentry. The minor gentry've either been in state service or else can't stay in one place, and as for the bigwigs – you can't recognize them any more. I've done my fill of looking at the big ones – for instance, over the redivision of land. And I've gotta tell you this: it fair gladdens the heart to see how caring and polite they are. Only what surprises me is that they've got all their learning and talk so fancy that one can't help being impressed, but they still don't understand real business and can't feel what's in their own best interest. Why, one of their peasants, a bailiff, say, can bend them any way he wants just like a bow! Well, you probably know Korolyov, Alexander Vladimirych – he's one of the gentry, isn't he? Good-looking, rich, attended universities, it seems, and been abroad, is a smooth talker, self-effacing and shakes everyone by the hand. Do you know who I mean? Well, then listen to this. Last week we all gathered in Beryozovka on the invitation of the mediator, Nikifor Ilyich. And the mediator Nikifor Ilyich said to us: "Gentlemen, we've got to revise our boundaries. It's a crying shame that our sector of land's got so behind-hand. Let's get down to business." So we got down to it. As usual, there were discussions and arguments and our legal adviser began to get really heated. But the first one to blow up was Porfiry Ovchinnikov. And what's he got to blow up about? He didn't own an inch of land, but he was acting on his brother's behalf. He shouted: "No, you won't get the better of me! No, I'm not going to be fooled! Give the plans here! Let me get my hands on that surveyor, just let me get hold of that Judas!" "In the end, what on earth do you want?" "My God, what a fool! Do you think I'm going to tell you right now what I want? No, just you let me have those plans!" And he brought his fist down on the plans. Marfa Dmitrievna was bitterly hurt. She shouted: "How do you dare cast a slur on my reputation?" He said: "I wouldn't want your reputation for my brown mare." They forced some madeira on them. He was calmed down and then others started up. Korolyov, Alexander Vladimirych, sat the whole time as good as gold in the corner and sucked the knob on his walking-stick and just nodded his head. I felt real bad about it all, but just didn't have the strength to get up and go. And I wondered what he was thinking about the lot of us? Then I saw that my Alexander Vladimirych had got up and was giving the impression he wanted to say something.

The mediator put on airs and said: "Gentlemen, gentlemen, Alexander Vladimirych would like to say a word." And you've gotta give the gentry credit, because they all stopped talking at that. So Alexander Vladimirych began and he said that we've, so to speak, forgotten what we're doing here, that although boundary revision is indisputably advantageous to landowners, what has it really been introduced for? Why, in order to ensure that the peasant has an easier lot, can work and fulfil his obligations more easily. As it is, he may not even know what land is his and frequently has to go five miles or more to do his ploughing and so you don't know how much to ask him to pay. Then Alexander Vladimirych said it was a sin for a landowner not to care about the welfare of his peasants, that peasants were entrusted to him by God and, finally, that, if one thought about it sensibly, their advantage was our advantage, that it was all one and the same: what was good for them was good for us, what was bad for them was bad for us, and that consequently it was sinful and foolish not to reach agreement because of trivial disputes, and so on, and so forth . . . Oh, the way he talked! He fairly seized one by the heart. The gentry all looked crestfallen and I myself was almost on the verge of tears. My word, you wouldn't find a speech like that in any of the old-fashioned books! But how did it all end? He didn't want to give up and sell just under a dozen acres of mossy bogland. He said: "I'll drain that bog with my own men and put up a cloth factory there, with all the latest improvements. I've specially chosen that place," he said, "and I've got my own reasons . . ." Though that was right and proper in its own way, it was only because Alexander Vladimirych's neighbour, Anton Karasikov, hadn't given Koroloyov's bailiff a hundred-rouble bribe in paper notes. So we dispersed without having done what we should've done. And Alexander Vladimirych still goes on thinking himself in the right and talks about a cloth factory, only he does nothing about draining the bog.'

'How does he run his estate?'

'Always bringing in new rules, he is. His peasants don't like it, but there's no point in listening to them. Alexander Vladimirych's doing the right thing.'

'How can you say that, Luka Petrovich? I thought you wanted to maintain the old ways.'

'I'm a different matter. You see, I'm not a member of the gentry and I'm not a landowner. What's my farm amount to, after all? In any case, I don't know how to do things otherwise. I try to conform to justice and the law – and I say thank God for 'em! The young gentlemen don't like the old ways and I praise them for it. It's time to start using our heads. Only the trouble is the young gents are too clever by half. They treat the peasant like a doll, playing with him, doing this and that to him, breaking him and throwing him away. And your bailiff, who's a peasant, too, or your manager, who's a transplanted German, they get their claws into the peasant as well. If only one of them young gents'd set an example and show how the peasants really should be treated! Where'd it end in that case? Am I literally going to die without seeing any new ways brought in? What a parable, eh? The old's died away but the young hasn't been born!'

I didn't know what to say to Ovsyanikov. He looked round, moved himself closer to me and continued in a low voice:

'Have you heard about Vasily Nikolaich Lyubozvonov?'

'No, I haven't.'

'Then please explain to me what wonders these are. I can't fathom it. His very own peasants have been telling me about it but I can't make head or tail of their talk. He's a young man, you know, and has recently come into his inheritance after the death of his mother. Well, he travelled to his estate. The peasants all gathered to have a glimpse of their master. Vasily Nikolaich went out to meet them. The peasants watched and – what a sight! – the master appeared wearing velveteen pantaloons just like a coachman and he'd put on fancy boots with trimmings and a red peasant shirt and a coachman's caftan.[5] He wore his beard long and had such a weird kind of hat on his head and his face was kinda weird – maybe he was drunk, maybe not, but he certainly wasn't in his right mind. "Greetings, lads," he said. "God be with you!" The peasants all bowed low to him, 'cept they didn't say anything, being shy, you know. And so he got all shy as well. He tried to make a speech. "I'm a Russian, like," he said, "and you're Russian. I love all things Russian ... Er, I've got a Russian soul, so to speak, and, er, I've got Russian blood ..." Then he suddenly gave an order: "Well, my children, sing me a real Russian, real folksy song!" The peasants' knees started fair shaking at that and they felt right idiots. One bold fellow struck up a song, only to sit flat down on the ground at once and hide himself behind the others ... This is what you've got to wonder at, you know: we've had landowners like that, bloody awful gents, mad as hatters, it's true, who've decked themselves out as coachmen and danced and played the guitar and sung and drunk with their own house servants and feasted with their peasants. But this one, this Vasily Nikolaich, is just like a girl, he's all the time reading and writing books or he goes around chanting verses, never talking to anyone, mind, fighting shy of people, strolling by himself in the garden as if he's bored or sad. The former bailiff was terrified at first. Before Vasily Nikolaich's arrival he dashed round all the peasant houses and fawned on 'em, just like a cat who knows he's eaten somebody else's meat. And the peasants raised their expectations and thought: "You're in for it, mate. O-oh, they'll get you to answer for what you done, you'll dance to a new tune, you old skinflint!" But instead it worked out – well, how can I put it? – I don't think the Good Lord himself really knows how it's worked out! Vasily Nikolaich summoned the bailiff to him and said: "You've got to be just in what you do, don't oppress anyone, do you hear?" But since then he's never spoken to him again! He's lived on his estate like a stranger. Well, of course, the bailiff heaved a deep sigh, and the peasants haven't dared approach Vasily Nikolaich because they're frightened to. And what's also worthy of surprise is that their master goes around bowing to them and giving them welcome looks, while they simply get stomach cramps from fright. What sort of wonders are these, eh? ... Or maybe I've grown old and stupid and just don't understand things any more ...'

I told Ovsyanikov that Mr Lyubozvonov was probably sick.

'Sick indeed! He's broader than he's tall and his face, God help him, is thick as thick, despite his being young ... Still, God knows!' (And Ovsyanikov gave a deep sigh.)

'Well,' I said, 'the gentry apart, what'll you tell me about the farmers, Luka Petrovich?'

'No, allow me to refuse on that one,' he declared hurriedly. 'True, I'd tell you a thing or two – but so what!' (Ovsyanikov gave a wave of the hand.) 'Let's have some tea. Peasants are peasants, that's the truth, and how could we be otherwise, eh?'

He fell silent. Tea was served. Tatyana Ilyinichna rose from where she'd been sitting and drew closer to us. In the course of the evening she'd several times gone out noiselessly and returned just as quietly. Silence reigned in the room. Ovsyanikov in a slow and dignified way drank cup after cup.

'Mitya came to see us today,' Tatyana Ilyinichna remarked quietly.

Ovsyanikov frowned.

'What did he want?'

'He came to make his apologies.'

Ovsyanikov shook his head.

'Well,' he continued, turning to me, 'tell me, what can you do about relatives? You can't turn your back on 'em . . . God's gone and rewarded me too with a nephew of sorts. He's a young fellow with brains, plenty of bounce, no denying it. He was good at learning, but I don't think he'll ever stick at anything. He was on government service and threw it up 'cos he didn't think he'd get anywhere with it . . . Well, he's not a gent, is he? And not all gentlemen get made generals rightaway, do they? So now he's got no work . . . And who knows where he'll get to next, maybe he'll become a government informer! He composes petitions for peasants, writes reports, tells the village constable what to do, gives the surveyors what for, goes round the pubs drinking and passes the time of day with soldiers on discharge, with townee types and porters from the post-stations. How long will it be before disaster strikes? He's already received threats from the police. It's a good thing, though, he's a bit of a joker. He can make 'em laugh, only to get them into a proper pickle afterwards . . . Enough of this, though, isn't he sitting in your little room right now?' he added, turning to his wife. 'I know you, you're much too kind-hearted. You've been protecting him, haven't you?'

Tatyana Ilyinichna bowed her head, smiled and blushed.

'Well, you see,' Ovsyanikov continued. 'Oh, you softie, you! Well, tell him to come in – on account of having a dear guest with us, I'll forgive him . . . Well, tell him, tell him . . .'

Tatyana Ilyinichna went to the door and called out: 'Mitya!'

Mitya, a fellow of about twenty-eight, tall, well-built and curly-haired, came into the room and, on seeing me, stopped in the doorway. He wore German-style clothes, but the puffing of the sleeves at the shoulders was of such unnatural size that they served as clear demonstration of the fact that it was not just a tailor but an All-Russian tailor who'd made them.

'Well, come in, come in,' said the old man, 'why're you so shy? Thank your aunt that you're forgiven. There you are, my dear sir, I'd like to introduce you,' he went on, pointing at Mitya. 'My very own nephew but I'll never see eye to eye with him, come the end of the world!' (We bowed to each other.) 'Well, tell us what you've been up to there? Why're they making complaints against you, eh?'

Mitya clearly didn't want to explain and justify himself in front of me.

'Later, uncle,' he muttered.

'No, not later, but right now,' the old man continued. 'I know you feel awkward in front of a landowner and a gentleman. So much the better, it'll serve you right. Come on, come on, tell us . . . we'll listen.'

'I've got nothing to be ashamed of,' Mitya began vivaciously and shook his head. 'Judge for yourself, uncle. The Reshetilov farmers came to me and said: "Help us, mate." "What's wrong?" "This is what's wrong: our grain stores are in tip-top shape, couldn't be better, but suddenly along comes an official and says he's got orders to inspect 'em. He looked 'em over and says: 'They're in a right mess, your stores, they've got serious shortcomings, I'll have to report to higher authority.' 'What are these shortcomings?' 'I know what they are,' he says . . . We got together and decided on the usual sort of bribe to give the official, when up spoke the old man Prokhorych and said, you'll only be whetting his appetite if you do that. What's the point of it? Or haven't we got any come-back at all? We listened to what the old man said and the official got real annoyed and put in a complaint and reported against us. And now they're making us answer for it." "Well, are your grain stores really in proper shape?" I asked. "As God is our witness, they're in tip-top shape and they contain the legal amount of grain . . ." "Well," I said, "you've got nothing to be ashamed of in that case," and I wrote out a statement for them . . . And it's still not clear which way the business'll go . . . But it's understandable you've had people complaining about me in this case because everyone knows which side his bread is buttered.'

'Yes, everyone knows that except you,' said the old man under his breath. 'But what fun and games have you been up to with the Shutolomovsky peasants?'

'How d'you know about that?'

'Oh, I know.'

'I'm in the right there, too. Again judge for yourself. The Shutolomovsky peasants' neighbour, Mr Bespandin, began ploughing up about a dozen acres of their land. It's mine, he said, mine. The Shutolomovsky people are on quit-rent and their landowner's gone abroad, so who've they got to stand up for them, eh? You be judge of that. And the land's theirs without doubt, peasant land, always has been. So they came to me and asked me to write out a petition. And I wrote it. And Mr Bespandin got to know about it and started making threats: "I'll pull that bloody Mitya's shoulder blades out of their sockets," he said, "and I'll just about tear his head from his shoulders . . ." Well, let's see if he tears it off. It's still on so far.'

'Well, don't you start boasting, that won't do your head much good,' said the old man. 'You're crazy, completely crazy!'

'Uncle, isn't it just what you've been telling me yourself . . .'

'I know it, I know exactly what you're going to say to me,' Ovsyanikov interrupted him. 'You're going to say: A man must live in justice and should help his neighbour. It's also true that he mustn't spare himself. Well, do you always behave as you should? Don't they sometimes take you into a pub, eh? Give you a drink, fawn on you and say: "Dmitry Alekseich, well, sir, you help us and we'll show you how grateful we are," and, you know, maybe there's a coin or a banknote slipping into your hand from somewhere, eh? Doesn't that happen? Say it doesn't, eh?'

'Sure, I'm guilty of that,' answered Mitya, looking down at the floor, 'but I don't take anything from poor people and I don't do anything to be ashamed of.'

'You don't take anything now, but when things start going wrong for you, you'll start taking. Nothing to be ashamed of indeed . . . Oh, you, you think you're taking the sides of the saints! Have you forgotten Borka Perekhodov? Who fussed over him? Who gave him protection, eh?'

'Perekhodov suffered because of what he did himself, true enough . . .'

'Stole government money . . . Some joke that!'

'Uncle, you've got to remember his poverty, his family . . .'

'His poverty, his family . . . He was a drunkard, a gambler, that's what!'

'He started drinking from sorrow,' remarked Mitya, lowering his voice.

'From sorrow! Well, you should've helped him if your heart's so fond and not sat in pubs with the drunkard. He's got a wonderful line in talk – never seen anything like it!'

'He's the soul of kindness, he is . . .'

'With you they're all the soul of kindness . . . Was, er,' Ovsyanikov went on, turning to his wife, 'something sent to him – well, you know where . . .'

Tatyana Ilyinichna nodded.

'So where've you been these last few days?' the old man started asking.

'In town.'

'I reckon you've been playing billiards and drinking tea and strumming the guitar and rushing round from one government office to another and concocting petitions in back rooms and parading about with merchants' sons? I'm right, aren't I? Go on, tell us!'

'OK, it was like that,' said Mitya with a smile. 'Oh, I almost forgot: Funtikov, Anton Parfenych, asked you to come and have dinner on Sunday.'

'I won't go to that big-bellied bloke. He'll give us good fish and then cover it all with rancid butter. Bless him, anyway!'

'And I met Fedosya Mikhaylovna.'

'What Fedosya?'

'The one belonging to Harpenchenko, the landowner, the one who bought Mikulino at auction. The Fedosya from Mikulino. She lived as a seamstress in Moscow paying quit-rent and paid her quit-rent punctually, 182 roubles and a half each year. And she knew her job, used to get good orders in Moscow. But now Harpenchenko's had her brought back and is keeping her there and not giving her any work. She'd like to buy her freedom and has spoken to her master, only he's not made any decision. Uncle, you know Harpenchenko, don't you? Couldn't you have a word with him? Fedosya'll pay well.'

'It's not your money, is it? Eh? Well, all right, I'll speak to him. 'Cept I don't know so much,' went on the old man, looking dissatisfied. 'God forgive me, but that Harpenchenko's a right skinflint, the way he buys up IOUs, lends at high rates and acquires estates under the hammer . . . Who the hell brought him our way? Oh, these outsiders! It'll take a while to get any sense from him, but anyhow, let's see.'

'Do your best, uncle.'

'All right, I'll do my best. Only just you look after yourself, just you watch out! I'm telling you that! No, no, don't make excuses . . . God be with you! Only just watch out for yourself, Mitya, otherwise you'll do yourself no good, you'll come a cropper, by God. Anyhow I don't want to have you round my neck all the time. I don't carry much weight, as it is. Well, be off with you, in God's name.'

Mitya went out. Tatyana Ilyinichna went after him.

'Give him some tea, you old softie, you,' Ovsyanikov shouted after her. 'The lad's no fool,' he continued, 'and he's got a kind heart, only I'm fearful for him . . . In any case, forgive me for bothering you so long with trifles.'

The door from the hallway opened. A small, slightly grey-haired man came in dressed in a velvet jacket.

'Ah, Franz Ivanych!' cried Ovsyanikov. 'Greetings! How's the Good Lord treating you?'

Permit me, dear reader, to acquaint you with this gentleman.

Franz Ivanych Lejeune, my neighbour and an Oryol landowner, achieved the honoured title of Russian nobleman and gentleman in a rather unusual way. He was born in Orléans, of French parents, and together with Napoleon set off on the conquest of Russia as a drummer. To start with everything went swimmingly, and our Frenchman entered Moscow with head held high. But on the return route the poor Monsieur Lejeune, half-frozen and without his drum, fell into the hands of Smolensk peasants. The Smolensk peasants locked him up for the night in an empty fullery and the next day led him to a hole in the ice near the dam and began begging the drummer '*de la grrrrande armée*' to do them the honour, that is to say to plunge under the ice. M. Lejeune was unable to agree to their suggestion and began in his turn to persuade the Smolensk peasants, in his French dialect, to let him go back to Orléans. 'There, *messieurs*,' he said, 'I have a mother living, *une tendre mère*.' But the peasants, doubtless through ignorance of the geographical location of the city of Orléans, went on suggesting to him that he take an under-water journey down the winding Gniloterka River and even began encouraging him with light shoves in his neck- and backbones when suddenly, to Lejeune's indescribable joy, there was a sound of horse-bells and on to the dam came a large sledge with the most colourful of covers laid over its exaggeratedly high back and drawn by a troika of light-brown Vyatka horses. In the sledge sat a stout and red-cheeked landowner in wolf fur.

'What're you doing there?' he asked the peasants.

'Drownin' a Frenchie, sir.'

'Ah!' the landowner responded indifferently and turned away.

'Monsieur! Monsieur!' exclaimed the poor fellow.

'Aha!' said the wolf fur reproachfully, 'with your dozen tongues you came to our Russia, burned Moscow, you scoundrel, stole the cross from off Ivan the Great's Tower and now it's all monsieur, monsieur! Now you've got your tail between your legs! A thief deserves what's coming to him . . . Off we go, Filka!'

The horses started away.

'Oh, by the way, stop a moment!' added the landowner. 'Hey you, monsieur, do you know any music?'

'Sauvez moi, sauvez moi, mon bon monsieur!' Lejeune begged.

'What a stupid people! Not a single one of them knows any Russian! Myuzik, myuzik, savvy myuzik voo? Savvy? Well, speak up! Comprenny? Savvy myuzik voo? On fortopiano zhooey savvy?'

Lejeune understood at last what the landowner was saying and nodded affirmatively.

'Oui, monsieur, oui, oui, je suis musicien; je joue de tous les instruments possibles! Oui, monsieur . . . Sauvez moi, monsieur!'

'Well, thank your lucky stars,' the landowner replied. 'Lads, let him go. Here's twenty copecks for a drink!'

'Thank you, sir, thank you. Please take him, sir.'

Lejeune was put in the sledge. He sighed with joy, wept, shivered, bowed to them and thanked the landowner, the coachman and the peasants. He was wearing only a green jersey with pink ribbons and there was a bitterly hard frost. The landowner gave one silent glance at his blue and freezing limbs and wrapped the unfortunate fellow in his own fur coat and took him home. The household ran to meet him. The Frenchman was quickly warmed up, fed and clothed. The landowner led him in to his daughters.

'Here, children,' he told them, 'a teacher's been found for you.

You were going on and on at me about wanting to learn music and that French dialect. Well, here's a Frenchman for you, and he plays the fortopiano ... Well, monsieur,' he continued, indicating a crummy little piano he'd bought five years before off a Jew, who was in any case an eau-de-cologne salesman, 'show us what you know: zhooey!'

Lejeune sat down on the chair with quaking heart because he'd never played a piano in his life.

'Zhooey, zhooey!' the landowner repeated.

In desperation the poor fellow struck the keys, just as if he were beating a drum, and played the first thing that came into his head. 'I literally thought,' he used to say afterwards, 'that my saviour would seize me by the scruff of the neck and throw me out of the house.' But, to the extreme surprise of the unwilling improviser, the land-owner after a short while tapped him appreciatively on the shoulder: 'Good, good,' he said. 'I see you know what to do. Now go and rest.'

After a couple of weeks Lejeune transferred from this landowner to another, a cultivated and wealthy man, caught his fancy through his happy and engaging character, married his pupil, entered the civil service, became a nobleman and a gentleman, married his own daughter off to an Oryol landowner called Lobyzanyev, a retired dragoon officer and amateur poet, and himself took up residence in Oryol.

It was this very Lejeune or, as he was now known, Franz Ivanych, who entered the sitting-room of Ovsyanikov, with whom he was on friendly terms ...

But perhaps the reader has already grown tired of sitting with me at Farmer Ovsyanikov's and so I will now eloquently fall silent.

LGOV

—————————— ❧ ——————————

'LET'S go to Lgov,' Yermolay, who is already known to our readers, said to me one day, 'we'll shoot duck there to our heart's content.'

Although wild duck is not particularly attractive to a real hunter, for want of any other kind of wildfowl (it was the beginning of September and the woodcock had not yet flown in and I was bored with scouring the fields for partridge) I listened to my hunter and set off for Lgov.

Lgov is a large steppe village with an exceedingly ancient stone, single-towered church and two mills on the marshy riverlet Rosota. About three miles from Lgov this riverlet turns into a broad stretch of pond water, overgrown at the edges and in parts of the middle by thick reeds which are known as 'mayer' in the Oryol region. On this pond, in the inlets and backwaters among the reeds, a great mass of ducks of every possible variety have found a habitat: mallard, half-mallard, pintail, teal, pochard, etc. Small flocks used continually to rise and fly about above the water, but at the sound of gunfire such clouds would rise that the hunter would be forced to hold down his hat and emit a prolonged 'Phe-e-ew!' Yermolay and I started off by going round the side of the pond but, firstly, the duck, being a cautious bird, does not come close to the bank and, secondly, if some slowcoach of an inexperienced teal should indeed have submitted itself to our shots and given up its life, then our dogs wouldn't have been in any condition to retrieve it from the thick reeds because, despite their noblest and most self-sacrificing efforts, they wouldn't have been able to swim or walk along the bottom and would only have cut their precious noses needlessly on the sharp edges of the reeds.

'No,' said Yermolay at last, 'it's no good, we've got to get a boat. Let's go back to Lgov.'

We set off. We'd scarcely gone a few steps when a rather undistinguished-looking setter rushed towards us from behind a thick clump of willow and there then appeared a man of medium height in a blue, badly torn coat, a yellowish waistcoat and trousers the colour of *gris de lin* or *bleu d'amour*[1] which had been hastily tucked into badly holed boots, with a red kerchief round his neck and a single-barrelled gun over his shoulder. While our dogs, with the usual Chinese ceremonial characteristic of their species, sniffed their new acquaintance, who, it appeared, got cold feet and tucked its tail between its legs, drew back its ears and rapidly twisted its body to and fro without bending its knees, its teeth bared, the stranger approached us and bowed exceedingly politely. He appeared to be about twenty-five. His long light-brown hair, liberally plastered with *kvas*, stuck up in fixed spikes, his small brown eyes blinked in welcome and his entire face, wound about with a black handkerchief as if he had toothache, was wreathed in a sugary smile.

'Permit me to introduce myself,' he began in a soft and insinuating voice. 'I'm the local hunter, Vladimir . . . Learning of your arrival and knowing that you'd graciously made your way on to the banks of our pond, I resolved, if you have no objections, to offer you my services.'

The hunter Vladimir spoke, without putting too fine a point on it, like a young provincial actor playing a juvenile lead. I agreed to his offer and before reaching Lgov had already learned the story of his life. He was a freed manorial serf. In his tenderest youth he'd learned music, then he'd worked as a valet, had learned to read and had read, so far as I could gather, one or two books, and, living now as do so many in Russia, without a penny to call his own and no permanent employment, he fed himself on scarcely anything save manna from heaven. He expressed himself unusually elegantly and evidently prided himself on his fancy manners. He was also, no doubt, a frightful one with the girls and probably successful, because Russian girls love eloquence. Besides, he let me know that he sometimes visited local landowners and received hospitality in the town and played whist and was on good terms with people from the capital. He was expert at smiling and had an extraordinarily wide range of smiles. One particularly suited him, a modest, withdrawn smile which played on his lips when he was listening to a stranger speaking to him. He would listen to you and agree with you completely, but never leave go of his sense of personal dignity, and he always sought to let you know that he could, if the occasion arose, give expression to his own opinion. Yermolay, as a man who was not too well-educated and in no way 'subtle', began by speaking to him as one of his own. It was a sight to see the way Vladimir condescended to him by saying: 'You, sir . . .'

'Why've you got that handkerchief wound round your face?' I asked him. 'Have you got toothache?'

'No, sir,' he replied, 'a far more ruinous consequence of inattention. I had a friend, a good man, sir, but in no sense a hunter, as things turned out, sir. One day, sir, he said to me: "My dear chap, take me hunting, I'm longing to know what sort of a sport it is." I, of course, didn't want to refuse a friend and obtained a weapon for him, for my part, sir, and took him hunting. Well, sir, we hunted, as we're accustomed to, and then we rested, sir. I sat down under a tree and he, for his part, sir, sat opposite, started playing tricks with his gun and aimed at me. I begged him to decease but, in his inexperience, he didn't pay any attention, sir. There was a loud shot and I lost my chin and the forefinger on my right hand.'

We reached Lgov. Both Vladimir and Yermolay had decided that it was impossible to hunt without a boat.

'Old Knot's got a punt,'* Vladimir remarked, 'but I don't know where he's hidden it. I'll have to go and see him.'

'Who's that?' I asked.

'There's a man lives here nicknamed Old Knot.'

Vladimir and Yermolay set off to find Old Knot. I told them I'd wait for them by the church. As I was looking at the gravestones in the churchyard I came across a blackened four-cornered urn with the following inscriptions: on one side in French: '*Ce gît Théophile Henri, vicomte de Blangy*', and on the other: 'Beneath this stone is laid the body of the Frenchman, Count Blanzhy, born 1737, died 1799, his life numbering in all 62 years'; on the third: 'May his Ashes Rest in Peace', and on the fourth:

> Beneath this stone there lies a Frenchman, immigrant;
> Noble lineage had he and outstanding talent,

---

* A flat boat made of old barge boards.

He mourned his murdered wife and family,
And left his country oppress'd by tyranny;
Come at last to shores of Russian earth,
In old age found he an hospitable hearth,
And children taught and parents much requited . . .
'Twas here with the Almighty was he reunited . . .

The arrival of Yermolay, Vladimir and the man with the strange nickname, Old Knot, interrupted my reflections. The barefoot, tattered and unkempt Old Knot seemed, to judge from appearances, a former manorial serf of about sixty.

'Have you a boat?' I asked.

'I have,' he answered in a hoarse and broken voice, 'but it's in a bad way.'

'How's that?'

'It's got leaky. An' the rivets've come out.'

'That's nothing!' exclaimed Yermolay. 'You can fill 'em with oakum.'

'Sure can,' Old Knot agreed.

'Who *are* you?'

'I'm the master's fisherman, sir.'

'How is it you're a fisherman, but your boat's in such a state of disrepair?'

'Well, there's no fish in the river.'

'Fish dislike marsh mildew,' my hunter remarked self-importantly.

'Well,' I said to Yermolay, 'go and get some oakum and patch up the boat as soon as possible.'

Yermolay went off.

'Surely we'll sink to the bottom very likely, won't we?' I said to Vladimir.

'God is merciful,' he answered. 'In any case, it must be supposed that the pond is not deep.'

'Sure it's not deep,' said Old Knot who spoke somewhat strangely, as if he'd only just woken up. 'Sure it's got a bottom full o' weeds an' grass, an' sure it's all overgrown with grass, it is. Mind you, it's also got some real deep holes, it has.'

'However, if the grass is so thick,' remarked Vladimir, 'it won't be possible to row in it.'

'Well, who rows in a punt, eh? You gotta punt it. I'll come with you, 'cos I gotta pole there. Or it's possible to use a shovel.'

'A shovel's awkward, sometimes you can't reach the bottom,' said Vladimir.

'It's true it's awkward.'

I sat down on a gravestone to wait for Yermolay. Vladimir went off a little to one side out of politeness and also sat down. Old Knot stayed standing in one place, his head lowered and his hands behind his back according to old custom.

'Tell me, please,' I began, 'have you been fisherman here long?'

'It'll be seven years, sir,' he answered, giving himself a shake.

'And what were you before?'

'Before I were a coachman.'

'Who stopped you being a coachman?'

'Our new lady.'

'Which lady?'

'The one who bought us. You're not knowing her, sir: Alyona Timofevna, the stout lady . . . not young.'

'What on earth made her turn you into a fisherman?'

'God knows. She came to us from her estate, from Tambov, an' ordered all us workers to gather in a group an' then she came out to see us. First of all we go an' kiss her hand and she doesn't mind, doesn't get upset . . . Then she started askin' us one after another what we do, what employment we have. When it was my turn, she asks: "What were you?" I said: "Coachman." "Coachman? Well, what sort of coachman do you think you are, just look at yourself, ask yourself that, eh? It's not right for you to be a coachman, but you can be my fisherman and shave off your beard. Whenever I have occasion to visit and come to dinner, you have fish ready, do you hear?" Since then I've been counted among the fishermen. "And see you keep my pond water in good condition," she said. But how can I do that?'

'Whose serf were you before?'

'Sergey Sergeich Pekhterev's. We were his by inheritance. An' he didn't own us long, just six years. It was for him I were coachman, though not in the town – he had others for town – only in the country.'

'Were you always a coachman?'

'Not always I weren't! I became a coachman under Sergey Sergeich, but before that I were a cook, but not a cook in town, just a cook here in the country.'

'Who were you a cook for?'

'A previous gentleman, Afanasy Nefedych, Sergey Sergeich's uncle. He bought Lgov, Afanasy Nefedych did, while Sergey Sergeich inherited his estate.'

'Who did he buy it from?'

'From Tatyana Vasilyevna.'

'Which Tatyana Vasilyevna?'

'The one who died last year near Bolkhov – that's to say, near Karachev – the spinster, the one who never got married. You perhaps know her? We passed to her from her father, from Vasily Semyonych. She owned us a long, long time – 'bout twenty years or so.'

'So you were a cook for her, were you?'

'At first I were just that, a cook, but then I became a cofficial.'

'A what?'

'A cofficial.'

'What sort of a job is that?'

'I don't really know, sir. Standing by the sideboard and being called Anton, not Kuzma. That's what our ladyship ordered.'

'Is your real name Kuzma?'

'Kuzma.'

'And you were a cofficial all the time?'

'No, not all the time. I was also an akhtor.'

'Really?'

'Sure I were. An akhtor in a keatre. Our ladyship had a keatre.'

'What parts did you play?'

'Pardon?'

'What did you do in the theatre?'

'You don't know what we did, eh? They'd take me and dress me up and I'd walk on dressed-up, or stand, or sit, as was needed. They'd say, You say this, and I'd say it. Once I were a blind man. They put a pea under each eyelid . . . That's what we did.'

'And then what?'

'Then I became a cook again.'

'Why did they demote you to cook?'

''Cos my brother ran away.'

'I see. But what were you under your first lady's father?'

'I had various employments. First I were a pageboy, then an outrider, then a gardener, then a huntsman.'

'A huntsman? So you rode to hounds?'

'I rode to hounds, but I got hurt. I fell with the horse and the horse got hurt. The old master, he were real strict with us. He ordered me flogged and sent off to Moscow, to be apprentice to a shoemaker.'

'To be an apprentice? You weren't a boy when you were made a huntsman, were you?'

'No, I were twenty years old or so.'

'What sort of an apprentice would you be if you were twenty?'

'That didn't matter, it's what had to happen if the master ordered. Luckily, he died soon afterwards and I were sent back to the country.'

'When did you learn to be a cook?'

Old Knot raised his thin and yellowish face and grinned.

'Do you have to learn that? It's women's work, cooking!'

'Well,' I said, 'you've seen some sights in your time, Kuzma! What do you do now as a fisherman if there are no fish?'

'I don't complain, sir. An' I thank God I were made a fisherman. There's another old man like me, Andrey Pupyr, her ladyship ordered him to work in the dipping-room in the paper factory. It's a sin, she said, for him to eat bread for nothing . . . But Pupyr'd hoped to gain her favour. He had a relative of his working as a clerk in her office. He promised to put in a good word for him with her ladyship, remind her, you know. Well, he reminded her right enough! Pupyr, you know, had bowed down to that relative's feet right before my very eyes . . .'

'Have you got a family? Were you married?'

'No, sir, I wasn't. The late Tatyana Vasilyevna – God rest her soul! – she wouldn't allow anyone to marry. Heaven preserve us! She'd say: "I live like a spinster, don't I, so what's the fuss? What more do they want?"'

'How do you make a living now? Do you get any pay?'

'Pay, sir! No! . . . Food is provided – so, glory be to God, I'm greatly content. May God grant our ladyship long life!'

Yermolay returned.

'The boat's put right,' he pronounced severely. 'You go off and get your pole, you!'

Old Knot ran off for his pole. Throughout my conversation with the poor old man the hunter Vladimir had been giving him glances and grinning disdainfully.

'A stupid fellow, sir,' he said when the other had gone, 'a completely uneducated fellow, sir, just a peasant, sir, nothing else. You can't call him a household servant, sir . . . and such a boaster . . . How could he be thought of as an actor, judge for yourself! You bothered with him for nothing, talking to him as you did, sir!'

Within a quarter of an hour we were already sitting in Old Knot's punt. (We left the dogs in a peasant hut in the care of the coachman Yehudi.) It wasn't very comfortable for us, but hunters are never very choosy. At the blunt rear end stood Old Knot and 'punted' with his pole. Vladimir and I sat on the centre cross-seat and Yermolay perched himself up front, in the bow. Despite the oakum, water soon appeared round our feet. Luckily the weather was calm and the pond water literally seemed to have gone to sleep.

We traversed the water fairly slowly. The old man had difficulty in pulling his long pole out of the sticky mud because it had become twined about with the green threads of underwater grasses and the solid round pads of the marsh lilies also hindered our boat's progress. Eventually we reached the clumps of reeds and the fun started. The ducks rose noisily, literally 'exploding' from the pond in fright at our sudden appearance in their domain and gunfire resounded in unison after them and it was a delight to see how the stumpy birds somersaulted in the air and splashed down heavily in the water. We didn't of course retrieve all the shot duck. Some of the slightly injured ones dived, some of the dead ones fell in such thick 'mayer' that even the lynx-eyed Yermolay couldn't spot them, but nevertheless by dinnertime our boat had become filled to the brim with our bag.

Vladimir, to Yermolay's great satisfaction, was by no means an expert shot and after each failure showed his surprise, inspected his gun, blew through it, expressed puzzlement and finally gave us his reasons for missing his target. Yermolay as usual shot victoriously and I, as usual, rather poorly. Old Knot studied us with the eyes of someone who'd been all his life in someone or other's service and from time to time cried out: 'There's one, there's a duck!' and all the while scratched his back not with his hands but with movements of his shoulders. The weather remained perfect. White round clouds hung high and calm above us, clearly reflected in the water. The reeds murmured softly all about us and in places the pond water glittered in the sunlight like steel. We were on the point of returning to the village when suddenly something rather unpleasant occurred.

We'd been aware for some time that water had slowly been seeping into the punt. Vladimir had been given the task of bailing it out with a ladle pinched for the purpose by my prudent hunter from a dozy old woman. Everything was all right so long as Vladimir remembered what he had to do. But towards the end of our hunt, as if in farewell, the ducks started to rise in such flocks that we scarcely had time to reload our guns. In the heat of firing we didn't pay any attention to the state of our punt, when suddenly, as a result of a strong movement from Yermolay, who had stretched out full-length along the gunwale in order to reach a shot bird, our ancient craft leaned to one side, keeled over and solemnly sank to the bottom, luckily in a shallow place. We cried out but it was already too late. In a moment we were standing up to our necks in water surrounded by the floating bodies of dead ducks. Now I can't help recalling without laughing the pale and frightened faces of my comrades (very likely my own face wasn't all that healthily pink at the time), but I must confess that at that moment it didn't occur to me to laugh at all. Each of us held our guns above our heads and Old Knot, no doubt through his habit of always copying his masters, also held his pole up. The first to break the silence was Yermolay.

'Phew, tipped right up!' he complained, spitting in the water. 'What an occasion! And it's all down to you, you old devil!' he added heatedly, turning to Old Knot. 'What sort of a boat is it you've got?'

'Sorry,' muttered the old man.

'Yes, and a lot of good you are,' my hunter went on, turning his head in the direction of Vladimir. 'Where were you looking? Why weren't you bailing? Oh, you, you, you . . .'

But Vladimir was in no mood to respond because he was shaking like a leaf, his teeth chattered without meeting and he was smiling completely senselessly. God knows what had happened to his eloquence and sense of elegant propriety and personal dignity!

The damned punt swayed about feebly under our feet. The instant after our shipwreck the water had seemed extremely cold, but we soon got used to it. When the first fright was over, I looked around and saw that ten or so paces from us were reeds and beyond, above their tips, could be seen the bank. 'Not good!' I thought.

'What can we do?' I asked Yermolay.

'Well, let's take a look, since we can't spend the night here,' he answered. 'Here, you, take hold of my gun,' he said to Vladimir.

Vladimir obeyed without a word.

'I'm going to look for a fording place,' continued Yermolay in the sure conviction that every stretch of pond water must have a fording place, seized hold of Old Knot's pole and set off in the direction of the bank, carefully feeling his way along the bottom.

'Do you know how to swim?' I asked him.

'No, I don't,' his voice resounded beyond the reeds.

'Well, he's bound to drown,' was the indifferent comment from Old Knot, who, as earlier, had been frightened not by the danger so much as by our anger and now, completely calm, merely emitted the occasional long breath and gave the impression of feeling no need to change his position.

'And he'll perish quite uselessly, sir,' Vladimir added piteously.

Yermolay didn't return for more than an hour. That hour seemed to us an eternity. To start with we exchanged shouts with him very eagerly, but later he began to answer our shouts more rarely and finally he ceased altogether. In the village the bells were tolling for the evening service. We didn't talk among ourselves and even tried to avoid each other's eyes. The ducks flew over our heads; some would be about to alight near us but would then suddenly rise up, as they say, 'in formation' and fly off with much quacking. We started to grow stiff. Old Knot started blinking his eyes as if he was preparing to go to sleep.

At last, to our indescribable joy, Yermolay returned.

'Well, what did you find?'

'I was on the bank and found a fording place . . . Let's go.'

We'd have liked to set off at once, but he first of all extracted some string from his pocket underwater and tied up all the shot duck by their feet, seized both ends of the string between his teeth and went ahead of us, Vladimir behind him and I behind Vladimir. Old Knot brought up the rear. It was about two hundred paces to the bank and Yermolay made his way boldly and without stopping (he'd noted the route that well), only occasionally shouting out: 'To the left! There's a hole on the right!' or: 'To the right! You'll get stuck on the left . . .' Sometimes the water rose to our necks and once or twice poor Old Knot, being smaller than us, started swallowing water and letting out bubbles. 'Hey, hey, hey!' Yermolay shouted at him threateningly and Old Knot would scramble along, jumping, his legs dangling and somehow managing to reach a shallower place, but even in extreme difficulty he never took hold of the edge of my coat. Finally worn out, filthy and wet through, we reached the bank.

A couple of hours later we were all seated, as dry as was possible, in a large hay barn and awaiting our supper. The coachman Yehudi, a man of extraordinarily slow movements, sluggish, deliberate and dopey, stood by the doors and zealously plied Old Knot with snuff. (I have noticed that coachmen in Russia are quick to make friends.) Old Knot gave frenzied sniffs, almost to the point of making himself ill. He spat and coughed and evidently enjoyed himself enormously. Vladimir looked languid, leaned his head to one side and said little. Yermolay cleaned our guns. The dogs wagged their tails at an exaggerated rate in anticipation of their oatmeal, while the horses stamped their hooves and neighed under the awning. The sun set slowly. Its last rays ran across the land in broad crimson lines. Little golden clouds spread out upon the sky in ever smaller shapes as if in a burst, splattered wave . . . The village resounded with a sound of singing.

BEZHIN LEA

❧ ───────────

IT was a beautiful July day, one of those days which occur only when the weather has been unchanged for a long time. From early morning the sky is clear and the sunrise does not so much flare up like a fire as spread like a mild pinkness. The sun – not fiery, not molten, as it is during a period of torrid drought, not murkily crimson as it is before a storm, but bright and invitingly radiant – peacefully drifts up beneath a long, thin cloud, sends fresh gleams through it and is immersed in its lilac haze. The delicate upper edge of the long line of cloud erupts in snakey glints of light: their gleam resembles the gleam of beaten silver. But then again the playful rays break out – and as if taking wing the mighty sun rises gaily and magnificently. About midday a mass of high round clouds appear, golden-grey, with soft white edges. They move hardly at all, like islands cast down on the infinite expanses of a flooding river which flows round them in deeply pellucid streams of level blue; away towards the horizon they cluster together and merge so that there is no blue sky to be seen between them; but they have themselves become as azure-coloured as the sky and are pervaded through and through with light and warmth. The light, pale-lilac colour of the heavens remains the same throughout the day and in all parts of the sky; there is no darkening anywhere, no thickening as for a storm, though here and there pale-blue columns may stretch downwards, bringing a hardly noticeable sprinkling of rain. Towards evening these clouds disappear. The last of them, darkling and vague as smoke, lie down in rosy mistiness before the sinking sun. At the point where the sun has set just as calmly as it rose into the sky, a crimson glow lingers for a short time over the darkened earth, and, softly winking, the evening star burns upon the glow like a carefully carried candle. On such days all the colours are softened; they are bright without being gaudy; everything bears the mark of some poignant timidity. On such days the heat is sometimes very strong and occasionally even 'simmers' along the slopes of the fields. But the wind drives away and disperses the accumulated heat, and whirling dust storms – a sure sign of settled weather – travel in tall white columns along roads through the ploughland. The dry pure air is scented with wormwood, harvested rye and buckwheat. Even an hour before nightfall you can feel no dampness. It is just such weather that the farmer wants for harvesting his grain.

It was on precisely such a day that I once went out grouse-shooting in Chernsk county in the province of Tula. I found, and bagged, a fair number of birds. My full game-pouch cut mercilessly at my shoulder. But I did not finally decide to make my way home until the evening glow had already died away and chill shadows began to thicken and proliferate in air that was still bright, though no longer illumined by the rays of the sunset. With brisk steps I crossed a long 'plaza' of bushy undergrowth, clambered up a hillock and, instead of the expected familiar moor with a little oak wood to the right of it and a low-walled white church in the distance, I saw completely different places which were unknown to me. At my feet there stretched a narrow valley; directly ahead of me rose, like a steep wall, a dense aspen wood. I stopped in bewilderment and looked around. 'Ah-ha!' I thought. 'I'm certainly not where I should be: I've swerved too much to the right' – and, surprised at my mistake, I quickly descended from the hillock. I was at once surrounded by an unpleasant, motionless damp, just as if I had entered a cellar. The tall, thick grass on the floor of the valley was all wet and shone white like a smooth tablecloth; it felt clammy and horrible to walk through. As quickly as possible I scrambled across to the other side and, keeping to the left, made my way along beside the aspen wood. Bats already flitted above its sleeping treetops, mysteriously circling and quivering against the dull paleness of the sky; a young hawk, out late, flew by high up, taking a direct, keen course in hurrying back to its nest. 'Now then, as soon as I reach that corner,' I said to myself, 'that's where the road'll be so what I've done is to make a detour of about three-quarters of a mile!'

I made my way finally to the corner of the wood, but there was no road there, only some low, unkempt bushes spread out widely in front of me and beyond them, in the far distance, an expanse of deserted field. Again I stopped. 'What's all this about? Where am I?' I tried to recall where I had been during the day. 'Ah, these must be the Parakhin bushes!' I exclaimed eventually. 'That's it! And that must be the Sindeyev wood . . . How on earth did I get as far as this? It's very odd! Now I must go to the right again.'

I turned to the right, through the bushes. Meanwhile, night was approaching and rose around me like a thunder cloud; it was as if, in company with the evening mists, darkness rose on every side and even poured down from the sky. I discovered a rough, overgrown track and followed it, carefully peering ahead of me. Everything quickly grew silent and dark; only quail gave occasional cries. A small night bird, which hurried low and soundlessly along on its soft wings, almost collided with me and plunged off in terror. I emerged from the bushes and wandered along the boundary of a field. It was only with difficulty that I could make out distant objects. All around me the field glimmered faintly; beyond it, coming closer each moment, the sullen murk loomed in huge clouds. My footsteps sounded muffled in the thickening air. The sky which had earlier grown pale once again began to shine blue, but it was the blue of the night. Tiny stars began to flicker and shimmer.

What I thought was a wood had turned out to be a dark, round knoll. 'Where on earth am I?' I repeated again out loud, stopping for a third time and looking questioningly at my yellow English piebald, Diana, who was by far the most intelligent of all four-legged creatures. But this most intelligent of four-legged creatures only wagged her small tail, dejectedly blinked her tired little eyes and offered me no practical help. I felt ill at ease in front of her and strode wildly forward, as if I had suddenly realized which way to go, circled the knoll and found myself in a shallow hollow which had been ploughed over. A strange feeling took possession of me. The hollow had the almost exact appearance of a cauldron with sloping sides. Several large upright stones stood in the floor of the hollow – it seemed as if they had crept down to that spot for some mysterious consultation – and the hollow itself was so still and silent, the sky above it so flat and dismal that my heart shrank within me. A small animal of some kind or other squeaked weakly and piteously among the stones. I hurried to climb back on to the knoll. Up to that point I had not given up the hope of finding a way home, but now I was at last convinced that I had completely lost my way and, no longer making any effort to recognize my surroundings, which were almost totally obliterated by the darkness, I walked straight ahead of me, following the stars and hoping for the best . . . For about half an hour I walked on in this way, with difficulty, dragging one foot after another. Never in my life, it seemed, had I been in such waste places: not a single light burned anywhere, not a single sound could be heard: one low hillock followed another, field stretched after endless field and bushes suddenly rose out of the earth under my very nose. I went on walking and was on the point of finding a place to lie down until morning, when suddenly I reached the edge of a fearful abyss.

I hastily drew back my outstretched leg and, through the barely transparent night-time murk, saw far below me an enormous plain. A broad river skirted it, curving away from me in a semicircle; steely gleams of water, sparkling with occasional faint flashes, denoted its course. The hill on which I was standing fell away sharply like an almost vertical precipice. Its vast outlines could be distinguished by their blackness from the blue emptiness of the air and directly below me, in the angle formed by the precipice and the plain, beside the river, which at that point was a dark, unmoving mirror, under the steep rise of the hill, two fires smoked and flared redly side by side. Figures clustered round them, shadows flickered and now and then the front half of a small curly head would appear in the bright light.

At last I knew the place I had reached. This meadowland is known in our region as Bezhin Lea. There was now no chance of returning home, especially at night; moreover, my legs were collapsing under me from fatigue. I decided to make my way down to the fires and to await the dawn in the company of the people below me, whom I took to be drovers. I made my descent safely, but had hardly let go of my last hand-hold when suddenly two large, ragged, white dogs hurled themselves at me with angry barks. Shrill childish voices came from the fires and two or three boys jumped up. I answered their shouted questions. They ran towards me, at once calling off the dogs who had been astonished by the appearance of my Diana, and I walked towards them.

I had been mistaken in assuming that the people sitting round the fires were drovers. They were simply peasant boys from the neighbouring villages keeping guard over the horses. During hot summer weather it is customary in our region to drive the horses out at night to graze in the field, for by day the flies would give them no peace. Driving the horses out before nightfall and back again at first light is a great treat for the peasant boys. Bareheaded, dressed in tattered sheepskin jackets and riding the friskiest ponies, they race out with gay whoops and shouts, their arms and legs flapping as they bob up and down on the horses' backs and roar with laughter. Clouds of fine sandy dust are churned up along the roadway; a steady beating of hooves spreads far and wide as the horses prick up their ears and start running; and in front of them all, with tail high and continuously changing his pace, gallops a shaggy chestnut stallion with burrs in his untidy mane.

I told the boys that I had lost my way and sat down among them. They asked me where I was from and fell silent for a while in awe of me. We talked a little about this and that. I lay down beside a bush from which all the foliage had been nibbled and looked around me. It was a marvellous sight: a reddish circular reflection throbbed around the fires and seemed to fade as it leaned against the darkness; a flame, in flaring up, would occasionally cast rapid flashes of light beyond the limit of the reflection; a fine tongue of light would lick the bare boughs of the willows and instantly vanish; and long sharp shadows, momentarily breaking in, would rush right up to the fires as if the darkness were at war with the light. Sometimes, when the flames grew weaker and the circle of light contracted, there would suddenly emerge from the encroaching dark the head of a horse, reddish brown, with sinuous markings, or completely white, and regard us attentively and gravely, while rapidly chewing some long grass and then, when again lowered, would at once disappear. All that was left was the sound as it continued to chew and snort. From the area of the light it was difficult to discern what was happening in the outer darkness, and therefore at close quarters, everything seemed to be screened from view by an almost totally black curtain; but off towards the horizon hills and woods were faintly visible, like long blurs. The immaculate dark sky rose solemnly and endlessly high above us in all its mysterious magnificence. My lungs melted with the sweet pleasure of inhaling that special, languorous and fresh perfume which is the scent of a Russian summer night. Hardly a sound was audible around us . . . Now and then a large fish would make a resounding splash in the nearby river and the reeds by the bank would faintly echo the noise as they were stirred by the outspreading waves ... Now and then the fires would emit a soft crackling.

Around the fires sat the boys, as did the two dogs who had been so keen to eat me. They were still unreconciled to my presence and, while sleepily narrowing their eyes and glancing towards the fire, would sometimes growl with a special sense of their personal dignity; to start with these were only growls, but later they became faint yelps, as if the dogs regretted their inability to satisfy their appetite for me. There were five boys in all: Fedya, Pavlusha, Ilyusha, Kostya and Vanya. (I learned their names from their conversation and I now intend to acquaint the reader with each of them.)

The first of them, Fedya, the eldest, would probably have been fourteen. He was a sturdy boy, with handsome and delicate, slightly shallow features, curly fair hair, bright eyes and a permanent smile which was a mixture of gaiety and absent-mindedness. To judge from his appearance, he belonged to a well-off family and had ridden out into the fields not from necessity but simply for the fun of it. He was dressed in a colourful cotton shirt with yellow edging; a small cloth overcoat, recently made, hung open somewhat precariously on his small narrow shoulders and a comb hung from his pale-blue belt. His ankle-high boots were his own, not his father's. The second boy, Pavlusha, had dishevelled black hair, grey eyes, broad cheekbones, a pale, pock-marked complexion, a large but well-formed mouth, an enormous head – as big as a barrel, as they say – and a thick-set, ungainly body. Hardly a prepossessing figure – there's no denying that! – but I none the less took a liking to him: he had direct, very intelligent eyes and a voice with the ring of strength in it. His clothes gave him no chance of showing off: they consisted of no more than a simple linen shirt and much-patched trousers. The face of the third boy, Ilyusha, was not very striking: hook-nosed, long, myopic, it wore an expression of obtuse, morbid anxiety. His tightly closed lips never moved, his frowning brows never relaxed; all the while he screwed up his eyes at the fire. His yellow, almost white, hair stuck out in sharp little tufts from under the small felt cap which he was continually pressing down about his ears with both hands. He had new bast shoes and foot cloths; a thick rope wound three times round his waist drew smartly tight his neat black top-coat. Both he and Pavlusha appeared to be no more than twelve years old. The fourth, Kostya, a boy of about ten, aroused my curiosity by his sad and meditative gaze. His face was small, thin and freckled, and pointed like a squirrel's; one could hardly see his lips. His large, dark, moistly glittering eyes produced a strange impression, as if they wanted to convey something which no tongue – at least not his tongue – had the power to express. He was small in stature, of puny build and rather badly dressed. The last boy, Vanya, I hardly noticed at first: he lay on the ground quietly curled up under some angular matting and only rarely poked out from under it his head of curly brown hair. This boy was only seven.

So it was that I lay down apart from them, beside the bush, and from time to time looked in their direction. A small pot hung over one of the fires, in which 'taters' were being cooked. Pavlusha looked after them and, kneeling down, poked the bubbling water with a small sliver of wood. Fedya lay, leaning on one elbow, his sheepskin spread round him. Ilyusha sat next to Kostya and continually, in his tense way, screwed up his eyes. Kostya, with his head slightly lowered, stared off somewhere into the distance. Vanya did not stir beneath his matting. I pretended to be asleep. After a short while the boys renewed their talk.

To start with, they gossiped about this and that – tomorrow's work or the horses. But suddenly Fedya turned to Ilyusha and, as if taking up from where they had left off their interrupted conversation, asked him:

'So you actually did see one of them little people, did you?'

'No, I didn't see him, and you can't really see him at all,' answered Ilyusha in a weak, croaky voice which exactly suited the expression on his face, 'but I heard him, I did. And I wasn't the only one.'

'Then where does he live around your parts?' asked Pavlusha.

'In the old rolling-room.'*

'D'you mean you work in the factory?'

'Of course we do. Me and Avdyushka, my brother, we work as glazers.'

---

* 'Rolling-rooms' or 'dipping-rooms' are terms used in paper factories to describe the place where the papers are baled out in the vats. It is situated right by the mill, under the mill-wheel.

'Cor! So you're factory workers!'

'Well, so how did you hear him?' asked Fedya.

'It was this way. My brother, see, Avdyushka, and Fyodor Mikheyevsky, and Ivashka Kosoy, and the other Ivashka from Redwold, and Ivashka Sukhorukov as well, and there were some other kids as well, about ten of us in all, the whole shift, see – well, so we had to spend the whole night in the rolling-room, or it wasn't that we had to, but that Nazarov, the overseer, he wouldn't let us off, he said: "Seeing as you've got a lot of work here tomorrow, my lads, you'd best stay here; there's no point in the lot o'you traipsing off home." Well, so we stayed and all lay down together, and then Avdyushka started up saying something about "Well, boys, suppose that goblin comes?" and he didn't have a chance, Avdey didn't, to go on saying anything when all of a sudden over our heads someone comes in, but we were lying down below, see, and he was up there, by the wheel. We listen, and there he goes walking about, and the floorboards really bending under him and really creaking. Then he walked right over our heads and the water all of a sudden starts rushing, rushing through the wheel, and the wheel goes clatter, clatter and starts turning, but them gates of the Keep★ are all lowered. So we start wondering who'd raised them so as to let the water through. Yet the wheel turned and turned, and then stopped. Whoever he was, he went back to the door upstairs and began coming down the stairway, and down he came, taking his time about it, and the stairs under him really groaning from his weight . . . Well, so he came right up to our door, and then waited, and then waited a bit more –and then that door suddenly burst open, it did. Our eyes were poppin' out of our heads, and we watch – and there's nothing there . . . And suddenly at one of the tubs the form† started moving, rose, dipped itself and went to and fro just like that in the air like someone was using it for swilling, and then back again it went to its place. Then at another tub the hook was lifted from its nail and put back on the nail again. Then it was as if someone moved to the door and started to cough all sudden-like, like he'd

★ 'The Keep' is the name used in our region for the place where the water runs over the wheel.

† The net with which the paper is scooped out.

got a tickle, and it sounded just like a sheep bleating . . . We all fell
flat on the floor at that and tried to climb under each other – bloody
terrified we were at that moment!'

'Cor!' said Pavlusha. 'And why did he cough like that?'

'Search me. Maybe it was the damp.'

They all fell silent.

'Are them 'taters done yet?' Fedya asked.

Pavlusha felt them.

'Nope, they're not done yet . . . Cor, that one splashed,' he added,
turning his face towards the river, 'likely it was a pike . . . And see
that little falling star up there.'

'Now, mates, I've really got something to tell you,' Kostya began
in a reedy voice. 'Just you listen to what my dad was talkin' about
when I was there.'

'Well, so we're listening,' said Fedya with a condescending air.

'You know that Gavrila, the carpenter in the settlement?'

'Sure we know him.'

'But d'you know why he's always so gloomy, why he never
says nothing, d'you know that? Well, here's why. He went out
once, my dad said – he went out, mates, into the forest to find
some nuts. So he'd gone into the forest after nuts and he lost his
way. He got somewhere, but God knows where it was. He'd been
walkin', mates, and no! he couldn't find a road of any kind, and
already it was night all around. So he sat down under a tree
and said to himself he'd wait there till mornin' – and he sat down
and started to snooze. So he was snoozin' and suddenly he hears
someone callin' him. He looks around – there's no one there. Again
he snoozes off – and again they're callin' him. So he looks and looks,
and then he sees right in front of him a water-fairy sittin' on a
branch, swingin' on it she is and callin' to him, and she's just killin'
herself laughin' . . . Then that moon shines real strong, so strong
and obvious the moon shines it shows up everythin', mates. So there
she is callin' his name, and she herself's all shiny, sittin' there all
white on the branch, like she was some little minnow or gudgeon,
or maybe like a carp that's all whitish all over, all silver . . . And
Gavrila the carpenter was just frightened to death, mates, and
she went on laughin' at him, you know, and wavin' to him to
come closer. Gavrila was just goin' to get up and obey the water-

fairy, when, mates, the Lord God gave him the idea to cross hisself... An' it was terrible difficult, mates, he said it was terrible
difficult to make the sign of the cross 'cos his arm was like stone,
he said, and wouldn't move, the darned thing wouldn't! But soon
as he'd managed to cross hisself, mates, that water-fairy stopped
laughin' and started in to cry ... An' she cried, mates, an' wiped
her eyes with her hair that was green and heavy as hemp. So
Gavrila kept on lookin' and lookin' at her, and then he started
askin' her, "What's it you're cryin' for, you forest hussy, you?"
And that water-fairy starts sayin' to him, "If you hadn't crossed
yourself, human being that you are, you could've lived with me
in joy and happiness to the end of your days, an' I'm cryin' and
dyin' of grief over what that you crossed yourself, an' it isn't
only me that'll be dyin' of grief, but you'll also waste away with
grievin' till the end of your born days." Then, mates, she vanished,
and Gavrila at once comprehended-like – how to get out of the
wood, that is; but from that day on he goes around everywhere
all gloomy.'

    'Phew!' exclaimed Fedya after a short silence. 'But how could that
evil forest spirit infect a Christian soul – you said he didn't obey her,
didn't you?'

    'You wouldn't believe it, but that's how it was!' said Kostya.
'Gavrila claimed she had a tiny, tiny, voice, thin and croaky like a
toad's.'

    'Your father told that himself?' Fedya continued.

    'He did. I was lyin' on my bunk an' I heard it all.'

    'What a fantastic business! But why's he got to be gloomy? She
must've liked him, because she called to him.'

    'Of course she liked him!' Ilyusha interrupted. 'Why not? She
wanted to start tickling him, that's what she wanted. That's what
they do, those water-fairies.'

    'Surely there'll be water-fairies here,' Fedya remarked.

    'No,' Kostya answered, 'this is a clean place here, it's free. 'Cept
the river's close.'

    They all grew quiet. Suddenly, somewhere in the distance, a
protracted, resonant, almost wailing sound broke the silence – one of
those incomprehensible nocturnal sounds which arise in the deep
surrounding hush, fly up, hang in the air and slowly disperse at last as

if dying away. You listen intently — it's as though there's nothing there, but it still goes on ringing. This time it seemed that someone gave a series of long, loud shouts on the very horizon and someone else answered him from the forest with sharp high-pitched laughter and a thin, hissing whistle which sped across the river. The boys looked at each other and shuddered.

'The power of the holy cross be with us!' whispered Ilyusha.

'Oh, you idiots!' Pavlusha cried. 'What's got into you? Look, the 'taters are done.' (They all drew close to the little pot and began to eat the steaming potatoes; Vanya was the only one who made no move.) 'What's wrong with you?' Pavlusha asked.

But Vanya did not crawl out from beneath his matting. The little pot was soon completely empty.

'Boys, have you heard,' Ilyusha began saying, 'what happened to us in Varnavitsy just recently?'

'On that dam, you mean?' Fedya asked.

'Ay, on that dam, the one that's broken. That's a real unclean place, real nasty and empty it is. Round there is all them gullies and ravines, and in the ravines there's masses of snakes.'

'Well, what happened? Let's hear.'

'This is what happened. Maybe you don't know it, Fedya, but that's the place where one of our drowned men is buried. And he drowned a long time back when the pond was still deep. Now only his gravestone can be seen, only there's not much of it — it's just a small mound ... Anyhow, a day or so ago, the bailiff calls Yermil the dog-keeper and says to him: "Off with you and fetch the mail." Yermil's always the one who goes to fetch the mail 'cos he's done all his dogs in — they just don't somehow seem to live when he's around, and never did have much of a life no-how, though he's a good man with dogs and took to it in every way. Anyhow, Yermil went for the mail, and then he mucked about in the town and set off home real drunk. And it's night-time, a bright night, with the moon shining ... So he's riding back across the dam, 'cos that's where his route came out. And he's riding along, this dog-keeper Yermil, and he sees a little lamb on the drowned man's grave, all white and curly and pretty, and it's walking about, and Yermil thinks: "I'll pick it up, I will, 'cos there's no point in letting it get lost here," and so he gets off his horse and picks it up in his arms — and the lamb doesn't turn a hair. So Yermil walks back to the horse, but the horse backs away from him, snorts and shakes its head. So when he's quieted it, he sits on it with the lamb and starts off again holding the lamb in front of him. He looks at the lamb, he does, and the lamb looks right back at him right in the eyes. Then that Yermil the dog-keeper got frightened: "I don't recall," he thought, "no lambs looking me in the eye like that afore." Anyhow, it didn't seem nothing, so he starts stroking its wool and saying "Sssh, there, sssh!" And that lamb bares its teeth at him sudden-like and says back to him: "Sssh, there, sssh! . . ."'

The narrator had hardly uttered this last sound when the dogs sprang up and with convulsive barks dashed from the fire, disappearing into the night. The boys were terrified. Vanya even jumped out from beneath his mat. Shouting, Pavlusha followed in hot pursuit of the dogs. Their barking quickly retreated into the distance. There was a noisy and restless scurrying of hoofs among the startled horses. Pavlusha gave loud calls: 'Gray! Beetle!' After a few seconds the barking ceased and Pavlusha's voice sounded far away. There followed another short pause, while the boys exchanged puzzled looks as if anticipating something new. Suddenly a horse could be heard racing towards them: it stopped sharply at the very edge of the fire and Pavlusha, clutching hold by the reins, sprang agilely from its back. Both dogs also leapt into the circle of light and at once sat down, their red tongues hanging out.

'What's there? What is it?' the boys asked.

'Nothing,' Pavlusha answered waving away the horse. 'The dogs caught a scent. I thought,' he added in a casual tone of voice, his chest heaving rapidly, 'it might have been a wolf.'

I found myself full of admiration for Pavlusha. He was very fine at that moment. His very ordinary face, enlivened by the swift ride, shone with bold courageousness and a resolute firmness. Without a stick in his hand to control the horse and in total darkness, without even so much as blinking an eye, he had galloped all by himself after a wolf . . . 'What a marvellous boy!' was my thought, as I looked at him.

'And you saw them, did you, those wolves?' asked the cowardly Kostya.

'There's plenty of them round here,' answered Pavlusha, 'but they're only on the prowl in the winter.'

He again settled himself in front of the fire. As he sat down he let a hand fall on the shaggy neck of one of the dogs and the delighted animal kept its head still for a long while as it directed sideward looks of grateful pride at Pavlusha.

Vanya once again disappeared under his mat.

'What a lot of horrible things you've been telling us, Ilyusha,' Fedya began. As the son of a rich peasant, it was incumbent upon him to play the role of leader (though for his own part he talked little, as if for fear of losing face). 'And it could've been some darned thing of the sort that started the dogs barking . . . But it's true, so I've heard, that you've got unclean spirits where you live.'

'In Varnavitsy, you mean? That's for sure! It's a really creepy place! More than once they say they've seen there the old squire, the one who's dead. They say he goes about in a coat hanging down to his heels, and all the time he makes a groaning sound, like he's searching for something on the earth. Once grandfather Trofimych met him and asked him: "What's it you are searching for on the earth, good master Ivan Ivanych?"'

'He actually asked him that?' broke in the astonished Fedya.

'He asked him that.'

'Well, good for Trofimych after that! So what did the other say?'

'"Split-grass," he says. "That's what I'm looking for." And he talks in such a hollow, hoarse voice: "Split-grass. And what, good master Ivan Ivanych, do you want split-grass for?" "Oh, my grave weighs so heavy," he says, "weighs so heavy on me, Trofimych, and I want to get out, I want to get away . . ."'

'So that's what it was!' Fedya said. 'He'd had too short a life, that means.'

'Cor, stone me!' Kostya pronounced. 'I thought you could only see dead people on Parents' Sunday.'

'You can see dead people at any time,' Ilyusha declared with confidence. So far as I could judge, he was better versed in village lore than the others. 'But on Parents' Sunday you can also see the people who're going to die that year. All you've got to do is to sit down at night in the porch of the church and keep your eyes on the road. They'll all go past you along the road – them who're going to die that year, I mean. Last year, grandma Ulyana went to the church porch in our village.'

'Well, did she see anyone?' Kostya asked him with curiosity.

'Sure she did. To start with she just sat there a long, long time, and didn't see no one and didn't hear nothing. Only there was all the time a sound like a dog starting to bark somewhere. Then suddenly she sees there's someone coming along the road – it's a little boy in nothing but a shirt. She looked close and she saw it was Ivashka Fedoseyev walking along.'

'Is that the boy who died in the spring!' Fedya broke in.

'That's the one. He walks along and doesn't even raise his head. But Ulyana recognized him. But then she looks again and sees a woman walking along, and she peers and peers and – God help us! – it's she herself, Ulyana herself, walking along.'

'Was it really her?' asked Fedya.

'God's truth. It was her.'

'But she hasn't died yet, has she?'

'No, but the year's not over yet either. You take a close look at her and then ask yourself what sort of body she's got to carry her soul around in.'

Again they all grew quiet. Pavlusha threw a handful of dry sticks on the fire. They blackened in sharp outline against the instantly leaping flames, and began to crackle and smoke and bend, curling up their burned tips. The reflections from the light, shuddering convulsively, struck out in all directions, but particularly upwards. Suddenly, from God knows where, a small white pigeon flew directly into the reflections, fluttered around in terror, bathed by the fierce light, and then vanished with a clapping of its wings.

'Likely it's lost its way home,' Pavlusha remarked. 'Now it'll fly until it meets up with something, and when it finds it, that's where it'll spend the night till dawn.'

'Look, Pavlusha,' said Kostya, 'mightn't that be the soul of some good person flying up to heaven, eh?'

Pavlusha threw another handful of sticks on the fire.

'Maybe,' he said after a pause.

'Pavlusha, tell us, will you,' Fedya began, 'were you able to see that heavenly foreboding* in Shalamavo?'

'You mean, when you couldn't see the sun that time? Sure.'

---

* The name given by the local peasants to an eclipse of the sun.

'Didn't you get frightened then?'

'Sure, and we weren't the only ones. Our squire, tho' he lets us know beforehand that "Well, there'll be a foreboding for you," but soon as it gets dark they say he got real scared. And in the servants' hut, that old granny, the cook, well – soon as it's dark, listen, she ups and smashes all the pots in the oven with a pair of tongs. "Who's going to need to eat now it's the end of the world," she says. The cabbage soup ran out all over everywhere. And, boy! What rumours there were going about in our village, such as there'd be white wolves and birds of prey coming to eat people, and there'd be Trishka★ himself for all to see.'

'What's this Trishka?' asked Kostya.

'Don't you know about Trishka?' Ilyusha started up heatedly. 'You're a dumb cluck, mate, if you don't know who Trishka is. It's just dunces you've got in your village, nothing but dunces! Trishka – he'll be a real astonishing person, who'll be coming, and he'll be coming when the last times are near. And he'll be the sort of astonishing person you won't be able to catch hold of, you won't be able to do nothing to him: that's the sort of astonishing person he'll be. The peasants, say, will want to try to catch him, and they'll go out after him with sticks and surround him, but what he'll do is lead their eyes astray – he'll lead their eyes astray so that they start beating each other. Say they put him in prison and he asks for some water in a ladle; they'll bring him the ladle and he'll jump right into it and vanish clean away, all trace of him. Say they put chains on him, he'll just clap his palms together and they'll fall right off him. So then this Trishka'll go walking through the villages and the towns; and this smart fellow, this Trishka, he'll tempt all Christian folk . . . but there won't be a thing you can do to him . . . That's the sort of astonishing, real cunning person he'll be.'

'Yes, that's the one,' Pavlusha continued in his unhurried way. 'He was the one that we were all waiting for. The old men said that soon as the heavenly foreboding begins, Trishka'll be coming. So the foreboding began, and everyone poured out into the street and into the field to see what'll happen. As you know, our place is high

★ The superstition about 'Trishka' probably contains an echo of the legend about Antichrist.

up and open so you can see all around. Everyone's looking – and suddenly down from the settlement on the mountain there's a man coming, strange-looking, with an astonishing big head . . . Everyone starts shouting: "Oy, oy, it's Trishka coming! Oy, oy, it's Trishka!" and they all raced for hiding, this way and that! The elder of our village, he crawled into a ditch and his wife got stuck in a gate and let out such a howling noise that she fair terrified her own watch-dog, and it broke its chain, rushed through the fence and into the wood. And Kuzka's father, Dorofeyich, jumped in among the oats, squatted down there and began to make cries like a quail, all 'cos he thought to himself: "For sure that soul-destroying enemy of mankind'll spare a poor wee birdie!" Such a commotion they were all in! . . . But all the time that man who was coming was simply our barrel-maker Vavila, who'd bought himself a new can and was walking along with that empty can perched on his head.'

All the boys burst out laughing and then once again fell quiet for an instant, as people talking out in the open air frequently do. I looked around me: the night stood guard in solemn majesty; the raw freshness of late evening had been replaced by midnight's dry mildness, and it still had a long time to lie like a soft quilt over the dreaming fields; there was still a long time to wait until the first murmur, the first rustlings and stirrings of morning, the first dew-beads of dawn. There was no moon in the sky: at that season it rose late. Myriads of golden stars, it seemed, were all quietly flowing in glittering rivalry along the Milky Way, and in truth, while looking at them, one sensed vaguely the unwavering, unstoppable racing of the earth beneath . . .

A strange, sharp, sickening cry resounded twice in quick succession across the river, and, after a few moments, was repeated farther off . . .

Kostya shuddered: 'What was that?'

'That was a heron's cry,' Pavlusha answered calmly.

'A heron,' Kostya repeated. 'Then what was it, Pavlusha, I heard yesterday evening?' he added after a brief pause. 'Perhaps you know.'

'What did you hear?'

'This is what I heard. I was walkin' from Stone Ridge to Shashkino, and at first I went all the way along by our nut trees, but afterwards I went through that meadow – you know, by the place where it comes out like a narrow file,* where there's a tarn.† You know it, the one that's all overgrown with reeds. So, mates, I walked past this tarn an' suddenly someone starts makin' a groanin' sound from right inside it, so piteous, piteous, like: Oooh – oooh ... oooh – oooh! I was terrified, mates. It was late an' that voice sounded like somebody really sick. It was like I was goin' to start cryin' myself ... What would that have been, eh?'

'In the summer before last, thieves drowned Akim the forester in that tarn,' Pavlusha remarked. 'So it may have been his soul complaining.'

'Well, it might be that, mates,' rejoined Kostya, widening his already enormous eyes. 'I didn't know that Akim had been drowned in that tarn. If I'd known, I wouldn't have got so terrified.'

'But they do say,' continued Pavlusha, 'there's a kind of little frog makes a piteous noise like that.'

'Frogs? No, that wasn't frogs ... what sort of ...' (The heron again gave its cry over the river.) 'Listen to it!' Kostya could not refrain from saying. 'It makes a noise like a wood-demon.'

'Wood-demons don't make a cry, they're dumb,' Ilyusha inserted. 'They just clap their hands and chatter ...'

'So you've seen one of them, a wood-demon, have you?' Fedya interrupted him scornfully.

'No I haven't, and God preserve that I should see one. But other people have seen one. Just a few days ago one such overtook one of our peasants and was leading him all over the place through the wood and round and round some clearing or other ... He only just managed to get home before it was light.'

'Well, did he see him?'

'He saw him. Big as big he was, he said, and dark, all wrapped up, just like he was behind a tree so you couldn't see him clearly, or like he was hiding from the moon, and looking all the time, peering with his wicked eyes, and winking them, winking ...'

'That's enough!' exclaimed Fedya, shuddering slightly and convulsively hunching his shoulders. 'Phew!'

---

* A 'narrow file' is a sharp turn in a ravine.
† A 'tarn' is a deep hole filled with spring water remaining after the spring torrents, which does not dry up even in summer.

'Why should this devilish thing be around in the world?' commented Pavlusha. 'I don't understand it at all!'

'Don't you scold it! It'll hear you, you'll see,' Ilyusha said.

Again a silence ensued.

'Look up there, look up there, all of you!' the childish voice of Vanya suddenly cried. 'Look at the little stars of God, all swarming like bees!'

He had stuck his small, fresh-complexioned face out from beneath the matting, was leaning on one little fist and slowly looking up with his large, placid eyes. The boys all raised their eyes to the sky, and did not lower them until quite a while had passed.

'Tell me, Vanya,' Fedya began to say in a gentle voice, 'is your sister Anyutka well?'

'She's well,' Vanya answered, with a faint lisp.

'You tell her she ought to come and see us. Why doesn't she?'

'I don't know.'

'Tell her that she ought to come.'

'I'll tell her.'

'Tell her that I'll give her a present.'

'And you'll give one to me, too?'

'I'll give one to you, too.'

Vanya sighed. 'No, there's no need to give me one. Better you give it to her, she's so good to us.'

And once more Vanya laid his head on the ground. Pavlusha rose and picked up the little pot, now empty.

'Where are you going?' Fedya asked him.

'To the river, to get some water. I'd like a drink.'

The dogs got up and followed him.

'See you don't fall in the river!' Ilyusha called after him.

'Why should he fall?' asked Fedya. 'He'll be careful.'

'All right, so he'll be careful. Anything can happen, though. Say he bends down, starting to dip up the water, but then a water-sprite grabs him by the hand and pulls him down below. They'll start saying afterwards that, poor boy, he fell in the water ... But what sort of a fall is that? Listen, listen, he's in the reeds,' he added, pricking up his ears.

The reeds were in fact moving, 'hushing', as they say in our parts.

'Is it true,' asked Kostya, 'that that ugly woman, Akulina, has been wrong in the head ever since she went in the water?'

'Ever since then . . . And look at her now! They say she used to be real good-looking before. The water-sprite did for her. Likely he didn't expect they'd drag her out so soon. He corrupted her down there, down in his own place at the bottom of the water.'

(I had come across this Akulina more than once. Covered with tatters, fearsomely thin, with a face as black as coal, a vacant gaze and permanently bared teeth, she used to stamp about on the same spot for hours at a time, at some point on the road, firmly hugging her bony hands to her breast and slowly shifting her weight from one foot to the other just like a wild animal in a cage. She would give no sign of understanding, no matter what was said to her, save that from time to time she would break into convulsions of laughter.)

'They do say,' Kostya went on, 'that Akulina threw herself in the river because her lover deceived her.'

'Because of that very thing.'

'But do you remember Vasya?' Kostya added sadly.

'What Vasya?' asked Fedya.

'The one who drowned,' Kostya answered, 'in this very river. He was a grand lad, a really grand lad! That mother of his, Feklista, how she loved him, how she used to love Vasya! And she sort of sensed, Feklista did, that ruin would come to him on account of water. That Vasya used to come with us boys in the summer when we went down to the river to bathe – and she'd be all bothered, his mother would. The other women wouldn't care, going waddling by with their washtubs, but Feklista would put her tub down on the ground and start calling to him: "Come back, come back, light of my life! O come back, my little falcon!" And how he came to drown, God alone knows. He was playing on the bank, and his mother was there, raking hay, and suddenly she heard a sound like someone blowing bubbles in the water – she looks, and there's nothing there 'cept Vasya's little cap floating on the water. From then on, you know, Feklista's been out of her mind: she goes and lies down at that place where he drowned, and she lies down, mates, and starts singing this song – you remember the song Vasya used to sing all the time – that's the one she sings, plaintive-like, and she cries and cries, and complains bitterly to God . . .'

'Here's Pavlusha coming,' Fedya said.

Pavlusha came up to the fire with a full pot in his hand.

'Well, boys,' he began after a pause, 'things aren't good.'

'What's happened?' Kostya quickly asked.

'I heard Vasya's voice.'

They all shuddered.

'What's that you're saying? What's it all about?' Kostya babbled.

'It's God's truth. I was just bending down to the water and suddenly I hear someone calling me in Vasya's voice, and it was just like it was coming from under the water: "Pavlusha, hey, Pavlusha!" I listen, and again it calls: "Pavlusha, come down here!" I came away. But I managed to get some water.'

'God preserve us! God preserve us!' the boys said, crossing themselves.

'It was a water-sprite for sure calling you, Pavlusha,' Fedya added. 'And we were only just talking about him, about that Vasya.'

'Oh, it's a real, bad omen,' said Ilyusha, giving due weight to each word.

'It's nothing, forget it!' Pavlusha declared resolutely and again sat down. 'Your own fate you can't escape.'

The boys grew quiet. It was clear that Pavlusha's words had made a profound impression on them. They began to lie down before the fire, as if preparing to go to sleep.

'What was that?' Kostya suddenly asked, raising his head.

Pavlusha listened.

'It's some snipe in flight, whistling as they fly.'

'Where would they be flying?'

'To a place where there's never any winter, that's what they say.'

'There isn't such a land, is there?'

'There is.'

'Is it far away?'

'Far, far away, on the other side of the warm seas.'

Kostya sighed and closed his eyes.

More than three hours had already flowed by since I joined the boys. Eventually the moon rose. I failed to notice it immediately because it was so small and thin. This faintly moonlit night, it seemed, was just as magnificent as it had been previously. But many stars which had only recently stood high in the sky were beginning to tilt towards its dark edge; all around absolute quiet descended, as usually happens only just before morning: everything slept the deep, still sleep of the pre-dawn hours. The air was not so strongly scented, and once again it seemed to be permeated with a raw dampness. O brief summer nights! The boys' talk died away along with the dying of the fires. Even the dogs dozed: and the horses, so far as I could make out by the vaguely glittering, feeble flux of the starlight, were also lying down with their heads bowed. A sweet oblivion descended on me and I fell into a doze.

A current of fresh air brushed my face. I opened my eyes to see that morning was beginning. As yet there was no sign of dawn's pinkness, but in the east it had begun to grow light. The surrounding scene became visible, if only dimly. The pale-grey sky shone bright and cold and tinged with blue; stars either winked their faint light or faded; the ground was damp and leaves were covered with the sweat of dew, here and there sounds of life, voices could be heard, and a faint, light wind of early morning began its wandering and fleet-footed journey across the earth. My body responded to it with a mild, joyful shivering. I got briskly to my feet and walked over to the boys. They slept the sleep of the dead about the embers of the fire; only Pavlusha raised himself half-way and glanced intently at me.

I nodded my head at him and set off to find my way home along the bank of the river, shrouded with smoky mist. I had hardly gone more than a mile when sunlight streamed all around me down the length of the wide damp lea, and ahead of me across the freshly green hills, from forest to woodland, and behind me along the far, dusty track, over the glistening blood-red bushes and across the river which now shone a modest blue under the thinning mist – flowed torrents of young, hot sunlight, crimson at first and later brilliantly red, brilliantly golden. Everything began quivering into life, awakening, singing, resounding, chattering. Everywhere, large drops of dew began to glow like radiant diamonds. There carried to me, pure and crystal-clear as if also washed clean by the freshness of the morning's atmosphere, the sound of a bell. And suddenly I was overtaken by the racing drove of horses, refreshed after the night, and chased along by my acquaintances, the boys.

I have, unfortunately, to add that in that same year Pavlusha died. He did not drown; he was killed in falling from a horse. A pity, for he was a fine lad!

KASYAN FROM THE BEAUTIFUL LANDS

I WAS returning from a hunting trip in a shaky little cart and, under the oppressive effects of an overcast summer day's stifling heat (it is notorious that on such days the heat can be even more insufferable than on clear days, especially when there is no wind), I was dozing as I rocked to and fro, in gloomy patience, allowing my skin to be eaten out by the fine white dust which rose incessantly from beneath the heat-cracked and juddering wheels on the hard earth track, when suddenly my attention was aroused by the unusual agitation and anxious body movements of my driver, who until that instant had been in an even deeper doze than I was. He pulled at the reins, fidgeted on his seat and began shouting at the horses, all the time glancing somewhere off to the side. I looked around. We were driving through a broad, flat area of ploughed land into which low hills, also ploughed up, ran down like unusually gentle, rolling undulations. My gaze encompassed in all about three miles of open, deserted country; all that broke the almost straight line of the horizon were distant, small groves of birch trees with their rounded, tooth-shaped tips. Narrow paths stretched through the fields, dipped into hollows and wound over knolls, and on one of these, which was due to cross our track about five hundred yards from us, I could distinguish a procession. It was at this that my driver had been glancing.

It was a funeral. At the front, in a cart drawn only by one small horse, the priest was riding at walking pace; the deacon sat next to him and was driving; behind the cart, four peasants with bared heads were carrying the coffin, draped in a white cloth; two women were walking behind the coffin. The fragile, plaintive voice of one of the women suddenly reached my ears; I listened: she was singing a lament. Pitifully this ululant, monotonous and helplessly grieving melody floated in the emptiness of the fields. My driver whipped up the horses in the desire to forestall the procession. It is a bad omen to meet up with a corpse on the road. He did, in fact, succeed in galloping along the track just in time before the procession reached it. But we had hardly gone a hundred yards farther on when our cart gave a severe lurch, keeled over and almost capsized. The driver stopped the wildly racing horses, leaned over from his seat to see what had happened, gave a wave of the hand and spat.

'What's wrong there?' I asked.

The driver got down without answering and with no sign of hurry.

'Well, what is it?'

'The axle's broken . . . burned through,' he answered gloomily, and, in a sudden fit of temper, tugged so sharply at the breech-band of the trace-horse that the animal almost toppled over on her side. However, she regained her balance, snorted, shook her mane and proceeded with the utmost calmness to scratch the lower part of her front leg with her teeth.

I got down and stood for a short while on the road, resigning myself to a vague and unpleasant sense of bewilderment. The right wheel had almost completely turned inwards under the cart and seemed to lift its hub in the air in dumb resignation.

'What's to be done now?' I asked eventually.

'That's to blame!' said my driver, directing his whip towards the procession which by this time succeeded in turning on to the track and was beginning to approach us. 'I've always noticed it,' he continued. 'It's always a bad omen to meet up with a corpse, that's for sure.'

Again he took it out on the trace-horse who, seeing how irritable and severe he was, decided to stand stock-still and only occasionally gave a few modest flicks with her tail. I took a few steps to and fro along the track and stopped again in front of the wheel.

In the meantime, the procession had caught up with us. Turning aside from the track on to the grass, the sad cortège passed by our cart. My driver and I removed our caps, exchanged bows with the priest and looks with the pall-bearers. They progressed with difficulty, their broad chests heaving under the weight. Of the two women who walked behind the coffin, one was extremely old and pale of face; her motionless features, cruelly contorted with grief, preserved an expression of stern and solemn dignity. She walked in silence, now and then raising a frail hand to her thin, sunken lips. The other woman, of about twenty-five, had eyes that were red and moist with tears, and her whole face had become swollen from crying. As she drew level with us, she ceased her lament and covered her face with her sleeve. Then the procession went past us, turning back on to the track once more, and her piteous, heart-rending lament was resumed. After following with his eyes the regular to-and-fro motion of the coffin without uttering a sound, my driver turned to me.

'It's Martin, the carpenter, the one from Ryabovo, that they're taking to be buried,' he said.

'How do you know that?'

'I could tell from the women. The old one's his mother and the young one's his wife.'

'Had he been ill, then?'

'Aye . . . the fever . . . The manager sent for the doctor three days back, but the doctor wasn't home. He was a good carpenter, he was. Liked his drink a bit, but he was a real good carpenter. You see how his wife's grieving for him. It's like they say, though – a woman's tears don't cost nothin', they just flow like water, that's for sure.'

And he bent down, crawled under the rein of the trace-horse and seized hold of the shaft with both hands.

'Well,' I remarked, 'what can we do now?'

My driver first of all leaned his knees against the shoulder of the other horse and giving the shaft a couple of shakes, set the shaft-pad back in its place, crawled back once again under the rein of the trace-horse and, after giving her a shove on the nose while doing so, walked up to the wheel – walked up to it and, without taking his eyes off it, slowly extracted a snuff-box from beneath the skirt of his long tunic, slowly pulled open the lid by a little strap, slowly inserted two thick fingers (the tips of them could hardly fit into the snuff-box at once), kneaded the tobacco, wrinkled up his nose in readiness, gave several measured sniffs, accompanied at each inhalation of the snuff with prolonged snorting and grunting, and, after painfully screwing up and blinking his tear-filled eyes, settled into deep thoughtfulness.

'So, what do you think?' I asked when all this was over.

My driver carefully replaced the snuff-box in his pocket, brought his hat down over his brows without touching it, simply by a movement of his head, and climbed thoughtfully up on to the seat.

'Where are you off to?' I asked, not a little amazed.

'Please be seated,' he answered calmly and picked up the reins.

'But how are we going to go?'

'We'll go all right.'

'But the axle . . .'

'Please be seated.'

'But the axle's broken . . .'

'It's broken, yes, it's broken all right, but we'll make it to the new village – at walking pace, that is. It's over there to the right, beyond the wood, that's where the new village is, what they call the Yudin village.'

'But d'you think we'll get there?'

My driver did not even deign to answer me.

'I'd better go on foot,' I said.

'As you please . . .'

He waved his whip and the horses set off.

We did, in fact, reach the new village, even though the right front wheel hardly held in place and wobbled in a most unusual fashion. It almost flew off as we negotiated a small knoll, but my driver shouted at it angrily and we successfully descended the far slope.

Yudin village consisted of six small, low-roofed huts which had already begun to lean to one side or the other despite the fact that they had no doubt been put up quite recently, and not even all the yards had wattle fencing. As we entered the village, we did not meet a living soul; there were not even any chickens to be seen in the village street; there were not even any dogs, save for one black, stubby-tailed animal that jumped hastily from a completely dried-up ditch, where it must have been driven by thirst, only to dash headlong under a gate without so much as giving a bark. I turned into the first hut, opened the porch door and called for the owners: no one answered me. I called again: a hungry miaowing came from behind the inner door. I shoved it with my foot and an emaciated cat flashed past me, its green eyes glittering in the dark. I stuck my head into the room and looked around: it was dark, smoky and empty. I went into the backyard and there was no one there. A calf gave a plaintive moo in the enclosure, and a crippled grey goose took a few waddling steps off to one side. I crossed to the second hut – and there was no one there either. So I went out into the backyard.

In the very middle of the brilliantly lit yard, right out in the middle of the sun, as they say, there was lying, face downward and with his head covered with a cloth coat, someone I took to be a boy. A few paces from him, beside a wretched little cart, a miserable little horse, all skin and bones, stood in a tattered harness under a straw overhang. Its thick reddish-brown coat was dappled with small bright splashes of sunlight that streamed through narrow openings in the dilapidated thatchwork. There also, high up in their little bird-houses, starlings chattered, looking down upon the world with placid inquisitiveness from their airy home. I walked up to the sleeping figure and began to rouse it.

The sleeper raised his head, saw me and at once jumped to his feet.

'What is it? What's happened?' he started muttering in bewilderment.

I did not answer him at once because I was so astonished by his appearance. Imagine, if you please, a dwarf of about fifty years old, with a small, swarthy, wrinkled face, a little pointed nose, barely discernible little brown eyes and abundant curly black hair which sat upon his tiny head just as broadly as the cap sits on the stalk of a mushroom. His entire body was extraordinarily frail and thin, and it is quite impossible to convey in words how unusual and strange was the look in his eyes.

'What is it?' he asked me again.

I explained the position to him and he listened to me without lowering his slowly blinking eyes.

'Is it not possible then for us to obtain a new axle?' I asked finally. 'I would gladly pay.'

'But who are you? Are you out hunting?' he asked, encompassing me with his glance from head to foot.

'I'm out hunting.'

'You shoot the birds of the air, eh? . . . And the wild animals of the forest? . . . Isn't it sinful you are to be killing God's own wee birds and spilling innocent blood?'

The strange little old man spoke with a very pronounced dwelling on each word. The sound of his voice also astonished me. Not only was there nothing decrepit about it but it was surprisingly sweet, youthful and almost feminine in its gentleness.

'I have no axle,' he added after a short interval of silence. 'This one won't do' – he pointed to his own little cart – 'because, after all, yours is a big cart.'

'But would it be possible to find one in the village?'

'What sort of village is it we have here! Here, there's not anyone of us has a single thing. And there's no one at home – aren't they all out at work for sure. Be off with you!' he said, suddenly, and lay down again on the ground.

I had certainly not expected an outcome of this kind.

'Listen, old man,' I started to say, touching him on the shoulder, 'have a heart, help me.'

'Be off with you in the name o' God! It's tired out I am, an' me having gone into town and back,' he told me and pulled his cloth coat over his head.

'Please do me a favour,' I went on, 'I . . . I'll pay you . . .'

'I'm not needin' your money.'

'Please, old man . . .'

He raised himself half-way and sat himself upright, crossing his delicate, spindly legs.

'It's takin' you I might be to where they've been cutting down the trees. 'Tis a place where some local merchants have bought a piece o' woodland, the Lord be the judge of 'em, an' they're getting rid of all the trees and putting up an office they are, the Lord judge 'em for it. That's where you might order an axle from 'em or buy one ready-made.'

'Excellent!' I exclaimed delightedly. 'Excellent! Let's go.'

'An oak axle, mind you, a good one,' he continued without rising from where he was sitting.

'Is it far to where they're cutting down the trees?'

'A couple o' miles.'

'Well, then, we can get there on your little cart.'

'Oh, but wait a moment . . .'

'Now come along,' I said. 'Come on, old man! My driver's waiting for us in the street.'

The old man got up reluctantly and followed me out into the

street. My driver was in a thoroughly vexed state of mind: he had wanted to water the horses, but it had turned out that there was very little water in the well and what there was had an unpleasant taste; and that was putting first things first, as drivers are accustomed to say ... However, as soon as he saw the old man he grinned broadly, nodded his head and cried out:

'If it's not little Kasyan! Good to see you!'

''Tis good to see you, Yerofey, righteous man that you are!' answered Kasyan in a despondent voice.

I at once told my driver about the old man's suggestion; Yerofey expressed his assent and drove into the yard. While Yerofey was quite deliberately making a great display of briskness in unharnessing the horses, the old man stood with one shoulder leaning against the gates and glanced unhappily either at him or me. He appeared to be at a loss and, so far as I could see, he was not unduly delighted by our sudden visit.

'Have they resettled you as well?' Yerofey suddenly asked him as he removed the shaft-bow.

'Me as well.'

'Yuck!' said my driver through his teeth. 'You know Martin, the carpenter ... Martin of Ryabovo, don't you?'

'That I do.'

'Well, he's dead. We just met up with his coffin.'

Kasyan gave a shudder.

'Dead?' he muttered, and stared at the ground.

'Yes, he's dead. Why didn't you cure him, eh? People say you do cures, that you've got the power of healing.'

My driver was obviously taunting and making fun of the old man.

'And that's your cart, is it?' he added, shrugging a shoulder in its direction.

''Tis mine.'

'A cart, is it, a cart!' he repeated and, taking it by the shafts, almost turned it upside down. 'A cart, indeed! But what'll you be using to get to the clearings? You won't be able to harness our horse into those shafts. Our horses are big, but what's this meant to be?'

'I wouldn't be knowing,' answered Kasyan, 'what you'll be using. For sure there's that poor creature,' he added with a sigh.

'D'you mean this?' asked Yerofey, seizing on what Kasyan had been saying, and, going up to Kasyan's miserable little horse, contemptuously stuck the third finger of his right hand in its neck. 'See,' he added reproachfully, 'gone to sleep, it has, the useless thing!'

I asked Yerofey to harness it up as quickly as possible. I wanted to go myself with Kasyan to the place where they were clearing the woodland, for those are the places where grouse are often found. When the little cart was finally ready, I somehow or other settled myself along with my dog on its warped, bast floor, and Kasyan, hunching himself up into a ball, also sat on the front support with the same despondent expression on his face — then it was that Yerofey approached me and, giving me a mysterious look, whispered:

'And it's a good thing, sir, that you're going with him. He's one of those holy men, you know, sir, and he's nicknamed The Flea. I don't know how you were able to understand him . . .'

I was about to comment to Yerofey that so far Kasyan had seemed to me to be a man of very good sense, but my driver at once continued in the same tone of voice:

'You just watch out and see that he takes you where he should. And make sure you yourself choose the axle, the stouter the better . . . What about it, Flea,' he added loudly, 'is there anywhere here to find a bite to eat?'

'Seek and it shall be found,' answered Kasyan, giving the reins a jerk, and we rolled away.

His little horse, to my genuine surprise, went far from badly. Throughout the entire journey Kasyan maintained a stubborn silence and answered all my questions peremptorily and unwillingly. We quickly reached the clearings, and once there we made our way to the office, a tall hut standing by itself above a small ravine which had been haphazardly dammed and turned into a pond. I found in this office two young clerks working for the merchants, both of them with teeth as white as snow, sugary sweet eyes, sugary sweet, boisterous chatter and sugary sweet, clever little smiles, did a deal with them for an axle and set off for the clearings. I thought that Kasyan would stay by the horse and wait, but he suddenly approached me.

'And is it that you're after shooting the wee birds?' he ventured. 'Is that it?'

'Yes, if I find them.'

'I'll go along with you. D'you mind?'

'Please do, please do.'

And we walked off. The area of felled trees extended for less than a mile. I confess that I looked at Kasyan more than at my dog. He had been aptly nicknamed the Flea. His black and hatless little head (his hair, by the way, was a substitute for any cap) bobbed up and down among the bushes. He walked with an extraordinarily sprightly step and literally took little jumps as he went, ceaselessly bending down, plucking herbs, stuffing them under his shirt, muttering words through his nose and shooting glances at me and my dog, giving us such keen and unusual looks. In the low bushes, the 'underbush' and in the clearings there are often little grey birds which all the time switch from sapling to sapling and emit short whistling sounds as they dive suddenly in their flight. Kasyan used to tease them, exchanging calls with them; a young quail would fly up shrilly from under his feet and he would call shrilly after it; a lark might start rising above him, fluttering its wings and pouring out its song – Kasyan would at once catch up its refrain. But to me he said not a word.

The weather was beautiful, still more beautiful than it had been before; yet there was still no lessening of the heat. Across the clear sky drifted, with scarcely a movement, a few distant clouds, yellowish-white, the colour of a late snowfall in the spring, flat in shape and elongated like furled sails. Their feathered edges, light and wispy as cotton, altered slowly but obviously with each passing instant; they were as if melting, these clouds were, and they cast no shadow. For a long while Kasyan and I wandered through the clearings. Young shoots which had not yet succeeded in growing more than a couple of feet high spread their thin, smooth stems round the blackened and squat stumps of trees; round, spongy fungoid growths with grey edges, the kind which they boil down to make tinder, adhered to these tree-stumps; wild strawberries spread their wispy pink runners over them; mushrooms were also ensconced there in tight family clusters. One's feet were continually becoming entangled and caught by the tall grass, drenched in the sun's heat; in all directions one's eyes were dazzled by the sharp, metallic flashes of light from the young, reddish leaves on the saplings; everywhere in gay abundance appeared sky-blue clusters of vetch, the little golden

chalices of buttercups, the partly mauve, partly yellow flowers of St
John and Mary daisies; here and there, beside overgrown tracks, in
which the traces of cart-wheels were marked by strips of short-
stemmed red grass rose piles of firewood, stacked in six-foot lengths
and darkened by the wind and rain; slight shadows extended from
them in slanting rectangles – otherwise there was no shade of any
kind. A light breeze sprang up occasionally and then died. It would
blow suddenly straight into one's face and caper around, as it were,
setting everything happily rustling, nodding and swaying about,
making the supple tips of the fern bow gracefully, so that one was
delighted at it; but then it would again fade away, and everything
would once more be still. Only the grasshoppers made a combined
whirring, as if infuriated – such an oppressive, unceasing, insipid, dry
sound. It was appropriate to the unabating, midday heat, as if
literally engendered by it, literally summoned by it out of the sun-
smelted earth.

Without coming across a single covey, we finally reached some
new clearings. Here, recently felled aspens were stretched sadly on
the ground, pressing down both grass and undergrowth beneath
their weight; on some of them the leaves, still green but already
dead, hung feebly from the stiff branches; on others they had already
withered and curled up. A special, extraordinarily pleasant acrid
scent came from the fresh, golden-white chips of wood which lay in
heaps about the moistly bright tree-stumps. Far off, closer to the
wood, there could be heard the faint clatter of axes and from time to
time, solemnly and quietly, as if in the act of bowing and spreading
out its arms, a curly-headed tree would fall.

For a long while I could find no game; finally, a landrail flew out
of an extensive oak thicket which was completely overgrown with
wormwood. I fired: the bird turned over in the air and fell. Hearing
the shot, Kasyan quickly covered his face with his hand and remained
stock-still until I had reloaded my gun and picked up the shot bird.
Just as I was preparing to move farther on, he came up to the place
where the bird had fallen, bent down to the grass which had been
sprinkled with several drops of blood, gave a shake of the head and
looked at me in fright. Afterwards I heard him whispering: 'A sin!
'Tis a sin, it is, a sin!'

Eventually the heat forced us to find shelter in the wood. I threw myself down beneath a tall hazel bush, above which a young and graceful maple had made a beautiful spread of its airy branches. Kasyan seated himself on the thick end of a felled birch. I looked at him. Leaves fluttered slightly high above, and their liquid, greenish shadows glided calmly to and fro over his puny figure, clad somehow or other in a dark cloth coat, and over his small face. He did not raise his head. Bored by his silence, I lay down on my back and began admiringly to watch the peaceful play of the entwined leaves against the high, clear sky. It is a remarkably pleasant occupation, to lie on one's back in a forest and look upwards! It seems that you are looking into a bottomless sea, that it is stretching out far and wide *below* you, that the trees are not rising from the earth but, as if they were the roots of enormous plants, are descending or falling steeply into those lucid, grassy waves, while the leaves on the trees glimmer like emeralds or thicken into a gold-tinted, almost jet-black greenery. Somewhere high, high up, at the very end of a delicate branch, a single leaf stands out motionless against a blue patch of translucent sky, and, beside it, another sways, resembling in its movements the ripplings upon the surface of a fishing reach, as if the movement were of its own making and not caused by the wind. Like magical underwater islands, round white clouds gently float into view and pass by, and then suddenly the whole of this sea, this radiant air, these branches and leaves suffused with sunlight, all of it suddenly begins to stream in the wind, shimmers with a fugitive brilliance, and a fresh, tremulous murmuration arises which is like the endless shallow splashing of oncoming ripples. You lie still and you go on watching: words cannot express the delight and quiet, and how sweet is the feeling that creeps over your heart. You go on watching, and that deep, clear azure brings a smile to your lips as innocent as the azure itself, as innocent as the clouds passing across it, and as if in company with them there passes through your mind a slow cavalcade of happy recollections, and it seems to you that all the while your gaze is travelling farther and farther away and drawing all of you with it into that calm, shining infinity, making it impossible for you to tear yourself away from those distant heights, from those distant depths . . .

'Master, eh, master!' Kasyan suddenly said in his resonant voice.

I raised myself up in surprise; until that moment he had hardly answered any of my questions and now he had suddenly started talking of his own accord.

'What do you want?' I asked.

'Why is it now that you should be killing that wee bird?' he began, looking me directly in the face.

'How do you mean: why? A landrail is a game bird. You can eat it.'

'No, it wasn't for that you were killing it, master. You won't be eating it! You were killing it for your own pleasure.'

'But surely you yourself are used to eating a goose or a chicken, for example, aren't you?'

'Such birds are ordained by God for man to eat, but a landrail — that's a bird of the free air, a forest bird. And he's not the only one; aren't there many of them, every kind of beast of the forest and of the field, and river creature, and creature of the marsh and meadow and the heights and the depths — and a sin it is to be killing such a one, it should be let to live on the earth until its natural end . . . But for man there is another food laid down; another food and another drink; bread is God's gift to man, and the waters from the heavens, and the tame creatures handed down from our fathers of old.'

I looked at Kasyan in astonishment. His words flowed freely; he did not cast around for them, but spoke with quiet animation and a modest dignity, occasionally closing his eyes.

'So according to you it's also sinful to be killing fish?' I asked.

'A fish has cold blood,' he protested with certainty, 'it's a dumb creature. A fish doesn't know fear, doesn't know happiness: a fish is a creature without a tongue. A fish doesn't have feelings, it has no living blood in it . . . Blood,' he continued after a pause, 'blood is holy! Blood does not see the light of God's sun, blood is hidden from the light . . . And a great sin it is to show blood to the light of day, a great sin and cause to be fearful, oh, a great one it is!'

He gave a sigh and lowered his eyes. I must admit that I looked at the strange old man in complete amazement. His speech did not sound like the speech of a peasant: simple people did not talk like this, nor did ranters. This language, thoughtfully solemn and unusual as it was, I had never heard before.

'Tell me, please, Kasyan,' I began, without lowering my eyes from his slightly flushed face, 'what is your occupation?'

He did not answer my question immediately. His gaze shifted uneasily for a moment.

'I live as the Lord ordains I should,' he said eventually, 'but as for an occupation, no, I don't have an occupation of any kind. 'Tis a poor mentality I have, right from when I was small. I work so long as I can, but it's a poor worker I'm being. There's nothing for me to do! My health's gone and my hands're all foolish. In the springtime, though, I catch nightingales.'

'You catch nightingales? Then why were you talking about not touching the beast of the forest and the field and other creatures?'

'Not to be killing 'em, that's the point; death will take what's due to it. Now there's Martin the carpenter: he lived his life, Martin the carpenter did, and he didn't have long and he died; and now his wife's grieving over her husband and her little ones . . . It's not for man nor beast to get the better of death. Death doesn't come running, but you can't run away from it, neither; nor must you be helping it along. I don't kill the nightingales, Good Lord preserve us! I don't catch them to cause them pain, nor to put their lives in any peril, but for man's enjoyment, for his consolation and happiness.'

'Do you go into the Kursk region to catch them?'

'I go into Kursk and I go farther, depending how things are. I sleep in the swamplands, and also I sleep in the woodlands, and I sleep all alone in the fields and in the wild places: that's where snipe do their whistling, where you can hear the hares crying, where the drakes go hissing . . . At eventide I take note where they are, and come morning I listen out for them, at dawn I spread my net over the bushes. There's a kind of nightingale sings real piteously, sweetly and piteously, it does . . .'

'Do you sell them?'

'I give 'em away to good people.'

'What d'you do apart from this?'

'What do I do?'

'What keeps you busy?'

The old man was silent for a moment.

'Nothing keeps me busy. 'Tis a poor worker I am. But I understand how to read and write.'

'So you're literate?'

'I understand how to read and write. The Lord God helped me, and some kind people.'

'Are you a family man?'

'No, I've got no family.'

'Why's that? They've all died, have they?'

'No, it's just like it wasn't my task in life, that's all. Everything's according to the will of God, we all live our lives according to the will of God; but a man's got to be righteous – that's what! That means he must live a fitting life in God's eyes.'

'And you haven't any relatives?'

'I have . . . I have, yes.' The old man became confused.

'Tell me, please,' I began. 'I heard my driver asking you, so to speak, why you hadn't cured Martin the carpenter? Is it true you can heal people?'

'Your driver's a just man,' Kasyan answered me thoughtfully, 'but he's also not without sin. He says I have the power of healing. What power have I got! And who is there has such power? It all comes from God. But there . . . there are herbs, there are flowers: they help, it's true. There's marigold, there's one, a kindly herb for curing human beings; there's the plantains, too; there's nothing to be ashamed of in talking about them – good clean herbs are of God's making. But others aren't. Maybe they help, but they're a sin and it's a sin to talk about them. Perhaps they might be used with the help of prayer . . . Well, of course, there are special words . . . But only he who has faith shall be saved,' he added, lowering his voice.

'Did you give anything to Martin?' I asked.

'I learned about him too late,' answered the old man. 'And what would've been the good! It is all ordained for man from his birth. He was not a dweller, was Martin the carpenter, not a dweller on this earth: and that's how it turned out. No, when a man's not ordained to live on this earth, the sweet sunlight doesn't warm him like it warms the others, and the produce of the earth profits him nothing, as if all the time he's being called away . . . Aye, God rest his soul!'

'Have you been resettled here among us for long?' I asked after a short silence.

Kasyan stirred.

'No, not long: 'bout four years. Under the old master we lived all the time where we were, but it was the custodians of the estate who resettled us. The old master we had was a meek soul, a humble man he was – God grant he enter the Kingdom of Heaven! But the custodians, of course, decided justly. It looks like this is how it was meant to be.'

'But where did you live before this?'

'We came from the Beautiful Lands.'[1]

'Is that far from here?'

''Bout sixty miles.'

'Was it better there?'

'It was better ... much better. The land's free and open there, with plenty of rivers, a real home for us; but here it's all enclosed and dried up. We've become orphans here. There where we were, on the Beautiful Lands, I mean, you'd go up a hill, you'd go up – and, Good Lord, what wouldn't you see from there? Eh? There'd be a river there, a meadow there and there a forest, and then there'd be a church, and again more meadows going far, far off, as far as anything. Just as far as far, that's how you'd go on looking and looking and wonderin' at it, that's for sure! As for here, true – the land's better: loamy soil it is, real good loam, so the peasants say. But so far as I'm concerned, there's sufficient food everywhere to keep me going.'

'But if you were to tell the truth, old fellow, you'd want to be where you were born, wouldn't you?'

'For sure I'd like to take a look at it. Still, it doesn't matter where I am. I'm not a family man, not tied to anywhere. And what would I be doing sittin' at home a lot? It's when I'm off on my way, off on my travels,' he began saying in a louder voice, 'that everything's surely easier. Then the sweet sunlight shines on you, and you're clearer to God, and you sing in better tune. Then you look-see what herbs is growing there, and you take note of 'em and collect the ones you want. Maybe there's water runnin' there, water from a spring, so you have a drink of it and take note of that as well. The birds of the air'll be singing ... And then on t'other side of Kursk there'll be the steppes, O such steppelands, there's a wonder for you, a real joy to mankind they are, such wide expanses, a sign of God's bounty. And they go on and on, people do say, right to the warm seas where Gamayun[2] lives, the bird of the sweet voice, to the place where no leaves fall from the trees in winter, nor in the autumn neither, and golden apples do grow on silver branches and each man lives in contentment and justice with another ... That's where I'd like to be going ... Though I've been about a bit in my time! I've been in

Romyon and in Sinbirsk, that fine city, and in Moscow herself, dressed in her golden crowns. And to Oka, river of mother's milk, I've been, and to Tsna, fair as a dove, and to our mother, the Volga, and many's the people I've seen, good Chrestians all, and many's the honest towns I've been in . . . But I'd still like to be going to that place . . . and that's it . . . and soon-like . . . And it's not only I, sinner that I am, but many other Chrestians that go walking and wandering through the wide world with nothin' but bast on their feet and seekin' for the truth . . . Sure they are! . . . But as for what's at home, eh? There's no justice in the way men live – that's what . . .'

Kasyan uttered these last words with great speed and almost inaudibly: afterwards he said something else, which I was unable even to hear, and his face took on such a strange expression that I was spontaneously reminded of the title 'holy man' which Yerofey had given him. He stared down at the ground, gave a phlegmy cough and appeared to collect his senses.

'O the sweet sun!' he uttered almost under his breath. 'O such a blessing, Good Lord! O such warmth here in the forest!'

He shrugged his shoulders, fell silent, glanced round distractedly and started singing in a quiet voice. I could not catch all the words of his protracted little song, but I heard the following words:

> But Kasyan's what they call me,
> And by nickname I'm the Flea . . .

'Ha!' I thought, 'he's making it up . . .'

Suddenly he shuddered and stopped his singing, gazing intently into the forest thicket. I turned and saw a little peasant girl of about eight years of age, dressed in a little blue coat, with a chequered handkerchief tied over her head and a small wattle basket on her bare, sunburnt arm. She had obviously not expected to come across us here at all; she had stumbled on us, as they say, and now stood stock-still on a shady patch of grass in a green thicket of nut trees, glancing fearfully at me out of her jet-black eyes. I had scarcely had time to notice her when she at once plunged out of sight behind a tree.

'Annushka! Annushka! Come here, don't be frightened,' the old man called to her in a gentle voice.

'I'm frightened,' a thin little voice answered.

'Don't be frightened, don't be frightened, come to me.'

Annushka silently left her hiding-place, quietly made her way round – her child's feet scarcely made any noise in the thick grass – and emerged from the thicket beside the old man. She was not a girl of about eight years of age, as it had seemed to me at first judging by her lack of inches, but of thirteen or fourteen. Her whole body was small and thin, but very well-made and supple, and her beautiful little face was strikingly similar to Kasyan's, although Kasyan was no beauty. The same sharp features, the same unusual look, which was both cunning and trustful, meditative and penetrating, and exactly the same gestures . . . Kasyan took her in at a glance as she stood sideways to him.

'You've been out picking mushrooms, have you?' he asked.

'Yes,' she answered with a shy smile.

'Did you find many?'

'Yes.' (She directed a quick glance at him and again smiled.)

'Are there any white ones?'

'There are white ones as well.'

'Come on, show them . . .' (She lowered the basket from her arm and partly raised the broad dock leaf with which the mushrooms were covered.) 'Ah!' said Kasyan, bending over the basket, 'they're real beauties! That's really something, Annushka!'

'Is she your daughter, Kasyan?' I asked. (Annushka's face crimsoned faintly.)

'No, she's just a relative,' Kasyan said with pretended indifference. 'Well, Annushka, you be off,' he added at once, 'and God be with you! Watch where you go . . .'

'But why should she go on foot?' I interrupted. 'We could take her home in the cart.'

Annushka blushed red as a poppy, seized hold of the basket by its string handle and glanced at the old man in alarm.

'No, she'll walk home,' he objected in the same indifferent tone of voice. 'Why shouldn't she? She'll get home all right . . . Off with you now!'

Annushka walked off briskly into the forest. Kasyan followed her with his eyes, then looked down at the ground and grinned to himself. In this protracted grin, in the few words which he had spoken to Annushka and in the sound of his voice as he was talking to her there had been ineffable, passionate love and tenderness. He again glanced in the direction that she had gone, again smiled and, wiping his face, gave several nods of the head.

'Why did you send her away so soon?' I asked him. 'I would have bought some mushrooms from her . . .'

'You can buy them there at home whenever you like, it's no matter,' he answered, addressing me with the formal 'You' for the first time.

'She's very pretty, that girl of yours.'

'No . . . how so? . . . she's just as they come,' he answered with apparent unwillingness, and from that very moment dropped back into his former taciturnity.

Seeing that all my efforts to make him start talking again were fruitless, I set off for the clearings. The heat had meanwhile dissipated a little; but my bad luck or, as they say in our parts, my 'nothing doing' continued the same and I returned to the village with no more than a single landrail and a new axle. As we were driving up to the yard, Kasyan suddenly turned to me.

'Master, sir,' he began, 'sure I'm the one you should blame, sure it was I who drove all the game away from you.'

'How so?'

'It's just something I know. There's that dog of yours, a good dog and trained to hunt, but he couldn't do anything. When you think of it, people are people, aren't they? Then there's this animal here, but what've they been able to make out of him?'

It would have been useless for me to start persuading Kasyan that it was impossible to 'cast a spell' over game and therefore I did not answer him. At that moment we turned in through the gates of the yard.

Annushka was not in the hut; she had already arrived and left behind her basket of mushrooms.

Yerofey fixed the new axle, having first subjected it to a severe and biased evaluation; and an hour later I drove away, leaving Kasyan a little money, which at first he did not wish to accept but which later, having thought about it and having held it in the palm of his hand, he placed inside the front of his shirt. During this whole hour he hardly uttered a single word; as previously, he stood leaning against the gates, made no response to my driver's reproachful remarks and was extremely cold to me in saying goodbye.

As soon as I had returned I had noticed that my Yerofey was once again sunk in gloom. And in fact he had found nothing edible in the village and the water for the horses had been of poor quality. So we drove out. With a dissatisfaction that expressed itself even in the nape of his neck, he sat on the box and dearly longed to strike up a conversation with me, but in anticipation of my initial question he limited himself to faint grumblings under his breath and edifying, occasionally caustic, speeches directed at the horses.

'A village!' he muttered. 'Call it a village! I asked for some *kvas* and they didn't even have any *kvas* . . . Good God! And as for water, it was simply muck!' (He spat loudly.) 'No cucumbers, no *kvas*, not a bloody thing. As for you,' he added thunderously, turning to the right-hand horse, 'I know you, you dissemblin' female, you! You're a right one for pretendin', you are . . .' (And he struck her with the whip.) 'That horse has gone dead cunnin', she has, and before it was a nice, easy creature . . . Gee-up there, look-see about it.'

'Tell me, please, Yerofey,' I began, 'what sort of a person is that Kasyan?'

Yerofey did not reply immediately: in general he was thoughtful and slow in his ways, but I could guess at once that my question had cheered and calmed him.

'The Flea, you mean?' he said eventually, jerking at the reins. 'A strange and wonderful man he is, truly a holy man, and you'd not find another one like him all that quick. He's, so to speak, as like as like our grey horse there: he's got out of hand just the same . . . that's to say, he's got out of the way of workin'. Well, of course, he's no worker. Just keeps himself going, but still . . . For sure he's always been like that. To start with he used to be a carrier along with his uncles: there were three of 'em; but after a time, well, you know, he got bored and gave it up. Started living at home, he did, but couldn't feel settled – he's restless as a flea. Thanks be to God, it happened he had a kind master who didn't force him to work. So from that time on he's been wanderin' here, there and everywhere, like a roaming sheep. And God knows, he's remarkable enough, with his being silent as a tree-stump one moment and then talking away all of a sudden the next – and as for what he says, God alone knows what that is. Maybe you think it's his manner? It's not his manner, because he's too ungainly. But he sings well – a bit pompous-like, but not too bad really.'

'Is it true he has the power of healing?'

'A power of healing! What would he be doing with that? Just ordinary he is. But he did cure me of scrofula ... A lot of good it does him! He's just as stupid as they come, he is,' he added, after a pause.

'Have you known him long?'

'Long enough. We were neighbours of his in Sychovka, on the Beautiful Lands.'

'And that girl we came across in the wood – Annushka – is she a blood relation of his?'

Yerofey glanced at me over his shoulder and bared his teeth in a wide grin.

'Huh ... Yes, they're relations. She's an orphan, got no mother and nobody knows who her mother was. But it's likely she's related to him: she's the spittin' image of him ... And she lives with him. A smart girl, she is, no denying that; and a good girl, and the old man, he dotes on her: she's a good girl. And likely he'll – you may not believe it – but likely he'll take it into his head to teach his Annushka readin' and writin'. You never know, it's just the sort of thing he'd start: he's as extrardin'ry as that, changeable-like he is, even untellable ... Hey, hey, hey!' My driver suddenly interrupted himself and, bringing the horses to a stop, leaned over the side and started sniffing. 'Isn't there a smell of burning? There is an' all! These new axles'll be the end of me. It seemed I'd put enough grease on. I'll have to get some water. There's a little pond over there.'

And Yerofey got down slowly from the box, untied a bucket, walked to the pond and, when he returned, listened with considerable pleasure to the way the axle-hole hissed as it was suddenly doused with water. About six times in the course of seven or so miles he had to douse the overheated axle, and evening had long since fallen by the time we returned home.

BAILIFF

TEN miles or so from my estate there lives a certain acquaintance of mine, a young landowner and retired guards officer, Arkady Pavlych Penochkin. His lands are rich in game, his house designed by a French architect, his servants dressed in the English fashion, he provides excellent dinners and extends a cordial welcome to his guests; yet it is only with reluctance that one visits him. He is a man of intelligence and substance, educated according to the best standards, has done his service in a guards regiment and gone the rounds of high society, and now looks after his estate with much success. To use his own words, Arkady Pavlych is stern but just, busies himself with the welfare of his menials and metes out punishments always for their own good. 'One must treat them like children,' he says on such occasions. 'It's due to ignorance, *mon cher; il faut prendre cela en considération.*' He himself, when there is occasion for so-called unfortunate strictness, avoids sharp and abrupt gestures and prefers not to raise his voice, but rather sticks his hand out directly in front of him saying quietly: 'Surely I asked you, my dear chap,' or 'What's the matter with you, my friend? Pull yourself together' – all the while slightly gritting his teeth and giving his mouth a slight twist. He is not tall, dapper in build, not at all bad-looking and he keeps his hands and nails admirably groomed; his rosy lips and cheeks exude good health. He has a resonant and carefree laugh and a jovial way of screwing up his bright hazel eyes. He dresses excellently and with taste; he orders French books, pictures and newspapers, but he is no book-worm: he hardly managed to finish *The Wandering Jew*.[1] He is an expert card-player. Generally speaking, Arkady Pavlych is considered to be one of the most cultured members of the gentry and the most sought-after prospective husband in our province; women are quite out of their minds about him and are particularly fulsome in their praise of his manners. He is amazingly good at conducting himself properly, is as cautious as a cat and has never for the life of him let himself be touched by a breath of scandal, although he occasionally permits the world to know what sort of man he is by taking a delight in teasing some shy wretch and snapping his head off. He stoutly avoids bad company for fear of compromising himself; though at a time of celebration he is fond of proclaiming himself a devotee of Epicurus, despite his generally poor opinion of philosophy which he calls the misty nourishment of German intellects or sometimes, quite simply, a lot of nonsense. He is also fond of music; while playing cards he sings through his teeth, but he does it with feeling; he knows part of *Lucia*[2] and *Les Somnambules*,[3] though he pitches his voice too high. During the winter he goes to St Petersburg. He keeps his house in exceptionally good order; even his coachmen have succumbed to his influence and not only give daily washings to the horse-collars and their own peasant coats, but also wash their own faces. Arkady Pavlych's house-serfs, it's true, have a habit of looking at you from under their brows – but then in Russia, it's no easy matter to tell a gloomy face from a sleepy one. Arkady Pavlych speaks in a soft and pleasant voice, lending his speech due measure and deriving enjoyment, as it were, from permitting each word to pass through his splendid, perfumed whiskers; he also makes use of many French turns of phrase, such as *'Mais c'est impayable!' 'Mais comment donc!'* and so on. Regardless of this, I at least visit him with the utmost reluctance, and if it had not been for the grouse and the partridges I would long ago no doubt have put an end to our acquaintanceship. A strange kind of unease seizes hold of you in his house; even the comforts of it evoke no pleasure, and each evening, when the frizzle-haired lackey appears before you in his sky-blue livery with its crested buttons and proceeds deferentially to pull off your boots, you feel that if only in place of his lean and hungry figure there were suddenly presented to you the strikingly wide cheekbones and impossibly blunt nose of a strapping lad just brought in from the plough by the master of the house, who had already succeeded in bursting through the seams of his newly loaned nankeen tunic in a dozen places – you would be indescribably pleased and would willingly submit to the danger of losing, along with your boot, the whole of your leg right up to the thigh . . .

Notwithstanding my dislike of Arkady Pavlych, I once had to spend a night at his house. Early the next morning I ordered my carriage to be harnessed, but he was unwilling to let me go without offering me an English breakfast and led me into his study. Tea was served together with cutlets, soft-boiled eggs, butter, honey, cheese and so on. Two menservants in peerless white gloves swiftly and silently anticipated our least wish. We were seated on a Persian divan. Arkady Pavlych was arrayed in wide silken trousers, a black velvet jacket, a fine fez with a blue tassel and yellow Chinese slippers without heels. He sipped his tea, laughed, studied his fingernails, smoked, stuffed cushions on either side of him and generally accounted himself to be in the best of moods. Having breakfasted substantially and with evident pleasure, Arkady Pavlych poured himself a glass of red wine, raised it to his lips and suddenly frowned.

'Why has the wine not been warmed?' he inquired of one of the menservants in a fairly sharp voice.

The man was confused, stood rooted to the spot and turned pale.

'Well, I am asking you, my dear chap,' Arkady Pavlych continued quietly, without taking his eyes off him.

The wretched man fidgeted, twisted his napkin and did not utter a word. Arkady Pavlych bent his head forward and meditated upon him from beneath his brows.

'*Pardon, mon cher,*' he said with a pleasant smile, giving me a friendly pat on the knee, and once again directed a stare at his manservant. 'Well, you may leave,' he added after a short silence, raised his brows and rang the bell.

There appeared a fat, dark-featured, black-haired man with a low forehead and eyes completely buried in his face.

'See about Fyodor,' said Arkady Pavlych in a low voice and with perfect self-control.

'Certainly, sir,' the fat man answered and went out.

'*Voilà, mon cher, les désagréments de la campagne,*' Arkady Pavlych gaily remarked. 'And where are you off to? Stay here and sit a while longer.'

'No,' I answered, 'it's time for me to go.'

'Always off hunting! You hunters'll be the death of me! Where are you off to today?'

'To Ryabovo, about twenty-five miles from here.'

'To Ryabovo, are you? Good Lord, in that case I'll come with you. Ryabovo is only about three miles from my own Shipilovka, and I haven't been in Shipilovka for ages – I haven't been able to find the time for it. See how things have worked out: you'll go hunting in Ryabovo today and this evening you'll be my guest. *Ce sera charmant*. We'll have dinner together – we can take my cook with us – and then you'll spend the night with me. Excellent! Excellent!' he added without waiting for my answer. '*C'est arrangé* . . . Hey, is there anyone there? Order them to get the carriage ready, and be quick about it! You've never been in Shipilovka, have you? I would hesitate to suggest that you spend the night in my bailiff's hut except that I know you're not averse to it and would probably spend the night in Ryabovo in a hay barn . . . Let's be off, let's be off!'

And Arkady Pavlych began singing some French love-song.

'Of course you very likely don't know,' he continued, rocking on his heels, 'that my peasants there are paying quit-rent. That's the Constitution for you – what else can one do? However, they pay me their rent correctly. I would long ago, I admit, have had them working for me directly, but there's not much land there to work: it surprises me really how they make ends meet. However, *c'est leur affaire*. The bailiff I've got there is a good chap, *une forte tête*, statesman-like! You'll see how well it's all worked out, that's for sure!'

I had no choice. Instead of leaving at nine in the morning we left at two in the afternoon. Hunters will understand my impatience. Arkady Pavlych liked, as he expressed it, 'to look after himself' on such an occasion and took with him such a fantastic amount of linen, supplies, clothes, scents, cushions and different cases that any economical and self-disciplined German would have found such an abundance of things sufficient to last him a whole year. At each downgrade Arkady Pavlych delivered a short but strongly worded speech to his driver, from which I was able to conclude that my acquaintance was unmistakably a coward. However, the journey was accomplished very satisfactorily; save that during the crossing of a small, recently repaired bridge, the cart carrying the cook broke down and his stomach was crushed by a rear wheel.

Arkady Pavlych, upon seeing the fall sustained by his home-bred Carême,[4] considered it no joking matter, and, in a fright, at once sent word to know whether the man's hands were unhurt. Having received an affirmative answer, he quickly regained his composure. All in all, we took a fairly long time travelling; I sat in the same carriage as Arkady Pavlych and towards the end of the journey became bored to death, the more so because in the course of several hours my acquaintance had become quite worn out and began pretending to be a liberal. Eventually we arrived, though not at Ryabovo but directly in Shipilovka; somehow or other that's how it had worked out. That day, regardless, I could not go out hunting, and with a heavy heart I submitted to my fate.

The cook had arrived a few minutes ahead of us and had evidently succeeded in giving orders and warning the people concerned, because upon entering the outskirts of the village we were met by the village elder (the Bailiff's son), a hefty red-haired peasant a good couple of metres high, on horseback and hatless, with a new coat unbuttoned at the front.

'But where's Sofron?' Arkady Pavlych asked him.

The elder first of all jumped briskly off the horse, bowed low in his master's direction, declared: 'Good day to you, good master, Arkady Pavlych,' then raised his head, gave himself a shake and announced that Sofron had set off for Perov, but that someone had been sent after him.

'Well, then, follow behind us,' said Arkady Pavlych.

Out of politeness the elder led his horse to one side, tumbled on to it and set off at a trot behind the carriage, holding his cap in his hand. We drove through the village. We came across several peasants in empty carts on the way; they were driving from the threshing and singing songs, being bounced up and down by their carts with their legs swinging in the air; but at the sight of our carriage and the elder they suddenly grew quiet, took off their winter caps (it was summer at the time) and raised themselves as if expecting to be given orders. Arkady Pavlych bowed graciously to them. An alarmed excitement was clearly spreading through the village. Women in woollen checked skirts flung bits of wood at unappreciative or unduly noisy dogs; a lame old man with a beard that started below his very eyes pulled a horse that had not finished drinking away from the well, struck it for some unknown reason on the flank and then bowed low. Little boys in long shirts ran howling towards the huts, placed their tummies over the high doorsteps, hung their heads down, kicked up their legs behind them and in this way rolled themselves very briskly through the doors and into the dark entrance-ways, from which they did not reappear. Even chickens streamed at a hurried trot through the spaces below the gates; one lively cock, with a black breast like a satin waistcoat and a red tail that twirled right round to its comb, would have remained on the road and was just on the point of crowing, but suddenly took fright and ran off like the others.

The Bailiff's hut stood on its own amid an allotment of thick green hemp. We stopped in front of the gates. Mr Penochkin stood up, picturesquely threw off his travelling cloak and stepped out of the carriage, looking affably around him. The Bailiff's wife greeted us with low bows and approached her master's small hand. Arkady Pavlych permitted her to kiss it to her heart's content and stepped on to the porch. In the entranceway to the hut, in a dark corner, stood the elder's wife, who also bowed, but she did not dare to approach the master's hand. In the so-called cold room, to the right of the entrance, two other women were already busy; they were carrying out all manner of rubbish, such as empty jugs, sheepskin coats of lath-like stiffness, butter jars, a cradle containing a pile of rags and a child arrayed in a motley of garments, and they were sweeping up the dirt with bath-house twigs. Arkady Pavlych sent them packing and set himself down on a bench under the icons. The drivers began to bring in trunks, boxes and other items for their master's comfort, endeavouring in every possible way to moderate the clattering made by their heavy boots.

Meanwhile, Arkady Pavlych was questioning the elder about the harvest, the sowing and other economic matters. The elder gave satisfactory answers, but somehow flabbily and awkwardly, as if he were doing up the buttons of his coat with frozen fingers. He stood by the door and all the time shrank back and glanced over his shoulder to make way for the bustling valet. Beyond his enormous shoulders I succeeded in catching sight of the Bailiff's wife quietly pummelling some other woman in the entranceway. Suddenly a cart clattered up and stopped in front of the porch. The Bailiff came in.

This statesman-like man, as Arkady Pavlych had described him, was small in stature, broad-shouldered, grey and thickset, with a red nose, little pale-blue eyes and a beard shaped like a fan. Let me remark in this regard that, ever since Russia has existed, there has never as yet been an example of a man gaining riches and corpulence who has not possessed a thoroughgoing beard; a man may all his life have worn nothing but a wispy goatee of a beard and suddenly, lo and behold, he's sprouted all over as if bathed in radiant light – and the wonder is where all the hairs came from! The Bailiff had assuredly been having a drop in Perov: his face had become thoroughly puffy and he dispensed around him strong whiffs of drink.

'Oh, our veritable father, our benefactor,' he began in a singsong voice and with such a look of exaltation on his face that it seemed he would instantly burst into tears, 'you've obliged yourself to visit us! Permit me your hand, your hand,' he added, stretching out his lips in anticipation. Arkady Pavlych satisfied his wish.

'Well, Sofron, my friend, how are your affairs going?' he asked in an unctuous voice.

'Oh, our veritable father,' Sofron exclaimed, 'how could they indeed go badly – our affairs, that is! You, our veritable father, our benefactor, you've most surely allowed light to shine into the life of our little village by your visit and you've given us pleasure to last the rest of our days! Glory be to thee, O Lord, Arkady Pavlych, glory be to thee, O Lord! Through your gracious kindness everything's in perfect order.'

At this point Sofron stopped a moment, looked at his master and, as though again carried away by an uncontrollable surge of emotion (the drink, mind you, had a part to play in this), once more asked for a hand and broke out in a singsong worse than before:

'Oh, our veritable father, our benefactor . . . and . . . See what's happened! My God, I've become a complete fool from the joy of it . . . My God, I look at you and I can't believe it . . . Oh, our veritable father!'

Arkady Pavlych glanced at me, smirked and asked: *'N'est-ce pas que c'est touchant?'*

'Indeed, good master, Arkady Pavlych,' the indefatigable Bailiff went on, 'how could you do such a thing? You have crushed me completely by not letting me know of your coming. After all, where'll you be spending the night? For sure, it's all filthy dirty here . . .'

'It's nothing, Sofron, nothing,' Arkady Pavlych answered with a smile. 'It's all right here.'

'But father of us all – who is it really all right for? It may be all right for our peasant friends, but surely you, my father, how can you . . . ? Forgive me, fool that I am, I've gone quite out of my wits, my God! I've lost all my senses!'

Supper was meanwhile served; Arkady Pavlych began to eat. The old man drove out his son, explaining that he wanted to make the room less stuffy.

'Well, me old dear, have you marked off the boundaries?' asked Mr Penochkin, who clearly wanted to give the impression of knowing peasant speech and kept on winking at me.

' 'Tis done, good master, all of it done through your kindness. The day afore yesterday documents an' all were signed. Them Khlynov people at first were for makin' difficulties, that they were . . . difficulties, father, an' no mistake. Such demands they made . . . demands . . . God alone knows what they weren't demanding, but it was all a lot of foolishness, good master, stupid people they are. But we, good master, by your kindness did give thanks and did what was right by Mikolay Mikolayich, the one as was mediatin', an' everything was done accordin' to your orders, good master. Just as you saw fit to order it, that is how it was done, and 'twas all done with the knowledge of Yegor Dmitrich.'

'So Yegor has informed me,' Arkady Pavlych remarked importantly.

'Aye, good master, Yegor Dmitrich.'

'Well, you ought to be satisfied now, eh?'

Sofron had been waiting for just this.

'Oh, our veritable father, our benefactor!' he commenced his singsong again. 'Have mercy on me, for isn't it, our veritable father, day in and day out, night in and night out, that we're all prayin' to God for ye? . . . Of course, the land's on the short side, smallish . . .'

Penochkin interrupted him:

'Well, all right, Sofron, I know you serve me conscientiously . . . Now what about the threshing?'

Sofron sighed.

'Well, father to us all that you are, the threshin's not goin' awful well. An' there's something, good master, Arkady Pavlych, let me inform you, some little matter as 'as cropped up.' (At this point he drew closer to Mr Penochkin with outspread arms, bent forward and screwed up one eye.) 'A dead body did 'appen to be on our land.'

'How so?'

'Can't apply my mind to understandin' it, good master, father of us all – likely an enemy, it was, 'as done some devilish work. The blessin' was that it was by someone else's hand, and yet – there's no good concealin' it – it was right on our land. So I straightaway ordered it to be dragged on t'other land, so long as we had chance of doin' it, and set a guard by it and told our people: "Don't no one breathe a word" – that's what I says. But in any event I explained it to the constable, I did. I said: "It's how things are" – that's what I says, and I give him a bit o' tea and somethin' what'd make him grateful . . . An' so what d'you think, good master? It stayed over on t'others' land, hangin' round their necks. An' after all a dead body's likely to cost us two hundred roubles – no tuppence-worth o' bread that isn't.'

Mr Penochkin laughed a great deal at his Bailiff's ruse and remarked to me several times, nodding in the old man's direction. *'Quel gaillard, hein?'*

In the meantime it had become quite dark outside. Arkady Pavlych ordered the table cleared and hay brought in. The valet laid out sheets for us and set out pillows; we lay down. Sofron retired to his quarters, having received the orders for the following day. Arkady Pavlych, on the point of going to sleep, persisted in chatting a little about the splendid qualities of the Russian peasant and remarked to me *à propos* of this that since Sofron had taken charge of the Shipilovka peasants there had been not so much as a farthing's-worth of quit-rent arrears . . . The night-watchman gave a rat-tat on his board; a child, who had evidently not yet succeeded in becoming imbued with the requisite spirit of self-denial, started whimpering somewhere in the hut. We fell asleep.

The next morning we rose fairly early. I had wanted to set off for Ryabovo, but Arkady Pavlych wanted to show me his estate and begged me to stay. For my own part, I was not exactly averse to convincing myself in practice of the splendid qualities of that statesman-like man, Sofron. He appeared. He wore a blue peasant coat tied with a red sash. He was a good deal less talkative than he had been the previous day, directed keen, steady looks into his master's eyes and gave cogent, business-like answers to questions.

Together with him we set off for the threshing-floor. Sofron's son, the seven-foot-tall elder, to all appearances a man of extreme stupidity, walked along behind us, and we were also joined by the Bailiff's clerk, Fedoseyich, an ex-soldier with enormous whiskers and a most unusual expression on his face which suggested that he had been extraordinarily startled by something a very long time ago and had not yet come to his senses. We looked around the threshing-floor, the barn, the store-houses, the outbuildings, the windmill, the cattle-shed, the vegetable allotments and land planted to hemp: everything was undoubtedly in splendid order and it was only the despondent faces of the peasants that gave me cause to feel slightly puzzled. Apart from practical matters, Sofron also concerned himself with making the place pretty: all the banks of the ditches had been planted with broom, paths had been made between the ricks on the threshing-floor and spread with sand, a weathervane had been fixed to the windmill in the shape of a bear with an open maw and red tongue, a kind of Grecian pediment had been stuck on the brick-built cattle-shed and beneath the pediment was written in white paint: 'Puilt in Shipilofka vilage in year one thousand aight hunted farty. This Cattle Shet.'

Arkady Pavlych was completely overwhelmed and embarked for my benefit on a dissertation in French about the benefits of the quit-rent system, although he remarked by the way that the system of direct work was more profitable for landowners – but what of it, anyhow! He began giving his Bailiff advice on how to plant potatoes, how to prepare fodder for the cattle and so forth. Sofron listened attentively to his master's words, occasionally making his own comments, but no longer endowing Arkady Pavlych with such grandiose titles as 'our veritable father' or 'our benefactor', and insisting all the time that the land, after all, was on the small side and that it would do no harm to buy some more.

'Buy it, then,' said Arkady Pavlych, 'in my name, I'm not against that.'

To which Sofron said nothing in return, simply stroked his beard.

'Now, however, there'd be no harm in riding into the forest,' remarked Mr Penochkin. At once horses were brought for us and we

rode into the forest or 'reserve', as we are accustomed to call forest
areas. In this 'reserve' we found a terrific abundance of thickets and
wild life, for which Arkady Pavlych praised Sofron and patted him
on the back. Mr Penochkin upheld Russian notions about forestry
and recounted to me on the spot a highly diverting – in his view –
instance of how a certain landowner, who was fond of joking, had
enlightened his woodsman by pulling out practically half the man's
beard as proof of the fact that felling trees does not make a forest
grow any thicker ... Nevertheless, in other respects, Sofron and
Arkady Pavlych did not fight shy of innovations. On returning to
the village, the Bailiff took us to see the winnowing machine which
he had recently ordered from Moscow. The winnowing machine, it
is true, worked well, but if Sofron had known the unpleasantness
that awaited both him and his master on this final walk, he would no
doubt have stayed at home with us.

This is what happened. As we left the outbuilding, we were
confronted with the following spectacle. A few steps from the door,
beside a muddy pool of water in which three ducks were carelessly
splashing about, two peasants were kneeling: one was an old man of
about sixty, the other a young fellow of about twenty, both barefoot,
in patched shirts made of coarse hemp with rope belts at the waist.
The clerk, Fedoseyich, was zealously fussing round them and would
probably have succeeded in persuading them to go away, if we had
stayed longer in the outbuilding, but on catching sight of us, he
straightened up taut as a violin string and froze on the spot. The elder
also stood there with wide-open mouth and fists clenched in bewilderment. Arkady Pavlych frowned, bit his lip and approached the
petitioners. Both of them bowed silently at his feet.

'What's up with you? What are you petitioning about?' he asked
in a stern voice and slightly through the nose. (The peasants looked
at each other and said not a word, simply screwed up their eyes, just
as if the sun were blinding them, and began to breathe faster.)

'Well, what is it?' continued Arkady Pavlych and at once turned
to Sofron. 'From which family?'

'From the Toboleyev family,' the Bailiff answered slowly.

'Well, what's it you're after?' Mr Penochkin started asking again.
'Haven't you got tongues, eh? Can't you tell me what it is?' he
added, giving a nod towards the old man. 'Don't be afraid, you fool.'

The old man stretched out his dark, coal-brown wrinkled neck, crookedly drew apart lips that had grown blue with age and uttered in a husky voice, 'Help us, lord and master!' and again struck the earth with his forehead. The young peasant also made an obeisance. Arkady Pavlych looked with dignity at the napes of their necks, threw back his head and placed his feet slightly apart.

'What is it? Who are you complaining about?'

'Have mercy on us, lord and master! Give us a chance to catch our breath . . . Completely done in we are!' (The old man spoke with difficulty.)

'Who's done you in?'

'Sofron Yakovlich, it is, good master.'

Arkady Pavlych was silent for a moment.

'What's your name?'

'Antip, good master.'

'And who's this?'

'My boy, good master.'

Arkady Pavlych was again silent for a moment and twitched his whiskers.

'Well, and how has he done you in?' he asked, looking at the old man over his moustache.

'Good master, ruined us he has, utterly. Two sons, good master, he's sent off out of turn to be recruits, and now he's taking away my third son . . . Yesterday, good master, he led away the last little cow from my yard and gave my wife a beating – that's his worship over there what done it.' (He pointed to the elder.)

'Hmmm!' pronounced Arkady Pavlych.

'Don't leave us to be completely ruined, bountiful master.'

Mr Penochkin frowned. 'What does this all mean?' he asked the Bailiff under his breath with a look of dissatisfaction.

'A drunkard, sir,' the Bailiff answered, using the formal 'sir' for the first time. 'Doesn't do any work. It's already the fifth year, sir, that he's behind with his payments.'

'Sofron Yakovlich's paid the arrears in for me,' continued the old man. 'It's the fifth year's gone by and he's paid in, and paid in he has so as I'm in bondage to him, good master, that's how it is . . .'

'And why did you get into arrears?' Mr Penochkin asked threateningly. (The old man bowed his head). 'Suppose it's because you like getting drunk, like roaming about from tavern to tavern?' (The old man was on the point of opening his mouth.) 'I know your sort,' Arkady Pavlych continued vehemently, 'all you do is drink and lie on the stove and let good peasants answer for you.'

'And insolent as well,' the Bailiff inserted into his master's speech.

'Well, that goes without saying. That's always the way of it – I've noticed that more than once. He'll spend the whole year lazing about and being insolent and now he flops down on his knees at your feet!'

'Good master, Arkady Pavlych,' the old man started saying desperately, 'be merciful, help me – how am I insolent? As I speak now before the Lord God I'm being made helpless by it all, I am. He's taken a dislike to me, Sofron Yakovlich has, and why he's done so only the Lord can judge! He's ruining me utterly, good master . . . Here's my last son – and now he's to go, too . . .' (Teardrops glittered in the old man's yellow and wrinkled eyes.) 'Be merciful, my lord and master, help me . . .'

'Aye, and it's not only us . . .' the young peasant was on the point of beginning.

Arkady Pavlych suddenly flared up:

'And who's asking you, eh? Nobody's asking you, so you be quiet . . . What is this? Be quiet, I'm telling you! Be quiet! Oh, my God, this is quite simply rebellion. No, my friend, I don't advise you to try being rebellious on my property . . . on my property . . .' (Arkady Pavlych took a step forward and then, no doubt, remembered my presence, turned away and placed his hands in his pockets.) *Je vous demande bien pardon, mon cher,*' he said with a forced smile, lowering his voice meaningfully. *'C'est le mauvais côté de la médaille* . . . Well, all right, all right,' he continued without looking at the peasants, 'I'll issue an order . . . all right, be off with you.' (The peasants did not rise.) 'Well, didn't I say to you . . . all right. Be off with you, I'll issue an order, I'm telling you that.'

Arkady Pavlych turned his back on them. 'No end of unpleasantness,' he uttered through his teeth and made for home with big strides. Sofron followed in his wake. The clerk's eyes almost popped out of his head, just as if he was preparing himself for a very high jump. The elder drove the ducks out of the pool. The petitioners remained for a short while where they were, looked at each other and then plodded off without looking back.

Two hours later I was already in Ryabovo, and together with Anpadist, a peasant acquaintance of mine, I was preparing to go hunting. Right up to my very departure Penochkin had been huffy towards Sofron. I struck up a conversation with Anpadist about the Shipilovka peasants and Mr Penochkin, and I asked whether he knew the Bailiff in that village.

'Sofron Yakovlich, you mean? Sure!'

'What sort of man is he?'

'He's a dog, not a man. You won't find another dog like him this side of Kursk.'

'What do you mean?'

'It's like this. Shipilovka's no more'n registered in the name of – what's he called? – that Penkin. He doesn't really own it. It's Sofron who owns it.'

'Do you really mean that?'

'He owns it like it's his own property. The peasants all around are owing him money. They work for him like they were in bondage to him. One he'll send off with a string of carts, another he'll send off somewhere else . . . bled them white he has.'

'It seems they haven't got much land?'

'Not much? He rents 216 acres just from the Khlynov peasants and 324 from our peasants – that's a good five hundred acres for you. And he isn't only trading in land: he does trade in horses, too, and cattle, and tar, and butter, and hemp, and this and that . . . Clever, awful clever, he is, and rich, too, the varmint! What's bad about him is – he's always knocking someone about. A wild beast, not a man. I tell you he's a dog, a cur, a real cur if ever there was one.'

'Then why don't they complain against him?'

'Phew! The master doesn't need to bother! There aren't any arrears, so what's it got to do with him? And just you try it,' he added after a short pause, 'try complaining. No, he'll get you . . . yes, you just try it. No, he'll just get you, just like that he will . . .'

I remembered about Antip and told him what I had seen.

'Well,' declared Anpadist, 'he'll eat him up now, eat him good and proper, he will. The elder'll start beating him up now. What bad luck he's had, the poor wretch, when you think of it! And what's he going through it for? . . . It was just that at a meeting he got cross with him, with the Bailiff, couldn't stand any more, you know . . .

Mighty big matter, that! So he began pecking at him, at Antip. Now he'll eat him right up. He's just that kind of a cur, a dog — the Lord forgive me for my sins — that he knows who to get his teeth into. The old men what are richer and with bigger families, them he doesn't touch, the bald-headed devil — but in this case he's lost his control! After all, he sent off Antip's sons out of turn to become recruits, the unpardonable rogue, the cur — the Lord forgive me for my sins!'

We went off hunting.

Salzbrunn, in Silesia
July 1847

THE OFFICE

❦

IT was in the autumn. I'd already been wandering about the fields with my gun for several hours and would probably not have returned before evening to the inn on the Kursk highway where my troika was waiting for me, if an extraordinarily fine and chilly rain, which had been plaguing me since early morning as fractiously and mercilessly as a complaining old maid, hadn't forced me finally to look somewhere close by for temporary shelter. While I was considering which way to go, my eyes were caught by a small shack beside a field sown with peas. I approached the shack, peered under the straw roof and saw an old man of such decrepitude that I immediately thought of the dying goat that Robinson Crusoe'd found in one of the caves on his island. The old man was squatting on his haunches, squeezing up his small darkened eyes and rapidly but carefully chewing like a hare (the poor fellow didn't have a single tooth) a hard, dried pea, rolling it ceaselessly from one side to the other. He was so preoccupied by this that he didn't notice my approach.

'Grandad! Hey, grandad!' I said.

He stopped chewing, lifted his brows high and with an effort opened his eyes.

'What?' he mumbled huskily.

'Where's a nearby village?' I asked him.

The old man again set about chewing. He hadn't heard me. I repeated my question more loudly.

'A village. Which one d'you want?'

'Just to shelter from the rain.'

'What?'

'To shelter from the rain.'

'Ah!' (He scratched the sunburnt nape of his neck.) 'Well, you go, see,' he started saying suddenly, waving his arms about disconnectedly, 'see over there . . . see, you go by that wood, see it – you go by that – and there's a road. Don't pay no attention to it, that road, see, but keep right, keep right, keep right . . . Well, you'll come to Ananyevo. The other way'll be Sitovka.'

I had difficulty understanding the old man. His whiskers got in the way and his tongue wouldn't obey him.

'Where are you from?' I asked him.

'What?'

'Where are you from?'

'From Ananyevo.'

'What are you doing here?'

'What?'

'What are you doing here?'

'I'm keeping guard.'

'On what?'

'The peas.'

I couldn't help laughing.

'For heaven's sake, how old are you?'

'God knows.'

'Maybe you don't see so well?'

'What?'

'Your eyesight's bad, isn't it?'

'It is. It does happen I don't hear nothin' neither.'

'So how can you be a guard, for heaven's sake?'

'That's for the guv'nors to know.'

'The guv'nors!' I thought and looked at the poor old man not without a certain pity. He felt about and got a piece of dry bread out of his breast pocket and started sucking at it like a baby, the effort pulling in his already sunken cheeks.

I went off in the direction of the wood, turned to the right and kept to the right, as the old man had advised me, and finally reached a large village with a stone church in the latest taste, that is, with columns, and an extensive manor house also with columns. From a distance, through the busy network of falling rain, I noticed a hut with a plank roof and two chimneys standing above the others, presumably the house of the village headman, and I directed my footsteps towards it in the hope of finding there a samovar, tea, sugar and cream that had not yet gone completely sour. Accompanied by my shivering dog I climbed on to the porch, went into the entrance-way and opened the door, but instead of the usual accoutrements of a peasant's hut I found several tables piled with papers, two large red cupboards, ink-stained inkwells, tin sand-boxes of enormous weight, the longest quill pens imaginable and so on and so forth. Seated on one of the tables was a young man of about twenty with a puffy and unhealthy face, the tiniest eyes, a fat forehead and endlessly receding temples. He was appropriately dressed in a grey nankeen caftan which had gone shiny with dirt at the collar and over the stomach.

'What do you want?' he asked me, jerking his head up like a horse which hadn't expected to be grabbed by the muzzle.

'Does the bailiff live here . . . or . . .'

'This is the main estate office,' he interrupted. 'I'm sitting here on duty. Didn't you see the notice? That's what the notice is there for.'

'Is there anywhere I can get dry round here? Does anyone in the village have a samovar?'

'Of course there are samovars,' the fellow in the grey caftan answered pompously. 'Try Father Timofey's, or if not there then the servants' hut, or if not there Nazar Tarasych, or if not there then Agrafena, the poultry-woman.'

'Who're you talking to, you bloody oaf? You're not letting me sleep, you oaf!' a voice shouted from the next room.

'A gentleman's come in, he's asking where he can get dried.'

'What gentleman?'

'I dunno. With a dog and a gun.'

A bed creaked in the next room. The door opened and a man of about fifty entered, fat, stocky, with a bull neck, protruding eyes, unusually round cheeks and a face shiny with sweat.

'What do you want?' he asked me.

'To get dried.'

'This isn't the place.'

'I didn't know this was an office. In any case, I'm prepared to pay . . .'

'Please, make yourself at home here,' the Fatso responded. 'Maybe you'd care to come this way.' (He led me into another room, but not the one he'd come out of.) 'Will it be all right for you here?'

'It's all right . . . Would it be possible to have some tea and some cream?'

'Of course, right away. You undress and have a rest, and the tea'll be ready right away.'

'Whose estate is this?'

'It belongs to Mrs Losnyakova, Yelena Nikolaevna.'

He went out. I looked round me. Along the partition which separated my room from the office stood a large leather divan. Two chairs, also of leather, with extremely high backs, stood on either side of the only window, which looked out on to the street. On the walls hung with green wallpaper decorated in rose-coloured patterns were three enormous oil paintings. One depicting a setter in a blue collar bore the title: 'Such is my Pleasure'. At the dog's feet there flowed a river, and on the opposite bank of the river under a fir tree sat a hare of unbelievably large proportions with one ear raised. Another painting depicted two old men eating a melon. In the background behind the melon could be seen a Greek portico bearing the device: 'The Temple of Contentment'.[1] The third picture represented a half-naked woman in a recumbent position *en raccourci* or so foreshortened that her knees were red and her heels exceedingly fat. Without a moment's hesitation my dog crawled under the divan with stupendous effort and evidently found a great deal of dust there, because it had an appalling sneezing fit. I went to the window. Lying diagonally across the street from the manor house to the office were wooden boards, which was a very useful precaution because all around, thanks to our black earth soil and the continuous rain, the mud was dreadful. In the vicinity of the manor itself, which stood with its back to the street, things were going on as they usually do in the vicinity of manors: maidservants in faded calico were dashing to and fro; menservants were wandering about in the mud, stopping occasionally and thoughtfully scratching their backs; the tethered horse of the local policeman lazily waved its tail and, its muzzle raised high, gnawed at the fence; hens clucked; consumptive-looking turkeys gobbled away endlessly. On the porch of a dark and rotting structure, very likely the bath-house, sat a hefty youth with a guitar, singing not without verve the well-known love-song:

Oy be offter deestant deeserts gone
Far away from thizere beauteous spots . . . (and so on) [2]

The Fatso came into my room.

'Your tea's just coming now,' he told me with a pleasant smile.

The fellow in the grey caftan, the duty clerk, set out on an old card-table a samovar, teapot, a glass on a cracked saucer, a jug of cream and a string of local pretzels which were as hard as flint. The Fatso went out.

'Who's he?' I asked the duty clerk. 'The steward?'

'No, sir, no way. He used to be the chief cashier, sir, but now he's been made a chief clerk.'

'Haven't you any stewards, then?'

'No, sir, no way. There's a bailiff, Mikhail Vikulov, but there ain't no stewards.'

'Is there a manager, then?'

'Why, 'course there is, a German, Lindamandol, Karlo Karlych, only he doesn't really manage.'

'Who does, then?'

'The mistress, she does, by herself.'

'Well, well! Tell me, do you have many people in your office?'

The fellow gave it some thought.

'There are six people.'

'Who are they?' I asked.

'This is who they are. First there'll be Vasily Nikolaevich, he's chief cashier. Then there's Pyotr the clerk, and his brother Ivan who's a clerk, and another Ivan who's a clerk. Koskenkin Narkizov, he's also a clerk, and then there's me. Oh, I can't remember how many there are.'

'So does your mistress keep a lot of servants?'

'No, not all that many . . .'

'How many then?'

'It'll run up to maybe hundred 'n' fifty.'

We were both silent.

'Well, do you write well?' I asked, setting things going again.

The fellow gave a broad smile, nodded, went off into the office and brought back with him a sheet of paper with writing on it.

'Here's how I write,' he said, still smiling.

I looked at it. On a quarto sheet of greyish paper the following was written in handsome, large handwriting:

AN ORDER

FROM THE CHIEF MANORIAL HOME OFFICE OF ANANYEVO TO
BAILIFF MIKHAIL VIKULOV

NO. 209

It is hereby demanded of you that immediately on receipt of this you ascertain who did last night, being pissed and singing indecent songs, pass near the English garden and did awaken and disturb the governess, the French lady, Madame Eugenie? And what were the nightwatchmen up to and who was on duty in the garden and who permitted such disorders to occur? It is hereby demanded that you inquire in detail into all the above and report immediately to the office.

Chief Clerk Nikolay Khvostov

The order bore a large heraldic stamp with the legend: 'Stamp of the Chief Manorial Office of Ananyevo', and below it a handwritten note: 'See to it precisely. Yelena Losnyakova.'

'Did your mistress write that herself?' I asked.

''Course, sir. She always writes on it herself. An order wouldn't be an order otherwise.'

'So you'll be sending this order to the bailiff, will you?'

'No, sir. He'll come an' read it. 'Cept it'll be read to him, 'cos he can't read.' (The duty clerk again fell silent.) 'What d'you think, sir,' he added, smiling, 'it's well written, isn't it?'

'It's well written.'

'I didn't make it up, I admit that. Koskenkin's best at doing that.'

'What? Do you mean your orders have to be made up first?'

''Course, sir. You can't write 'em out straight off.'

'How much do you get paid?' I asked him.

'Thirty-five roubles and five roubles for shoes.'

'Are you satisfied with that?'

'Sure I am. It's not everyone gets a job in the office. I admit it was an order from above, 'cos my uncle's a butler.'

'And you're all right, are you?'

'I'm all right, sir. Truth to tell,' he went on with a sigh, 'it's better for people like us working for merchants. People like us're very well off working for merchants. Look, just last night a merchant came to us from Venyovo and his workman was telling me . . . it's all right, all right with them, no matter what you say.'

'Are you telling me that merchants pay better wages?'

'God forbid! You'd really get it in the neck if you asked him for wages. No, at a merchant's you live in faith and fear. He gives you food and drink and clothes and everything. You do well by 'im and he'll give you more . . . What's wages! You don't need 'em . . . And your merchant, he lives simple-like, Russian-like, like we do. If you go travelling with 'im, he'll drink tea and you'll drink tea, what he eats, you'll eat. A merchant . . . how can I say? he's not like a master. A merchant doesn't have whims. Well, he'll fly off the handle and bash you one, but that's the end of it. He doesn't whine, he doesn't nag . . . But work for a master and it's hell! Nothing's ever right for 'im. This is wrong, that doesn't please him. Why, you give 'im a glass of water or some food – "Ah, this water stinks! This food stinks!" You take it away, stand outside the door a bit and bring it in again – "Well, now this is good, this doesn't stink at all." And as for the mistress of the house, oh, I can tell you, they're something else! And as for the young ladies!'

'Fedyushka!' came the voice of the Fatso in the office.

The duty clerk dashed out. I finished my glass of tea, lay down on the divan and went to sleep. I slept for about two hours.

After waking up I was on the point of getting to my feet, but fatigue got the better of me. I closed my eyes but didn't go back to sleep. People were talking quietly in the office beyond the partition. I started listening willy-nilly.

'Yessir, yessir, Nikolay Yeremeich,' said one voice, 'yessir. Zat's gotta be taken into account. Exactly, not possible otherwise, no, sir . . . Hm!' The speaker coughed.

'Just you believe me, Gavrila Antonych,' the Fatso's voice objected. 'Judge for yourself, but I'm the one who knows how things are round here.'

'Who better than you, Nikolay Yeremeich. Yessir, one might say you're the real boss round here. Well, then, how'll it be?' the unfamiliar voice went on. 'How'll we decide it, Nikolay Yeremeich? I'm bound to ask that.'

'How'll we decide it, Gavrila Antonych? It all depends on you, so to speak. It seems you're not desirous.'

'Please, Nikolay Yeremeich, what're you saying? It's our business to trade, to purchase. That's what we're here for, you might say, Nikolay Yeremeich.'

'Eight roubles,' the Fatso said, pausing between the words.

There was an audible gasp.

'Nikolay Yeremeich, that's an awful lot you're asking.'

'I can't do it otherwise, Gavrila Antonych. In God's name I tell you I can't.'

Silence ensued.

I quietly raised myself and looked through a slit in the partition. The Fatso was sitting with his back to me. Facing him sat the merchant, about forty years old, lean and pale, looking literally as if he'd been smeared with grease. He ceaselessly fussed with his beard and blinked his eyes rapidly and his lips worked.

'Surprisingly good, one might say, the fields this year, yes, indeed,' he began again. 'I've been admiring 'em on my travels. From Voronezh onwards, they've been amazin', first class you might say.'

'Exactly, they're not bad,' said the chief clerk. 'But you know what they say, Gavrila Antonych, seeds in autumn's no use lest spring needs 'em.'

'Definitely so, Nikolay Yeremeich, it's all in God's hand. That's the absolute truth, what you've just said . . . Ah, I think your guest's awake.'

The Fatso turned round and listened.

'No, he's asleep. Still, I'll just . . .'

He went to the door.

'No, he's asleep,' he repeated and returned to his place.

'Well, how's it to be, Nikolay Yeremeich?' the merchant began again. 'We've got to conclude our little bit o' business . . . It'll be like this, Nikolay Yeremeich, like this,' he went on, ceaselessly blinking. 'Two little grey 'uns and a little white 'un for your good self,[3] but over there –' he nodded towards the manor house – 'six and a half. Shake on it, eh?'

'Four little grey 'uns,' answered the chief clerk.

'Let's say three.'

'Four little grey 'uns without the white 'un.'

'Three, Nikolay Yeremeich.'

'Not a word more, Gavrila Antonych.'

'What a difficult one you are!' muttered the merchant. 'It'd be better if I completed the deal with the mistress.'

'Suit yourself,' answered the Fatso. 'You should've done so long ago. What in fact worries you about that? Far better if you did!'

'No, no, that's enough, Nikolay Yeremeich. I lost my temper just now! Zat's what I'd said, after all.'

'No, in fact . . .'

'Enough, I tell you, I was joking, that's all. Look, take your three and a half, if there's no other way of dealing with you.'

'I should've got four, but I'm a fool, I was in a hurry,' muttered the Fatso.

'So over in the house there they'll be paying six and a half, Nikolay Yeremeich, sir, six and a half for the grain?'

'That's what we agreed, six and a half.'

'Well, let's shake on it, Nikolay Yeremeich!' The merchant struck his outspread fingers on to the chief clerk's palm. 'Thank God!' The merchant stood up. 'So, sir, Nikolay Yeremeich, I'll be going over to the mistress now and have myself announced and I'll be telling 'er Nikolay Yeremeich says he's settled for six and a half.'

'You say that, Gavrila Antonych.'

'Now here's what I owe you.'

The merchant handed the chief clerk a small wad of notes, bowed, gave a shake of the head, picked his hat up between two fingers, shrugged his shoulders, gave a wavy movement to his waist and went out with a polite squeaking of his boots. Nikolay Yeremeich went to the hall and, so far as I could see, began counting through the notes handed him by the merchant. A red head with thick sideburns was poked in through the door.

'Well?' the head asked. 'Is it as it should be?'

'As it should be.'

'How much?'

The Fatso waved his hand irritably and pointed to my room.

'Ah, right!' the head said and disappeared.

The Fatso went to the table, sat down, opened a book, got hold of an abacus and began running the bone beads backwards and forwards, using not his index finger but the third finger of his right hand because it was more respectable.

The duty clerk came in.

'Whadya want?'

'Sidor's come from Golopleki.'

'Ah! Well, let him in. Just a moment, just a moment . . . Take a look first and see if that 'un, the gent who's not from round 'ere, see if he's woken up.'

The duty clerk came cautiously into my room. I laid my head down on my game-bag, which served as a pillow, and closed my eyes.

'He's asleep,' whispered the duty clerk, returning to the office.

The Fatso mumbled something through his teeth.

'Well, call in Sidor,' he said at last.

I once again raised myself up. An enormous peasant came in, about thirty years old, a picture of health, red-cheeked, with brown hair and a small curly beard. He made the sign of the cross towards the icon, bowed to the chief clerk, held his hat in both hands and straightened his back.

'Good day, Sidor,' said the Fatso, making a noise with the abacus.

'Good day, Nikolay Yeremeich.'

'Well, how was the road?'

'All right, Nikolay Yeremeich. A bit muddy.' (The peasant had a slow, quiet way of speaking.)

'Is your wife well?'

'She's all right!'

The peasant sighed and stuck out one foot. Nikolay Yeremeich put the pen behind his ear and blew his nose.

'So why've you come?' he went on questioning, tucking the checkered handkerchief away in his pocket.

'Listen, Nikolay Yeremeich, they're asking us for carpenters.'

'Well, you've got some, haven't you?'

''Course there are, Nikolay Yeremeich. Everyone knows our homes're made of wood. But it's the work season, Nikolay Yeremeich.'

'The work season! That's it! You're glad to work for others, but you don't want to work for your mistress . . . It's all the same work!'

'The work's all the same, true, Nikolay Yeremeich, but . . .'

'Well?'

'The pay's poor . . . you know . . .'

'I don't know any such thing! Just look how spoilt you are. Be off with you!'

'An' it's gotta be said, Nikolay Yeremeich, the work'll only be for a week, but they'll keep us a month. Or there won't be enough material, or we'll be sent to sweep the paths in the garden.'

'I don't know anything of the sort! The mistress herself gave the order, so there's no point in you and me discussin' it.'

Sidor fell silent and began moving his weight from one foot to the other.

Nikolay Yeremeich twisted his head on one side and started assiduously clicking away on the abacus.

'Our . . . p-peasants . . . N-nikolay Yeremeich,' Sidor said at last, stumbling over each word, 'o-ordered me, for y-your g-good s-self . . . H-here it is . . . it'll . . .' (He put his hand in the chest pocket of his sheepskin coat and started drawing out a rolled-up cloth with red designs on it.)

'What're you doing, you fool, have you gone mad?' the Fatso hurriedly interrupted him. 'Go off to my hut,' he went on, almost pushing the astonished peasant out. 'Ask for my wife, she'll give you some tea. I'll be along in a minute. Go on. I'm telling you, go . . .'

Sidor went out.

'What a bloody bear!' the chief clerk muttered at his back, shook his head and once more turned to his accounts.

Suddenly there were cries of 'Kuprya! Kuprya! Kuprya's OK!' out in the street and in the porch and a moment later there entered the office a man of small stature, consumptive in appearance, with an unusually long nose, large staring eyes and a very haughty air. He was dressed in an ancient, torn coat of light lilac colour, or what we call Odeloid (after the name Adelaide), which had a velveteen collar and tiny buttons. He was carrying a bundle of firewood on his shoulders. He was surrounded by five or so manorial servants all shouting: 'Kuprya! Kuprya's OK! Kuprya's been made a stoker, Kuprya's been made a stoker!' But the man in the coat with the velveteen collar didn't pay the slightest attention to the wild cries of his comrades and his expression did not change. With measured strides he went over to the stove, flung down his burden, straightened up, got a tobacco pouch out of his back pocket, scrunched up his eyes and stuffed up his nose a snuff of sweet clover mixed with ash.

At the entry of the exuberant gang the Fatso made to frown and rise from his seat but, seeing what all the fuss was about, he smiled and simply ordered them not to shout because there was a hunter asleep in the next room.

'What hunter?' two of the men asked simultaneously.

'A landowner.'

'Ah!'

'Let 'em shout,' said the fellow with the velveteen collar, spreading his arms, 'it doesn't bother me! So long as they don't touch me, 'cos I've been made a stoker . . .'

'A stoker! A stoker!' the crowd chimed in joyfully.

'The mistress gave the order,' he went on with a shrug of the shoulders, 'an' just you watch out, you lot, they'll turn you into pig keepers, you know. An' I'm a tailor, an' a good one, learned to tailor with the best teachers in Moscow and worked for generals, I did. No one'll ever take that away from me. But what've you got to boast about, eh? Got free of the power of the masters, have you? You're just bloody spongers, you are, just a lot of layabouts, nothing else! If I get my freedom, I won't die of hunger, I'll get by. Give me a passport an' I'll pay good quit-rent and satisfy my masters. But what'll you do? You'll be done for, done for, like so many flies, that's for sure!'

'That's a bloody lie!' broke in a pockmarked and flaxen-haired lad with a red tie and arms out at the elbows. 'You had a passport, you did, and the masters didn't see one penny from you in quit-rent, an' you didn't earn a penny neither. You just had enough to drag yourself back home here, an' ever since then you've been livin' in nothin' but that caftan thing you've got on!'

'So what, Konstantin Narkizych?' replied Kuprian. 'A fellow fell in love – and was done for, finished. You live like what I did, Konstantin Narkizych, and then you can judge me.'

'And look who he fell in love with! A real fright she was!'

'No, you mustn't say that, Konstantin Narkizych.'

'Who're you trying to kid? I saw 'er with my own eyes. Last year in Moscow I saw 'er with my own eyes.'

'Last year she'd really gone downhill a bit, sure,' Kuprian remarked.

'No, gentlemen, what I'd . . .' interrupted in a contemptuous and offhand voice a tall, thin man, with a face covered in spots, evidently a valet with his curled, pomaded hair, 'er, let Kuprian Afanasych sing his little song. Come on, Kuprian Afanasych, get going!'

'Yes, yes!' the others all shouted. 'Come on, Alexandra! You're done for, Kuprya! Come on, sing, Kuprya! Come on, Alexandra!' (Manorial servants frequently, when speaking about a man, use a feminine form out of greater fondness.) 'Come on, sing!'

'This isn't a place for singing,' Kuprian objected with firmness, 'it's an office.'

'So what's that matter to you? You're aimin' to become a clerk, aren't you?' Konstantin responded with a coarse laugh. 'Goes without sayin'!'

'Everything's in the mistress's hands,' the poor fellow remarked.

'See, see, that's what he's after, isn't he? Ooh! Ooh! Ah!'

And they all burst out laughing, and some started jumping with joy. One laughed louder than all the rest, a boy of about fifteen, apparently the son of an aristocrat from among the manorial staff because he was wearing a waistcoat with brass buttons and a lilac-coloured tie and had already developed a little pot-belly.

'Just listen a moment, admit it, Kuprya,' said Nikolay Yeremeich self-importantly, evidently delighted and thoroughly mollified. 'It's no good being a stoker, is it? It's an empty job, isn't it?'

'Look, Nikolay Yeremeich,' said Kuprian, 'you're now our chief clerk, that's true. There's no dispute about that, none at all. But you were in disgrace once and had to live in a peasant hut as well.'

'Just you watch out, and don't you forget it!' the Fatso interrupted him angrily. 'They're joking with you, you fool. You, you fool, you ought to sense how things are and be grateful that they're taking some interest in you, fool that you are.'

'I didn't mean it, Nikolay Yeremeich, I'm sorry . . .'

'You'd better mean that.'

The door was flung open and in ran a servant-boy.

'Nikolay Yeremeich, the mistress's askin' for you.'

'Who's with her?' he asked the boy.

'Aksinya Nikitishna and the merchant from Venyovo.'

'I'll be there in a moment. And you, my lads,' he went on in a persuasive voice, 'you'd best be off out of here with the newly appointed stoker, 'cos that German'll likely drop in and he'll lay a complaint at once.'

The Fatso put his hair to rights, coughed into a hand that was almost completely covered by his coat sleeve, buttoned himself up and set off to see his mistress, walking with his feet placed wide apart. A short while later the whole gang followed in his wake together with Kuprya. The only one remaining was my old friend the duty clerk. He set about sharpening quills, but while sitting there he fell asleep. Several flies immediately took advantage of this good fortune and settled on his mouth. A mosquito alighted on his forehead, correctly spread its little feet and slowly plunged its whole sting into his soft body. The former red-headed man with sideburns again appeared in the doorway, glanced in once or twice and then entered along with his rather unattractive torso.

'Fedyushka! Fedyushka! You're always sleeping!' he said.

The duty clerk opened his eyes and rose from his chair.

'Has Nikolay Yeremeich gone to see the mistress?'

'He's gone to see the mistress, Vasily Nikolaich.'

Ah, I thought, here he is – the chief cashier. He began walking about the room. Though it was more of a prowl than a walk and was generally rather cat-like. An ancient black frock-coat with very narrow tails bounced up and down on his shoulders, while one hand was held on his breast and the other ceaselessly fingered a high, tight, horsehair cravat, and he turned his head to and fro with an effort. He wore goatskin boots which did not squeak and he padded about very softly.

'Today the Yagushka landowner was asking for you,' the duty clerk added.

'Was he? What did he have to say?'

'He said to say he'd be going to Tyutyurev in the evening and he'd wait for you there. He said to say he'd wanted to discuss something with Vasily Nikolaich, but he didn't say what it was 'cos, he said, Vasily Nikolaich'd already know.'

'Hm!' exclaimed the chief cashier and went to the window.

'Is Nikolay Yeremeich in the office?' a voice resounded in the porch and a tall man, evidently extremely angry, with irregular, but expressive and bold features, and fairly neatly dressed, strode into the room.

'So he's not here?' he asked, glancing quickly round.

'Nikolay Yeremeich is with the mistress,' answered the cashier. 'Tell me what you want, Pavel Andreich. You know you can tell me . . . What d'you want?'

'What do I want? You want to know what I want?' (The cashier nodded painfully.) 'I want to teach him a lesson, the useless Fatso he is, the low-down sneak . . . I'll give him something to sneak about!'

Pavel threw himself into a chair.

'What's up with you, what's up, Pavel Andreich? Calm down . . . Aren't you ashamed of yourself? You'll not forget who you're speaking about, Pavel Andreich!' the cashier started babbling.

'Who I'm speaking about? What's it to me that he's been made chief clerk? A fine one they've found to promote, say what you like! What can be said is that they've gone and let the old goat into the cabbage patch!'

'Enough's enough, Pavel Andreich! That's enough! Stop it! What sort of rubbish is that?'

'Well, so the old fox is off a-hunting, is he! I'll wait for him!' said Pavel in a temper, and struck the table with his fist. 'Ah, there he is!' he added, glancing through the window. 'The devil himself! Greetings, sir!' He stood up.

Nikolay Yeremeich came into the office. His face glowed with satisfaction, but at the sight of Pavel he appeared slightly embarrassed.

'Hallo, Nikolay Yeremeich,' said Pavel meaningfully, slowly moving forwards to meet him, 'hallo.'

The chief clerk did not answer. The merchant's face appeared in the doorway.

'Why don't you do me the courtesy of answering?' Pavel went on. 'Besides, no . . . no,' he added, 'that's not the way, you won't get anything by shouting and cursing. No, it'd be better if you did the right thing by me and told me, Nikolay Yeremeich, why you're persecuting me. Why d'you want to ruin me, eh? Well, speak up, speak up.'

'This isn't the place for explanations,' the chief clerk retorted, not without a certain feeling. 'And it's not the time either. Except, I confess, I'm surprised by one thing. Wherever did you get the idea that I wanted to ruin you or was persecuting you? After all, how could I persecute you? You're not working here in the office.'

'Right,' answered Pavel, 'that's all that's missing! But why go on pretending, Nikolay Yeremeich? You know what I mean.'

'No, I don't.'

'Yes, you do.'

'No, by God, I don't.'

'And it's by God, too! If it comes to that, you tell me: don't you have any fear of God? Why're you ruining a poor girl's life? What d'you need from her?'

'Who're you speaking about, Pavel Andreich?' asked the Fatso with feigned astonishment.

'Hey, so he doesn't know, eh? I'm talking about Tatyana. You ought to have the fear of God in you – why're you being so vengeful? You should be ashamed! You're a married man, you've got children the same size as me and I'm not any different, I want to get married. I'm acting honourably.'

'Why am I to blame, Pavel Andreich? The mistress doesn't permit you to get married – she's the one with authority! What've I got to do with it?'

'What! So you haven't been up to your old tricks behind our backs with that old witch, the housekeeper, eh? So you haven't been sneaking about this and that, eh? Say you haven't been telling all sorts of lies, eh, about that poor defenceless girl? So it wasn't through your efforts, eh, that she got demoted from the laundry to the scullery? And isn't it through your efforts they're beating her and making her wear rags, eh? You ought to be ashamed of yourself, you ought, you old man! You'll be struck down by paralysis, you will, just you wait and see! You'll have to answer to God for this!'

'That's bad language, Pavel Andreich, bad language . . . But you won't go on with that much longer!'

Pavel exploded.

'What? So it's threats now, is it?' he burst out angrily. 'You think I'm frightened of you, do you? No, mate, you've met your match with me! What've I got to be frightened of? I can earn a living wherever I like. But you – that's a different matter! You can only live here, and do your sneaking and your thieving . . .'

'Oh, listen to him, putting on airs!' broke in the chief clerk, who was also beginning to lose patience. 'A medic, just a medic, a bloody little quack! But just listen to him, what an important person he is!'

'Yes, a medic, but without this medic your honour'd be rotting in a graveyard now! I don't know what possessed me to cure you,' he added through his teeth.

'You cured me? No, you wanted to poison me, you made me drink aloes,' the chief clerk objected.

'So what, if nothing but aloes had any effect on you?'

'Aloes are forbidden by the medical authorities,' Nikolay went on, 'and I'll lay a complaint against you. I'll say you wanted to kill me, so I will! But the Good Lord didn't allow it.'

'Enough, gentlemen, enough . . .' the cashier started saying.

'Shut up!' screamed the chief clerk. 'He wanted to poison me! Don't you understand?'

'A lot I care . . . Listen, Nikolay Yeremeich,' Pavel exclaimed in desperation, 'for the last time I'm asking you – you've been pressuring me, you've made things impossible for me – leave us alone, understand? Or else, by God, it'll be the worse for one of us, that I can tell you!'

The Fatso went crazy.

'I'm not scared of you,' he screamed, 'd'you hear me, you milksop! I did for your father, too, I broke his antlers I did – an' I'll do the same for you, you'll see!'

'Don't you mention my father, Nikolay Yeremeich, leave him out of it!'

'Well I never! So who're you to tell me what to do?'

'I'm telling you, leave him out!'

'An' I'm telling you, don't forget yourself . . . No matter how much the mistress, in your opinion, needs you, if she had to choose between the two of us, you wouldn't stand a chance, my fine friend!' (Pavel shook with rage.) 'And the girl Tatyana deserves what she's got . . . Just wait and see what'll be coming to her next!'

Pavel hurled himself at the man with raised fists and the chief clerk fell heavily to the floor.

'Put him in chains, in chains!' groaned Nikolay Yeremeich.

I will not take it upon myself to describe the end of this scene because I'm already afraid I've insulted the reader's feelings.

I returned home that day. A week later I learned that Mrs Losnyakova had kept both Pavel and Nikolay in her employment but had sent the girl Tatyana away: she evidently wasn't needed.

LONER

❦

ONE evening I was by myself in my racing droshky after going hunting. There were still some half-dozen miles before I got home. My good trotting mare went happily along the dusty road, occasionally giving snorts and twitching her ears; my tired dog, as though literally tied there, never for a moment fell back behind the rear wheels. A thunderstorm was threatening. Straight ahead an enormous lilac cloud rose slowly beyond the forest and long grey lengths of cloud hung above me and stretched towards me. The willows rustled and murmured in alarm. The muggy heat was suddenly replaced by moist cool air and the shadows thickened. I struck the horse with a rein, descended into a gully, made my way across a dry stream completely overgrown with willow bushes, went uphill and drove into the forest. The road wound its way ahead of me between thick clumps of nut, already immersed in darkness, and my progress was difficult. The droshky jumped about as the wheels struck the hard roots of centuries-old oaks and limes which criss-crossed the deep ruts made by cartwheels, and my horse began to stumble. A strong wind suddenly began roaring on high, the trees began thrashing about, huge raindrops started pounding sharply on the leaves and splashing over them, lightning flashed and thunder exploded. The rain fell in torrents. I went at a walking pace and was soon obliged to stop because my horse had got stuck and I couldn't see a thing. Somehow or other I found shelter by a large bush. Hunched down and covering up my face, I was waiting patiently for the storm to end, when suddenly by the light of a lightning flash I thought I saw a tall figure on the road. I began looking intently in that direction and saw that the figure had literally sprung from the earth just beside my droshky.

'Who is it?' asked a loud voice.

'Who are you?'

'I'm the local forester.'

I named myself.

'Ah, I know you. On your way home, are you?'

'Yes. But you can see, what a storm . . .'

'Yes, a storm,' the voice responded.

A white lightning flash lit up the forester from head to toe. A crackling thunderclap followed immediately afterwards. The rain beat down with redoubled force.

'It'll not be over soon,' the forester went on.

'What's to be done?'

'Let me lead you to my cottage,' he said sharply.

'Please.'

'Kindly take your seat.'

He went up to the head of the horse, took hold of the bridle and gave a tug. We set off. I clung to the cushion on the droshky which swayed 'like a boat on the waves'[1] and called to my dog. My poor mare splashed about heavily in the mud, slipping and stumbling, while the forester hovered to right and left in front of the shafts like a ghost. We travelled for quite a long while until my guide finally came to a stop.

'Here we are at home, sir,' he said in a calm voice.

The garden gate creaked and several dogs started barking in unison. I raised my head and saw by the light of a lightning flash a small cottage set in a large courtyard surrounded by wattle fencing. From one small window a light shone faintly. The forester led the horse up to the porch and banged on the door. 'Coming! Coming!' rang out a thin, small voice, followed by a sound of bare feet and the squeaky drawing of the bolt, and a little girl of about twelve, in a shirt tied with selvedge and with a lantern in her hand, appeared on the doorstep.

'Show the gentleman the way,' he said to the little girl. 'Meanwhile I'll put your droshky under cover.'

She glanced at me and went in. I followed her.

The forester's cottage consisted of one room, smoke-blackened, low and bare, without slats for bedding or partitions. A torn sheepskin coat hung on the wall. On a bench lay a single-barrelled gun and in one corner a pile of rags; beside the stove stood two large jugs. A taper burned on the table, sadly flaring up, then guttering. In the very centre of the cottage hung a cradle tied to the end of a long pole. The little girl extinguished the lantern, seated herself on a tiny bench and began with her right hand to rock the cradle and with her other to adjust the taper. I looked around me and my heart sank, because it's not a happy experience to enter a peasant cottage at night. The baby in the cradle breathed heavily and quickly.

'Are you all by yourself here?' I asked the little girl.

'I am,' she said scarcely audibly.

'You're the forester's daughter?'

'Yes,' she whispered.

The door squeaked and the forester came across the threshold, ducking his head. He lifted the lantern off the floor, went to the table and lit the wick.

'It's likely you're not used to just a taper, are you?' he said and shook his curls.

I looked at him. I'd rarely seen such a fine figure of a man. He was tall, broad-shouldered, with a splendid physique. Beneath the damp, coarse cloth of his shirt his powerful muscles stood out clearly. A black curly beard covered half his severe, masculine features and beneath broad eyebrows which met in the middle there gazed out small hazel eyes. He lightly placed his hands on his hips and stood in front of me.

I thanked him and asked him his name.

'I'm called Foma,' he answered, 'but I'm nicknamed Loner.'*

'So you're the one called Loner?'

I looked at him with redoubled interest. From my Yermolay and others I'd often heard stories about the Loner whom all the local peasants feared like fire. According to them there wasn't a better master of his job in the world: 'He won't let you take so much as a bit o' brushwood! It doesn't matter when it is, even at dead o' night, he'll be down on you like a ton o' snow, an' you'd best not think of puttin' up a fight – he's as strong and skilful as a devil! An' you can't bribe him, not with drink, not with money, not with any trickery. More'n once there's good folks've tried to drive him off the face of the earth, but he's not given up.'

* In the province of Oryol a man of solitary and gloomy character is called a Loner.

That's how the local peasants spoke about Loner.

'So you're Loner,' I repeated. 'I've heard about you, my friend. They say you won't let a thing go.'

'I look after my job,' he answered sombrely. 'I'm not eating my master's bread for nothing.'

He took a chopper from his belt, squatted down on the floor and began to hack out a taper.

'You've no lady of the house?' I asked him.

'No,' he answered and struck a heavy blow with the chopper.

'She's dead, is she?'

'No . . . Yes . . . She's dead,' he added and turned away.

I said nothing. He raised his eyes and looked at me.

'She ran off with a passer-by, a fellow from the town,' he pronounced with a cruel smile. The little girl bowed her head. The baby woke up and started crying. The little girl went to the cradle. 'Here, give him this,' said Loner, thrusting a dirty feeding bottle into her hand. 'She even abandoned him,' he went on in a low voice, pointing at the baby. He went to the door, stopped and turned round.

'You'll likely, sir,' he began, 'not want to eat our bread, but apart from bread I've . . .'

'I'm not hungry.'

'Well, you know how it is. I'd light the samovar, only I've got no tea . . . I'll go out and see how your horse is.'

He went out and banged the door. I again looked around. The cottage seemed to me even more miserable than before. The bitter odour of stale woodsmoke made it hard for me to breathe. The little girl didn't move from where she was and didn't raise her eyes. From time to time she gave the cradle a rock and modestly drew her shirt over her shoulders. Her bare feet hung down motionlessly.

'What's your name?' I asked her.

'Ulita,' she said, lowering her sad little face even further.

The forester came in and sat on the bench.

'The storm's passing,' he remarked after a short silence. 'If you say so, I'll lead you out of the forest.'

I rose. Loner picked up his gun and examined the breech-block.

'What's that for?' I asked.

'There's something going on in the forest . . . Someone's felling wood up on Mare's Ridge,'* he added, in answer to my questioning look.

'Can you hear it from here?'

'Outside I can.'

We left together. The rain had stopped. In the far distance heavy masses of cloud still crowded together and long streaks of lightning flickered, but above our heads dark-blue patches of sky could be seen here and there and tiny stars twinkled through sparse, swiftly fleeting clouds. The outlines of trees, drenched in rain and shaken by the wind, began to emerge from the darkness. We started listening. The forester took off his cap and bent his head.

'There! . . . There!' he said suddenly and pointed. 'My, what a night he's chosen for it!'

I didn't hear a thing apart from the noise of leaves. Loner led the horse out from under the awning.

'It's likely,' he added aloud, 'I'll not get there in time.'

'I'll come with you . . . Is that all right?'

'All right,' he answered and put the horse back. 'We'll catch him and then I'll lead you out. Let's go.'

We set off, Loner in front and I behind him. God knows how he knew the way, but he stopped only occasionally and then just to listen to the sound of the axe.

'See,' he hissed through his teeth, 'd'you hear it? D'you hear it?'

'But where?'

Loner shrugged his shoulders. We descended into a gully, the wind dropped for a moment and the regular sounds of an axe clearly reached my hearing. Loner looked at me and nodded. We went further through wet bracken and nettles. A muffled and prolonged cracking sound was heard.

'He's felled it,' said Loner.

Meanwhile the sky continued to clear and in the forest it became just a bit brighter. Finally we made our way out of the gully.

'You wait here,' the forester whispered to me, bent down and, raising his gun aloft, disappeared among the bushes. I began listening intensely. Through the wind's constant noise I thought I heard such

* A 'Ridge' is the name for a ravine in Oryol province.

faint sounds as an axe carefully cutting off branches, the creaking of wheels and the snorting of a horse.

'Where're you going? Stop!' the iron voice of Loner suddenly cried out.

Another voice cried out plaintively, like a trapped hare. Then a struggle ensued.

'Li-ar! Li-ar!' asserted Loner, breathing hard. 'You'll not get away . . .'

I dashed off in the direction of the noise and, stumbling at each step, ran to the site of the struggle. The forester was busy with something on the ground beside a felled tree: he was holding the thief under him and twisting his arm round his back with a belt. I approached. Loner straightened up and set the other on his feet. I saw a peasant all damp and in tatters, with a long straggly beard. A wretched little horse, half-covered by an awkward piece of matting, also stood there along with the flat cart. The forester didn't say a word, the peasant also. He merely shook his head.

'Let him go,' I whispered in Loner's ear. 'I'll pay for the wood.'

Loner silently seized the horse by its mane with his left hand while with his right he held the thief by his belt.

'Well, get a move on, you good-for-nothing,' he said sternly.

'There's my axe there,' mumbled the thief.

'No point it getting lost!' exclaimed the forester and picked the axe up.

We set off and I followed along behind. The rain started again and soon it began to pour. We made our way with difficulty back to the cottage. Loner abandoned the little horse in the middle of the yard, led the peasant into the room, slackened the knotted belt and set him down in a corner. The little girl, who'd been asleep beside the stove, jumped up and started looking at us in silent fright. I sat down on a bench.

'It's such a downpour,' remarked the forester, 'we'll have to wait a bit. Would you like to lie down?'

'Thank you.'

'I'd lock 'im up in that cupboard, for your sake,' he went on, pointing at the peasant, 'only there's no bolt, as you can see . . .'

'Leave him be, don't touch him,' I broke in.

The peasant glanced at me from under his brows. Inwardly I made myself promise to free the poor wretch no matter what happened. He was sitting motionless on a bench. By the light of the lantern I could make out his haggard, wrinkled face, the jaundiced overhanging brows, restless eyes and thin limbs. The little girl lay down on the floor at his very feet and went to sleep again. Loner sat at the table, leaning his head on his hands. A cricket chirruped in the corner. The rain beat down on the roof and slid down the windows. We were all silent.

'Foma Kuzmich,' the peasant began suddenly in a hollow, broken voice, 'Foma Kuzmich . . .'

'What's up wi' you?'

'Let me go.'

Loner didn't answer.

'Let me go . . . It's bein' hungry . . . Let me go.'

'I know your sort,' the forester said sombrely. 'You're all the same where you come from, a bunch of thieves!'

'Let me go,' repeated the peasant. 'It's the bailiff, you know . . . ruined is what we are . . . Let me go!'

'Ruined! . . . No one's got a right to thieve.'

'Let me go, Foma Kuzmich! Don't do me in! Your master, you know yourself, he'll gobble me up, just you see!'

Loner turned away. The peasant shivered as if in a fever. He continuously shook his head and breathed unevenly.

'Let me go,' he repeated in miserable despair, 'for God's sake! I'll pay, just you see, by God I will! By God, it's bein' hungry . . . an' the babes cryin', you know what it's like. It gets real hard, just you see.'

'But you none the less shouldn't go thieving.'

'My little horse,' the peasant went on, 'let 'er go, she's all I got . . . Let 'er go!'

'I'm telling you I can't. I'm also one who takes orders and I'll have to answer for it. And I've got no reason to be kind to the likes of you.'

'Let me go! Need, Foma Kuzmich, need as ever was, that's what . . . Let me go!'

'I know your sort!'

'Just let me go!'

'What's the point of talking to you, eh? You sit there quietly, otherwise you know what you'll get from me, don't you? Can't you see there's a gentleman here?'

The poor fellow dropped his eyes. Loner yawned and rested his head on the table. The rain still went on. I waited to see what would happen.

The peasant suddenly straightened himself. His eyes were burning and his face had gone red.

'Well, eat me, go on, stuff yourself!' he began, screwing up his eyes and turning down the corners of his mouth. 'Go on, you bloody bastard, suck my Christian blood, go on, suck!'

The forester turned round.

'I'm talkin' to you, you bloody Asian, you bloodsucker!'

'Drunk, are you, that's why you've started swearing at me, eh?' said the forester in astonishment. 'Lost your senses, have you?'

'Drunk, ha! Not on your money I wouldn't, you bloody bastard, bloody animal you, animal, animal!'

'Hey, that's enough from you! I'll give you what for!'

'What's it to me! It's all the same – I'll be done for! What can I do without a horse? Kill me – it'll be the same end, if it's from hunger or from you, it's all the same to me! It's all over, wife, children – it's all done for! Just you wait, though, we'll get you in the end!'

Loner stood up.

'Hit me! Hit me!' shouted the peasant in a voice of fury. 'Come on, hit me! Hit me!' (The little girl quickly scrambled up from the floor and stared at him.) 'Hit me! Hit me!'

'Shut up!' thundered the forester and took two steps towards him.

'Enough, Foma, enough!' I cried. 'Leave him be! God be with him!'

'I won't shut up!' the wretch went on. 'It's all the same to me – I'll be done for! You bloody bastard, you animal, you, there's no end to what you do, but just you wait and see, you won't be lordin' it round here much longer! There'll be a tight noose round your neck, just you wait!'

Loner seized him by the shoulder. I hurled myself to the peasant's aid.

'Don't touch him, sir!' the forester shouted at me.

I didn't pay any attention to his threat and was about to stretch out my hand when, to my extreme astonishment, he pulled the belt from the peasant's elbows with one twist, seized him by the nape of the neck, shoved his hat on his head, flung open the door and pushed him out.

'Go to hell with your horse!' he shouted after him. 'Take care you don't come my way again!'

He returned to the cottage and began fussing about in a corner.

'Well, Loner,' I said at last, 'you've astonished me! I realize you're an excellent fellow.'

'Enough of that, sir,' he interrupted me in annoyance. 'Please be good enough not to talk about it. I'd better be leading you out,' he added, ''cos you know the rain's not going to wait for you . . .'

The wheels of the peasant's cart rattled away out of the yard.

'Look, he's off!' he said. 'I'll give 'im what for!'

Half an hour later I said goodbye to him at the edge of the forest.

TWO LANDOWNERS

❦

I HAVE already had the honour, kind readers, of acquainting you
with some of my neighbouring landowners; please permit me
now, appropriately (for the likes of us writers everything is appropriate), to acquaint you with two further landowners, on whose
lands I have frequently hunted, men who are highly esteemed and
well-intentioned, and who enjoy universal respect in several counties.

To begin with, I will describe to you the retired Major-General
Vyacheslav Illarionovich Khvalynsky. Imagine a tall man, at one
time possessing a graceful build, though now a little flabby, but by
no means decrepit, not even really old – a man of mature age, in his
prime, as they say. True, the formerly straight – even so, still
pleasing – features of his face have changed a little, his cheeks have
sagged, frequent wrinkles form ray-like surrounds to his eyes, here
and there a tooth is gone, as Saadi[1] was reputed to have said,
according to Pushkin; the auburn hair – at least, what has remained
of it – has turned a lilac grey, thanks to a preparation bought at the
Romen horse fair from a Jew who passed himself off as an Armenian;
but Vyacheslav Illarionovich has a lively manner of speaking, laughs
boisterously, jingles his spurs, twirls his moustache and – to cap it all
– speaks of himself as an old cavalry officer, whereas it is common
knowledge that real oldsters never speak of themselves as old. He
usually wears a coat buttoned up to the neck, a tall cravat with
starched collar and wide grey speckled trousers of military cut; his
cap he wears pulled straight down over his forehead, leaving the
back of his head completely bare.

He is a man of great kindness, but with some fairly strange notions
and habits. For example: he can never treat impoverished noblemen
or those with no rank as people who are his equals. Conversing with
them, he usually looks at them sideways, leaning his cheek strongly

against his firm, white collar, or he suddenly ups and glowers at them with a lucid and unwavering stare, stops talking and starts twitching the skin all over his scalp; he even takes to pronouncing words differently and does not say, for instance: 'Thank you, Pavel Vasilych', or 'Please approach, Mikhaylo Ivanych', but: 'Sonk you, Pall Asilich', or 'Pl-laase apprarch, Mikhal Vanych'. He deals even more oddly with those who occupy the lowest rungs of society: he does not look at them at all and, prior to explaining to them what he wants or giving an order, he has a way of repeating, several times in a row and with a perplexed and dreamy look on his face: 'What's your name? . . . What's your name?', placing unusually sharp emphasis on the first word 'what' and uttering the rest very rapidly, which gives his manner of speaking a fairly close resemblance to the cry of a male quail. He is a terrible one for fussing and frightfully grasping, but he is poor at managing his own affairs, having taken on as administrator of his estate a retired sergeant-major who is a Little Russian and an extraordinarily stupid man.

In the matter of estate-management, by the way, not one of us has yet outdone a certain important St Petersburg official who, having observed from the reports of his steward that the store-barns on his estate were frequently catching fire (as a result of which a great deal of his grain was being lost), issued the strictest edict to the effect that corn sheaves should not be placed in the barns until all fires were completely extinguished. This very same personage took it into his head to sow all his fields with poppies on the evidently very simple principle, so he claimed, that poppy-seed was dearer than rye, consequently poppies were more profitable. It was he who also ordered all his peasant women to wear tall headdresses designed according to a pattern sent from St Petersburg and in fact, right up to the present day, the womenfolk on his estates still wear such headdresses – except that the tall tops have been folded down . . . But we must return to Vyacheslav Illarionovich.

Vyacheslav Illarionovich is terribly keen on the fair sex and he no sooner catches sight of some pretty girl or other on the street of his local town than he at once sets off in hot pursuit, only to develop a sudden limp – which is a remarkable state of affairs. He likes to play cards, but only with people of lower rank, so that they will address him as 'Your Excellency' while he can huff and puff at them and abuse them as much as he wishes. Whenever he happens to be playing with the Governor or some high-ranking official, a surprising change comes over him: he even smiles and nods his head and looks them intently in the eyes – he positively exudes honey and sweetness . . . He even loses without grumbling.

Vyacheslav Illarionovich reads little and, when he does, he continuously moves his moustache and eyebrows – first his moustache, then his eyebrows, just as if a wave was passing upwards across his face. This wave-like movement on the face of Vyacheslav Illarionovich is particularly noteworthy when he happens – in the presence of guests, naturally – to be reading through the columns of the *Journal des Débats*. At the elections of marshals of nobility he plays a fairly important role, but out of meanness he always refuses the honourable title of marshal. 'Gentlemen,' he says to the members of the nobility who usually approach him on the subject, and he says it in a voice redolent with condescension and self-confidence, 'I am much obliged for the honour; but I have resolved to devote my leisure hours to solitude.' And, having once uttered these words, he will jerk his head several times to right and left, and then, with dignity, let the flesh of his chin and cheeks lap over his cravat.

In the days of his youth he was adjutant to some important personage, whom he never addressed otherwise than by his name and patronymic. They say that he assumed rather more than the duties of an adjutant, that decked out, for example, in full parade uniform, with everything buttoned-up and in place, he used to attend to his master's needs in the bath-house – but one can't believe everything one hears. Besides, General Khvalynsky is himself by no means fond of mentioning his service career, which is in general a somewhat odd circumstance; he also, it seems, has no experience of war. He lives, does General Khvalynsky, in a small house, by himself; he has had no experience of married happiness in his life, and consequently is regarded as an eligible bachelor even now – indeed, an advantageous match. Yet he has a housekeeper, a woman of about thirty-five, black-eyed and black-browed, buxom, fresh-faced and bewhiskered, who walks about on weekdays in starched dresses, adding muslin sleeves on Sundays.

Splendid is Vyacheslav Illarionovich's behaviour at large banquets given by landowners in honour of Governors and other persons in authority: on such occasions, it might be said, he is truly in his element. It is usual for him on such occasions to sit, if not directly to the Governor's right, then not far from him; at the beginning of the banquet he is concerned more than anything with preserving a sense of his own dignity and, leaning back, though without turning his head, directs his eyes sideways at the stand-up collars of the guests and the round napes of their necks; then, towards the end of the sitting, he grows expansively gay, smiles in all directions (he had smiled in the Governor's direction from the beginning of the meal) and even occasionally proposes a toast in honour of the fair sex – an ornament to our planet, as he puts it. Likewise, General Khvalynsky makes a good showing on all solemn and public occasions, at in-quiries, assemblies and exhibitions; masterly, also, is his fashion of receiving a blessing from a priest. At the end of theatrical perform-ances, at river-crossings and other such places, Vyacheslav Illarion-ovich's servants never make a noise or shout; on the contrary, making a path for him through a crowd or summoning a carriage, they always say in pleasant, throaty baritones: 'If you please, if you please, make way for General Khvalynsky' or 'General Khvalynsky's carriage ...' His carriage, if the truth be told, is of fairly ancient design; his footmen wear fairly tattered livery (it is hardly worth mentioning that it is grey with red piping); his horses are also fairly antiquated and have given service in their time; but Vyacheslav Illarionovich makes no pretensions to dandyishness and does not even consider it proper for a man of his rank to throw dust in people's eyes.

Khvalynsky has no particular gift for words, or it may be that he has no chance of displaying his eloquence since he cannot tolerate either disputes or rebuttals and studiously avoids all lengthy conver-sations, particularly with young people. Indeed, this is the proper way to handle things; any other way would be disastrous with the people as they are today: in no time at all they'd stop being servile and start losing respect for you. In the presence of those of higher rank Khvalynsky is mostly taciturn, but to those of lower rank, whom he evidently despises but who are the only ones he knows, he delivers sharp, abrupt speeches, endlessly using such expressions as: 'You are, however, talking rubbish,' or 'At last I find it necessary, my good fellah, to put you in your place,' or 'Now, damn it all, you surely ought to know who you're talking to,' and so on. Postmasters, committee chairmen and station-masters are especially awed by him. He never receives guests at home and lives, so rumour has it, like a regular Scrooge. Despite all this, he is an excellent landowner. Neighbours refer to him as 'an old fellow who's done his service, a man who's quite selfless, with principles, *vieux grognard*, old grouser that he is'. The public prosecutor of the province is the only man to permit himself a smile when mention is made in his presence of General Khvalynsky's splendid and solid qualities – but, then, such is the power of envy!

Let me pass now to another landowner.

Mardary Apollonych Stegunov bore no resemblance at all to Khvalynsky; he was hardly likely to have served anywhere and was never accounted handsome. Mardary Apollonych is a squat little old man, roly-poly and bald, with a double chin, soft little hands and a thoroughgoing paunch. He is a great one for entertaining and has a fondness for pranks; he lives, as they say, in clover; and winter and summer he walks about in a striped quilted dressing-gown. In only one respect is he similar to General Khvalynsky: he is also a bachelor. He has five hundred serfs. Mardary Apollonych takes a fairly superficial interest in his estate; ten years ago, so as not to be too far behind the times, he bought from the Butenops in Moscow a threshing machine, locked it in his barn and then rested content. On a fine summer day he may indeed order his racing buggy to be harnessed and then ride out into the field to see how the grain is ripening and to pick cornflowers.

He lives, does Mardary Apollonych, completely in the old style. Even his house is of antiquated construction: the entrance hall, as one might expect, smells of *kvas*, tallow candles and leather; on the right stands a sideboard with pipes and hand-towels; the dining-room contains family portraits, flies, a large pot of geraniums and a down-in-the-mouth piano; the drawing-room has three divans, three tables, two mirrors and a wheezy clock of blackened enamel with fretted, bronze hands; the study has a table piled with papers, a bluish draught-screen pasted with pictures cut from various works of the last century, cupboards full of stinking books, spiders and thick black dust, a stuffed armchair and an Italian window and a door into the garden that has been nailed up ... In a word, everything is quite appropriate. Mardary Apollonych has a mass of servants, and they are all dressed in old-fashioned style: long blue coats with high collars, trousers of some muddy colouring and short yellowish waist-coats. They use the old-fashioned address 'good master' in speaking to guests. His estate is managed by a bailiff drawn from among his peasants, a man with a beard as long as his sheepskin coat; his house is run by an old woman, wrinkled and tight-fisted, with a brown kerchief wound round her head. His stables contain thirty horses of various sizes; he rides out in a home-made carriage weighing well over two and a half tons. He receives guests with the utmost warmth and entertains them lavishly – that is to say, thanks to the stupefying characteristics of Russian cookery, he deprives them, until right up to the evening, of any opportunity of doing anything apart from playing preference. He himself never occupies himself with anything and has even given up reading his dream-book. But we still have a good many such landowners in Russia. It may be asked: what's led me to mention him and why? In place of a straight answer, let me tell you about one of my visits to Mardary Apollonych.

I went over to his place one summer, about seven o'clock in the evening. Evening prayers had just concluded, and the priest, a young man, evidently very shy and only recently graduated from his seminary, was sitting in the drawing-room beside the door, perched on the very edge of a chair. Mardary Apollonych, as was his custom, received me exceptionally fondly: he was genuinely delighted to receive guests and, by and large, he was the kindest of men. The priest rose and picked up his hat.

'One moment, one moment, my good fellow,' said Mardary Apollonych without leaving hold of my arm. 'You mustn't be going. I've ordered them to bring you some vodka.'

'I don't drink, sir,' the priest mumbled in confusion and reddened up to his ears.

'What rubbish! You say you're a priest and you don't drink!' Mardary Apollonych retorted. 'Mishka! Yushka! Vodka for the gentleman!'

Yushka, a tall and emaciated old man of about eighty, came in with a glass of vodka on a dark-painted tray covered with a variety of flesh-coloured splodges.

The priest proceeded to refuse.

'Drink, my good fellow, and no fussing, it's not proper,' the landowner remarked in a reproachful tone.

The poor young man acquiesced.

'Well now, my good fellow, you can go.'

The priest started bowing.

'All right, all right, be off with you ... An excellent fellow,' Mardary Apollonych continued, watching him depart, 'and I'm very satisfied with him. The only thing is – he's still young. Preaches sermons all the time, and he doesn't drink. But how are you, my good fellow? What're you doing, how're things? Let's go out on to the balcony – you see what a fine evening it is.'

We went out on to the balcony, sat down and began to talk. Mardary Apollonych glanced downwards and suddenly became frightfully excited.

'Whose are these chickens? Whose are these chickens?' he started shouting. 'Whose are these chickens walking about the garden? Yushka! Yushka! Off with you and find out at once whose are these chickens walking about the garden. Whose are these chickens? How many times I've forbidden this, how many times I've said so!'

Yushka ran off.

'What disorders there are!' repeated Mardary Apollonych. 'It's terrible!'

The unfortunate chickens – as I recall it now, there were two speckled and one white one with a crest – continued walking under the apple trees with the utmost lack of concern, occasionally expressing their feelings by making prolonged cluckings, when suddenly Yushka, hatless and armed with a stick, and three other house-serfs who were well on in years made a combined attack on them. A riot followed. The chickens squawked, flapped their wings, leapt about and cackled deafeningly; the house-serfs ran to and fro, stumbling and falling; and their master shouted from the balcony like one possessed: 'Catch them, catch them! Catch them, catch them! Catch them, catch them, catch them! Whose are these chickens, whose are these chickens?' Finally, one of the house-serfs succeeded in catching the crested chicken by forcing its breast to the ground, and at that very moment a girl of about eleven years of age, thoroughly dishevelled and with a switch in her hand, jumped over the garden fence from the street.

'So that's who the chickens belong to!' the landowner exclaimed triumphantly. 'They're Yermila the coachman's! See, he's sent his little Natalya to drive them back! It's not likely he'd send Parasha,' the landowner interjected under his breath and grinned meaningfully. 'Hey, Yushka! Forget the chickens and bring little Natalya here.'

But before the puffing Yushka could reach the terrified little girl, she was grabbed by the housekeeper, who had appeared from nowhere, and given several slaps on her behind.

'That's right, that's right,' the landowner said, accompanying the slaps. 'Yes, yes, yes! Yes, yes, yes! And mind you take the chickens off, Avdotya,' he added in a loud voice and turned to me with a shining face: 'Quite a chase, my good fellow, what? I've even worked myself into a sweat – just look at me!'

And Mardary Apollonych rattled off into thunderous laughter.

We remained on the balcony. The evening was really unusually beautiful. Tea was served to us.

'Tell me,' I began, 'Mardary Apollonych, are they yours, those settlements out there on the road, beyond the ravine?'

'They're mine. What of it?'

'How could you allow such a thing, Mardary Apollonych? It's quite wrong. The tiny huts allotted to the peasants are horrible, cramped things; there's not a tree to be seen anywhere; there's nothing in the way of a pond; there's only one well, and that's no use. Surely you could have found somewhere else? And rumour has it that you've even taken away their old hemp-fields.'

'But what's one to do about these redistributions of the land?' Mardary Apollonych asked me in turn. 'This redistribution's got me right here.' He pointed to the back of his neck. 'And I don't foresee any good coming from it. And as to whether I took away their hemp-fields and didn't dig out a pond for them there – about such matters, my good fellow, I haven't the foggiest. I'm just a simple man and I have old-fashioned ways. In my way of thinking, if you're the master, you're the master, and if you're a peasant, you're a peasant. And that's that.'

It goes without saying that such a lucid and convincing argument was unanswerable.

'What's more,' he continued, 'those peasants are a bad sort, not in my good books. Particularly two families over there. Even my late father, God rest his soul in the Kingdom of Heaven, even he wasn't fond of them, not at all fond of them. And I'll tell you something I've noticed: if the father's a thief, then the son'll be a thief, it doesn't matter how much you want things to be otherwise . . . Oh, blood-ties, blood-ties – they're the big thing! I tell you quite frankly that I've sent men from those two families to be recruits out of their turn and shoved them around here, there and everywhere. But what's one to do? They won't give up breeding. They're so fertile, damn them!'

In the meantime, the air grew completely quiet. Only occasionally a light breeze eddied around us and, on the last occasion, as it died down around the house it brought to our ears the sound of frequent and regular blows which resounded from the direction of the stables. Mardary Apollonych had only just raised a full saucer to his lips and was already on the point of distending his nostrils, without which, as everyone knows, no true Russian can imbibe his tea, when he stopped, pricked up his ears, nodded his head, drank and, setting the saucer down on the table, uttered with the kindest of smiles and as if unconsciously in time with the blows: 'Chooky-chooky-chook! Chooky-chook! Chooky-chook!'

'What on earth is that?' I asked in astonishment.

'It's a little rascal being punished on my orders. Do you by any chance know Vasya the butler?'

'Which Vasya?'

'The one who's just been waiting on us at dinner. He's the one who sports those large side-whiskers.'

The fiercest sense of outrage could not have withstood Mardary Apollonych's meek and untrammelled gaze.

'What's bothering you, young man, eh?' he said, shaking his head. 'You think I'm wicked, is that why you're staring at me like that? Spare the rod and spoil the child, you know that as well as I do.'

A quarter of an hour later I said goodbye to Mardary Apollonych. On my way through the village I saw Vasya the butler. He was walking along the street and chewing nuts. I ordered my driver to stop the horses and called to him.

'Did they give you a beating today, my friend?' I asked him.

'How do you know about it?' Vasya answered.

'Your master told me.'

'The master did?'

'Why did he order you to be beaten?'

'It served me right, good master, it served me right. You don't get beaten for nothing here. That's not how things are arranged here – oh, no. Our master's not like that, our master's . . . you won't find another master like ours anywhere else in the province.'

'Let's go!' I told my driver. *Well, that's old-style Russia for you!* I thought as I travelled home.

LEBEDYAN

❦

ONE of the principal advantages of hunting, my dear readers, is that it forces you to travel ceaselessly from place to place, which for someone without any occupation is very pleasant. True, sometimes (particularly in rainy weather) it's not too much fun to go wandering about on country roads, taking things 'all in all' and stopping every peasant along the way with the question: 'Hey, my friend, how do we get to Mordovka?' and then in Mordovka trying to elicit from some dim woman (all the workers being out in the fields) how far it is to the hostelries on the main road and how to get there, and then, having gone half-a-dozen miles, instead of finding hostelries finding oneself in the badly run-down little village of Dud-Diamond, to the extreme astonishment of a whole herd of pigs up to their ears in dark-brown mud in the middle of the street and quite unaware that anyone would be coming along to disturb them. It's also an unhappy business to try crossing rickety bridges, descending into ravines and traversing marshy streams; there's nothing joyful about travelling, day after day travelling through the greenish sea of main roads awash with water or, God forbid, getting stuck in mud for several hours by a signpost which says 22 on one side and 23 on the other; there's no fun in spending whole weeks eating nothing but eggs, milk and over-rated rye bread . . . But all these inconveniences and mishaps are compensated for by advantages and satisfactions of another kind. However, let's get on with the story.

As a consequence of all the above-said I've no need to inform the reader how, five years ago, I found myself in Lebedyan at the height of the horse fair. Hunters like us can set off one fine morning from their more or less ancestral estates with the intention of returning on the evening of the following day and little by little, without ceasing for a moment to shoot snipe, can end up finally by reaching the blessed banks of the Pechora;[1] additionally, anyone keen on gun and gun-dog is also likely to be a passionate admirer of the noblest animal on earth, the horse. So I arrived in Lebedyan, stopped at a hotel, changed my clothes and set off for the horse fair. (A waiter, a tall, lean fellow of twenty with a sweet nasal tenor voice had already managed to inform me that His Highness, Prince N., Remount Officer of such-and-such a regiment, had dined there, that many other gentlemen had arrived, that there were gypsy singers performing in the evenings and *Pan Tvardovsky*[2] was being performed at the theatre and that the horses were fetching good prices because good horses had after all been brought to the fair.)

On the fairground endless rows of carts stretched away, and behind the carts horses of every description: trotters, stud horses, cart-horses, dray-horses, coach-horses and ordinary peasant horses. Some, sleek and well-fed, arranged according to their colour, covered with cloths of varying hues and tethered on short leashes to tall ladder-backs of waggons, glanced timidly behind them at the all-too-familiar whips of their owners and masters. Landowners' horses, dispatched by nobility of the steppes for a hundred and more miles in the charge of some decrepit coachman and two or three big-headed stableboys, waved their long necks, stamped their hoofs and gnawed their stakes out of boredom. Light-brown Vyatka horses pressed tightly against each other. In magnificent immobility, as if they were lions, stood the trotters with their broad hindquarters, wavy tails and shaggy manes, dappled grey, black and bay-coloured. Connoisseurs of horses stopped respectfully in front of them. In the thoroughfares created by the lines of carts were crowds of people of every calling, age and appearance: dealers in blue caftans and tall hats were craftily on the watch awaiting buyers; curly-haired gypsies with popping eyes rushed to and fro like mad things looking horses in the teeth, lifting their hoofs and tails, shouting, swearing, acting as go-betweens, making bets or swarming about some remount officer in his army cap and beaver-lined greatcoat. A hefty cossack perched on top of a gaunt gelding with a neck like a stag's was offering it 'with the bloody lot', meaning with saddle and reins. Peasants in sheepskin jackets torn under the armpits desperately pushed their way through the crowds and poured in their dozens on to a cart to which a horse

had been harnessed for 'trying-out' or, somewhere on the side, with
the help of a shifty gypsy, engaged in trading to the point of
exhaustion, slapping their hands together a hundred times over and
each one insisting on their price while the object of their dispute, a
wretched little nag covered in some warped matting, scarcely blinked
her eyes as if the whole thing were no concern of hers . . . And in fact
it didn't matter to her a damn who'd be beating her from now on!
Broad-browed landowners with tinted whiskers and dignified expressions, in peakless, rectangular caps and camlet cloth jackets worn
on one arm only, chatted condescendingly to stout merchants in
fluffy hats and green gloves. Officers of various regiments crowded
there as well. An unusually tall cuirassier, of German extraction,
coldly asked a limping dealer how much he wanted for 'zet chestnut
'oss'. A fair-haired little hussar of about nineteen tried to match a
side-horse to a sinewy pacer. A coachman in a low hat wound about
with a peacock feather and in brown coat with leather sleeves
inserted under a narrow greenish belt was searching for a shaft-horse.
Drivers were plaiting the tails of their horses, moistening their manes
and offering respectful advice to their masters. All those who'd done
deals dashed to a hostelry or a pub, depending on their status . . .

And all this bustling and shouting and hassling and quarrelling and
dealing and swearing and laughing was going on among men with
mud up to their knees. I wanted to purchase a trio of decent horses
for my carriage because my present ones were getting past their best.
I found two, but couldn't pick up a third. After dinner, which I
won't undertake to describe (after all Aeneas knew long ago how
unpleasant it is to recall past misfortune),[3] I set off for the so-called
coffee-house where each evening there were gatherings of remount
men, horse-breeders and others. In the billiard-room, fuggy with
leaden waves of tobacco smoke, there were about twenty men.
Among them were dissolute young landowners in riding jackets and
grey trousers, with long whiskers and waxed moustaches, looking
grandly and boldly around them. Other members of the nobility in
long frockcoats, with extraordinarily short necks and eyes swimming
in fat, wheezed their way painfully about. Merchants sat to one side
'on their tod', as they say, while officers chattered freely among
themselves. A game was being played by Prince N., a young man of
about twenty-two in an open jacket, red silk shirt and wide velvet

trousers, with a jolly and slightly condescending face. He was playing with a retired lieutenant, Victor Khlopakov.

Retired Lieutenant Victor Khlopakov, a small, dark, thin fellow of about thirty, with cropped black hair, brown eyes and a snouty turned-up nose, is an assiduous visitor of elections and fairs. He has a springy walk, a fancy way of moving his rounded hands about, a hat worn at a smart angle and turned-back sleeves of his military coat showing the grey calico lining. Mister Khlopakov possesses an ability for sucking up to rich St Petersburg men-about-town, smokes, drinks and plays cards with them and is always on familiar terms with them. Why they put up with him it is not all that easy to understand. He's not clever, nor is he even witty: he'd be no good as a jester. True, they treat him in a carelessly amiable way as a good-enough, empty-headed fellow whom they can knock around with for two or three weeks and then suddenly not even bow to, just as he doesn't bow to them. A peculiarity of Lieutenant Khlopakov is that, for a year, sometimes two, he constantly uses one and the same expression, appropriately and inappropriately, an expression in no way humorous which, God knows why, makes everyone laugh. Eight or so years ago he would say at every opportunity: 'My honouring to you, sir, the very humblest gratitude,' and his patrons of those days would die laughing on each occasion and force him to repeat 'My honouring to you, sir.' Later he took to using a more complex expression: 'No, you're doing your *qu'est-ce que ça*, what's come out comes out,' and with the same brilliant success. A couple of years ago he came out with a new catchphrase: 'Don't *vous* get hot *pas*, you man of God, you sheepskin clod!' and so on. So there it is! These, as you can see, wholly unimportant sayings are his food, drink and clothing. (He's long ago used up his own estate and now lives solely off his friends.) Take note that there are absolutely no other niceties associated with him. It's true that he smokes a hundred pipefuls of Zhukov tobacco a day and while playing billiards raises his right foot above his head and, in taking aim, makes a great show of playing with his cue – well, of course, not everyone's keen on such accomplishments. He also drinks like a fish, but it's hard to be remarkable for doing that in Russia. In a word, his success is to me a complete mystery. Maybe it's because he's careful, he doesn't spread dirt about people and never says a bad word about a soul . . .

'Well,' I thought on seeing Khlopakov, 'what's his latest expression, I wonder?'

The prince addressed the cue ball.

'Thirty, love,' cried out a consumptive marker with a dark face and lead-grey bags under his eyes.

The prince sent a yellow ball banging into a far pocket.

'Heck!' a stoutish merchant wheezed approvingly, his stomach quivering as he sat in a corner at a shaky, one-legged little table, wheezed and stopped in embarrassment. But fortunately no one took any notice. He sighed and stroked his beard.

'Thirty-six and little chance!' cried the marker through his nose.

'What d'you think of that, old chap?' the prince asked Khlopakov.

'What do I think? It's a right old rrrrapscalliooon, a right old rrrrapscalliooon that is!'

The prince exploded with laughter.

'What? What? Say it again!'

'Rrrrapscalliooon!' the retired lieutenant repeated smugly.

'So that's the new one!' I thought.

The prince pocketed a red ball.

'Hey! Not like that, prince, not like that,' suddenly babbled a small, fair-haired officer with little bloodshot eyes, tiny nose and a childishly sleepy face. 'Don't play like that! You shouldn't do that!'

'What's that?' the prince asked him over his shoulder.

'You should've played a triplet.'

'Is that so?' the prince muttered through his teeth.

'What about going to the gypsies this evening, prince?' the young man hurriedly asked in confusion. 'Styeshka'll be singing . . . and Ilyushka . . .'

The prince didn't answer him.

'Rrrrapscalliooon, old chap,' said Khlopakov, slyly screwing up his left eye.

And the prince burst into torrents of laughter.

'Thirty-nine, love,' proclaimed the marker.

'Love . . . Just look what I'll do to that yellow . . .'

Khlopakov made a great show with using his cue, took aim and missed.

'Oh, rrrrapscalliooon!' he cried in annoyance.

The prince again laughed.

'What? what? what?'

But Khlopakov didn't want to repeat his special word. He had to be sparing with his party piece.

'You made a mis-hit,' remarked the marker. 'Allow me to offer some chalk . . . Forty and very little!'

'Yes, gentlemen,' the prince began, turning to the entire company and not looking at anyone in particular, 'you know, today we must ensure an ovation for Verzhembitskaya in the theatre.'

'Of course, of course, without doubt,' exclaimed several gentlemen in friendly rivalry, astonishingly flattered by the opportunity to respond to the prince's words. 'For Verzhembitskaya . . .'

'Verzhembitskaya is an outstanding actress, much better than Sopnyakova,' squeaked from one corner a shabby man with whiskers and glasses. Poor fellow, he secretly yearned after Sopnyakova, but the prince didn't deign so much as to give him a glance!

'I say, a pipe!' pronounced into his cravat a tall man with regular features and the grandest of bearing, to all appearances a cardsharp.

A waiter dashed off to fetch him a pipe and, on returning, informed His Highness that Baklaga, the driver, had apparently been asking for him.

'Ah! Well, tell him to wait and fetch him some vodka, there's a good chap.'

'Yes, sir.'

Baklaga, as I was told later, was the nickname of a young, handsome and exceedingly spoiled driver. The prince was very fond of him, gave him gifts of horses, went racing with him and spent whole nights with him . . . This very same prince, former playboy and spendthrift, you wouldn't recognize now, so perfumed he's become, so stiff and proud! So busy he is now with his government service, but, chiefly, how extremely circumspect!

However, the tobacco smoke began to hurt my eyes. Having heard for the last time Khlopakov's exclamation and the prince's answering laugh, I went to my room where my manservant had made up a bed for me on a narrow, broken-down horsehair divan with a high bent back.

The next day I went to look at the horses in the various yards and began by going to the well-known dealer Sitnikov. By way of a gate I went into a yard spread with sand. Before the wide-open door of the stables stood the proprietor himself, a man no longer young, tall and stout, in a hare-skin jacket with a raised, turned-back collar. Seeing me, he moved slowly in my direction, holding his hat above his head with both hands and pronouncing in a singsong voice:

'Our respects to you, sir. Is it some horses you'll be after seein'?'

'Yes, I've come to have a look at horses.'

'What kind precisely, if I may ask?'

'Show me what you have.'

'With our pleasure.'

We went into the stables. Several small white dogs rose from the hay and ran towards us wagging their tails. An old goat with a long beard withdrew to one side in dissatisfaction. Three stable-boys in strong but greasy sheepskin coats bowed to us in silence. To left and right, in artificially raised stalls, stood about thirty horses cleaned and groomed to perfection. Among the rafters pigeons flew to and fro and cooed.

'For what is it you'll be wantin' a horse, for ridin', is it, or for breedin'?' Sitnikov asked me.

'Both for riding and for breeding.'

'We get your meanin', sir, we get your meanin', sir, we do,' said the dealer, pausing between the words. 'Petya, show Ermine to the gentleman.'

We went out into the yard.

'Shall I have a bench brought out? You don't want it? As you wish . . .'

Hoofs resounded on the floorboards, there was a whip-crack and Petya, a fellow of about forty, with a pitted, swarthy complexion, jumped out of the stables with a grey, fairly stately stallion, made him rise up on his hind legs, ran him round the yard once or twice and skilfully halted him at a point for showing him off. Ermine stretched his neck, gave a whistling neigh, flourished his tail, moved his mouth and nostrils and gave us a sideways look.

'He knows a thing or two,' I thought.

'Let 'im be, let 'im be,' said Sitnikov and looked hard at me.

'How d'you t'ink? Will he do, sir?' he asked eventually.

'The horse is not bad, except that his forelegs are not quite right.'

' 'Tis fine legs he has!' Sitnikov retorted with conviction. 'Look at his hindquarters, just look at 'em, broad as a stove they are, you could sleep on 'em!'

'He's got long pasterns.'

'Long, indeed – have a care, sir! Run him a bit, Petya, run him, at a trot, a trot, a trot – don't let 'im gallop!'

Petya again ran round the yard with Ermine. We were all silent.

'Well, put 'im back now,' said Sitnikov, 'and then show us Falcon.'

Falcon, a stallion black as a beetle, of Dutch breed, wiry with drooping hindquarters, was a little better than Ermine. He belonged to that kind of horse of which hunters say that 'they cut and hew and imprison you', meaning that when being ridden they thrash about with their forelegs to right and left and make little headway forwards. Middle-aged merchants have a fondness for them. As they run they remind you of the flashy walk of a lively floor-waiter. They are good singly for going out after dinner because, striding out fine and dandy, their necks arched, they can busily pull a gaudily painted droshky loaded with a driver who's eaten himself paralytic, an overweight merchant suffering from heartburn and his podgy wife in a light-blue silk coat and a small lilac kerchief on her head. I turned down Falcon as well. Sitnikov showed me several more horses. Finally, one, a dappled grey stallion of the famous Voeikovsky breed, appealed to me. I couldn't restrain myself and patted him approvingly on the withers. Sitnikov immediately pretended to be indifferent.

'Tell me, does he ride well?' I asked. (One never says 'run' about a trotter.)

'He rides,' the dealer answered calmly.

'Can't I have a look?'

'Of course you can, sir. Hey, Kuzya, harness Catch-up to the droshky.'

Kuzya, a master-jockey, drove past us at least three times along the street. The horse ran well, didn't stray, didn't throw up its hind-quarters, lifted its legs freely, kept its tail high and held itself well – in short, a good trotter.

'What are you asking for it?'

Sitnikov named an unheard-of price. We began bargaining right there on the street when suddenly there flew thunderously round the corner a splendidly matched troika which stopped boldly outside the gates of Sitnikov's house. Prince N. sat in the fancy hunting carriage and Khlopakov next to him. Baklaga was driving the three horses – and how he drove! The villain could've driven them through an earring! The bay outrunners were small, lively, black-eyed, black-legged and literally on fire, literally raring to go – one whistle and they'd be off! The dark-bay shaft-horse stood there calmly, his neck thrust back like a swan's and his chest out, his legs like arrows, shaking his head and proudly closing his eyes. A splendid team! Tsar Ivan Vasilyevich himself could have ridden behind them for his Easter outing!

'Your Highness! We beg you welcome!' cried Sitnikov.

The prince jumped down from the carriage. Khlopakov slowly alighted the other side.

'Hello, my good man . . . Have you any horses?'

'For your Highness – of course! Please, come this way . . . Petya, bring out Peacock! And see that Commendable's got ready! And with you, sir,' he went on, turning to me, 'we'll finish our business later . . . Fomka, a seat for his Highness!'

Peacock was led out of a special stables which I'd not noticed at first. The powerful dark-bay horse literally pawed the air with its hoofs. Sitnikov even turned his head away and squeezed up his eyes.

'Oo, the rrapscallion!' declared Khlopakov. 'J'aime ça!'

The prince roared with laughter.

Peacock was stopped with some difficulty. He literally pulled the stable-boy round the yard until they finally pressed him up against a wall. He snorted, quivered and rared to go while Sitnikov went on taunting him by waving a whip at him.

'Who're you looking at? Oh, I'll teach you! Ooo!' said the dealer in a fondly threatening tone, admiring his horse despite everything.

'How much?' asked the prince.

'To your Highness, five thousand.'

'Three.'

'Impossible, your Highness, if you don't mind . . .'

'Three, he says, you rrapscallion!' chimed in Khlopakov.

I didn't wait for the conclusion of the deal and left. At the far corner of the street I noticed a large sheet of paper fixed to the gates of a small grey house. At the top was a pen-drawing of a horse with an enormously long neck and a tail looking like a trumpet and under the horse's hoofs were the following words, written in an old-fashioned hand:

On Sale Here are Horses of Diverse Hues, Conveyed to the Lebedyan Fair from the Famed Steppeland Stud of Anastasey Ivanych Chernobay, Landowner of Tambov. These Horses have Outstanding Points; Trained to Perfection and of Meek Habits. Gentlemen intending to Purchase are Requested to ask for Anastasey Ivanych Himself; in his Absence, ask for the coachman Nazar Kubyshkin. Gentlemen intending to Purchase are Kindly Requested to Spare a Thought for an Old Man!

I stopped. Right, I thought, I'll have a look at the horses of the famed steppeland stud-owner, Mr Chernobay.

I was about to go in by the gate but, contrary to usual practice, found it shut. I knocked.

'Who's there? A buyer?' squeaked a female voice.

'A buyer.'

'At once, sir, at once.'

The gate was opened. I saw a woman of about fifty, her head uncovered, wearing boots and with an open sheepskin jacket.

'Please come in, good sir. I'll go and tell Anastasey Ivanych this minute . . . Nazar, Nazar!'

'Wha-a-at?' mumbled the voice of a seventy-year-old from the stables.

'Get the horses ready. A buyer's come.'

The old woman ran off into the house.

'A buyer, a buyer,' grumbled Nazar in response to her. 'I 'aven't yet washed the tails on all of 'em.'

'O, Arcadia!' was my thought.

'Good day, sir, and welcome,' resounded a slow, fruity and pleasant voice behind me. I glanced round and saw standing there, in a long, blue overcoat, an old man of medium height, with white hair, a charming smile and beautiful sky-blue eyes.

'Are you looking for horses? Certainly, sir, certainly . . . Wouldn't you care to come in and have some tea first?'

I thanked him and refused.

'Well, it's as you wish. You must forgive me, sir, but I'm old-fashioned.' (Mr Chernobay spoke slowly and emphasized his 'o's.) 'I like things to be simple, you know. Nazar! Naza-a-ar!' he added, elongating the vowel and not raising his voice.

Nazar, a wrinkled old fellow with a small, hawk-like nose and goatee beard, appeared in the stables doorway.

'What kind of horses would you be wanting, sir?' Mr Chernobay went on.

'Not too expensive, well-trained and for harnessing.'

'Certainly, we have some like that, certainly . . . Nazar, Nazar, show the gentleman that little grey gelding, you know, the one in the corner, and the bay mare with the bald patch, no, not that one — the other bay, the one out of Little Beauty, d'you know which one?'

Nazar returned to the stables.

'Oh, and bring them out just as they are!' Mr Chernobay shouted after him. 'With me, sir,' he went on, looking me clear-eyed and calmly in the face, 'it's not as it is with the dealers, who don't feed 'em properly. They use various gingers and salt and malt dregs* and God knows what! But with me, as you can see for yourself, everything's above-board and no tricks.'

The horses were led out. They didn't appeal to me.

'Well, put them back where they came from,' said Anastasey Ivanych. 'Show us some others.'

Others were shown. Finally I chose one cheaper than the others. We began to bargain. Mr Chernobay did not get heated, spoke so reasonably and called upon God as his witness with such self-importance that I couldn't help 'sparing a thought for an old man' and put down a deposit.

'Well, now,' muttered Anastasey Ivanych, 'allow me, in the old-fashioned way, to let you have this one under the counter . . . You'll be grateful to me, after all it's fresh as a ripe nut, untouched, just off the steppes! It'll go into any harness.'

He crossed himself, then crossed his palm with the hem of his overcoat, took the bridle and handed over the horse to me.

'Keep it in God's name . . . Are you sure you don't want some tea?'

'No, thank you most humbly. I must be getting home.'

'As you wish . . . Shall my coachman bring the horse to you now?'

'Yes, right away, if you please.'

'Certainly, my dear chap, certainly . . . Vasily, hey, Vasily, go with the gentleman. Take the horse and receive the money. Well, goodbye, sir. God be with you.'

'Goodbye, Anastasey Ivanych.'

* A horse will quickly grow fat on salt and malt dregs.

The horse was led to where I was staying. The next day it turned out to be broken-winded and lame. I thought of harnessing it but my horse backed away and when the whip was applied it grew stubborn, reared its hindquarters and then lay down. I at once set off to find Mr Chernobay.

'Is he at home?' I asked.

'He's at home.'

'What've you been up to?' I asked. 'You've sold me a broken-winded horse.'

'Broken-winded? God preserve us!'

'It's lame as well and it's temperamental.'

'Lame? I don't know anything about that. Evidently your driver's mishandled it . . . As for me, as God is my witness . . .'

'You really ought to take it back, Anastasey Ivanych.'

'No, sir, don't be annoyed, but once it's out of the yard the matter's finished. You should've seen to all that beforehand.'

I understood what it was all about, accepted my fate, gave vent to laughter and left. Fortunately I'd not paid too highly for my lesson.

A couple of days later I left and a week later again stopped by in Lebedyan on my return journey. In the coffee-house I found almost exactly the same people and once more came across the prince in the billiard-room. But the usual change had occurred in the fortunes of Mr Khlopakov. The little fair-haired officer had taken his place in the prince's affections. The poor retired lieutenant tried once again in my presence to do his party piece, to see whether it'd meet with its former favour, but the prince not only didn't smile, he even frowned and gave a shrug of the shoulder. Mr Khlopakov was crestfallen, shrank away into a corner and began quietly filling his pipe . . .

TATYANA BORISOVNA AND HER NEPHEW

❧

GIVE me your hand, dear reader, and come on an outing. The weather is beautiful. The May sky glows a gentle blue. The smooth young leaves of the willow shine as if newly washed. The broad, level road is entirely covered with that short grass with reddish stems which sheep so love to nibble. To left and right, along the long slopes of the low hills green rye quietly ripples. The shadows of small clouds slide across it like globules of moisture. In the distance gleam dark woodlands, ponds glisten and villages shine yellow. Larks rise by the hundreds, sing and fall precipitately and, with small outstretched necks, are seen conspicuously on small out-crops of soil. Rooks stop on the road, look at you, crouch down to let you pass and, giving a couple of jumps, fly off heavily to one side. On an upland beyond a shallow valley a peasant is ploughing. A dappled foal with short little tail and ruffled mane runs on uncertain legs behind its mother and one can hear its high-pitched neighing. We drive into a birch wood and the strong, fresh scent pleasantly takes one's breath away. We're on the outskirts of a village. The coachman alights, the horses snort, the trace-horses looking round them and the shaft-horse waving its tail and leaning its head against the shaft ... The gate opens with a loud creaking. The coachman takes his seat – and off we go! The village is in front of us. Passing half-a-dozen houses, we turn to the right, descend into a hollow and drive across a dam. Beyond a small pond, from behind the round tops of apple trees and lilacs, can be seen a wooden roof, at one time painted red, and two chimneys. The coachman chooses a way to the left along a fence and to the accompaniment of the hoarse, yelping barks of three exceedingly ancient small dogs drives through wide-open gates, dashes boldly round a wide yard past stables and barn, bows with a flourish to an old housekeeper who has just gone sideways over a high doorstep into an open store-room doorway, and comes to a stop finally in front of the entrance to a dark little house with shining windows . . . We've reached Tatyana Borisovna's. And there she is herself, opening the little window and nodding to us . . .

Hello, auntie!

Tatyana Borisovna is a lady of about fifty with large, grey, bulging eyes, a slightly blunt nose, pink cheeks and a double chin. Her face breathes welcome and warmth. She was married at one time but was quickly widowed. Tatyana Borisovna is a very remarkable lady. She lives permanently on her little estate, has little to do with her neighbours and only likes and receives young people. She was the daughter of extremely poor landowners and received no education – that is to say, she doesn't speak French; nor has she ever been to Moscow and yet, despite these many handicaps, she conducts herself so simply and well, feels and thinks so freely and is so little affected by the usual ailments of ladies on small estates that one cannot help being amazed at her . . . And, to be sure, for a lady living the whole year round in one village in the heart of the country not to be engaged in gossip, talking with a squeaky voice, dropping curtsies, becoming emotional, choking with horror and quivering with curiosity is quite miraculous! She usually wears a grey taffeta dress and white bonnet with hanging lilac ribbons. She's fond of eating but not to excess and she leaves the jam-making, drying and salting to her housekeeper.

What does she do all day, you may ask. Does she read? No, she doesn't read, and, truth to tell, books are not printed for the likes of her. If she has no guests, my Tatyana Borisovna sits in winter by the window and knits stockings; in the summer she walks in the garden, plants flowers and waters them, plays for hours at a time with her kittens and feeds the pigeons. She takes little interest in the running of her house. But as soon as a guest arrives, some young neighbour of whom she's fond, Tatyana Borisovna at once grows lively, sits him down, pours him tea, listens to his stories, laughs, occasionally pats him on the cheek, but says little herself. In misfortune and in grief she always offers comfort and gives good advice. How many people have entrusted her with their most private and domestic secrets and cried in her arms! It's usual for her to sit down opposite her guest, lean on one elbow and look him in the eye with such sympathy and smile with such friendliness that the guest can't help thinking: 'What a wonderful lady you are, Tatyana Borisovna! I'll be glad to tell you everything in my heart.' In her small, comfortable rooms one always feels warm; there is always beautiful weather in her house, if one may put it that way. Tatyana Borisovna is a surprising lady and yet no one is surprised at her. Her common sense, firmness and frankness, her passionate immersion in others' sorrows and joys — in a word, all her talents — were given her at birth and never cost her any labour or fuss ... It would be impossible to imagine her in any other way, just as there's really nothing to thank her for.

She's especially fond of watching the games and pranks of the young. She folds her arms below her bosom, tosses back her head, screws up her eyes and sits there smiling, and then she suddenly sighs and says: 'Oh, you young things, you!' It makes you want to go up to her and take her hand and say: 'Tatyana Borisovna, listen, you don't know your own worth, why, with all your simplicity and artlessness, you're a simply extraordinary person!' Her name itself has a familiar ring, is welcomed and uttered with pleasure and gives rise to friendly smiles. The number of times, for example, I've had occasion to ask a peasant how to get to Grachovka, say, and heard 'Well, sir, go first to Vyazovoe and from there to Tatyana Borisovna's and anyone'll tell you the way from Tatyana Borisovna's.' And at Tatyana Borisovna's name the peasant'll give a special shake of the head. She keeps only a small number of servants, according to her needs. The house, laundry, store-room and kitchen are the preserve of her housekeeper Agafya, her former nurse, the kindest of creatures, toothless and prone to tears. She has charge of two healthy girls with strong dusky cheeks the colour of ripe apples. The positions of valet, butler and steward are filled by the seventy-year-old servant Polikarp, a very unusual old chap, well-read, a retired violinist and devotee of Viotti,[1] personal enemy of Napoleon or 'Old Boney', as he calls him, and passionately fond of nightingales. He always has five or six of them in his room and in early spring spends whole days sitting beside the cages waiting for the first 'burst of song' and, on hearing it, covers his face with his hands and bursts into tears, moaning

'Oh my! Oh, my!' Polikarp has a grandson to help him, Vasya, a boy of about twelve, with curly hair and lively eyes. Polikarp loves him to distraction and grumbles at him from dawn to dusk. He also occupies himself with his education.

'Vasya,' he says, 'say: Old Boney's a robber.'

'What'll you give me, grandad?'

'What'll I give you? I won't give you nuthin'. Who d'you think you are? You're Russian, aren't you?'

'I'm an Amchenian, grandad. I was born in Amchensk.'*

'Oh, you silly thing! Where d'you think Amchensk is?'

'How should I know?'

'Amchensk's in Russia, silly!'

'So what if it's in Russia?'

'So what? 'Cos His Magnificence, the late-lamented Prince Mikhaylo Illarionovich Golenishchev-Kutuzov, with God's help, drove that Old Boney right beyond the Russian borders. An' on account of it a song was made up: "Old Boney's gone and lost 'is fasteners, so he can't go to no more dances . . ." He liberated the fatherland, understand?'

'What's it to me?'

'Oh, you silly boy, you! If His Magnificence Prince Mikhaylo Illarionovich hadn't driven out Old Boney, some monsewer or other'd be beatin' you about the head with a stick. He'd come up to you an' say: Koman vu porty vu? an' bash, bash he'd go!'

'Then I'd give 'im my fist in the stomach!'

'An' he'd say to you: Bonjur, bonjur, veney issy an' grab hold of your hair, he would!'

'I'd grab 'im by the legs, I would! I'd grab 'im by the goat's legs!'

'It's true they've got legs like goats! . . . But what if he started tying your hands?'

'I wouldn't let 'im! I'd call Mickey the coachman to come an' help.'

'So, Vasya, you don't think a Frenchie'd be a match for Mickey?'

''Course he wouldn't! Mickey's real strong!'

'Well, what'd you do to him?'

---

* In peasant speech the town of Mtsensk is called Amchensk and the inhabitants are called Amchenians. Amchenians are boisterous. It's no wonder that among us we tell people we don't like that we'll 'send an Amchenian to live with you'.

'We'd bash 'im on the back, that's what!'

'An' he'd start shoutin': Pardon, pardon, sivuplay!'

'An' we'd tell 'im no sivuplay to you, you Frenchie, you!'

'Bravo, Vasya! Well, go on, shout out: "Old boney's a robber!"'

'You give me some sugar!'

'Oh, you're a one!'

Tatyana Borisovna has little to do with local ladies. They don't like visiting her and she doesn't know how to entertain them, falls asleep under the sound of their talk, then shakes herself, forces herself to open her eyes and once more falls asleep. Tatyana Borisovna is not fond of women in general. One of her friends, a decent and quiet young man, had a sister who was an old maid of thirty-eight and a half, the kindest creature but extremely artificial, intense and emotional. Her brother frequently spoke to her about their neighbour. One fine morning my old maid, without a word of warning, ordered a horse saddled for her and set off for Tatyana Borisovna's. In her long dress, with a hat on her head, a green veil and curls let down, she walked into the hallway and, slipping past an astonished Vasya who took her for a water sprite, ran into the drawing-room. Tatyana Borisovna was frightened out of her wits, tried to get up, but her legs failed her.

'Tatyana Borisovna,' her guest started saying in a pleading voice, 'forgive me for being so bold. I'm the sister of your neighbour Aleksey Nikolaevich K— and have heard so much about you I decided to make your acquaintance.'

'It's a great honour,' murmured the astonished hostess.

Her guest tossed off her hat, shook out her curls, seated herself beside Tatyana Borisovna and took her hand.

'So here she is,' she began in a thoughtful and affected voice, 'here is the kind, placid, noble, holy being herself! Here she is, the simple and yet profound lady! How delighted I am, how delighted! How fond we'll be of each other! I'm content at last! . . . You are just as I'd imagined you'd be,' she added in a whisper, directing her eyes into Tatyana Borisovna's. 'Tell me the truth, you're not annoyed with me, my dear one, my fine one, are you?'

'Not at all, I'm very glad . . . Would you care for some tea?'

The guest smiled condescendingly. *'Wie wahr, wie unreflektiert,'* she whispered as if to herself. 'Permit me to embrace you, my darling!'

The old maid spent three hours at Tatyana Borisovna's without being quiet for an instant. She tried to demonstrate to her new acquaintance her own importance. The moment the unexpected guest had left the poor lady of the house set off for the bath-house, drank plentifully of lime tea and took to her bed. But the next day the old maid returned, spent four hours with her and left promising to visit Tatyana Borisovna every day. She'd taken it upon herself, you see, to complete the development of – or the education of – such a rich nature, as she put it, and probably she'd have carried it through completely if, firstly, after a couple of weeks she hadn't become 'utterly' disillusioned by her brother's friend and, secondly, if she hadn't fallen in love with a young student who came her way and with whom she immediately entered into a vigorous and passionate correspondence. In her letters she gave him, as is customary, her blessing for a sacred and beautiful life, offered 'every bit of herself' as a sacrifice, demanded only that he call her his sister, embarked on descriptions of nature, mentioned Goethe, Schiller, Bettina von Arnim[2] and German philosophy and finally drove the poor lad to grim despair. But youth asserted itself. One fine morning he awoke in such a frenzy of loathing for this 'sister and best friend' of his that he barely restrained himself from giving his valet a thumping in the heat of the moment and for a long while felt like biting anyone who made the slightest mention of exalted and disinterested love . . . But from that moment on Tatyana Borisovna began to avoid contact with her female neighbours even more than before.

Alas, nothing is certain on this earth! Everything I've told you so far about the life and times of my kind lady is a matter of the past. The calm which reigned in her house has gone forever. She has already had living with her for more than a year her nephew, an artist from St Petersburg. This is how it came about.

About eight years ago Tatyana Borisovna had living with her a boy of about twelve called Andryusha, an orphan without mother or father and the son of her late brother. Andryusha had large, bright, moist eyes, a small mouth, straight nose and fine high forehead. He spoke in a quiet, sweet voice, was neat and well-behaved, polite and considerate to guests and always kissed his aunt's hand with an orphan's appropriate tenderness. You'd scarcely have put in an appearance when, lo and behold, he'd be bringing in an armchair for you.

He was not one for pranks of any kind and never made a noise, but would sit in a corner with a book so deferentially and quietly he wouldn't even lean back against the back of the chair. A guest would arrive and my Andryusha'd be up on his feet, smile politely and turn pink. When the guest left, he'd sit down again, take a little brush and mirror from his pocket and start brushing his hair. From a very early age he had a fondness for drawing. Should a scrap of paper come his way, he'd at once beg a pair of scissors from Agafya, the housekeeper, carefully set about cutting the paper into a perfect rectangle, make a border round it and start work, drawing an eye with an enormous pupil, or a Grecian nose, or a house with a chimney and smoke rising in a spiral, or a dog *en face* looking like a park bench, or a small tree with two little pigeons, and he'd sign it: 'Drawn by Andrey Belovzorov on such-and-such a day of such-and-such a year in the village of Lower Kicking.' He used to be especially zealous for a couple of weeks before Tatyana Borisovna's name-day. He'd be the first to appear with best wishes and he'd be carrying a rolled-up sheet of paper tied with pink ribbon. Tatyana Borisovna'd kiss her nephew on the forehead and untie the ribbon. The paper would unroll and reveal to the curious eye of the beholder a briskly shaded picture of a round temple with columns and an altar in the middle. On the altar there glowed a heart and lay a wreath, while above it, on a winding scroll, was the printed legend: 'To my Auntie and Benefactress Tatyana Borisovna Bogdanova from her Respectful and Loving Nephew as a Token of my Most Profound Affection.' Tatyana Borisovna would kiss him again and present him with a coin. However, she never felt any great attachment to him and Andryusha's fawning attitude didn't appeal to her at all. In the meantime Andryusha grew up. Tatyana Borisovna began to be concerned about his future. An unexpected event provided a way out of her difficulties . . .

It was this: once, some eight years before, she had been visited by a certain Mr Benevolensky, Pyotr Mikhaylych, a collegiate counsellor and knight. Mr Benevolensky had at one time been in the civil service in the nearest county town and had visited Tatyana Borisovna assiduously. Later he had moved to St Petersburg, served in a ministry, achieved a fairly important post and, on one of his frequent journeys on official business, he'd remembered his old acquaintance and made a detour to call on her with the intention of spending a couple of days resting from the cares of the service 'in the bosom of rural tranquillity'.[3] Tatyana Borisovna received him with her usual warmth and Mr Benevolensky ... But before we go on with our story, permit me, dear reader, to acquaint you with this new personage.

Mr Benevolensky was on the fat side, of medium height, soft in appearance, with tiny feet and plump little hands. He used to wear a capacious and extraordinarily neat frockcoat, a tall and broad cravat, linen that was white as snow, a gold chain in his silk waistcoat, a cameo ring on his index finger and a blond wig. He had a way of speaking convincingly and deferentially, would pace about noiselessly, smile pleasantly, roll his eyes about pleasantly and pleasantly bury his chin in his cravat. Generally speaking, he was a pleasant man. The Good Lord had also endowed him with the kindest of hearts with the result that he used to cry and grow emotional easily. Above all, he burned with a selfless passion for art, and it was genuinely selfless, because it was precisely in art that Mr Benevolensky, truth to tell, had absolutely no insight whatever. It was even a matter of some amazement as to how on the strength of what mysterious and incomprehensible laws such a passion had gained such a hold on him. It seems he was a positive man, quite ordinary ... None the less in Russia we have a good many such people.

Love of art and artists gives such people an inexplicably cloying affectedness. To know them and talk to them is torture because they're real blockheads smeared with honey. For example, they never refer to Rafael as Rafael or Correggio as Correggio, it's always, as they say: 'Oh, the divine Sanzio, oh, the inimitable de Allegris,' always emphasizing the 'oh'. Any homegrown, ambitious, overrated and mediocre talent they proclaim a genius or – more correctly – a 'henius'. They never stop babbling about the blue sky of Italy, southern lemons, the fragrant airs of Brenta's banks. 'Oh, Vanya, Vanya,' or 'Oh, Sasha, Sasha,' they say to each other with feeling, 'we must be off to the south, the south ... We're Greeks in spirit, you and I, ancient Greeks!' They can be observed at exhibitions standing in front of the works of Russian painters. (It has to be noted that for the most part all these gentlemen are frightful patriots.) They will take a couple of steps back and throw back their heads, then once more advance towards the picture, their little eyes fattily misting over. 'My God, there you are!' they tend to say at last in voices hoarse with emotion. 'The soulfulness of it, the soulfulness! Oh, the feeling in it, the feeling! Oh, he's shown such soulfulness, a mass of soulfulness! Oh, the way it's done! Masterfully!' And yet what paintings they have in their own drawing-rooms! What artists they have visiting them in the evenings, drinking tea with them and listening to their talk! And what perspective views of their own rooms they bring them, with a broom on the right-hand side, a pile of rubbish on a polished floor, a yellow samovar on a table next the window and the master of the house himself in a dressing-gown and skull-cap with a bright splodge of highlight on his cheek! What long-haired devotees of the Muses visit them with their feverishly condescending smiles! What pale-green young ladies screech their way through songs at their pianos! Because with us in Russia it's now ordained that one cannot be devoted only to one branch of art: it's all or nothing now. And therefore it's not at all surprising that these gentlemen amateurs are also showing strong protective feeling towards Russian literature, particularly the drama ... The *Giacobo Sannazaros*[4] of this world are written for them: the struggle of unrecognized talent against people, against the whole world, something told a thousand times before, shakes their souls to their very depths ...

The day after Mr Benevolensky's arrival, Tatyana Borisovna over tea ordered her nephew to show their guest his drawings.

'So he draws, does he?' uttered Mr Benevolensky, not without surprise, and turned with interest towards Andryusha.

'Certainly he does,' said Tatyana Borisovna. 'He's very fond of it! And he does it by himself without a teacher.'

'Oh, show me, show me,' chimed in Mr Benevolensky.

Andryusha, reddening and smiling, brought their guest his drawing-book.

Mr Benevolensky began to look through it with the air of an expert.

'Good, young man,' he said finally. 'Good, very good.' And he stroked Andryusha on the head. Andryusha gave his hand a flying kiss. 'Well, well, what a talent! I congratulate you, Tatyana Borisovna, I congratulate you.'

'But you see, Pyotr Mikhaylych, I simply cannot find a teacher anywhere here. It's expensive having one from the town. Our neighbours, the Artamonovs, have a painter and they say he's very good, but the young lady there forbids him to teach anyone else for fear he may spoil his taste, as she puts it.'

'Hmm,' said Mr Benevolensky, reflected a while and looked at Andryusha from under his brows. 'Well, we'll give it some thought,' he added and rubbed his hands.

That very day he asked Tatyana Borisovna permission to speak to her alone. They locked themselves away. After half an hour they summoned Andryusha. He entered. Mr Benevolensky was standing by the window with a slightly pink face and shining eyes. Tatyana Borisovna was sitting in a corner and wiping away tears.

'Well, Andryusha,' she began at last, 'you must be grateful to Pyotr Mikhaylych, he is taking you into his keeping and is carrying you off to St Petersburg.'

Andryusha literally froze where he stood.

'You must tell me sincerely,' began Mr Benevolensky in a voice filled with dignity and deference, 'do you wish to be an artist, young man, do you feel a sacred calling towards art?'

'I want to be an artist, Pyotr Mikhaylych,' Andryusha confirmed haltingly.

'In that case I'm very glad. It will be hard for you, of course,' Mr Benevolensky went on, 'to say goodbye to your honoured auntie. You must feel towards her the liveliest gratitude.'

'I adore my auntie,' interrupted Andryusha and blinked his eyes.

'Of course, of course, that is very understandable and does you much credit. But on the other hand, just imagine what joy you'll have in due course . . . your successes . . .'

'Embrace me, Andryusha,' murmured the kind lady of the house. Andryusha flung himself on her neck. 'Well, now thank your benefactor . . .'

Andryusha embraced Mr Benevolensky's stomach, stood on tiptoe and reached out for his hand, which the benefactor, true, was ready to deliver to him, but in no great hurry, as if to say: one's got to play along with a child's wishes and satisfy them but one can have a bit of fun oneself, too. A couple of days later Mr Benevolensky left and carried off his new protégé.

In the course of the first three years of separation Andryusha wrote fairly often and sometimes attached drawings to his letters. Occasionally Mr Benevolensky also added a few words of his own, for the most part words of approval. Later the letters became less and less frequent and finally stopped altogether. For a whole year her nephew was silent and Tatyana Borisovna began to grow worried, when suddenly she received a note with the following content:

Dear auntie!

Three days ago Pyotr Mikhaylych, my protector, passed away. A cruel paralytic stroke deprived me of this final support. Of course, I'm already nearly twenty. In the course of seven years I've had considerable success. I have strong hopes for my talent and am able to live off it. I am not downhearted but nevertheless, if you can, send me as soon as possible 250 roubles in banknotes. I kiss your hand and remain, etc., etc.

Tatyana Borisovna dispatched 250 roubles to her nephew. After a couple of months he made the same demand again. She collected together the last money she had and sent it to him. Six weeks had scarcely gone by since the last parcel had been sent when he made a third demand, ostensibly to buy paints for a portrait commissioned from him by Princess Terteresheneva. Tatyana Borisovna refused. 'In that case,' he wrote to her, 'I intend to travel to you in the country for the benefit of my health.' And in fact, in May of that very year, Andryusha returned to Lower Kicking.

Tatyana Borisovna didn't recognize him at first. Judging by his letter, she'd expected to see someone ill and thin, but what she saw was a broad-shouldered, fat young man, with a broad, red face and lush curly hair. The slender and pale-faced Andryusha had turned into a robust Andrey Ivanov Belovzorov. It wasn't only his appearance that had changed. The punctilious bashfulness, carefulness and neatness of former years had been replaced by the neglectful arrogance of youth and an intolerable slovenliness. He would sway to left and right as he walked and fling himself down into armchairs, sprawl on to the table, lounging about and yawning loudly. He was rude to his auntie and the servants. It was as if he were saying: 'I'm an artist, a free-spirited Cossack! You ought to know how we behave!' It would happen that for whole days at a time he never touched a paint brush. When so-called inspiration got hold of him he'd posture and show off as if drunk, heavily, ineptly and noisily. His cheeks would burn with crude colour and his eyes mist over and he'd launch himself into tirades about his talent, his successes, about how he was developing and progressing . . .

In fact, it turned out that his abilities were barely up to doing decent small portraits. He was an all-round ignoramus and read nothing – and what's the point of reading for an artist? Nature, freedom and poetry – those are his elements. All he needs to know is how to shake his curls and sing like a nightingale and inhale Zhukov tobacco! Russian panache is a fine thing, though only a few can carry it off; the untalented, secondhand artists of this world are impossible. Andrey Ivanych made himself at home at his auntie's because the free food and lodging were evidently to his taste. He bored all her guests to death. He'd sit at a grand piano (Tatyana Borisovna had one) and begin with one finger to pick out 'And races fast the dashing troika';[5] or he'd play chords, pounding on the keys; or for hours at a time he'd murder the romances of Varlamov 'O-O so-olitary pine!' or 'No, doctor, no, come no more',[6] all the while his eyes swimming in fat and his cheeks shining tight as drums . . . Then he'd suddenly burst out with 'Be gone, you restless passions!'[7] and Tatyana Borisovna'd literally shudder.

'It's astonishing,' she remarked to me once, 'the sorts of songs they write nowadays, such melancholy stuff. They wrote different ones in my time. They were sad songs, but still pleasant to listen to. For instance:

> 'Come, come to me in meadowland,
> Where I'll await you vainly;
> Come, come to me in meadowland,
> Where I shed tears all hours . . .
> Alas, you'll come to me in meadowland,
> But late 'twill be, my dearest friend!'[8]

Tatyana Borisovna gave a sly smile.

'I'm su-uffering, I'm su-uffering,' howled her nephew in the next room.

'That's enough, Andryusha.'

'My spirit droops now that you're go-one,' went on the indefatigable singer.

Tatyana Borisovna shook her head. 'My, oh my, these artistic types!'

A year has passed since then. Belovzorov is still living with his auntie and still planning to go to St Petersburg. He's grown broader than he's tall since being in the country. His aunt — who'd have thought it? — can't do enough for him and young ladies of the region are falling in love with him . . .

Many of her former friends have stopped visiting Tatyana Borisovna.

DEATH

I HAVE a neighbour, a youthful squire and youthful hunter. One beautiful July morning I rode over to his place with a proposal that he should join me on a grouse shoot. He agreed. 'Only,' he said, 'let's go by way of some small property of mine in the Zusha[1] direction. I'd like to have a look at Chaplygino, my oak wood, d'you know it? They're cutting it down.'

'Let's be off, then.'

He ordered a horse to be saddled and dressed himself in a short green jacket with bronze buttons bearing the image of a boar's head, pulled on a worsted game-bag and silver flask, and having thrown a new French sports-gun over his shoulder, disported himself before the mirror, not without some approbation, and shouted for his dog, Esperance, a gift from a cousin, an elderly maiden lady with a warm heart but without a hair on her head.

We set off. My neighbour took with him the local guardian of the peace, Arkhip, a stout and thick-set peasant with a square-shaped face and cheekbones of positively antediluvian dimensions, and a young man of about nineteen, lean, fair-haired and shortsighted, with sloping shoulders and a long neck, Mr Gottlieb von der Kock, recently engaged as a manager from the Baltic provinces. My neighbour had not long before inherited his estate. It had come to him as an inheritance from his aunt, Kardon-Katayeva, the widow of a state's counsellor, a woman of unusual obesity who, even when lying in bed, had a habit of emitting protracted and piteous groans. We reached his small property and Ardalion Mikhaylich (my neighbour) said, addressing his companions: 'Wait for me out here in the clearing.'

The German bowed, slid from his horse, extracted a small book from his pocket – a novel, it appeared, by Johanna Schopenhauer[2] –

and seated himself in the shade of a bush, while Arkhip remained out in the sun for a solid hour without budging an inch. Ardalion Mikhaylich and I made a round of the undergrowth, but were unable to find a single bird. My friend announced that he was determined to set off for his wood. I was also far from convinced that our hunting would be successful on such a day and trailed along behind him. We returned to the clearing. The German made a note of his page, stood up, placed his book in his pocket and, not without some difficulty, mounted his short-tailed reject of a mare which neighed and kicked at the slightest touch. Arkhip sprang to life, gave a sharp tug at both reins, clapped his legs against the animal's flanks and eventually managed to set off on his cowed and shaken little steed. Off we went.

Ardalion Mikhaylich's wood had been known to me since my childhood. I had often gone to Chaplygino in the company of my French tutor, Monsieur Désiré Fleury, an excellent chap (who, however, only just avoided ruining my health irretrievably by forcing me to take the medicines of Leroy every evening). The entire wood consisted of some two or three hundred enormous oaks and ash trees. Their stately, powerful trunks used to stand out in magnificent dark relief against the golden transparency of the green-leaved rowans and nut trees; rising on high they composed their fine proportions against the lucid blue sky and there spread out the domes of their far-reaching, angular branches; hawks, merlins, kestrels, all whistled and hovered above their motionless crests and colourful woodpeckers tapped away loudly at their thick bark; the resonant song of the blackbird suddenly rang out amid the thick foliage in the wake of the lilting call of the oriole; below, in the undergrowth, robins, siskins and chiffchaffs chirruped and sang; finches darted to and fro across the paths; white hares ran along the edge of the wood in cautious stops and starts, and nut-brown squirrels leapt friskily from tree to tree, suddenly stopping with tails raised above their heads. In the grass, around tall ant-hills and in the mild shadiness offered by the beautiful fretwork of ferns, violets used to flower, and lilies of the valley, and reddish mushrooms grew, russula, emetic agaric, milk agaric, fairy clubs and red fly agaric; and in the meadows, among the widespread bushes, wild strawberries would grow crimson . . . And what deep shade there was in the wood! At noon, when the heat was

greatest, it would be dark as night: peaceful, fragrant, moist ...
Time would pass for me so gaily at Chaplygino that it was, I
admit, not without a feeling of sadness that I now rode into this
all-too-familiar wood. The bitter, snowless winter of 1840 had not
spared my old friends, the oaks and ash trees. Desiccated and naked,
covered here and there with diseased leaf, they rose sadly above
the young trees which 'had supplanted them but not replaced
them' ...*3 Some, well covered with foliage on their lower
boughs, raised on high, as if in reproach and desperation, their
lifeless, broken upper branches; from other trees amidst foliage
which was still quite thick, although not as abundant or overflowing as it was formerly, there stuck out fat, dry limbs of dead
wood; from others, the bark had already fallen away; and there
were some that had fallen down completely and lay rotting on the
ground like corpses. Who could have foreseen that there would
have been shadows in Chaplygino, where once there wasn't a
single shadow to be found! As I looked at the dying trees, I
thought: surely you must know shame and bitterness? And I
recalled the lines from Koltsov:[4]

> Where have you gone to
> Speech high and mighty,
> Strength so haughty,
> Courage so kingly?
> Where is it now
> The green sap and the power?

'Why was it, Ardalion Mikhaylich,' I began, 'that these trees
weren't cut down the year afterwards? They won't give you a tenth
of what they were worth before.'

He simply shrugged his shoulders.

'You should have asked my aunt – merchants came to her, brought
money, badgered her.'

* In 1840 there were most cruel frosts and snow did not fall before the end of
December; all the foliage was frozen to death, and many fine oak forests were
destroyed by this merciless winter. It is difficult to replace them; the fertility of the
earth is obviously declining; on waste lands that have been 'reserved' (that is to say,
which have had icons carried round them) birches and aspens are growing up of
their own accord in place of the noble trees which used to grow there; for we know
no other way of propagating our woodlands.

'*Mein Gott! Mein Gott!*' von der Kock exclaimed at every step. 'Such a sham! Such a sham!'

'What sham?' my neighbour remarked with a smile.

'This eez a shame, what I wishes to te*ll*.' (It is well known that all Germans, once they have finally mastered our Russian letter 'l', dwell on it amazingly.)

His compassion was particularly aroused by the oaks which lay on the ground – and no wonder, for many a miller would have paid a high price for them. But our guardian of the peace, Arkhip, maintained an imperturbable composure and showed not the least sign of regret; on the contrary, it was even with a certain pleasure that he jumped over them and lashed at them with his riding crop.

We made our way to the place where the felling was going on, when suddenly, after the sound of a falling tree, there resounded cries and talk, and a few seconds later a young peasant, pale and dishevelled, raced towards us out of a thicket.

'What's the matter? Where are you running?' Ardalion Mikhaylich asked him.

He stopped at once.

'Ardalion Mikhaylich, sir, there's been an accident.'

'What's the matter?'

'Maxim, sir, has been knocked down by a tree.'

'How did it happen? Do you mean Maxim the contractor?'

'Yes, sir, the contractor. We started cutting down an ash tree, and he stood and watched ... He was standing there a long time, and then he went to the well to get water, like he wanted to have a drink, see. Then all of a sudden the ash tree starts creaking and falling right down on him. We shout to him: run, run, run ... He could've thrown himself to one side, but instead he decides to run straight on ... he got scared, you know. The ash tree's top boughs fell on him and covered him. God only knows why it fell so quickly. Probably it was all rotten inside.'

'So it struck Maxim, did it?'

'It struck him, sir.'

'Did it kill him?'

'No, sir, he's still alive, but it's no good: his legs and arms are broken. I was just running to get Seliverstych, the doctor.'

Ardalion Mikhaylich ordered the guardian of the peace to gallop into the village for Seliverstych and himself set off at a brisk trot for the site of the felling. I followed him.

We found the wretched Maxim on the ground. Ten or so peasants were gathered round him. We alighted from our horses. He was hardly groaning at all, though occasionally he opened wide his eyes, as if looking around him with surprise, and bit his blue lips. His chin quivered, his hair was stuck to his temples and his chest rose irregularly: he was clearly dying. The faint shadow of a young lime tree ran calmly aslant his face. We bent down to him, and he recognized Ardalion Mikhaylich.

'Sir,' he began to say in a scarcely audible voice, 'the priest . . . send for him . . . order to send . . . God has . . . has punished me . . . my legs, arms, all broken . . . today . . . Sunday . . . but I . . . but I . . . you see . . . I didn't let the lads off.'

He fell silent. His breath came in short gasps.

'My money . . . the wife . . . give it to the wife . . . after what's owing . . . Onisim knows . . . who I . . . owe what . . .'

'We've sent for the doctor, Maxim,' my neighbour said. 'Perhaps you won't die after all.'

He wanted to open wide his eyes and with an effort raised his brows and eyelids.

'No, I'll die. See . . . see, there she's coming, there she is, there . . . Forgive me, lads, if I've in any way . . .'

'God'll forgive you, Maxim Andreyich,' the peasants said in husky unison and removed their caps. 'And you forgive us.'

He gave a sudden desperate shake of the head, lifted his chest regretfully and again sank back.

'He shouldn't have to die here,' Ardalion Mikhaylich exclaimed. 'Lads, get the mat from the cart over there and let's carry him to the hospital.'

A couple of men rushed to the cart.

'Off of Efim . . . Sychovsky,' the dying man began to babble, 'I bought a horse yesterday . . . I put money down . . . So the horse is mine . . . see the wife gets that as well . . .'

They began to lay him on the mat. He started trembling all over, like a shot bird, and straightened up.

'He's dead,' the peasants said.

Silently, we mounted our horses and rode off.

The death of the wretched Maxim put me in a reflective mood. What an astonishing thing is the death of a Russian peasant! His state of mind before death could be called neither one of indifference, nor one of stupidity; he dies as if he is performing a ritual act, coldly and simply.

A few years ago a peasant belonging to another country neighbour of mine was burned in a barn. (He would, in fact, have remained in the barn had not a visitor from town pulled him out half dead: he doused himself in a pitcher of water and at a run broke down the door under the overhang which was already alight.) I visited him in his hut. It was dark inside, the atmosphere stuffy and smoky. 'Where is the sick man?' I inquired.

'Over there, sir, above the stove,' answered the singsong voice of an old woman weighed down by her burden of grief.

I approached and found a peasant covered in a sheepskin, breathing painfully.

'Well, how are you feeling?'

The sick man grew restless, wanted to raise himself, but he was covered in wounds and close to death.

'Lie down, lie down. Well? How is it?'

'I'm poorly, that's for sure,' he said.

'Does it hurt you?'

No answer.

'Is there anything you need?'

Silence.

'Shall I order some tea to be sent to you, eh?'

'There's no need.'

I left him and sat down on a bench. I sat for a quarter of an hour, half an hour, and all the while the silence of the grave reigned in the hut. In one corner, by a table under the icons, a five-year-old girl was hiding, eating bread. From time to time her mother warned her to be quiet. Out on the porch people walked about, clattered and talked and a sister-in-law of the dying man was chopping cabbage.

'Ha, Aksinya!' he mumbled eventually.

'What is it?'

'Give me a little *kvas*.'

Aksinya gave him some. The silence once more returned. I asked in a whisper: 'Have they given him the last rites?'

'Yes.'

In that case, everything was in order: he was simply awaiting death, nothing else. I could not stand it any more and left.

On another occasion, I remember, I called in at the hospital in Red Hills village to see the assistant doctor, Kapiton, an acquaintance of mine and a devoted hunter.

The hospital occupied what had formerly been the wing of the manor. The lady of the manor had herself established it – that is, she had ordered to be placed over the door a blue sign with letters in white reading: 'Red Hills hospital', and she had herself entrusted to Kapiton a beautiful album for noting down the names of the sick. On the first page of this album one of the benevolent lady's sycophants and time-servers had inscribed the following trite verses:

> *Dans ces beaux lieux, où règne l'allégresse,*
> *Ce temple fut ouvert par la Beauté;*
> *De vos seigneurs admirez la tendresse,*
> *Bons habitants de Krasnogorié!*★

And another gentleman had added below:

> *Et moi aussi j'aime la nature!*
> Jean Kobyliatnikoff

The assistant doctor had purchased six beds out of his own money and, after calling down a blessing on his work, had set about caring for all God's people. Apart from himself, the hospital had a staff of two; Pavel, a wood-carver, given to fits of madness, and a woman with a withered arm, Melikitrisa, who was the hospital cook. Both of them made up medicines, dried herbs and concocted herbal infusions; they also used to subdue patients if they became delirious. The mad wood-carver was sullen in appearance and a man of few words: by night he used to sing a ditty concerning 'a beautiful Venus' and he would importune every visitor to the hospital with the request that he be allowed to marry a certain Malanya, a girl long since dead. The woman with the withered arm used to beat him and made him look after the turkeys.

One day I was sitting with Kapiton. We had just begun to chat

★ Krasnogorié = Red Hills.

about our most recent hunting expedition when suddenly a cart drove into the yard with an unusually fat grey horse in harness (of the dray-horse variety only used by millers). In the cart sat a solid-looking peasant, in a new coat, sporting a mottled beard.

'Hey there, Vasily Dmitrich,' Kapiton shouted out of the window, 'you're welcome to come in ... It's the Lybovshinsky miller,' he whispered to me.

The peasant climbed down from the cart, groaning as he did so, and entered Kapiton's room, where he glanced round for the icon and crossed himself.

'Well, Vasily Dmitrich, what's new? You're ill, that's obvious: your face looks pasty.'

'Yes, Kapiton Timofeyich, something's wrong.'

'What's the trouble?'

'It's like this, Kapiton Timofeyich. Not long ago I bought mill-stones in the town. Well, I brought them home, but when I started unloading them from the cart, I put too much into it, you know, and something went pop in my stomach, just as if it'd got torn. And from then on I've felt bad all the time. Today it hurts real bad.'

'Hmmm,' murmured Kapiton and sniffed some tobacco, 'that means a hernia. How long ago did this happen to you?'

'It's ten days ago, now.'

'Ten?' Kapiton drew in breath through his teeth and shook his head. 'Let me feel. Well, Vasily Dmitrich,' he said at last, 'I'm sorry for you, because I like you, but that condition of yours is not at all good. You're ill right enough, and no joking. Stay here with me, and I'll do all I can for you, but I don't promise anything.'

'You really mean it's that bad?' muttered the astonished miller.

'Yes, Vasily Dmitrich, it's that bad. If you'd come to me a couple of days earlier, I'd have been able to put you right with a flick of the wrist. But now you've got an inflammation here, that's what it is, and before long it'll turn into St Anthony's fire.'

'But it's just not possible, Kapiton Timofeyich.'

'And I'm telling you it is.'

'But how can it be!' (In response Kapiton shrugged his shoulders.) 'Am I going to die because of this silly business?'

'I'm not saying that. I'm simply telling you to stay here.'

The peasant thought about this a bit, looked at the floor, then glanced up at us, scratched the nape of his neck and was ready to put his cap on.

'Where are you off to, Vasily Dmitrich?'

'Where to? It's obvious where to – home, if things are that bad. If things are like that, there's a lot to be put in order.'

'But you'll do yourself real harm, Vasily Dmitrich. I'm surprised that you even got here at all. Stay here, I beg you.'

'No, Brother Kapiton Timofeyich, if I'm going to die, I'll die at home. If I died here, God knows what a mess there'd be at home.'

'It's still not certain, Vasily Dmitrich, how it's going to turn out ... Of course, it's dangerous, there's no doubt about that, and that's why you ought to stay here.'

The peasant shook his head. 'No, Kapiton Timofeyich, I won't stay. Just you write out a prescription for a little medicine.'

'Medicine by itself won't help.'

'I'm not staying, I'm telling you that.'

'Well, as you wish ... Mind you, you've only yourself to blame afterwards!'

Kapiton tore a little page out of the album and, after writing out a prescription, gave some advice on what still had to be done. The peasant took the sheet of paper, gave Kapiton a half-rouble piece, walked out of the room and sat in his cart.

'Goodbye, then, Kapiton Timofeyich. Think kindly of me and don't forget the little orphans, if it should happen ...'

'Stay here, Vasily, stay here!'

The peasant merely gave a shake of the head, struck the horse with the reins and rode out of the yard. I went out on to the street and looked after him. The road was muddy and pot-holed. The miller drove carefully, without hurrying, skilfully guiding the horse and bowing to those he met on the way ... Four days later he was dead.

In general, Russians surprise one when it comes to dying. I can recall to mind now many who have died. You I recall, my friend of old, the student who never completed his education, Avenir Sorokoumov, fine and most noble person! I see again your consumptive, greenish face, your thin, russet-coloured hair, your timid smile, your fascinated gaze and long-limbed body; I hear your weak, kindly voice. You lived at the house of the Great Russian landowner, Gur Krupyanikov, taught Russian grammar, geography and history to his children, Fofa and Zyoza, and patiently endured the heavy-handed humour of Gur himself, the crude familiarity of his butler, the tasteless pranks of his wicked little boys and not without a bitter smile, but also without complaint, fulfilled all the capricious demands made upon you by his bored wife; despite this, how you used to enjoy your leisure, how filled with beatitude were your evenings, after supper, when, finally rid of all obligations and duties, you would sit by the window, thoughtfully smoking your pipe or greedily thumbing through some mutilated and much-fingered copy of a thick journal which had been brought from town by a surveyor who was just as homeless a wretch as you were! How you used to enjoy in those days all kinds of verses and stories, how easily tears would be brought to your eyes, with what pleasure you used to laugh, how rich was your childishly pure soul in sincere love for mankind and in high-minded compassion for all that was good and beautiful! True, you were not remarkable for undue wit: nature had endowed you neither with a good memory, nor with diligence; at the university you were considered one of the worst students; you used to sleep during lectures and preserved a solemn silence at examinations. But whose eyes lit up with joy, who used to catch his breath at the success and accomplishments of a fellow-student? You did, Avenir ... Who believed blindly in the high calling of his friends, who took such pride in extolling them, who was so fierce in their defence? Who knew neither envy nor ambition, who selflessly sacrificed his own interests, who gladly deferred to people who were unworthy so much as to unlatch the buckle of his shoes? ... You did, you did, my good Avenir! I remember how you said goodbye to your comrades with a heavy heart when you went off to your 'temporary employment'; evil forebodings tormented you ... And for good reason: in the country things were bad for you; there was no one in the country at whose feet you could sit in reverent attentiveness, no one to wonder at, no one to love .... Both the provincials and the educated landowners treated you simply as a schoolteacher, some displaying rudeness, others indifference. And you, for your own part, cut a poor figure with your shyness, and blushing, and sweatiness, and your stammer ... Even your health was not improved by the country air; you melted away, poor fellow, like a wax candle! True, your little room looked out on to the garden; cherry trees, apple trees and limes sprinkled their delicate blossoms on your table, your ink-pot and your books; on the wall hung a little pale-blue silk cushion for a watch, given to you as a parting gift by a warm-hearted and sensitive little German governess with fair curls and sweet blue eyes; and sometimes an old friend from your Moscow days would visit and put you in an ecstasy of excitement over his own or another's verses; but your loneliness, the unbearable grind of your vocation as a teacher, the impossibility of freeing yourself, but the endless autumns, the endless winters, the relentless advance of disease . . . Wretched, wretched Avenir!

I visited Sorokoumov shortly before his death. He was almost unable to walk. The landowner, Gur Krupyanikov, had not driven him from his house, but had ceased to pay him and had hired another teacher for Zyoza. Fofa had been put in the cadet corps. Avenir was sitting beside the window in an ancient Voltairean armchair. The weather was wonderful. A bright autumn sky shone a gay blue above a dark-brown row of naked limes; here and there on their boughs the last, radiantly golden leaves fluttered and rustled. The frost-bound earth perspired and thawed in the sunlight; its slanting, pink-tinged rays struck lengthwise across the pale grass; a faint crackling seemed to dwell in the air, and in the garden the voices of workmen had a clear, sharp resonance.

Avenir wore an antiquated Bokhara dressing-gown; a green neckerchief cast a deathly hue upon his terribly wasted face. He was extremely delighted to see me, stretched out his hand, began to say something and started coughing. I gave him time to compose himself and took a seat near him. On Avenir's knees lay an exercise book into which the poems of Koltsov had been painstakingly copied. Giving a smile, he tapped the book with his hand.

'That's a poet,' he managed to say, with an effort holding back his cough, and embarked on declaiming some of the verse in a scarcely audible voice:

> What if a falcon's
> Wings are tied?
> What if all ways
> Are to him denied?[5]

I stopped him; the doctor had forbidden him to talk. I knew how to indulge him. Sorokoumov had never, as they say, 'followed' science, but he was always curious to know what, so to speak, the great minds of the present day had been thinking and what conclusions had been reached. There had been a time when he used to catch a fellow-student in a corner and began plying him with questions: he would listen, wonder, believe every word and afterwards repeat it all as his own. German philosophy held a particularly strong fascination for him. I began to tell him about Hegel (as you can appreciate, these matters relate to days long since gone by). Avenir gave affirmative nods of the head, raised his eyebrows, smiled, saying in a whisper, 'I understand, I understand! . . . Ah, that's good, that's good!' The child-like curiosity of the dying man, of this poor, neglected, homeless fellow, touched me, I confess, to the point of tears. It must be said that Avenir, in contrast to most consumptives, never deluded himself in the least about his illness. And why should he? He did not sigh over it, and was not crushed in spirit by it, nor did he once make reference to his condition.

Gathering his strength, he began to talk about Moscow, about fellow-students, about Pushkin and the theatre and Russian literature; he recalled our feastings, the heated debates which occurred in our circle and with regret he uttered the names of two or three friends who had died . . .

'Do you remember Dasha?' he added finally. 'There was a soul of pure gold! A pure heart! And how she loved me! . . . What's happened to her now? Probably dried up, wasted away, hasn't she, poor thing?'

I did not dare to disenchant the sick man – and, indeed, there was no reason for him to be told that his Dasha was now fatter than she was tall and carrying on with merchants, the brothers Kondachkov, and powdered and rouged herself, and spoke in a squeaky voice and used bad language.

However, I thought, looking at his exhausted features: is it impossible to drag him out of this place? Perhaps there is still a chance of curing him . . . But Avenir would not let me finish what I was proposing.

'No, thank you, good friend,' he murmured, 'it doesn't matter where one dies. You can see I won't live until the winter, so why bother people unnecessarily? I'm used to this house. It's true that the people in charge here . . .'

'. . . are bad people, do you mean?' I inserted.

'No, not bad, just rather like bits of wood. But I haven't any reason to complain about them. There are neighbours: Kasatkin, the landowner, has a daughter who is educated, kind, the sweetest of girls . . . not one of the proud kind . . .'

Sorokoumov once again had a fit of coughing.

'It would be all right,' he continued, having got his breath back, 'if they'd just allow me to smoke a pipe . . . No, I'm not going to die before I smoke a whole pipe!' he added, winking slyly at me. 'Good Lord, I've lived enough, and I've known some good people . . .'

'You ought at least to write to your relatives,' I interrupted him.

'What for? To ask for help? They won't be able to help me, and they'll learn about me soon enough when I die. There's no point in talking about it . . . Better, tell me what you saw when you were abroad.'

I began to tell him. He stared at me, drinking in my words. Towards evening, I left, and about ten days later I received the following letter from Mr Krupyanikov:

With this letter I have the honour to acquaint you, my dear sir, with the fact that your friend, the student Mr Avenir Sorokoumov, who has been residing at my house, passed away four days ago at two o'clock in the afternoon and was today given a funeral in my parish at my expense. He begged me to send you the accompanying volumes and exercise books. It transpired that he had twenty-two and one half roubles in his possession, which, together with his other things, will be delivered into the possession of his relatives. Your friend passed away in full command of his senses and, it may be said, with a similar degree of insensitiveness, without exhibiting the slightest signs of regret even when we were saying goodbye to him in a family group. My wife, Kleopatra Alexandrovna, sends you her respects. The death of your friend could not but have an adverse effect on her nerves; so far as I am concerned, I am well, God be praised, and I have the honour to remain –
                    Your most humble servant,
                    G. Krupyanikov.

There are many other examples that occur to me, so many that it would be impossible to tell them all. I will limit myself to one only.

An elderly lady, a landowner, was dying in my presence. The priest began to read the prayer for the dying over her, when he suddenly noticed that the sick woman was in fact passing on and hurriedly handed her the cross. The elderly lady took umbrage at this.

'Why all the hurry, sir?' she said with a tongue that was already stiffening. 'You'll be in time . . .'

She lay back and she had just placed her hand under her pillow when she drew her last breath. There was a rouble piece lying under the pillow: she had wanted to pay the priest for reading the prayer for her own death . . .

Yes, Russians surprise one when it comes to dying!

SINGERS

————————— ❧ —————————

T HE small village of Kolotovka, which belonged at one time to a female landowner who had been nicknamed locally The Stripper on account of her fast and lively temperament (her real name remained unknown), but which now belongs to some St Petersburg German, is situated on the slope of a bare hill, split from top to bottom by an awful ravine that gapes like an abyss and winds its pitted and eroded course right down the centre of the main street, dividing the two sides of the miserable settlement more effectively than a river since a river can at least be bridged. A few emaciated willows straggle timidly down its sandy sides; on the very bottom, which is dry and yellow as copper, lie enormous slabs of clayey stone. There is no denying that its appearance is far from happy, and yet all who live in the locality are thoroughly familiar with the road to Kolotovka, travelling there gladly and often.

At the head of the ravine, a few steps from the point where it begins as a narrow crevice, there stands a small, square hut, quite by itself and apart from the others. It is roofed with straw and it has a chimney; one window is turned towards the ravine like a watchful eye, and on winter evenings, when illumined from within, may be seen far off through the faint frost-haze twinkling like a lodestar for many a passing peasant. A small blue sign has been fixed above the door of the hut, since this hut is a tavern, nicknamed The Welcome.* Drink cannot be said to be sold in this tavern below the normal price but it is patronized much more assiduously than all the other establishments of this kind in the locality. The reason for this is mine host, Nikolay Ivanych.

* The Welcome is the name given to any place where people gather willingly, any kind of shelter.

Nikolay Ivanych — at one time a well-built, curly-headed, red-cheeked youngster, but now an extraordinarily stout, greying man with a plump face, slyly good-humoured eyes and fleshy temples crisscrossed with wrinkles as fine as threads — has lived more than twenty years in Kolotovka. He is a busy and competent man, like the majority of tavern-keepers. Though outstanding neither for unusual kindliness, nor for a gift of the gab, he possesses the knack of attracting and keeping his patrons, who are happy after their fashion to sit in front of his brew under the calm and welcoming, albeit watchful, gaze of such a phlegmatic host. He has a great deal of sound good sense; he is equally familiar with the way of life of the landowners, the peasants and the townspeople; when difficulties arise he can offer advice that is not at all stupid, but, being a man of cautious and egotistical nature, he prefers to remain on the sidelines and only by remote, as it were, hints, uttered without the least apparent intent, does he suggest to his patrons — and then only his favourite patrons — the right course to take. He has a good grasp of all the important or interesting things a Russian should know: of horses, cattle, forestry, brick-making, crockery, textiles, and leatherware, singing and dancing. When he has no patrons, he usually sits like a sack on the ground outside the door of his hut, his thin little legs drawn up under him, and exchanges pleasantries with all who pass by. He has seen a great deal in his time and has survived more than his fair number of small-time gentry who have dropped in on him for 'a spot of the pure stuff'; he knows all that's going on in the entire region and yet he never gossips, never even so much as gives a sign that he knows what a policeman with the keenest nose for crime could not even suspect. He keeps what he knows to himself, occasionally chuckling and shuffling his tankards about. Neighbours show him respect: General Sherepetenko, the highest ranking of the landowners in the county, gives him a deferential bow every time he drives past his little hut. Nikolay Ivanych is a man with influence: he forced a well-known horse thief to return a horse which he had taken from the yard of one of his friends and talked persuasively to peasants from a neighbouring village who were reluctant to accept a new manager, and so on. But one mustn't imagine that he does such things out of a love of justice or community zeal — oh, no! He simply endeavours to put a stop to whatever might disturb his own peace of mind. Nikolay Ivanych is married and he has children. His wife, a brisk, sharp-nosed woman of middle-class origins, with eyes that dart to and fro, has recently grown plump, like her husband. He relies upon her for everything, and it is she who keeps the money under lock and key. Loud-mouthed drunkards are wary of her, nor is she fond of them: there is little profit to be got from them, only a lot of noise; the taciturn and serious patrons are more to her liking. Nikolay Ivanych's children are still little; the first children all died in infancy, but the surviving ones have grown to look like their parents. It is a pleasure to see the intelligent little faces of those healthy boys.

It was an intolerably hot July day when, slowly dragging one foot after another, I and my dog climbed up the hill beside the Kolotovka ravine in the direction of The Welcome tavern. The sun blazed in the sky, as if fit to explode; it steamed and baked everything remorselessly, and the air was full of suffocating dust. Glossy-feathered rooks and crows hung their beaks and gazed miserably at those who passed by, as if literally imploring their sympathy. Only the sparrows kept their spirits up and, spreading their feathers, chirruped away more fiercely than ever, squabbled round the fences, took off in flight from the dusty roadway and soared in grey clouds above the plantations of green hemp. I was tormented by thirst. There was no water to be got close by: in Kolotovka, as in so many other steppe villages, the peasants, for want of springs and wells, are accustomed to drink a kind of liquid mud from the ponds ... But who would call that beastly drink water? I wanted to beg a glass of beer or *kvas* from Nikolay Ivanych.

It has to be confessed that at no time of year does Kolotovka offer a spectacle to please the eye; but it evokes an especially sad feeling when the glittering July sun pours its merciless rays down on the rust-coloured and only partly thatched roofs of the huts, and the deep ravine, and the scorched, dust-laden common ground where gaunt chickens roam about hopelessly on spindly legs, and the grey, skeletal frame of a house of aspen wood, which has holes in place of windows and is all that remains of the former manor house (now overgrown with nettles, wormwood and other weeds), and the dark-green, literally sun-smelted pond, covered with bits of goose fluff and edged with half-dried mud, and a dam knocked askew, beside which, on earth so finely trodden it resembles ash, sheep huddle miserably together, sneezing and scarcely able to draw breath from the heat, and with patient despondency hang their heads as low as possible, as if awaiting the time when the intolerable heat will finally pass.

With weary steps I drew close to Nikolay Ivanych's dwelling, arousing, quite naturally, a state of excitement in the little boys which grew into an intently senseless staring, and in the dogs a state of dissatisfaction which expressed itself in barks so shrill and malicious that it seemed their innards were being torn out of them and they were left with nothing to do but cough and catch their breaths – when suddenly there appeared in the tavern doorway a tall, hatless man in a frieze overcoat tied low down with a blue sash. To all appearances he was a house-serf; clusters of grey hair rose untidily above his dry and wrinkled face. He called to someone, making hurried motions with his arms which clearly waved about a good deal more expansively than he wished. It was obvious that he had already managed to have something to drink.

'Come on, come on now!' he burbled, with an effort raising his thick eyebrows. 'Come on, Winker, will you! You just go at a crawl, you do, mate. It's no good, it isn't. Here they're waitin' for you, and you just goin' at a crawl . . . Come on.'

'Well, I'm coming, I'm coming,' responded a querulous voice, and there appeared from behind the hut on the right a smallish man, who was fat and lame. He wore a fairly smart cloth jacket, with his arm through one of the sleeves; a tall, pointed cap, tilted directly forward over his brows, lent his round, puffy face a sly and comic look. His little yellow eyes darted about and a strained, deferential smile never left his thin lips; while his nose, long and sharp, projected impudently in front of him like a rudder. 'I'm coming, my dear fellow,' he continued, limping in the direction of the drinking establishment. 'Why're you calling to me? Who's waiting for me?'

'Why'm I callin' to you?' the man in the frieze overcoat said reproachfully. 'Oh, you, Winker, you're a wonder, mate, you are – they're callin' you to the tavern, and you go askin' why? It's all good fellows that're waitin' for you – Yashka the Turk's there, and Gentleman Wildman, and Barrowboy from Zhizdra. Yashka's made a bet with Barrowboy – a pot of ale he's staked on whoever gets the better of whom, who sings the best, that's to say . . . See?'

'Yashka'll be singing?' the man nicknamed Winker asked with lively interest. 'Do you really mean that, you Nit?'

'I do mean that,' the Nit answered with dignity, 'and there's no need for you to be askin' silly questions. 'Course he'll be singin' if he's made a bet, you old bumbler you, you ruddy menace, Winker!'

'Well, get going, then, you dimwit!' Winker retorted.

'Come on, then, and give me a kiss, me old dear,' the Nit said in his prattling way, holding wide his arms.

'Look at him, gone soft in the head in his old age,' Winker responded contemptuously, thrusting him aside with his elbow, and both of them, bending down, went in through the low door.

The conversation I had heard strongly aroused my curiosity. More than once rumours had reached me about Yashka the Turk as the best singer in the region, and now I was suddenly presented with a chance of hearing him in competition with another master. I redoubled my steps and entered the establishment.

Probably few of my readers have had a chance of seeing the inside of a rural tavern; but we hunters drop in anywhere and everywhere! They are exceedingly simply arranged. They consist usually of a dark entrance and a parlour divided in two by a partition beyond which none of the patrons has the right to go. In this partition, above a wide oak table, there is a big longitudinal opening. The drink is sold at this table, or counter. Labelled bottles of various sizes stand in rows on the shelves directly opposite the opening. In the forward part of the hut, which is given over to the patrons, there are benches, one or two empty barrels and a corner table. Rural taverns are for the most part fairly dark, and you will hardly ever see on the log walls any of those brightly coloured popular prints with which most peasant huts are adorned.

When I entered The Welcome tavern, quite a large company was already gathered there.

Behind the counter, as usual, and occupying almost the whole width of the opening, stood Nikolay Ivanych, dressed in a colourful calico shirt and, with a lazy smirk on his plump cheeks, pouring out with his large white hand two glasses of liquor for the two friends who had just entered, Winker and the Nit; while at his back, in a corner beside the window, his sharp-eyed wife could be seen. In the middle of the parlour stood Yashka the Turk, a thin, lithe man of about twenty-three dressed in a long-hemmed coat of a light shade of blue. He looked like a daredevil factory lad and, so it seemed, could hardly boast of perfect health. His sunken cheeks, large restless grey eyes, straight nose with delicate spirited nostrils, white sloping forehead below backswept light-auburn curls, large but beautiful, expressive lips – his entire face betokened a man of sensibility and passion. He was in a state of great excitement: he blinked his eyes, breathed irregularly and his hands shook feverishly – indeed, he was in a fever, that anxious, sudden state of fever which is familiar to everyone who speaks or sings before an assembled company. Beside him stood a man of about forty, broad-shouldered, with broad cheekbones, a low forehead, narrow Mongol eyes, short flat nose, square chin and black shiny hair as hard as bristles. The expression on his dark, lead-coloured face, especially on his pale lips, could have been called savage, had it not also been so tranquilly thoughtful. He hardly stirred at all and did no more than look slowly round him from time to time, like an ox looking round from beneath a yoke. He was dressed in a kind of very worn frockcoat with smooth bronze buttons; an old black silk kerchief encased his huge neck. He was called Gentleman Wildman. Directly opposite him, on a bench beneath the icons, sat Yashka's rival, Barrowboy from Zhizdra. He was a thickset man of about thirty, small in stature, pock-marked and curly-headed, with a blunt turned-up nose, lively brown eyes and a wispy little beard. He was glancing rapidly about him, his hands tucked under him, carelessly chattering and now and then tapping his dandified, fancifully decorated boots. His dress consisted of a new thin peasant coat of grey cloth with a velveteen collar, to which the edge of the red shirt tightly fastened round his neck stood out in sharp contrast. In the opposite corner, to the right of the door, there sat at a table some little peasant or other wearing a narrow, worn-out coat with an enormous tear in the shoulder. Sunlight streamed in a pale yellow flood through the dusty panes of the two small windows and seemed to be unable to overcome the habitual darkness of the parlour: everything was so meagrely lit that it seemed blurred. Despite this, the air was almost cool, and all sense of the suffocating and oppressive heat slipped from my shoulders like a discarded burden as soon as I stepped through the porch.

My arrival, as I could sense, somewhat confused Nikolay Ivanych's guests to start with; but seeing that he bowed to me as to someone familiar, they were put at their ease and paid no more attention to me. I asked for some beer and sat down in the corner next to the peasant in the torn coat.

'Well, what's doing?' the Nit suddenly roared, drinking back his glass at a gulp and accompanying his exclamation with the same strange waving gestures, without which he evidently never pronounced a single word. 'What're we waiting for? Begin now, if you're goin' to begin. Eh? Yashka?'

'Get started, get started,' Nikolay Ivanych added by way of encouragement.

'We'll begin, presuming it's all right,' Barrowboy announced with cold-blooded audacity and a self-confident smile. 'I'm ready.'

'And I'm ready,' Yakov declared excitedly.

'Well, get going, lads, get going,' Winker hissed squeakily.

But, despite the unanimously expressed wish, no one began; Barrowboy did not even rise from the bench. There was a general air of expectancy.

'Begin!' said Gentleman Wildman in a sharp, sullen voice.

Yakov shuddered. Barrowboy rose, gave a tug at his sash and coughed.

'An' who's to begin?' he asked in a slightly less confident voice, speaking to Gentleman Wildman who continued to stand motionlessly in the middle of the room, his stout legs set wide apart and his powerful arms thrust into the pockets of his broad trousers, almost up to the elbows.

'It's you, you, Barrowboy,' the Nit started babbling, 'you're the one, mate.'

Gentleman Wildman looked at him from beneath his brows. The Nit gave a faint croak, got confused, glanced somewhere up towards the ceiling, shrugged his shoulders and became silent.

'Throw for it,' Gentleman Wildman announced in measured tones. 'Put the ale on the counter.'

Nikolay Ivanych bent down, lifted the pot of ale from the floor with a groan and set it on the table.

Gentleman Wildman glanced at Yakov and said: 'Well!' Yakov dug around in his pockets and produced a copper which he tested between his teeth. Barrowboy extracted from beneath the hem of his coat a new leather money-bag, slowly untied the string and, having poured a mass of small change into his hand, picked out a new copper coin. The Nit shoved his threadbare cap with its torn, battered peak down in front of them: Yakov threw his coin in it, as did Barrowboy.

'You choose,' said Gentleman Wildman, turning to Winker.

Winker gave a self-satisfied grin, seized the cap in both hands and began shaking it. Momentarily a profound silence reigned while the coins chinked faintly against each other. I looked attentively around: all the faces expressed tense expectancy; Gentleman Wildman screwed up his eyes; my neighbour, the little peasant in the torn coat, even he stretched his neck forward in curiosity. Winker put his hand into the cap and drew out Barrowboy's coin; everyone sighed with relief. Yakov reddened, and Barrowboy drew his hand through his hair.

'Didn't I say it was you!' the Nit exclaimed. 'Sure I did!'

'Now, now, none o' that squawking,' Gentleman Wildman remarked contemptuously. 'Begin!' he went on, nodding his head to Barrowboy.

'What song ought I to sing?' asked Barrowboy, becoming upset.

'Sing what you like,' answered Winker. 'Whatever comes into your head, sing that.'

'Of course, sing what you like,' added Nikolay Ivanych, slowly folding his arms across his chest. 'Nobody's giving you any orders. Sing what you like, only sing it well. Afterwards we'll decide as our conscience dictates.'

'Nacherly, as conscience dictates,' the Nit inserted, and licked the edge of his empty glass.

'Give me time, mates, to get my throat cleared a bit,' Barrowboy started saying, passing his fingers along the collar of his coat.

'Now, now, don't start trying to get out of it – begin!' Gentleman Wildman said decisively, and lowered his eyes to the floor.

Barrowboy thought for a moment, gave a shake of the head and took a step forward. Yakov fixed his eyes on him, drinking him in . . .

But before I embark on a description of the contest itself, I consider it necessary to say a few words about each of the participants in my story. The lives of some of them were already known to me before I encountered them in The Welcome tavern; about the others I picked up information at a later date.

Let's begin with the Nit. This man's real name was Yevgraf Ivanov; but no one in the region knew him as anything save the Nit, and he prided himself on such a nickname because it suited him so well. And there is no doubt that nothing could have been more appropriate for describing his insignificant and eternally agitated countenance. He was a feckless, bachelor house-serf, long ago given up for good by his masters, who, though having no post and not receiving a penny in wages, nevertheless found means each day of making merry at other people's expense. He had a mass of acquaintances who plied him with drink and tea, they themselves not knowing why, because not only was he far from entertaining company but he even, to the contrary, bored everyone stiff with his senseless chatter, intolerable sponging, feverish body-movements and endless unnatural laughter. He did not know how to sing or dance; since birth he had never once spoken not only an intelligent, but even a sensible, word; he rattled on the whole time and talked whatever nonsense came into his head – he was a real nit, in fact! Even so, no drinking bout could occur within a twenty-five mile radius without his lanky figure milling round among the guests, to such an extent had people grown used to him and accustomed to his presence like an unavoidable evil. True, he was treated with contempt, but Gentleman Wildman was the only one who knew how to tame his witless outbursts.

Winker bore no sort of resemblance to the Nit. The title of Winker also suited him, although he did not wink his eyes more than other people; everyone knows, though, what past-masters Russians are at contriving nicknames. Despite my attempting to gain a fuller picture of this man's past, his life still contained for me – and probably for many others as well – dark spots, areas, as bookish people like to say, obscured by profound mists of uncertainty. I learnt simply that he had at one time been a coachman for an elderly childless lady, that he had run off with the troika of horses left in his charge, had disappeared for a whole year and, having no doubt discovered for himself the disadvantages and perils of a vagrant's life, returned of his own accord, but already lame, threw himself at the feet of his mistress and, having erased his crime during the course of several years of exemplary behaviour, gradually regained her favour, finally earned her complete trust, became one of her bailiffs and, at her death, turned out in some mysterious way to have been given his freedom, enrolled himself among the petit-bourgeois stratum of the population, began renting areas of kitchen garden from his neighbours, grew rich and now lived in the pink. He was a man of experience, with a mind to his own affairs, neither malicious nor kindly, but chiefly prudent; he was a tough nut, who knew what people were like and had learned how to make use of them. He was cautious and at the same time as resourceful as a vixen; he was as garrulous as an old woman and yet he never used to say too much, but always made everyone else speak their minds; mind you, he never tried to pass himself off as a simpleton, as some rascals of that ilk do, and it would have been difficult for him to pretend because I had never seen more perspicacious and intelligent eyes than his crafty little 'peepers'.* Their gaze was never simple and straightforward – they were always looking you up and down, always investigating you. Sometimes Winker would spend whole weeks thinking over some apparently simple operation, and then in a flash he would make up his mind to launch into a desperately audacious business; it would seem that he was about to come a cropper, and yet before you'd had time to give a second look everything was a howling success, everything was going along swimmingly. He was fortunate and he believed in his good fortune, just as he believed in omens. He was in general very superstitious. He was not liked, because he did not concern himself with other people's business, but he was respected. His entire family consisted of one small son, on whom he doted, and who, being educated by such a father, would no doubt go a long way. 'Wee Willy Winker takes after his father' were the words already being spoken under their breaths by old men sitting on earthen seats and discussing this and that between themselves on summer evenings; and everybody understood what was meant by that and felt no need to add anything to it.

About Yakov the Turk and Barrowboy there is no reason to say a great deal. Yakov, nicknamed the Turk, because he was in fact the offspring of a captured Turkish girl, was by nature an artist in every sense of that word, whereas by calling he was a

---

* People of the Orlov region refer to eyes as 'peepers', just as they call mouths 'eaters'.

dipper in the paper factory of a local merchant; as for Barrowboy, whose fate, I admit, has remained unknown to me, he seemed to be a slippery and lively product of the small-town bourgeoisie. But it is worth being a little more detailed about Gentleman Wildman.

The first impression produced by the sight of this man was a sense of crude, heavy but irresistible strength. He had an awkward build, as if he had been 'knocked together', as they say, but he exuded an air of unbreakable good health and, strange though it may seem, his bear-like figure was not without its own kind of grace, which may have been due to a completely calm assurance of his own powers. At a first glance it was difficult to decide to what social stratum this Hercules belonged; he did not look like a house-serf, or one of the petit-bourgeois, or an impoverished retired clerk, or a bankrupt member of the minor nobility turned huntsman and strong-arm man: he was precisely himself and no more. Nobody knew where he had come from before dropping in on our county; gossip had it that he came from small-time landowning stock and was supposed to have been in the government service previously; but nothing positive was known about him and, besides, there was nobody from whom one could learn anything about him – certainly not from the man himself, because no one was more morose and taciturn. Also, no one could say for sure how he lived: he occupied himself with no special trade, never travelled off to work with anyone, had practically no acquaintances, yet he never seemed to be without money – not much, it was true, but some. It was not so much that he conducted himself modestly – there was in general nothing modest about him whatever – but he conducted himself quietly; he lived literally without taking notice of anyone around him and quite definitely without needing anyone. Gentleman Wildman (that was his nickname; his real name was Perevlesov) enjoyed enormous authority throughout the entire region; he was obeyed instantly and without question, although he not only had no right at all to order people about, but he did not even make the slightest pretence of expecting obedience from anyone he might chance to meet. He had only to speak and they obeyed; strength will always exact its due. He hardly drank at all, did not consort with women and was passionately fond of singing. There was much that was enigmatic about this man; it seemed as if certain mighty powers sullenly lurked within him, knowing, as it were, that if they were once roused, if they once broke free, they would be sure to destroy both the man himself and everything they came in contact with; and if I am not terribly mistaken, precisely such an outburst had occurred in the life of this man, and he, schooled by the experience and barely saved from perishing, implacably held himself in check with a rod of iron. I was particularly struck by the mixture in him of a certain in-born, natural ferocity and a similarly in-born nobility of spirit – a mixture which I had not encountered before in anyone else.

Meanwhile, Barrowboy took a pace forward, half closed his eyes and began to sing in an exceptionally high falsetto. He had a fairly pleasant, sweet voice, although it was a little husky; he played with his voice, twisting it round and round like a top, ceaselessly running up and down the scale and all the time returning to the high notes, which he endeavoured particularly to hold and prolong, dropping into silence and then suddenly catching up the earlier refrain with a certain carefree, arrogant audacity. His shifts from one to the other were sometimes fairly bold, sometimes quite amusing: to an expert they would have given a good deal of pleasure; a German would have been annoyed by them. He was a Russian *tenore di grazia*, *ténor léger*. The song he sang was gay, for dancing, the words of which, so far as I could make them out through the endless embellishments, additional consonants and ejaculations, were as follows:

> I'll plough, my young one so pretty,
> A small patch for thee;
> I'll sow, my young one so pretty,
> Bright red flowers for thee.

He sang, and everyone listened to him with great attention. He was obviously conscious of performing in front of people experienced in the art of singing and therefore, as they say, gave it all he'd got. Certainly, in our parts people know something about singing, and it is not for nothing that the village of Sergiyevsky, on the main Orlov highway, is famed throughout Russia for its especially pleasant and harmonious melodies. Barrowboy sang for a long time without arousing any exceptionally strong sympathy in his listeners; he lacked support, a chorus; finally, after one particularly successful shift which

made even Gentleman Wildman smile, the Nit could not contain
himself and shouted with joy. Everyone became animated. The Nit
and Winker began in low voices to catch up the refrain, joining in
and occasionally shouting:

'Great, man, great! Get it, boyo! Get it, hold it, keep at it, stretch
it, you snake! Stretch it, go on, and again! Make it hot again, man,
you old dog, you! Oh, the devil take your soul, man!' and so on.

Behind the counter Nikolay Ivanych approvingly shook his head
to right and left. The Nit eventually started tapping his feet, mincing
on tiptoe and jerking one shoulder, and Yakov's eyes simply burst
into flame like coals and his whole body quivered like a leaf as he
smiled all over his face. Only Gentleman Wildman did not alter the
look on his face and remained in his former posture without moving;
but his gaze, directed at Barrowboy, softened a little, although the
expression on his lips remained contemptuous. Encouraged by these
signs of general enjoyment, Barrowboy completely gave himself up
to a veritable whirling frenzy of sounds and began to execute such
convolutions, such clickings and drummings with his tongue, began
such wild throaty trills that when, finally, exhausted, pale and covered
in hot perspiration, he flung back his whole body and emitted a last
dying cry, a general and unanimous shout of approval greeted him in
a fierce outburst. The Nit threw himself at Barrowboy's neck and
began to hug him to the point of suffocation with his long bony
arms; a blush appeared on the fleshy face of Nikolay Ivanych which
literally made him look younger; Yakov, like a madman, started
shouting: 'O boy, O boy, O boy!' Even my neighbour, the peasant
in the ragged coat, could not restrain himself, and, striking the table
with his fist, gave a cry of 'Bah-gum that was good, the devil take it,
that was good!' and resolutely spat to one side.

'Well, mate, that was a delight!' cried the Nit without releasing
the utterly exhausted Barrowboy from his embraces. 'That was a
delight, no denyin'! You've won, mate, you've won! Congratulations! That pot of ale's all yours! Yashka won't come near you, I'm
tellin' you he won't come near . . . Just you remember what I've
said!' (And he once more clasped Barrowboy to his chest.)

'Let him go, let him go, like a ruddy clingin' vine you are!'
Winker started saying in annoyance. 'Let him sit down on the bench.
You can see he's tired. A bloody idiot you are, mate, a right bloody

idiot! What's the good o' stickin' to 'im like a wet leaf in a steambath, eh?'

'So all right, let him sit down, and I'll drink to his health,' said the Nit and approached the counter. 'You'll do the payin', mate,' he added, turning to Barrowboy.

The latter gave a nod of the head, sat down on the bench, took a cloth out of his cap and began wiping his face; while the Nit drank down a glass with greedy swiftness and, after the manner of heavy drinkers, grunted and assumed a sadly preoccupied look.

'You sing well, mate, real well,' Nikolay Ivanych remarked gently. 'And now it's your turn, Yashka. Don't be bashful. We'll see who's better than whom, we'll just see ... But Barrowboy sings awful well, my God he does!'

'Ve-ery well,' commented his wife and looked with a smile towards Yakov.

'Ah, that was good!' my companion repeated in a soft voice.

'Hey, you twister-Woody!'* the Nit all of a sudden started yelling and, going up to the little peasant with the tear in the shoulder of his coat, stuck his finger out at him, began jumping about and pouring out a torrent of rumbustious laughter. 'Woody! Woody! Ha, bah-gum harry-on, you twister!† Waddya come here for, twister?' he shouted through his laughter.

The wretched peasant was confused and was on the point of leaving as soon as possible when suddenly there boomed out the resonant voice of Gentleman Wildman:

'What kind of bloody awful animal's making that noise?' he rasped through his teeth.

'I wasn't doin' nothin',' the Nit mumbled, 'it weren't nothin' ... Just like I was ...'

'Well, then, shut up!' retorted Gentleman Wildman. 'Yakov, begin!'

Yakov seized hold of his own throat.

---

* 'Woodies' is the name given to inhabitants of the southern forest areas (*poles'ye*), a long forest belt which originates on the boundary between Bolkhov and Zhizdra counties. They are distinguished by having many peculiarities in their way of life, habits and speech. They are called twisters owing to their suspicious and tight-fisted disposition.

† 'Woodies' add the exclamation 'Ha!' and 'Bah-gum!' to almost every word. 'Harry-on' instead of 'hurry-on'.

'Well, mate, it's . . . something's wrong . . . Hmm . . . Honest, I
don't know what's wrong wi' it . . .'

'Enough of that, don't start being bashful. You ought to be
ashamed! What's all the squirming for? Sing just the way God makes
you.'

And Gentleman Wildman lowered his eyes to the floor, expecting
no more fuss.

Yakov said nothing, glanced around and covered his face with his
hand. Everyone drank him in with their eyes, especially Barrowboy,
on whose face there appeared, through his normal self-assured look
and look of triumph at his success, an involuntary faint uneasiness.
He leaned back against the wall and again placed both hands under
him, but he no longer swung his feet about. When, at last, Yakov
uncovered his face, it was pale as death; his eyes scarcely gleamed
through his lowered eyelashes. He drew in a deep breath and began
to sing.

The first sound his voice gave was weak and uneven, seeming
to emerge not from his chest but to have been carried from somewhere far away, just as if it had flown by accident into the room.
This quivering, ringing sound acted strangely upon all of us; we
glanced at each other, and Nikolay Ivanych's wife literally stif-
fened. The first sound was followed by another, much firmer and
long-drawn, but still clearly sobbing like a violin string when, after
being suddenly plucked by a strong finger, it wavers in one final,
quickly fading *tremolo* of sound, after which there followed a third
and, little by little growing in intensity and volume, the plaintive
song poured forth. 'More than one path through the field wound
its way' was the song he sang, and each one of us felt a wave of
sweetness and shivery anticipation creeping over us. I confess that
I had rarely heard such a voice: it was slightly broken and rang
as if cracked; to start with it even had a suggestion of sickliness
about it; but it also contained unfeigned depth of passion, and
youthfulness, and strength, and sweetness, and a kind of attractively
uncaring, mournful piteousness. The honest, fiery soul of Russia
resounded and breathed through it and quite simply seized us by the
heart, plucked directly at our Russian heart-strings. The song grew
and overflowed. Yakov was obviously possessed by inspiration: all
shyness gone, he was giving himself completely to his exaltation;

his voice no longer quivered – it sobbed, but with that scarcely noticeable, inner tremor of passion which plunges like an arrow into the soul of the listener, and ceaselessly it grew in strength, firmness and volume.

I remember how one evening, at the ebbing of the tide, on the smooth sandy shore of a sea thundering and roaring with the breaking of heavy waves in the far distance, I saw a large white seagull; it stood motionless, its silky breast turned to the crimson brilliance of the evening, and only now and then slowly spread out its long wings in a gesture of welcome to the familiar sea and low, blood-red sun; this I recalled as I listened to Yakov. He sang, quite oblivious of his rival and all of us, yet evidently uplifted, as a spirited swimmer is borne up by the waves, by our silent, devotional participation. He sang, and in every sound his voice made there breathed something familiar as our birthright and so vast no eye could encompass it, just as if the Russian steppe were being unrolled before us, stretching away into an endless distance. I felt emotions throb in my heart and tears rose to my eyes. I was suddenly surprised by the sound of mute, suppressed crying. I glanced round – it was mine host's wife weeping, her bosom pressed to the window. Yakov cast a quick glance in her direction and began to pour out the song still more resonantly, still more sweetly than before; Nikolay Ivanych fixed his eyes on the floor and Winker turned away; the Nit, quite sodden with emotion, stood there, his mouth stupidly gaping; the colourless little peasant was quietly sobbing in his corner and rocking his head to the accompaniment of a tearful whispering; and down the iron face of Gentleman Wildman, from beneath eyebrows that had been drawn completely together, a single heavy tear slowly trickled; Barrowboy had raised a clenched fist to his forehead and was absolutely still . . .

I do not know how the universal tension would have been dispersed had not Yakov suddenly finished on a high, unusually thin note, just as if his voice had broken. Nobody shouted, nobody even stirred; they all waited, as it were, to see whether he was going to continue; but he simply opened his eyes, literally astonished by our silence, looked round at us with an inquiring gaze and recognized that he had won.

'Yasha,' said Gentleman Wildman, placed a hand on his shoulder – and stopped.

We were all motionless as if stunned. Barrowboy quietly stood up and approached Yakov. 'You ... it's yours ... you've won,' he uttered at last with difficulty and flung himself out of the room.

His quick, decisive movement seemed to break the spell: everyone suddenly burst into loud and joyful talking. The Nit jumped in the air, began babbling and waving his arms about like the vanes of a windmill; Winker walked lamely up to Yakov and kissed him on both cheeks; Nikolay Ivanych straightened himself and solemnly announced that he would provide another pot of ale on his own account; Gentleman Wildman gave a series of jovial laughs, of a kind which I had never expected to see on his face; the colourless little peasant over and over again muttered in his corner as he drew both sleeves over his eyes, cheeks, nose and beard: 'Ha, that was good, by God it was good; bah-gum I'll be a son of a bitch, but that was good!'; and Nikolay Ivanych's wife, quite red in the face, quickly stood up and withdrew. Yakov delighted in his victory like a child; his whole face was transformed; his eyes in particular glittered with happiness. They dragged him to the counter, and he summoned the tearful little peasant to join in and sent one of mine host's little sons after Barrowboy, who, however, was not to be found, and the celebrating began. 'You're goin' to sing again, you'll sing to us till it's dark,' the Nit kept on repeating, raising his arms high in the air.

I took a final look at Yakov and went out. I did not want to remain – I was frightened of spoiling my impression. But the heat was as unbearable as before. It seemed to hang over the very surface of the earth in a thick, heavy layer; against the dark-blue sky certain tiny, bright fires appeared to lick up through the very fine, almost black, dust. Everything was silent; there was something hopeless, depressed about this profound silence of exhausted nature. I made my way to a hayloft and lay down on the recently mown grass which had already dried out almost completely. For a long while I was unable to doze off; the enthralling voice of Yakov still rang in my ears ... Finally heat and weariness exacted their due and I fell into a dead sleep.

When I awoke, everything was already dark; the grass scattered round me had a strong scent and was ever so slightly damp; through the thin laths of the half-covered roof pale stars winked feebly. I went out. The glow of sunset had long since died away and its final traces hardly showed at all on the horizon; but in the recently white-hot air the heat could still be felt even through the night's freshness, and one's lungs still yearned for a cooling breeze. There was no wind, nor were there any clouds; the sky stood all about me, clear and transparently dark, quietly flickering with numberless but scarcely visible stars. Lights flashed in the village; from the brightly lit tavern near by there came a dissonant, vague hubbub, through which I seemed to make out the voice of Yakov. Wild laughter broke out explosively from time to time. I went up to the little window and pressed my face to the glass.

I saw an unhappy, though a motley and lively enough scene: everyone was drunk – everyone, beginning with Yakov. With bared breast he was sitting on a bench and, singing in a husky voice some dancing song of the streets, idly fingered and plucked the strings of a guitar. His damp hair hung in clusters over his terribly pale face. In the middle of the tavern the Nit, completely 'unwound' and without his coat, was dancing with skips and jumps in front of the peasant in the colourless overcoat; the little man, in his turn, was with difficulty tapping and scraping his dog-tired feet and, smiling senselessly through his dishevelled beard, gave occasional waves of the hand, as though wishing to say: 'So what the hell!' Nothing could have been more comic than his face; no matter how much he jerked his brows up, his heavy eyelids refused to rise and remained fallen over his barely visible, bleary, though extremely syrupy little eyes. He was in the pleasant condition of someone who is rolling drunk, to whom every passer-by, upon glancing in his face, invariably remarks: 'You're doing fine, mate, you're doing fine!' Winker, red-faced as a crab and with widely distended nostrils, was giving roars of venomous laughter from one corner; only Nikolay Ivanych maintained his unvarying composure, as befitted a true tavern-keeper. Many new faces had gathered in the room; but I did not see Gentleman Wildman there.

I turned away and began quickly to descend the hill on which Kolotovka is situated. At the foot of this hill there is a broad plain; flooded with murky waves of evening mist, it appeared to be even vaster than it was and seemed to flow into the darkened sky. I was taking large steps down the road alongside the ravine, when suddenly somewhere far off in the plain a boy's shrill voice cried out. 'Antropka! Antropka-a-a!' he shouted with insistent and tearful desperation, prolonging and prolonging the last syllable.

He was silent for several instants and then resumed his shouting. His voice carried resonantly through the still, lightly dreaming air. At least thirty times he called out Antropka's name, when suddenly from the opposite end of the wide field, as if from another world, came the hardly audible answer:

'Wh-a-a-a-at?'

The boy's voice at once cried out with gleeful spite:

'Come here, you devil pip-sque-e-e-eak!'

'Why-y-y-y?' the other answered after a short time.

''Cos dad wants to be-e-eat you,' the second voice hurriedly shouted.

The second voice made no further reply, and the boy again started calling for Antropka. His shouts, more and more infrequent and faint, still reached my ears by the time it had grown completely dark and I was skirting the edge of the forest which surrounds my little village and lies about three miles from Kolotovka.

'Antropka-a-a!' still seemed to resound in the air, filled with shades of night.

PYOTR PETROVICH KARATAEV

❦

ABOUT five years ago one autumn, on the road from Moscow to Tula, I had to spend almost a whole day in a post house due to a lack of horses. I was returning from hunting and was incautious enough to send my troika on ahead. The post-master, an old man of gloomy character, with hair that hung down to his nose and with small, sleep-filled eyes, answered all my complaints and requests with short-tempered grumbling, angrily slammed the door in my face as if he were bringing down curses on his own calling and, going out on to the porch, swore at the drivers who either slowly dragged their way through the mud with heavy items of harness in their arms or sat on a bench, yawning and scratching themselves and not giving any particular attention to the angry exclamations of their boss. I'd already drunk tea on three occasions, tried several times without success to have a snooze and read all the announcements on the windows and the walls and was bored to death. With unfeeling and hopeless despair I gazed at the raised shafts of my tarantass when suddenly a harness-bell started tinkling and a small cart drawn by a troika of worn-out horses stopped in front of the porch. The new arrival jumped down from the cart and with a cry of 'Horses! Step lively there!' entered the room.

While he was listening with the usual strange astonishment to the post-master saying that there weren't any horses, I managed, with all the greedy curiosity of a bored man, to survey my new companion from head to toe. To all appearances he seemed to be in his late twenties. Smallpox had left ineradicable traces on his face, which was dry-skinned and yellowish with an unpleasant coppery tinge to it. His long blue-black hair lay in rings over his collar at the back, while in front it was twisted into fancy curls. His small puffy eyes gazed out – and that's all one can say about them. A few small hairs were prominent on his upper lip. He was dressed like an out-and-out landowning type, a frequenter of horse fairs, in a colourful, rather greasy coat, a faded silk cravat of a mauve colour, a waistcoat with copper buttons and grey trousers with enormous bell-bottoms beneath which the tips of his unpolished shoes were only just visible. He emitted a strong smell of tobacco and vodka. Silver and Tula-made rings could be seen on his stubby, red fingers, almost covered by his coat sleeves. Such figures can be encountered not by the dozen but by the hundreds in Russia. Acquaintanceship with them, it has to be said, does not afford any pleasure, but despite the prejudice with which I studied the new arrival I couldn't help noticing the unheedingly kind and passionate look on his face.

'This gentleman here's been waiting for more than an hour, sir,' said the post-master, pointing to me.

More than an hour, indeed! The villain was having a laugh at my expense.

'Perhaps he doesn't need them as badly as we do,' answered the new arrival.

'That, sir, we cannot know, sir,' said the post-master gloomily.

'So you can't do a thing? There are absolutely no horses?'

'Not a thing, sir. There's not a single horse.'

'Well, then, have the samovar brought in for me. If we've got to wait, there's nothing to be done about it.'

The new arrival sat down on a bench, threw his cap on the table and ran his hand through his hair.

'You've already had some tea to drink?' he asked me.

'I have.'

'Would you care to have some more just for the company?'

I agreed. The large reddish samovar appeared on the table for the fourth time. I got out a bottle of rum. I wasn't mistaken in taking my companion for a small-time landowner. He was called Pyotr Petrovich Karataev.

We started talking. Scarcely half an hour had passed since his arrival and he'd already told me the story of his life with the most good-natured candour.

'Now I'm on my way to Moscow,' he told me, finishing his fourth glass. 'There's nothing left for me here in the country.'

'Why nothing?'

'Just that – there's nothing left. The estate's in a mess, I've got to admit, and I've ruined the peasants. Bad years've arrived, what with harvest failures and, you know, various misfortunes. Besides,' he added, glancing away despondently, 'I'm no good at managing!'

'How come?'

'Look,' he interrupted me, 'a fine owner I am! I mean,' he went on, twisting his head to one side and busily sucking at his pipe, 'you might think, taking a look at me as I am now, that I, well ... and yet I've got to confess I received an ordinary sort of education because there wasn't a lot of money about. You must forgive me, I'm an honest sort of chap and after all ...'

He didn't finish what he was saying and gave a wave of the hand. I began assuring him he was wrong, that I was very glad we'd met and so on, and then I remarked that one didn't need too strong an education to manage an estate, or so it would seem.

'Sure,' he responded. 'I agree with you. But at least something's needed, like a special disposition. Some fleece the peasant like nobody's business and get away with it, but I ... Permit me to inquire, are you yourself from Peter or Moscow?'

'I'm from St Petersburg.'

He emitted a long stream of smoke through his nostrils.

'I'm off to Moscow to enter the civil service.'

'Where do you intend to find a place?'

'I don't know. Whatever comes along. I confess to you I'm frightened of joining because you're instantly responsible to someone. I've lived all the time in the country, got used to it, you know ... Still, there's nothing to be done about it – necessity demands! Oh, what this necessity does to me!'

'No matter, you'll be living in the capital.'

'In the capital ... Well, I don't know what'll be good about that. We'll see, perhaps it'll be good. But I don't think there can be anything better than the country.'

'Are you sure you can't live any longer in the country?'

He gave a sigh.

'It's impossible. My estate's now no longer my own.'

'Why's that?'

'A kind chap there, my neighbour, has acquired it ... an IOU ...'

Poor Pyotr Petrovich ran his hand across his face, thought a moment and shook his head.

'Well, that's all there is to it! . . . And I've got to confess,' he added after a short silence, 'I can't blame anyone, it's all my own fault. I liked making a bit of a show! I still do like making a bit of a show, devil take it!'

'You had a good time when you lived in the country?' I asked him.

'I had in my possession, sir,' he answered, pausing between the words and looking me directly in the eyes, 'a dozen pair of hunting dogs,[1] the like of which, I'll tell you, there can't be many.' (He practically sang out this last word.) 'They'd be on to a hare in an instant, and as for red deer – like snakes they were, absolute vipers. And I could boast of my borzoi as well. Now it's all a matter of the past, there's no point in telling tales. I also went hunting with a gun. I had a dog called Contessa, an exceptional pointer she was, she'd fetch anything with her sixth sense. Say I'd come to a marsh, and I'd tell her: charge! If she didn't start seeking, you could send a dozen dogs through there and you'd be wasting your time, you wouldn't find a thing! But if she did, she'd gladly die on the spot! . . . And at home she was so polite. You'd give her a piece of bread with your left hand and say: "A Jew's eaten that," and she wouldn't take it, but give it her with your right hand and say: "A young lady's eaten that," she'd take it at once and eat it. I had a puppy from her, an excellent puppy, and wanted to bring it with me to Moscow, but a friend of mine asked me to give it him along with my gun. He said: "You won't be needing that in Moscow, my dear chap. There'll be quite different things going on in Moscow, my dear fellow." So I let him have the puppy and my gun. It's all remained behind there, you see.'

'But even in Moscow you could go shooting.'

'No, what'd be the point? I couldn't restrain myself, so now I've just got to bide my time. But it'd be better if you could tell me, is life in Moscow expensive?'

'No, not too expensive.'

'Not too expensive? Then tell me, please, do gypsies live in Moscow?'

'What kind of gypsies?'

'The kind that travel round the horse fairs.'

'Yes, in Moscow . . .'

'Well, that's splendid. I love gypsies, the devil take 'em, I love 'em . . .'

And Pyotr Petrovich's eyes flashed with daredevil happiness. But suddenly he twisted about on the bench, then grew thoughtful, lowered his head and held out to me his empty glass.

'Give me a drop of your rum,' he said.

'The tea's run out, you know.'

'It doesn't matter, I'll have it like that, without tea . . . Oh, hell!'

Karataev placed his head in his arms and leaned his elbows on the table. I watched him in silence and waited for those emotional outbursts, those tears even, of which drunkards are so prodigal, but when he raised his head what struck me, I confess, was the profoundly sad expression on his face.

'What's wrong?'

'Nothing . . . I was just remembering old times. It's a long story. I'd tell you, only I don't want to take up your time . . .'

'Please!'

'Yes,' he went on with a sigh, 'there are instances . . . Take, for instance, my case. If you like I'll tell you. Still, I don't know . . .'

'Tell me, my dear Pyotr Petrovich.'

'May be, though it's . . . Well, you see,' he began, 'but really I don't know if I should . . .'

'That's enough shilly-shallying, my dear Pyotr Petrovich.'

'Well, probably. This, then, is what happened in my case, so to speak. I was living in the country, sir. Suddenly a girl caught my eye, oh, what a girl she was – good-looking, clever and as kind-hearted as you can imagine! Her name was Matryona. She was a simple girl, a peasant girl, you understand, no more'n a serf. And she wasn't mine but somebody else's, that was the problem. Well, I fell in love with her – it's an old story, true – and she fell in love with me. So she starts begging me: buy me from my mistress. And I'd been thinking about the same thing myself. But her mistress was rich, a really frightful old woman. She lived about ten miles away from me. Well, one fine day, as they say, I ordered my droshky to be harnessed with three horses – between the shafts went my ambling horse, an un-usually barbarous animal, which is why he was called Lampurdos – and I dressed up in my best clothes and set off to see Matryona's

mistress. I arrived and found a large house with wings and a garden
... At the turn in the road Matryona was waiting for me and had
wanted to say something to me, but simply kissed my hand and
stepped back. So I went into the entrance and asked: "Is there anyone
home?" And a tall footman then asked me: "How shall I announce
you, sir?" I said: "Announce, my dear fellow, that the landowner
Karataev has arrived to discuss a matter of business." The footman
went off. I waited about and wondered whether anything'd come of
it. Very likely the old woman'd demand a frightfully high price,
since she wasn't rich for nothing. She'd very likely ask about 500
roubles, I thought. Then the footman returned and said: "Follow
me, please." I followed him into a drawing-room. There sitting in an
armchair was a tiny, yellowish old woman blinking her eyes all the
time. "What can I do for you?" The first thing I considered necessary,
you know, was to say how glad I was to make her acquaintance, so
to speak. "You are mistaken, I'm not the mistress here but her
relative ... What can I do for you?" I remarked to her at once that I
had something to discuss with the mistress. "Marya Ilinichna is not
receiving today. She is unwell. What can I do for you?" Well, I
thought, it's no good, I'll have to explain everything to her. The old
woman heard me out. "Matryona, what Matryona?" "Matryona
Fyodorova, Kulik's daughter." "Fyodor Kulik's daughter ... How
do you come to know her?" "In a chance manner." "Is she aware of
your intentions?" "She is." The old woman was silent for a while.
"Well, I'll give her what for, the good-for-nothing!" I was astonished, I can tell you. "Why d'you say that? I'm prepared to offer
money for her. Just name the sum please." The old hag literally
started hissing. "Surprise, surprise, a lot of good your money'll do us!
Just let me get my hands on her, just let me, I'll soon knock the nonsense
out of her!" The old woman burst out coughing in her annoyance. "So
she doesn't like it here, is that it? Oh, the little she-devil, God forgive
me for saying such a thing!" I can tell you I lost my temper at that.
"What're you threatening the poor girl for? What's she done
wrong?" The old woman crossed herself. "Oh, you can say that, my
God, Jesus Christ! Can't I treat my serfs just as I wish?" "But she's
not yours!" "Well, Marya Ilinichna knows all about that. It's none of
your business, my good man. But I'll just show that Matryoshka
whose serf she is!" I can tell you I almost flung myself on to the old

woman, but I remembered Matryona and let my hands fall to my sides. I felt so chastened, I can't tell you, and began pleading with the old woman. "Take whatever you want." "What's she mean to you?" "I'm fond of her, my dear lady. See the position I'm in and permit me to kiss your charming hand!" And I literally kissed the hand of the old witch! "Well," mumbled the old witch, "I'll tell Marya Ilinichna. It'll be up to her. You come back here in two days' time." I returned home in a state of great unease. I was beginning to sense that I'd got things wrong and had let my feelings be known for nothing and then had realized my mistake too late. A couple of days later I set off to see the lady again. They showed me into her boudoir. A mass of flowers everywhere, splendid furnishings, and she herself was sitting in such a strange-looking armchair and her head resting back on cushions; and the relative who'd been there last time was also sitting there, as well as some other white-haired lady in a green dress, with a lopsided mouth – I guessed she was a companion. "Please be seated," said the old lady nasally. I sat down. She started asking me how old I was, where I'd done my government service, what I was intending to do – and all in a high-and-mighty, self-important way. I answered everything in detail. The old lady seized a handkerchief from a table and started fanning herself with it. "Katerina Karpovna," she said, "has informed me of your intentions, but I have made it a rule not to allow my servants to be released for service elsewhere. It is not decent, and it is unsuitable for an orderly home: it is disorderly. I have already dealt with the matter," she said, "so you won't be bothered any more." "Bothered, but . . . D'you need Matryona Fyodorova?" "No," she said, "I don't need her." "Then why don't you want to let her come to me?" "Because I don't have a mind to, I don't want to, and that's final. I've already dealt with the matter: she's been sent away to a steppe village." That struck me like a thunderclap. The old lady spoke a couple of words in French to the green lady and the green lady left. "I am a woman," she said, "of strict rules and my health is weak. I can't endure upsets of any kind. You're still a young man, but I'm an old woman and I've earned the right to give you some advice. Surely you'd be better off settling down, marrying, looking for a good match. Rich brides are rare, but it's possible to find some poor girl, though of good morals." You know, I stared at the old lady and didn't understand a thing she was babbling about. I heard her saying something about marriage, but what rang in my ears was what she'd said about a steppe village. Get married! Devil take that!'

At this point the narrator suddenly stopped in what he was saying and looked at me.

'You're not married, are you?'

'No.'

'Well, of course, you can guess what happened. I couldn't contain myself. "Well, my good woman," I said, "what rubbish are you talking? What's all this about marriage? I simply want to know from you whether or not you're prepared to let me have your girl Matryona." The old lady started groaning. "Oh, he's upset me! Oh, tell him to go! Oh! . . ." Her relative rushed to her and started shouting at me, but the old lady went on groaning and saying: "Why've I deserved this? So I'm no longer mistress in my own house, is that it? Oh! Oh!" I seized my hat and dashed out of the house like a mad thing.

'Perhaps,' the narrator went on, 'you'll blame me for becoming so strongly attached to a girl from a lower class. I don't intend to justify myself – it's just how things worked out! Believe me, day and night I had no peace! I suffered tortures! What've I ruined the poor girl for? I thought. As soon as I'd think of her having to wear a coarse coat to go driving the geese and being kept in the harshest of conditions on her mistress's orders and having the village elder, a peasant in tarred boots, swearing at her, I'd literally break out in a cold sweat. Well, I couldn't stand it any longer. I discovered which village she'd been sent to, got on my horse and rode there. It was the evening of the next day when I arrived. Obviously they'd not expected me to do such a thing and given no orders how to deal with me. I went straight to the elder as if I were a neighbour. I went into the yard and saw Matryona sitting on the porch, with her head resting on her hand. She was on the point of crying out, but I made her a sign that she shouldn't and pointed in the direction of the backyard and the fields. I went into the peasant hut, started chattering with the elder, told him the devil's own nonsense and when the opportunity came went out to Matryona. She, poor girl, literally threw herself on my neck. She'd got pale and thin, my darling had. I told her, you know: "It's all right, Matryona, don't cry," but my own tears just poured down my face. Well, anyhow, in the end I felt quite ashamed of myself and I told her: "Matryona, tears'll get us nowhere, the thing is we've got to act decisively, as the saying goes. You've got to come away with me. That's what we've got to do." Matryona simply froze. "We can't do that! I'll be lost, they'll swallow me whole!" "You're being silly – who'll come looking for you?" "Someone'll come looking for sure. Thank you, Pyotr Petrovich, I'll never forget your kindness, but you must give me up now. I can see what my fate is." "Oh, Matryona, Matryona, and I took you for a girl with character!" And she did have a lot of character – and she had a heart, a heart of gold! "A lot of good it'll do you staying here! All in all it won't be worse coming away with me. Tell me, have you had a taste of those elder's fists?" Matryona just flared up at that and her lips started trembling. "'Cos of me my family's in trouble." "Well, your family – will they be sent away?" "They'll be sent away. My brother'll be sure to be sent to the army." "And your father?" "No, he won't be, he's the only good tailor in these parts." "Well, you see, then. And your brother won't be done for either." Believe you me, I had a hard time persuading her and she took it into her head to start telling me I'd have to take responsibility for everything . . . "That," I said, "is none of your business." However, I did take her away – not that time but another. I came with a cart at night and took her.'

'You took her away with you?'

'Yes, I did. Well, she came and lived with me. My house wasn't large and I didn't have many servants. I can say without fear of contradiction that my servants respected me and wouldn't have given me away for any kind of bribes. I started living to my heart's content. Matryona took a little time to rest and adjust – and I grew so attached to her, what a girl she was! Where'd she get it all from? She could sing and dance and play the guitar . . . I never showed her to the neighbours – lot of good that'd do, they'd only gossip! But I had a friend, a bosom friend, Panteley Gornostaev – you may have heard of him? He simply adored her. He'd kiss her hand just as if she were a high-born lady. And I must tell you that Gornostaev was quite unlike me. He was an educated man, had read the whole of Pushkin. Sometimes when he'd start talking to Matryona and me we'd just listen open-mouthed. He taught her to write, oddball that he was! And the way I used to dress her up – simply better than a

Governor's wife! I had a little coat made for her out of bright-red velvet with fur hems – and how that little coat looked on her! A Moscow *madame* made that little coat in the latest style, with a narrow waist. And what a strange and wonderful girl that Matryona was! Sometimes she'd fall into deep thought and sit there for hours staring at the floor, not moving an eyebrow. I'd sit there too and watch her and I couldn't have enough of looking at her as if I'd never seen her before in my life. She'd smile and my heart'd literally jump as if someone'd tickled it. Or she'd suddenly take to laughing and joking and dancing and give me such passionate, strong hugs my head would start going round. From morning to night I'd be thinking only about how I could please her. And, believe me, I only gave her presents so as to see how overjoyed my darling was, how she'd go all red from joy, how she'd try on what I'd given her and come to me in her new array and kiss me. I don't know how her father, Kulik, got wind of the affair, but he came to take a look at us and shed some tears. Surely they were tears of joy, or you'd have thought that, wouldn't you? We gave him a few things. She, my darling, even gave him a five-rouble note in the end – and he went flop down at her feet, such a silly old fool he was! So that's how we lived five months or so together and I wouldn't have objected to living the whole of my life with her in that way, 'cept I've had such damned awful bad breaks!'

Pyotr Petrovich stopped.

'What on earth happened?' I asked him with feeling.

He waved his hand.

'It all went to pot. I was the one that spoiled her. My Matryona was terribly fond of sledge rides and liked driving herself. She'd put on her little coat and wear her embroidered Torzhok mittens and do nothing but shriek. We'd always go sledge-riding at night so as, you know, not to meet anyone. Then there was one of those days, you know, quite splendid – frosty, clear, no wind – and we went riding. Matryona took the reins. Then I saw where she was going. Wasn't she going towards Kukuevka, her mistress's estate? Yes, she was. I said to her: "You're mad! D'you know where you're going?" She glanced at me over her shoulder and grinned, so much as to say: Let's risk it! Ah, I thought, in for a penny, in for a pound – it'd be fun to drive past the mistress's house, wouldn't it? Don't you think it would be? Well, we drove on. My shaft-horse literally floated along and the side-horses went like the wind. The Kukuevka church was already in sight when we saw an old green contraption crawling along the road with a footman sticking up at the back. It was the mistress out for a drive! I was for turning back, but Matryona struck the horses with the reins and rushed straight at the contraption! The coachman, the mistress's, that is, saw this Alchimerical wonder racing towards him, tried, you know, to get out of the way, swerved sharply and overturned the contraption into a snowdrift. The glass was broken and the mistress cried out: "Ay-ay-ay! Ay-ay-ay!" Her lady companion squeaked: "Hold on! Hold on!" We rushed by at God's speed and galloped on, but I thought it wouldn't work out and knew I'd been wrong to let Matryona drive to Kukuevka. Well, wouldn't you know it! Her mistress had of course recognized Matryona and me, old hag that she was, and laid a complaint to the effect that her runaway servant-girl was living with the landowner Karataev and of course expressed her gratitude to the authorities in the appropriate way. The next thing I saw was the constable riding up, and the constable was an acquaintance of mine, Stepan Sergeich Kuzovkin, a good fellow, that's to say, not really a good fellow at all. Well, he came to me and said words to the effect that it's like this and that, Pyotr Petrovich, can't you see that, eh? There's a serious responsibility and the laws are quite clear on the point . . . I said to him: "Well, we ought to talk about it, of course we ought, so won't you have a bite to eat after your journey?" He agreed to have a bite to eat, but he said: "Justice demands this, Pyotr Petrovich, judge for yourself." "Oh, of course, it's justice," I said, "of course it is . . . I hear, though, you've got a little black horse. Wouldn't you like to swap it for my Lampurdos? In any case, the girl Matryona Fyodorova isn't here!" "Well," he said, "Pyotr Petrovich, we know the girl's here, we're not living in Switzerland, you know . . . But as for Lampurdos, I'll swap my horse for him, or you know, I could just take him." Anyhow, that time I fooled him. But the old woman, the mistress, now started making more fuss than before. "I don't mind if it costs me ten thousand roubles," she said. You see, the thing was that, on seeing me, she'd suddenly taken it into her head to marry me off to her green lady companion – or that's what I learnt later, which is why she'd got so angry. The things these ladies think up! It must be out of boredom. So things were working out badly for me, what with the money I'd been spending and hiding Matryona – no, far worse, I was being pestered and quite driven out of my mind! I fell into debt, my health suffered. One night I was lying on my bed and thinking, Good God, why've I got to endure all this? What am I to do if I can't give her up? Well, I can't, and that's final! when suddenly Matryona came into my room. At that time I'd been hiding her on a farm a mile or so from my house. I was scared stiff. "What's happened? Have they found where you were?" "No, Pyotr Petrovich," she said, "no one's been after me in Bubnovo. But how long's this got to go on? My heart's breaking, Pyotr Petrovich," she said. "I feel so sorry for you, my darling. All my life I'll never forget your kindness, Pyotr Petrovich, but now the time's come to say goodbye to you." "What're you saying? Are you mad? Say goodbye – what do you mean?" "Just that. I'm going to give myself up." "Then I'll put you up in the attic, because you're out of your mind . . . Or have you decided to ruin me for good and all? You're set on finishing me off, are you?" She didn't say anything and just looked at the floor. "Well, tell me, tell me!" "I don't want to cause you any more trouble, Pyotr Petrovich." Well, I tried to reason with her, I tried . . . I said: "Don't you know, you silly girl, can't you see, you crazy . . . crazy . . ."'

And Pyotr Petrovich burst into bitter tears.

'So what d'you think?' he went on, striking his fist on the table and trying to frown as the tears ran down his burning cheeks. 'The girl gave herself up, she went and gave herself up . . .'

'The horses are ready, sir!' the post-master exclaimed triumphantly as he came into the room.

We both stood up.

'What happened to Matryona?' I asked.

Karataev gave a wave of the hand.

A year after my meeting with Karataev I had occasion to travel to Moscow. One day, just before dinner, I happened to go into the coffee-house on Hunter's Row, the original Moscow coffee-house.[2] In the billiard-room, through waves of smoke, one could glimpse beetroot-red faces, moustaches, topknots, old-fashioned Hungarian short jackets and the latest thing in Slavophile wear. Scrawny old gents in modest frock-coats were reading Russian newspapers. The waiters darted briskly about the place with trays, their footsteps softened by the green carpets. Merchants drank their tea with painful concentration. Suddenly a man came out of the billiard-room looking slightly dishevelled and a little unsteady on his feet. He put his hands in his pockets, let his head drop forward and glanced mindlessly around him.

'But, it's, it's, it's . . . Pyotr Petrovich! How are you?'

Pyotr Petrovich almost threw himself on my neck and then, swaying slightly, dragged me off to a small private room.

'Here,' he said, carefully directing me to an armchair, 'we'll be all right. Waiter, beer! No, make it champagne! Well, I must say, I'd never have expected, never . . . Have you been here long? Are you staying long? Well, it's an act of God, as they say, that brought . . .'

'So you remember, do you . . .'

'How can I forget, how can I forget,' he interrupted me hurriedly. 'It's all in the past . . . all in the past . . .'

'Well, what're you doing with yourself here, my dear Pyotr Petrovich?'

'I live, as you can observe. Living's good here, the people here are welcoming. I've found peace here.'

He sighed and raised his eyes to the ceiling.

'Are you in the civil service?'

'No, sir, I'm not in the civil service yet, but I think I'll find a post soon. Anyhow, what's government service? People – that's the main thing. What people I've got to know here!'

A boy came in with a bottle of champagne on a black tray.

'Well, there's a good chap . . . Isn't it true, Vasya, you're a good chap, eh? Here's to your health!'

The boy waited a moment, politely shook his little head, smiled and went out.

'Yes, they're good people, here,' Pyotr Petrovich went on, 'people with feeling, people with heart . . . If you like, I'll introduce you? Such grand lads they are, they'll be glad to see you. I'll tell them . . . Bobrov's dead, such a pity.'

'What Bobrov?'

'Sergey Bobrov. He was a splendid chap. He supported me financially, provincial ignoramus that I was. And Panteley Gornostaev's died. They've all died, all of them!'

'Have you been here in Moscow all the time? Haven't you been to the country at all?'

'To the country . . . My estate's been sold.'

'Sold?'

'Auctioned . . . It's a pity you didn't buy it!'

'What on earth will you live on, Pyotr Petrovich?'

'I won't die of hunger, God grant! There'll be no money, but there'll be friends. Anyhow, what's money? It's just dust! Gold's just dust!'

He screwed up his eyes, rummaged about in his pocket and then held out to me in the palm of his hand two fifteen-copeck coins and a ten-copeck coin.

'What's that? It's just dust!' The money was flung on the floor. 'Tell me now, have you read Polezhaev?'

'Yes.'

'Have you seen Mochalov[3] in *Hamlet*?'

'No, I haven't.'

'You've never seen, never . . . ' (And Karataev went pale, his eyes roved restlessly about. Turning away, his lips gave slight quivers.) 'Oh, Mochalov, Mochalov! "To die, to sleep,"[4] he declared in a hoarse voice.

> ' "No more – and by a sleep to say we end
> The heartache and the thousand natural shocks
> That flesh is heir to. 'Tis a consummation
> Devoutly to be wished. To die, to sleep . . ."

'To sleep, to sleep!' he muttered several times.

'Tell me, please,' I started to say, but he went on heatedly:

> ' "For who would bear the whips and scorns of time,
> Th'oppressor's wrong, the proud man's contumely,
> The pangs of despised love, the law's delay,
> The insolence of office, and the spurns
> That patient merit o' the unworthy takes,
> When he himself might his quietus make
> With a bare bodkin? . . . Nymph, in thy orisons
> Be all my sins remembered." '

And he let his head fall on the table. He began to stammer and blabber.

'"A little month",' he pronounced with renewed effort,

> '"A little month, or e'er these shoes were old
> With which she followed my poor father's body
> Like Niobe, all tears, why she, even she –
> O God, a beast that wants discourse of reason
> Would have mourned longer . . ."'

He raised the glass of champagne to his lips, but he didn't drink and went on:

> '"For Hecuba!
> What's Hecuba to him, or he to her,
> That he should weep for her? . . . Yet I,
> A dull and muddy-mettled rascal . . . Am I a coward?
> Who calls me villain? Gives me the lie i'th'throat?
> Ha, 'swounds, I should take it. For it cannot be
> But I am pigeon-livered and lack gall
> To make oppression bitter . . ."'

Karataev dropped his glass and clutched his head in his hands. I realized that I understood him.

'Well, that's it,' he said eventually. 'The past's a foreign country, you shouldn't go there . . . Isn't that right?' He gave a laugh. 'Here's to your health!'

'Will you stay in Moscow?' I asked him.

'I'll die in Moscow!'

'Karataev!' came a shout from the next room. 'Karataev, where are you? Come here, there's a good fe-ow!'

'They're calling me,' he said, rising heavily from where he'd been sitting. 'Goodbye. Call on me if you can. I'm living in —.'

But the next day, due to unforeseen circumstances, I had to leave Moscow and I never saw Pyotr Petrovich Karataev again.

MEETING

———————— ❦ ————————

I WAS sitting in a birch wood one autumn, about the middle of September. From early morning there had been occasional drizzle, succeeded from time to time by periods of warm sunny radiance; a season of changeable weather. The sky was either covered with crumbling white clouds or suddenly clear for an instant in a few places, and then, from behind the parted clouds, blue sky would appear, lucid and smiling, like a beautiful eye. I sat and looked around me and listened. The leaves scarcely rustled above my head; by their very noise one could know what time of year it was. It was not the happy, laughing *tremolo* of spring, not the soft murmuration and long-winded talkativeness of summer, not the shy and chill babblings of late autumn, but a hardly audible dreamy chattering. A faint wind ever so slightly moved through the treetops. The interior of the wood, damp from the rain, was continually changing, depending on whether the sun was shining or whether it was covered by cloud; the interior was either flooded with light, just as if everything in it had suddenly smiled: the delicate trunks of the not-too-numerous birches would suddenly acquire the soft sheen of white silk, the wafer-thin leaves which lay on the ground would suddenly grow multi-coloured and burn with crimson and gold, while the beautiful stems of tall curly bracken, already embellished with their autumn colouring which resembles the colour of overripe grapes, would stand there shot through with light, endlessly entangling and crisscrossing before one's eyes; or suddenly one would again be surrounded by a bluish dusk: the bright colours would instantly be extinguished and the birches would all stand there white, without a gleam on them, white as snow that has only just fallen and has not yet been touched by the chilly sparkling rays of the winter sun; and secretively, slyly, thinly drizzling rain would begin to filter and whisper through the wood.

The foliage on the birches was still almost completely green, although it had noticeably faded; only here and there stood a young tree all decked out in red or gold, and one could not help watching how brightly it flared up when the sun's rays broke, gliding and scintillating, through the myriad network of fine branches only just washed by glittering rain. There was not a single bird to be heard: all had taken cover and fallen silent; only the mocking little voice of the tom-tit tinkled occasionally like a little steel bell.

Before I had stopped in this little birch wood, I had gone with my dog through a grove of tall aspens. I confess that I am not particularly fond of that tree – the aspen – with its pale-mauve trunk and grey-green, metallic foliage which it raises as high as possible and spreads out in the air like a quivering fan; nor do I like the continual flutterings of its round untidy leaves which are so awkwardly attached to their long stalks. It acquires beauty only on certain summer evenings when, rising on high in isolation among low bushy undergrowth, it meets the challenge of the ebbing rays of the sunset and gleams and trembles, suffused from its topmost branches to its roots by a uniform yellow and purple light; or when, on a clear windy day, it is all noisily streaming and babbling against the blue sky, and every leaf, seized by the wind's ardour, appears to want to tear itself free, fly away and hurry off into the distance. But in general I dislike this tree and therefore, without stopping to rest in the aspen grove, I made my way to the little birch wood, settled myself under a tree whose branches began close to the ground and were able, in consequence, to shelter me from the rain, and, having gazed admiringly at the surrounding view, fell into the kind of untroubled and mild sleep familiar only to hunters.

I cannot say how long I was asleep, but when I opened my eyes the entire interior of the wood was filled with sunlight and in all directions through the jubilantly rustling foliage a bright blue sky peered and seemed to sparkle; the clouds had vanished, dispersed by the wind that had sprung up; the weather had cleared, and in the air could be felt that special dry freshness which, imbuing the heart with a feeling of elation, almost always means a peaceful and clear evening after a rainy day.

I was on the point of rising and again trying my luck, when suddenly my eyes lighted on a motionless human form. I looked closely and saw that it was a young peasant girl. She was sitting twenty paces from me, her head lowered in thought and both hands dropped on her knees; in the half-open palm of one of them lay a thick bunch of wild flowers and at each breath she took the bunch slipped quietly down on to her checked skirt. A clean white blouse, buttoned at the neck and at the wrists, gathered in short soft folds about her waist; two rows of large yellow beads fell from her neck on to her bosom. She was very pretty in her own way. Her thick fair hair of a beautiful ash colour was parted into two carefully styled semi-circles below a narrow crimson ribbon drawn almost down to her temples, which were white as ivory; the rest of her face was faintly sunburned to that golden hue which is only acquired by a delicate skin. I could not see her eyes because she did not raise them; but I clearly saw her fine, high eyebrows and long eyelashes, which were damp, and on one of her cheeks I saw the dried trace of a tear that had come to rest at the edge of her slightly pale lips and glittered in the sunlight. The whole appearance of her head was very charming; even the slightly thick and rounded nose did nothing to spoil it. I particularly liked the expression on her face for the way in which it was so artless and gentle, so melancholy and full of childish bewilderment at her own grief.

She was evidently waiting for someone. Something crackled faintly in the wood and she at once raised her head and looked round; in the transparent shade her large eyes, bright and frightened, flashed quickly before me like the eyes of a doe. She listened for a few moments without taking her wide-open eyes from the place where the faint sound had been made, then heaved a sigh, turned her head calmly back, bent still farther down and began slowly to finger the flowers. Her eyelids reddened, her lips gave a quiver of bitterness and another tear slipped from beneath her thick lashes, coming to rest on her cheek where it glittered radiantly. Some time passed in this way, and the poor girl did not move save to make a few regretful gestures with her hands and to go on listening and listening. Again something made a noise in the wood and she was instantly alerted. The noise continued, grew louder as it approached, and finally could be heard the noise of rapid, decisive footsteps. She straightened herself and appeared to be overcome with shyness; her attentive features began to quiver and burn with expectation. The figure of a man could be glimpsed through the thicket. She peered in that direction, blushed suddenly, gave a joyful and happy smile, got ready to stand up and once again suddenly lowered her head, growing pale and confused – and she only raised her faltering, almost imploring gaze to the newcomer when he had stopped beside her.

I examined him with curiosity from my hiding-place. I confess that he produced an unpleasant impression on me. To all appearances he was the pampered valet of some rich young master. His clothes displayed pretensions to good taste and dandified casualness: they consisted of a short, bronze-coloured top-coat buttoned up to the neck and inherited, more than likely, from his master, a little rose-tinted neck-tie with mauve tips and a black velvet cap with gold lace edging worn pulled down over the eyebrows. The rounded collar of his white shirt pressed unmercifully up against his ears and bit into his cheek, while his starched cuffs covered his hands right down to the red and crooked fingers which were embellished with gold and silver rings containing turquoise forget-me-nots. His face – ruddy, fresh-complexioned and impudent – belonged to the category of faces which, so far as I have been able to judge, almost invariably annoy men and, unfortunately, are very often pleasing to women. He clearly made an effort to endow his rather coarse features with an expression of superciliousness and boredom; he endlessly screwed up his already tiny milk-grey eyes, frowned, let his mouth droop at the edges, gave forced yawns and with a casual, though not entirely skilled, air of abandon either patted the reddish, artfully coiled hair on his temples or twiddled the little yellow hairs that stuck out on his fat upper lip – in a word, he showed off insufferably. He began to show off as soon as he saw the young peasant girl waiting for him; he slowly approached her at a lounging pace, came to a stop, shrugged his shoulders, stuck both hands into the pockets of his top-coat and, with hardly more than a fleeting and indifferent glance at the poor girl, lowered himself to the ground.

'Well,' he began, still looking away to one side, swinging his leg and yawning, 'have you been here long?'

The girl was unable to answer him immediately.

'A long time, sir, Victor Alexandrych,' she said eventually in a scarcely audible voice.

'Ah!' He removed his cap, grandly drew his hand through his

thick, tightly coiled hair, which began almost at his eyebrows, and glancing round with dignity, once more carefully covered his priceless head. 'And I'd almost completely forgotten. After all, look how it rained!' He yawned once more. 'There's a mass of things to be done, what with everything to be got ready and the master swearing as well. Tomorrow we'll be off . . .'

'Tomorrow?' the girl said and directed him a look of fright.

'That's right – tomorrow. Now, now, now, please,' he added hastily and with annoyance, seeing that she had begun to tremble all over and was quietly lowering her head, 'please, Akulina, no crying. You know I can't stand crying.' And he puckered up his snub nose. 'If you start, I'll leave at once. What silliness – blubbering!'

'No, I won't, I won't,' Akulina uttered hurriedly, making herself swallow her tears. 'So you're leaving tomorrow?' she added after a brief pause. 'When will God bring you back to see me again, Victor Alexandrych?'

'We'll meet again, we'll meet again. If not next year, then later. It seems the master wants to enter government service in St Petersburg,' he continued, speaking the words casually and slightly through the nose, 'and maybe we'll go abroad.'

'You'll forget me, Victor Alexandrych,' Akulina said sadly.

'No, why should I? I won't forget you. Only you've got to be sensible, not start playing up, obey your father . . . I'll not forget you – no-o-o.' And he calmly stretched himself and again yawned.

'You mustn't forget me, Victor Alexandrych,' she continued in an imploring voice. 'I've loved you so much, it seems, and it seems I've done everything for you . . . You tell me to listen to my father, Victor Alexandrych . . . There's no point in listening to my father . . .'

'Why not?' He uttered these words as it were from his stomach, lying on his back with his arms behind his head.

'There's no point, Victor Alexandrych. You know that yourself . . .'

She said nothing. Victor played with the steel chain of his watch.

'You're not a fool, Akulina,' he started saying at last, 'so don't talk nonsense. I want what's best for you, do you understand me? Of course, you're not stupid, you're not a complete peasant girl, so to speak; and your mother also wasn't always a peasant girl. But you're without any education, so you've got to listen when people tell you things.'

'I'm frightened, Victor Alexandrych.'

'Hey, there, that's a lot of nonsense, my dear. What's there to be frightened of! What's that you've got there,' he added, turning to her, 'flowers?'

'Flowers,' answered Akulina despondently. 'They're some field tansies I've picked,' she continued, brightening slightly, 'and they're good for calves. And these are marigolds, they help against scrofula. Just look what a lovely little flower it is! I've never seen such a lovely little flower before in all my born days. Then there are some forget-me-nots, here are some violets. But these I got for you,' she added, taking out from beneath the yellow tansies a small bunch of blue cornflowers tied together with a fine skein of grass, 'would you like them?'

Victor languidly stretched out his hand, took the bunch, casually sniffed the flowers and began to twiddle them in his fingers, gazing up in the air from time to time with thoughtful self-importance. Akulina looked at him and her sad gaze contained such tender devotion, such worshipful humility and love. Yet she was also afraid of him, and fearful of crying; and taking her own leave of him and doting on him for the last time; but he lay there in the lounging pose of a sultan and endured her worship of him with magnanimous patience and condescension. I confess that his red face vexed me with its pretentiously disdainful indifference through which could be discerned a replete and self-satisfied vanity. Akulina was so fine at that moment, for her whole heart was trustfully and passionately laid open before him, craving him and yearning to be loved, but he . . . he simply let the cornflowers drop on the grass, took a round glass in a bronze frame out of the side pocket of his top-coat and started trying to fix it in place over his eye; but no matter how hard he tried to keep it in place with a puckered brow, a raised cheek and even with his nose, the little eyeglass kept on falling out and dropping into his hand.

'What's that?' Akulina asked finally in astonishment.

'A lorgnette,' he answered self-importantly.

'What's it for?'

'So as to see better.'

'Show it me.'

Victor frowned, but he gave her the eyeglass.

'Don't break it, mind.'

'You needn't worry, I won't.' She raised it timidly to her eye. 'I don't see anything,' she said artlessly.

'It's your eye, you've got to screw up your eye,' he retorted in the voice of a dissatisfied mentor. She screwed up the eye before which she was holding the little glass. 'Not that one, not that one, idiot! The other one!' exclaimed Victor and, giving her no chance to correct her mistake, took the lorgnette from her.

Akulina reddened, gave a nervous laugh and turned away.

'It's obviously not for the likes of me,' she murmured.

'That's for sure!'

The poor girl was silent and let fall a deep sigh.

'Oh, Victor Alexandrych, what'll I do without you?' she suddenly said.

Victor wiped the lorgnette with the edge of his coat and put it back in his pocket.

'Yes, yes,' he said eventually, 'it sure will be hard for you to start with.' He gave her several condescending pats on the shoulder; she ever so quietly lifted his hand from her shoulder and timidly kissed it. 'Well, all right, all right, you're a good kid,' he went on, giving a self-satisfied smile, 'but what can I do about it? Judge for yourself! The master and I can't stay here; it'll be winter soon now and to spend the winter in the country – you know this yourself – is just horrible. But it's another matter in St Petersburg! There are simply such wonderful things there, such as you, stupid, wouldn't be able to imagine even in your wildest dreams! What houses and streets, and the sochiety, the culture – it's simply stupendous!' Akulina listened to him with greedy interest, her lips slightly parted like a child's. 'Anyhow,' he added, turning over, 'why am I telling you all this? You won't be able to understand it.'

'Why say that, Victor Alexandrych? I've understood it, I've understood everything.'

'What a bright one you are!'

Akulina lowered her head.

'You never used to talk to me like that before, Victor Alexandrych,' she said without raising her eyes.

'Didn't I before? Before! You're a one! Before indeed!' he commented, pretending to be indignant.

Both were silent for a while.

'However, it's time for me to be going,' said Victor, and was on the point of raising himself on one elbow.

'Stay a bit longer,' Akulina declared in an imploring voice.

'What's there to wait for? I've already said goodbye to you.'

'Stay a bit,' Akulina repeated.

Victor again lay back and started whistling. Akulina never took her eyes off him. I could tell that she was slowly working herself into a state of agitation: her lips were working and her pale cheeks were faintly crimsoning.

'Victor Alexandrych,' she said at last in a breaking voice, 'it's sinful of you . . . sinful of you, Victor Alexandrych, in God's name it is!'

'What's sinful?' he asked, knitting his brows, and he raised himself slightly and turned his head towards her.

'It's sinful, Victor Alexandrych. If you'd only say one kind word to me now you're leaving, just say one word to me, wretched little orphan that I am . . .'

'But what should I say to you?'

'I don't know. You should know that better than me, Victor Alexandrych. Now you're going away, and if only you'd say a word . . . Why should I deserve this?'

'What a strange girl you are! What can I say?'

'Just say one word . . .'

'Well, you've certainly gone on and on about the same thing,' he said in disgruntlement and stood up.

'Don't be angry, Victor Alexandrych,' she added quickly, hardly restraining her tears.

'I'm not angry, it's only that you're stupid . . . What do you want? You know I can't marry you, don't you? Surely you know I can't? So what's it you want? What is it?' He stuck his face forward in expectation of her answer and opened wide his fingers.

'I don't want anything . . . anything,' she answered, stammering and scarcely daring to stretch her trembling hands out towards him, 'only if you'd just say one word in farewell . . .'

And tears streamed from her eyes.

'Well, so there it is, you've started crying,' Victor said callously, tipping his cap forward over his eyes.

'I don't want anything,' she went on, swallowing her tears and covering her face with both hands, 'but what'll it be like for me in the family, what'll there be for me? And what's going to happen to me, what's going to become of me, wretch that I am! They'll give their orphan girl away to someone who doesn't love her . . . O poor me, poor me!'

'Moan away, moan away!' muttered Victor under his breath, shifting from one foot to the other.

'If only he'd say one little word, just one word . . . Such as, Akulina, I . . . I . . .'

Suddenly heart-rending sobs prevented her from finishing what she was saying. She flopped on her face in the grass and burst into bitter, bitter tears. Her whole body shook convulsively, the nape of her neck rising and falling. Her long-restrained grief finally poured forth in torrents. Victor stood for a moment or so above her, shrugged his shoulders, turned and walked away with big strides.

Several moments passed. She grew quiet, raised her head, jumped up, looked about her and wrung her hands; she was on the point of rushing after him, but her legs collapsed under her and she fell on her knees. I could not hold myself back and rushed towards her, but she had hardly had time to look at me before she found the strength from somewhere to raise herself with a faint cry and vanish through the trees, leaving her flowers scattered on the ground.

I stopped there a moment, picked up the bunch of cornflowers and walked out of the wood into a field. The sun was low in the pale clear sky and its rays had, as it were, lost their colour and grown cold; they did not shine so much as flow out in an even, almost watery, light. No more than half an hour remained until evening, but the sunset was only just beginning to crimson the sky. A flurrying wind raced towards me across the dry, yellow stubble; hastily spinning before it, little shrivelled leaves streamed past me across the track and along the edge of the wood; the side which faced on to the field like a wall shuddered all over and glistened with a faint sparkling, distinctly though not brightly; on the red-tinted grass, on separate blades of grass, on pieces of straw, everywhere innumerable strands of autumn cobwebs glittered and rippled. I stopped, and a feeling of melancholy stole over me, for it seemed to me that the sombre terror associated with the approaching winter was breaking through the cheerless, though fresh, smile of nature at this time of withering. High above me, ponderously and sharply sundering the air with its wings, a vigilant raven flew by, turned its head, looked sidewards at me, took wing and disappeared beyond the wood with strident cawings; a large flock of pigeons rose smartly from a place where there had been threshing and after suddenly making a huge wheeling turn in the air settled busily on to the field — a sure sign of autumn! Someone rode by on the other side of a bare hillock, his empty cart clattering noisily . . .

I returned home; but the image of the poor Akulina took a long time to fade from my mind, and her cornflowers, which have long since withered, remain with me to this day . . .

HAMLET OF THE
SHCHIGROVSKY DISTRICT

———————— ❧ ————————

O N one of my trips I received an invitation to dine with a
wealthy landowner and hunter, Alexander Mikhailych G—.
His village was situated about three miles from a small group of
dwellings where I was staying at that time. I dressed up in my frock-
coat, without which I advise no one to leave home, even though it
be only for a hunting trip, and set off for Alexander Mikhailych's
place. Dinner was to begin at six; I arrived at five and found, already
assembled, a large number of members of the nobility in uniforms,
evening dress and other less specific types of costume. My host
greeted me cordially, but at once hurried off into the servants' hall.
He was awaiting the arrival of an eminent dignitary and felt a degree
of excitement over it that was hardly in keeping with his independent
position in the world and his wealth. Alexander Mikhailych had
never been married and disliked women; his parties were attended
only by men. He lived on a big scale, had enlarged and done up his
ancestral home in magnificent fashion, every year ordered from
Moscow wines to the tune of fifteen thousand roubles and in general
enjoyed the greatest respect. He had long ago retired from service
and was not seeking honours of any kind ... Why on earth, then,
should he have fussed himself over the visit of an official guest and
been so excited by it ever since the morning of his banquet? That
remains obscured by the mists of uncertainty, as a notary of my
acquaintance used to say when he was asked whether he took bribes
from willing donors.

Parting with my host, I began to wander about the rooms. Almost
all the guests were complete strangers to me; about twenty of them
were already seated at the card tables. Among those playing preference were two military men with distinguished, if slightly down-at-

heel, faces, and a few civilian gentlemen wearing high, tight collars and the kind of pendant, dyed whiskers affected only by resolute but well-disposed people (these well-disposed people were engaged in importantly sorting their cards and casting sideward glances at new-comers without moving their heads); also five or six district officials with round tummies, puffy, sticky little hands and modestly im-mobile little feet (these gentlemen spoke in soft voices, regaled everyone with timid smiles, held their cards close to their shirt-fronts and, when playing trumps, did not thump them down on the table but, on the contrary, let them drop with a floating motion on the green cloth and, as they gathered in their winnings, produced a slight, but very decorous and polite creaking sound). Other members of the nobility were sitting on divans or clustered in groups about the doorways and windows; a no longer young, though outwardly effeminate, landowner was standing in one corner, trembling and blushing and agitatedly twisting the watch signet on his stomach, though no one was paying any attention to him; other gentlemen, adorned in round frock-coats and chequered trousers of Moscow workmanship tailored by the foreigner, Fiers Klyukhin, master of his guild in perpetuity, were engaged in unusually free and lively discussion, liberally turning the fat, bare napes of their necks in one direction or another; a young man of about twenty, blond and myopic, dressed from head to foot in black, was visibly embarrassed, but continued to smile venomously.

I was, however, beginning to grow a little bored when suddenly I was joined by a certain Voinitsyn, a young man who had failed to complete his education and was now living in Alexander Mik-hailych's house in the capacity of ... it would be difficult to say precisely in what capacity. He was an excellent shot and adept at training dogs. I had known him earlier in Moscow. He belonged to the run of young men who used to 'play dumb as a post' at every examination – that is to say, who never uttered a word in answer to the professor's questions. These gentlemen were also known, in stylish parlance, as 'sideburn-ites'.[1] (These matters relate to the distant past, as you can readily appreciate.) It would be arranged as follows: they would call upon Voinitsyn, for instance. Voinitsyn, who until that moment had been sitting straight and motionless on his bench, perspiring hotly from head to toe and slowly, though fatuously, rolling his eyes around – he would rise, hastily button up his uniform right to the top and saunter crabwise to the examiners' table.

'Be good enough to take a ticket,' a professor would say affably.

Voinitsyn would stretch out a hand and agitatedly finger the little pile of tickets.

'You don't have to choose one, if you don't mind,' would remark the querulous voice of some tetchy old man, a professor from another faculty, who had conceived a sudden dislike for the unfortunate 'sideburn-ite'. Voinitsyn would submit to his fate, take a ticket, show its number and walk to the window to sit down while a previous examinee answered a question. At the window Voinitsyn would not take his eyes off the ticket, save perhaps once again to roll his eyes slowly around, and would remain stock-still in every limb. Eventually, however, the previous examinee would be finished. He would be told: 'Good, you may go,' or even 'Good, sir, very good, sir,' depending upon his abilities. Then they would call upon Voinitsyn. Voinitsyn would rise and approach the table with a firm step.

'Read out the question,' they would tell him.

Holding it in both hands, Voinitsyn would raise the ticket to the tip of his nose, read out the question slowly and slowly lower his arms.

'Well, sir, be so good as to answer,' the first professor would say casually, resting back in his chair and crossing his hands on his chest.

A silence deep as the grave would fall upon the proceedings.

'What's wrong with you?'

Voinitsyn would be silent. The old man from another faculty would begin to grow annoyed.

'Come on, say something, man!'

This Voinitsyn of mine would remain silent, as if he had given up the ghost. The shaven nape of his neck would jut out still and sharp before the curious gaze of his comrades. The old man's eyes were ready to jump out of his head: he had finally begun to loathe Voinitsyn.

'Isn't it rather strange, after all,' another examiner would remark, 'that you should stand there dumb as a post? So you don't know the answer, is that it? If that's so, say so.'

'Permit me to take another ticket,' the unfortunate chap would mumble. The professors exchanged looks.

'Very well, then,' says the chief examiner with a wave of his hand.

Voinitsyn again takes a ticket, again goes to the window, again returns to the table and again is as silent as a corpse. The old fellow from another faculty is just about to eat him alive. Finally they send him packing and award him a zero mark. By now you would think he'd at least make tracks. Not at all! He returns to his place and adopts the same motionless pose until the conclusion of the examination, when he leaves, exclaiming: 'What a sweat that was! What a business!' And all day he strolls around Moscow, occasionally clutching his head and bitterly cursing his wretched fate. Never once, of course, does he so much as glance at a book, and the next day the same thing happens all over again.

It was this Voinitsyn who took his place next to me. We talked together about our Moscow days, about our hunting experiences.

'If you wish,' he suddenly whispered to me, 'I'll introduce you to our leading local wit?'

'Do me that honour.'

Voinitsyn led me up to a man of small stature, with a tall tuft of hair on the top of his head and whiskers, dressed in a brown frock-coat and a colourful necktie. His embittered, lively features conveyed a real air of wit and vindictiveness. A sour, fugitive smile endlessly contorted his lips; his small, dark, puckered eyes looked boldly out from beneath uneven eyelashes. Standing beside him was a land-owner, broad of beam, soft, sugary – a real Lord Honeybun – and one-eyed. His laughter always anticipated the little man's witticisms and he was literally melting with pleasure. Voinitsyn introduced me to the local wit, one Pyotr Petrovich Lupikhin by name. We made our introductions and exchanged the initial words of greeting.

'And now allow me to introduce you to my best friend,' said Lupikhin suddenly in a sharp tone of voice, seizing the sugary landowner by the arm. 'Now don't you be retiring, Kirila Seli-fanych,' he added, 'they won't bite you. Here, my dear sirs,' he continued, while the embarrassed Kirila Selifanych gave such awk-ward bows that it seemed his stomach was about to collapse, 'here, sir, I recommend to you a most excellent member of the gentry. He enjoyed splendid health until he was fifty years of age, and then he suddenly took it into his head to cure his eyesight, as a result of which he lost the use of one eye. Since then he's been dispensing cures to his peasants with the same degree of success . . . And they, it goes without saying, have shown a similar devotion . . .'

'What a fellow,' Kirila Selifanych muttered and burst into laughter.

'Do complete what you were saying, my friend, do go on,' Lupikhin inserted. 'After all, they could well elect you to the judges' bench, and they will elect you, you'll see. Well, suppose, of course, that the court assessors do all the thinking for you, there'd still be a need in any event to express somebody else's ideas, let's say. What if the Governor should unexpectedly drop by and ask: "What's the judge stammering for?" Well, suppose they say it's an attack of paralysis, then he'll say: "Bleed him, then, bleed him!" And that in your position, you'll agree, wouldn't be right and proper.'

The sugary landowner went off into a drum-roll of laughter.

'Look at him laughing,' Lupikhin continued, gazing wickedly at the quivering stomach of Kirila Selifanych. 'And why shouldn't he laugh?' he added, turning to me. 'He's well fed, healthy, childless, his peasants aren't mortgaged – after all, he's curing them – and his wife's a bit dotty.' (Kirila Selifanych turned slightly to one side, feigning not to catch this, and continued to roar with laughter.) 'I can laugh just the same, and my wife's run off with a land surveyor.' (He showed his teeth in a grin.) 'Perhaps you didn't know that? Yessir! She just upped and ran off and left me a letter which read: "Dear Pyotr Petrovich, forgive me, carried away by passion. I'm going off with the friend of my heart . . ." And the land surveyor only captured her heart by not cutting his nails and wearing his pants skin-tight. You're surprised? "Such a frank fellow," you'll say . . . And, my God! we men of the steppes know how to open up the womb of truth. However, let's go to one side. There's no need for us to go on standing next to a future judge . . .'

He took me by the arm and we went to the window.

'I pass here for a wit,' he said to me in the course of conversation, 'but you mustn't believe that. I'm simply an embittered man and I speak my mind out loud. That's why I'm so unrestrained. And why should I stand on ceremony, in fact? I don't give a damn for any opinions and I'm not out for anything for myself. I have a wicked tongue – so what of it? A man with a wicked tongue at least doesn't need to have a mind. But how refreshing it is, you wouldn't believe it . . . Well, take a look, for example, at our host! Now I ask you, why on earth is he scurrying about like that, all the time glancing at the clock, smiling, perspiring, making himself look important and leaving us to die of hunger? A high-ranking dignitary's not so unusual a sight, after all! There he is, there he is, again running – he's even started hobbling about, look at him!'

And Lupikhin gave a screeching laugh.

'One thing wrong is that there are no ladies,' he continued with a deep sigh. 'It's a stag occasion – otherwise it would've been useful for the likes of us. Take a look, take a look,' he exclaimed suddenly. 'Prince Kozelsky's coming – there he is, that tall man with a beard and yellow gloves. You can tell at once that he's been abroad . . . And he makes a habit of arriving so late. That man alone, I tell you, is as stupid as a couple of merchant's horses, but you just take the trouble to notice how condescendingly he addresses the likes of us, how magnanimously he permits himself to smile at the pleasantries of our famished mothers and daughters! Sometimes he even tries to be witty on his own account, although he doesn't live here permanently; and the kind of witty remarks he makes! Just like trying to saw at a tow-rope with a blunt knife! He can't stand the sight of me . . . I'll go and pay my respects to him.'

And Lupikhin ran off in the prince's direction.

'And here comes my private enemy,' he announced, suddenly turning back to me. 'See that stout man with the tanned face and bristles on his head – there, the one who's grasping his hat in his hand and stealing along by the wall, glancing all around him like a veritable wolf? For 400 roubles I sold him a horse that was worth a thousand, and this lowly creature now has every right to despise me; and yet he is so devoid of the capacity for understanding, especially in the morning, before he's taken his tea, or immediately after dinner, that if you say "How d'you do?" to him he'll answer: "How what, sir?" And here comes a general,' Lupikhin went on, 'a civil-service general in retirement, a general who's lost all his money. He has a daughter of sugar-beet refinement and a factory of scrofula – I'm sorry, I didn't get that right . . . Anyhow, you understand what I mean. Ah! and here's an architect just dropped by! A German, replete with whiskers and no idea of his business – wonders'll never cease! But as a matter of fact there's no need for him to know his business: all he has to do is take bribes and put up more columns, more pillars, that is, for the pillars of our aristocracy!'

Lupikhin again gave vent to laughter. But suddenly an anxious excitement spread through the entire house. The dignitary had arrived. Our host literally plunged into the entrance hall. Several devoted members of his staff and some eager guests rushed after him. The noisy conversation changed into soft, pleasant talk, similar to the springtime humming of bees in their native hives. Only the indefatigably waspish Lupikhin and the superb drone Kozelsky did not lower their voices ... And finally came the queen herself – the dignitary entered. Hearts were wafted to meet him, sitting torsos were raised a trifle; even the landowner who had bought the horse cheaply from Lupikhin, even he thrust his chin into his chest. The dignitary maintained his dignity with the utmost aplomb: nodding his head back as though bowing, he spoke a few appreciative words, each of which began with the letter 'a' uttered protractedly through the nose, and with a disapproval amounting to ravening hunger he glanced at Prince Kozelsky's beard and offered the index finger of his left hand to the penniless civil-service general with the factory and daughter. After a few minutes, in the course of which the dignitary succeeded in remarking twice how glad he was that he had not arrived late for the dinner, the entire company proceeded into the dining-room, the bigwigs leading the way.

It is hardly necessary to tell the reader how the dignitary was given the seat of honour between the civil-service general and the provincial marshal of nobility, a man of unrestrained and dignified expression entirely in keeping with his starched shirt-front, infinitely broad waistcoat and round snuff-box full of French tobacco; how our host fussed, dashed about, busied himself importantly, urged his guests to partake of what was offered, smiled in passing at the dignitary's back and, standing in one corner like a schoolboy, hastily spooned down a plate of soup or had a bite of beef; how the butler brought in a fish more than three feet long with a floral bouquet in its mouth; how the servants, all liveried and severe of face, morosely approached each member of the gentry either with Malaga or dry madeira and how almost all these gentlemen, especially the elderly, drank glass after glass as though submitting unwillingly to a sense of duty; how finally bottles of champagne began to pop and toasts began to be made: the reader is, no doubt, only too familiar with such matters. But particularly noteworthy, it seemed to me, was an anecdote told by the dignitary himself amid a universally joyous hush.

Someone – it may have been the penniless general, a man acquainted with the latest literary trends – remarked on the influence of women in general and particularly their influence on young men. 'Yes, indeed,' said the dignitary in amplification, 'that is true. But young men should be kept under the strictest control, otherwise they tend to go out of their minds over any and every kind of skirt.' (Childishly happy smiles sped across the faces of all the guests; one landowner's expression even lit up with gratitude.) '*Bee*-cause young men are stupid.' (The dignitary, probably for the sake of grandness, sometimes altered the accepted accentuation of words.) 'Take, for example, my son Ivan,' he continued. 'The fool's only just twenty, but he comes to me suddenly and says: "Permit me, sir, to get married." I tell him: "You're a fool, do your service first . . ." Well, of course, despair, tears . . . But in my view that's it . . .' (The dignitary pronounced the words 'that's it' more with his stomach than his lips; he paused and directed a majestic glance at his neighbour, the general, at the same time raising his brows quite unexpectedly high. The civil-service general inclined his head pleasantly a little on one side and with extraordinary rapidity blinked one eye, which was turned towards the dignitary.) 'And now what d'you think,' the dignitary started up again, 'now he himself writes to me and says: "Thank you, sir, for teaching me not to be so foolish." That's how one ought to handle such matters.' All the guests, needless to say, were in full agreement with the speaker and apparently grew quite enlivened at receiving such pleasure and such injunctions. After dinner the entire company rose and moved into the drawing-room with a great deal more noisiness, though it was still within the bounds of decency and on this occasion literally justified. They all sat down to cards.

Somehow or other I passed the time until it was evening and, having ordered my driver to have my carriage ready for five o'clock the next morning, I retired to bed. But during the course of that same day it still remained for me to make the acquaintance of a certain remarkable person.

Owing to the number of guests no one slept in a room by himself. The small, greenish, dampish room, to which my host's butler led me, was already occupied by another guest, who had already undressed completely. Seeing me, he swiftly plunged under the counterpane, with which he covered himself right up to his nose, twisted and turned a little on the crumbling feather mattress and grew still, looking sharply up from beneath the rounded rim of his cotton nightcap. I went up to the other bed (there were only two of them in the room), undressed and lay down between the damp sheets. My neighbour began turning over in his bed. I wished him good night.

Half an hour passed. Despite all my efforts, I was quite unable to get to sleep: an endless succession of vague, unnecessary thoughts dragged one after another persistently and monotonously through my mind just like the buckets of a water-lifting machine.

'It seems you're not asleep?' my neighbour said.

'As you see,' I answered. 'And you're also wakeful?'

'I'm always wakeful.'

'How is that?'

'That's how it is. I go to sleep without knowing why; I lie and lie and then I'm asleep.'

'Why, then, do you get into bed before you feel like sleeping?'

'What do you suggest I should do?'

I did not reply to my neighbour's question.

'It surprises me,' he continued after a short silence, 'that there are no fleas here. Where, one wonders, have they got to?'

'You sound as if you regret not having them,' I remarked.

'No, I don't regret not having them; but I do like things to be consistent.'

Listen to the words he's using, I thought.

My neighbour again grew silent.

'Would you like to make a bet with me?' he suddenly asked fairly loudly.

'About what?' My neighbour was beginning to amuse me.

'Hmm . . . about what? About this: I feel sure that you take me for a fool.'

'If you please . . .' I mumbled in surprise.

'For a country bumpkin, an ignoramus . . . Admit it.'

'I do not have the pleasure of knowing you,' I protested. 'How can you deduce . . .'

'How! I can deduce from the very sound of your voice: you've been answering me so casually . . . But I'm not at all what you think.'

'Allow me . . .'

'No, *you* allow me. In the first place, I speak French no worse than you, and German even better. In the second place, I spent three years abroad: in Berlin alone I lived about eight months. I have studied Hegel, my good sir, and I know Goethe by heart. What is more, I was for quite a while in love with the daughter of a German professor and then, back here, I got married to a consumptive lady – a bald-headed but very remarkable individual. It would seem, then, that I'm of the same breed as you. I'm not a country bumpkin, as you suppose . . . I'm also consumed by introspection and there's nothing straightforward about me whatever.'

I raised my head and looked with redoubled interest at this odd fellow. In the faint illumination of the night-light I could scarcely make out his features.

'There you are now, you're looking at me,' he continued, adjusting his nightcap, 'and no doubt you're asking yourself: how is it that I didn't notice him today? I'll tell you why you didn't notice me – because I do not raise my voice; because I hide behind others, standing behind doors, talking with no one; because when the butler passes me with a tray he raises his elbow beforehand to the level of my chest . . . And why do all these things happen? For two reasons: firstly, I am poor, and secondly, I have become reconciled . . . Tell me the truth, you didn't notice me, did you?'

'I really did not have the pleasure . . .'

'Oh, sure, sure,' he interrupted me, 'I knew it.'

He raised himself a little and folded his arms; the long shadow of his nightcap bent round from the wall to the ceiling.

'But admit it,' he added, suddenly glancing sideways at me, 'I must seem to you to be an extremely odd fellow, an original character, as they say, or perhaps something even worse, let's suppose: perhaps you think I'm trying to make myself out to be an eccentric?'

'Again I must repeat to you that I don't know you . . .'

He lowered his head for an instant.

'Why I should've started saying these things quite out of the blue to you, someone I don't know at all – the Lord, the Lord alone knows!' (He sighed.) 'It's not due to any kinship of souls! Both you and I, we're both respectable people – we're egoists, that's to say. My business is not the slightest concern of yours, nor yours of mine, isn't that so? Yet neither of us can get to sleep . . . So why not talk a little? I'm in my stride now, which doesn't happen to me often. I'm shy, you see, but not shy on the strength of being a provincial, a person of no rank or a pauper, but on the strength of the fact that I'm an awfully conceited fellow. But sometimes, under the influence of favourable circumstances and eventualities, which, by the way, I'm in no condition either to define or foresee, my shyness vanishes completely, as now, for instance. Set me face to face now with, say, the Dalai Lama himself and I'd ask even him for a pinch of snuff. But perhaps you'd like to go to sleep?'

'On the contrary,' I protested in haste, 'I find it very pleasant conversing with you.'

'That is, I entertain you, you mean . . . So much the better. Well, then, sir, I'll tell you that in these parts people do me the honour of calling me original – those people, that's to say, who may casually happen to let fall my name along with the rest of the rubbish they talk. "With my fate is no one very much concerned . . ."[2] They aim to hurt my pride. Oh, my God! If they only did but know that I'm perishing precisely because there's absolutely nothing original about me whatever, nothing except such childish pranks, for instance, as my present conversation with you; but such pranks aren't worth a jot. They're the cheapest and most despicable form of originality.'

He turned to face me and threw wide his arms.

'My dear sir!' he exclaimed. 'I am of the opinion that life on this earth is intended, generally speaking, for original people; only they have the right to live. *Mon verre n'est pas grand, mais je bois dans mon verre*,[3] someone once said. You see, don't you,' he added in a low voice, 'what pure French pronunciation I have? What's it to me if your head's leonine and roomy and you understand everything, know a great deal, keep up with the times, but you've got nothing at all that's uniquely your own, uniquely special, uniquely personal! You'll be just one more lumber-room of commonplaces with which to clutter up the world – and what sort of enjoyment is to be derived from that? No, at least be stupid, but stupid in your own way! At least have your own smell, some personal smell! And don't think my demands as regards this smell are formidable . . . God forbid! There's a bottomless pit of such kinds of original people: wherever you look you'll find one; every man alive's an original person in that sense – except that I haven't happened to be one of them!'

'Nevertheless, though,' he continued, after a short pause, 'what expectations I aroused in my youth! What an exalted opinion I had of my own person before going abroad and immediately after my return! Abroad, of course, I kept my ears pinned back, made my own way in the world, just as people of our sort should – people who know it all, see the point of everything, but, in the end, when you look at them you realize they haven't learned the first blessed thing!'

'Original, original!' he elaborated, giving a reproachful shake of the head. 'They call me original, but it turns out in fact that there's no one on earth less original than your most humble servant. I most likely was born in imitation of someone else . . . Yes, by God! I live my life as well in imitation of a few authors whom I've studied, living by the sweat of my brow: I've done my bit of studying and falling in love and, at last, getting married, not as it were of my own free will, but just as if I was performing some duty, doing some lesson – who knows which it was?'

He tore his nightcap from his head and flung it down on the bed.

'If you like, I'll tell you the story of my life,' he asked me in an abrupt tone of voice, 'or, better, a few features of my life?'

'Do me that honour.'

'Or, no, I'd better tell you how I got married. After all, marriage is a serious affair, the touchstone of the whole man; in it is reflected, as in a mirror . . . no, that analogy's too banal. If you don't mind, I'll take a pinch of snuff.'

He extracted a snuff-box from beneath his pillow, opened it and began talking again while waving the opened snuff-box in the air.

'My good sir, you should appreciate my position. Judge for yourself what – what, if you'll be so kind – what good I might derive from the encyclopedia of Hegel?[4] What is there in common, will you tell me, between this encyclopedia and Russian life? And how would you want it applied to our circumstances – and not only it alone, the encyclopedia, but in general German philosophy – and more than that – German science?'

He jumped up and down on his bed and began muttering in a low voice, gritting his teeth maliciously:

'So that's how it is, that's how it is! So why on earth did you drag yourself abroad? Why didn't you sit at home and study the life around you on the spot? You would then have recognized its needs and future potential, and so far as your vocation, so to speak, was concerned you'd have been able to reach a clear understanding . . . Yet, if you'll allow me,' he continued, again altering his tone of voice as if justifying himself and succumbing to shyness, 'where can people of our sort learn to study something that not a single scholar has yet set down in a book? I would have been glad to take lessons from it – from Russian life, that is; but the trouble is, the poor darling thing doesn't say a word in explanation. "Take me as I am," it seems to say. But that's beyond my powers. It ought to give me something to go on, offer me something conclusive. "Something conclusive?" they ask; "here's something conclusive: Lend your ear to our Moscow sages,[5] don't they sing as sweetly as nightingales?" But that's just the trouble: they whistle away like Kursk nightingales and don't talk like human beings . . . So I gave the matter a good deal of thought and came to the conclusion that science was apparently the same the world over, just as truth was, and took the plunge by setting out, with God's help, for foreign lands to live among heathens . . . What more d'you want me to say in justification? Youth and arrogance got the better of me. I didn't want, you know, to develop a premature middle-aged spread, although they say it's worth it. What's more, if nature hasn't given you much flesh on your bones to start with, you won't get much fat on your body no matter what happens!'

'However,' he added, after a moment's thought, 'I promised to tell you, it seems, how my marriage came about. Listen now. In the first place, I should tell you that my wife is no longer among the living, and in the second place . . . in the second place I see that I will have to tell you about my boyhood, otherwise you won't understand anything . . . Surely you want to get to sleep?'

'No, not at all.'

'Excellent. Just listen to it, though – there's Mister Kantagryukhin

snoring in the next room like a postillion! I was born of poor
parents – I say parents because legend has it that, besides a mother,
I also had a father. I don't remember him. They say he was rather
dim-witted, with a large nose and freckles, light-brown hair and a
habit of taking in snuff through one nostril; there was a portrait of
him hanging in my mother's bedroom, in a red uniform with a
black collar standing up to the ears – extraordinarily ugly. I used
to be taken past it whenever I was being led in for a beating, and
my mama, under such circumstances, would always point to it
and declare: "He wouldn't treat you so lightly." You can imagine
what an encouraging effect that had on me! I had neither brothers
nor sisters – that's to say, if the truth be told, there was a little
brother bedridden with rickets of the neck and he soon died . . .
And why, d'you think, should the English disease of rickets find
its way into the Shchigrovsky district of Kursk Province? But that's
beside the point. My mama undertook my education with all the
headstrong ardour of a *grande dame* of the steppes; she undertook it
right from the magnificent day of my birth until the moment I
reached sixteen years of age . . . Are you following what I'm
saying?'

'Of course; do go on.'

'Very well. As soon, then, as I reached sixteen, my mama, without
the slightest delay, expelled my French tutor – a German by the
name of Philipovich who'd taken up residence among the Nezhin
Greeks – and carted me off to Moscow, entered me for the university
and then gave up her soul to the Almighty, leaving me in the hands
of a blood-relation of mine, the attorney Koltun-Babura, an old bird
famous not only in the Shchigrovsky district. This blood uncle of
mine, the attorney Koltun-Babura, fleeced me of all I'd got, as is
customary in such cases . . . But again that's beside the point. I
entered the university well enough prepared – I must give that much
due to my maternal parent; but a lack of originality was even then
beginning to make itself apparent in me. My boyhood had in no way
differed from the boyhood of other youths: I had grown up just as
stupid and flabby, precisely as if I'd lived my life under a feather-bed,
just as early I'd begun repeating verses by heart and moping about on
the pretext of having a dreamy disposition . . . With what in mind?
With the Beautiful in mind, and so on. I went the same way at the

university: I at once joined a circle. Times were different then ...
But perhaps you don't know what a circle is? I recall that Schiller
said somewhere:

> 'Gefährlich ist's den Leu zu wecken,[6]
> Verderblich ist des Tigers Zahn,
> Jedoch der schrecklichste der Schrecken –
> Das ist der Mensch in seinem Wahn!*

'I assure you that wasn't what he wanted to say; what he wanted to
say was:

> 'Das ist ein "kruzhok" in der Stadt Moskau!'†

'But what do you find so horrible about a student's circle?' I
asked.

My neighbour seized his nightcap and tilted it forward on to his
nose.

'What do I find so horrible?' he cried. 'This is what: a circle – a
circle's the destruction of any original development; a circle is
a ghastly substitute for social intercourse, for women, for living; a
circle ... Wait a minute, I'll tell you what a circle really is! A
circle is a lazy and flabby kind of communal, side-by-side existence,
to which people attribute the significance and appearance of an
intelligent business; a circle replaces conversation with discourses,
inclines its members to fruitless chatter, distracts you from isolated,
beneficial work, implants in you a literary itch; finally, it deprives
you of freshness and the virginal strength of your spirit. A circle –
it's mediocrity and boredom parading under the name of brother-
hood and friendship, a whole chain of misapprehensions and pretences
parading under the pretext of frankness and consideration; in a circle,
thanks to the right of each friend to let his dirty fingers touch on the
inner feelings of a comrade at any time or any hour, no one has a
clean, untouched region left in his soul; in a circle, respect is paid to
empty gasbags, conceited brains, young men who've acquired old
men's habits; and rhymesters with no gifts at all but with
"mysterious" ideas are nursed like babies; in a circle, young,

---

* Fearful it is the lion to waken, And dreadful is the tiger's tooth, But most awful of
  all things together taken – Is man in his madness and lack of truth!
† Is a students' circle in the city of Moscow!

seventeen-year-old boys talk saucily and craftily about women and love, but in front of women they are either silent or they talk to them as if they were talking to a book – and the things they talk about! A circle is a place where underhand eloquence flourishes; in a circle, the members watch one another no less closely than do police officials . . . Oh, students' circles! They're not circles, they're enchanted rings in which more than one decent fellow has perished!'

'But surely you're exaggerating, allow me to remark,' I interrupted.

My neighbour glanced at me in silence.

'Perhaps – the Good Lord knows the sort of person I am – perhaps I am exaggerating. For people of my sort there's only one pleasure left – the pleasure of exaggerating. Anyhow, my dear sir, that's how I spent four years in Moscow. I am quite incapable of describing to you, kind sir, how quickly, how awfully quickly that time passed; it even saddens and vexes me to remember it. You would get up in the morning and just like tobogganing downhill, you'd soon find you were rushing to the end of the day; suddenly it was evening already; your sleepy manservant'd be pulling your frock-coat on to you – you'd dress and plod off to a friend's place and light up your little pipe, drink glass after glass of watery tea and talk away about German philosophy, love, the eternal light of the spirit and other lofty matters. But here I also used to meet independent, original people: no matter how much they might try to break their spirits or bend themselves to the bow of fashion, nature would always in the end assert itself; only I, miserable fellow that I was, went on trying to mould myself like soft wax and my pitiful nature offered not the least resistance! At that time I reached the age of twenty-one. I entered into ownership of my inheritance or, more correctly, that part of my inheritance which my guardian had been good enough to leave me, entrusted the administration of my estate to a freed house-serf, Vasily Kudryashev, and left for abroad, for Berlin. Abroad I spent, as I have already had the pleasure of informing you, three years. And what of it? There also, abroad, I remained the same unoriginal being. In the first place, there's no need to tell you that I didn't acquire the first inkling of knowledge about Europe itself and European circumstances; I listened to German professors and read German books in the place of their origin – that was all the difference there was. I led a life of isolation, just as if I'd been a monk of some kind; I took up with lieutenants who'd left the service and were cursed, as I was, with a thirst for knowledge, but were very hard of understanding and not endowed with the gift of words; I was on familiar terms with dim-witted families from Penza and other grain-producing provinces; I dragged myself from coffee-house to coffee-house, read the journals and went to the theatre in the evenings. I had little intercourse with the natives, would converse with them in a somewhat strained way and never had a single one of them to visit me, with the exception of two or three importunate youngsters of Jewish origin who kept on running after me and borrowing money from me – it is a good thing *der Russe* has a trustful nature.

'A strange trick of fortune brought me finally to the home of one of my professors. This is how it happened: I came to him to sign on to his course, but he suddenly took it into his head to invite me home for an evening. This professor had two daughters, about twenty-seven years old, such dumpy things – God be with them – with such majestic noses, hair all in frizzly curls, eyes of the palest blue and red hands with white fingernails. One was called Linchen, the other Minchen. I started visiting the professor's house. I ought to tell you that this professor was not so much foolish as literally punch-drunk: when he lectured he was fairly coherent, but at home he stumbled over his words and wore his spectacles stuck up all the time on his forehead; yet he was a most learned chap ... And then what? Suddenly it seemed to me I'd fallen in love with Linchen – and this seemed to be the case for a whole six months. I talked with her little, it's true, mostly just looked at her; but I read aloud to her various touching works of literature, squeezed her hands in secret and in the evenings used to sit dreaming beside her, gazing fixedly at the moon or simply up in the air. At the same time, she could make excellent coffee! What more could one ask for? Only one thing bothered me: at this very moment, as they say, of inexplicable bliss there would be a sinking feeling at the pit of my stomach and my abdomen would be assailed by a melancholy, cold shivering. In the end I couldn't abide such happiness and ran away. I spent a further two years abroad even after that: I went to Italy, in Rome I stood for a while in front of the Transfiguration, and in Florence I did the same thing in front of the Venus; I became subject to sudden, exaggerated enthusiasms, just like fits of bad temper; in the evenings I would do a little writing of verses, begin keeping a diary; put in a nutshell, I did exactly what everyone else did. And, yet, look how easy it is to be original! For instance, I'm a complete philistine when it comes to painting and sculpture, but to admit such a thing out loud – no, quite impossible! So you hire a guide, dash off to see the frescos . . .'

He again lowered his head and again flung down his nightcap.

'So I returned finally to my native country,' he continued in a tired voice, 'and came to Moscow. In Moscow I underwent a surprising change. Abroad I had mostly kept my mouth shut, but now I suddenly began talking with unexpected vigour and at the same time conceived God knows how many exalted ideas about myself. Indulgent people cropped up to whom I seemed to be almost a genius; ladies listened considerably to my blatherings; but I did not succeed in remaining at the height of my fame. One fine day gave birth to some gossip on my account (I don't know who trotted it out into the light of God's world; probably some old maid of the male sex – the number of such old maids in Moscow is infinite), it was born and started putting out shoots and runners as fast as a strawberry plant. I got entangled in them, wanted to jump free, break through the sticky threads, but there was nothing doing. So I left. That's where I showed what an empty person I was; I should have waited until it had blown over, in the way people wait for nettle-rash to pass, and those very same indulgent people would again have opened their arms to me, those very same ladies would again have smiled at my eloquence . . . But that's just my problem: I'm not original. A feeling of honesty, you understand, awoke in me: I became somehow ashamed of chattering ceaselessly all the time, holding forth yesterday in the Arbat, today in Truba Street, tomorrow in the Sitsevo-Vrazhok, and always about the same thing. What if that's what they expect of you? Take a look at the real old battleaxes in that line of the country: it doesn't mean a thing to them; on the contrary, that's all they want; some of them have been wagging their tongues for twenty years and all the time in the same direction. That's real self-assurance, real egotistical ambition for you! I had it, too – ambition, that is – and even now it's not completely left me. But the bad part of it is that, I repeat, I'm not original. I've stopped half-way: nature should either have allowed me a great deal more ambition or have given me none at all. But in the first stages things really got very steep for me; at the same time, my journey abroad had finally exhausted my means and I had no desire to marry a merchant's daughter with a body already as flabby as jelly, even though young. So I retreated to my place in the country. I suppose,' my neighbour added, again glancing at me sideways, 'I can pass over in silence the first impressions of country life, all references to the beauties of nature, the quiet charm of a life of solitude and so on . . .'

'You can, you can,' I responded.

'So much the better,' the speaker continued, 'since it's all nonsense, at least so far as I'm concerned. I was as bored in the country as a puppy put under lock and key, although, I admit, as I returned for the first time in springtime past a birch grove that was familiar to me my head was dizzy and my heart beat fast in vague, delightful anticipation. But such vague expectations, as you yourself know, never come to anything; on the contrary, the things that actually happen are always those one had somehow never expected: epidemics among the cattle, arrears of rent, public auctions and so on, and so forth. Making out from day to day with the help of my bailiff Yakov, who had taken the place of the former manager and turned out subsequently to be just as much of a pilferer, if not a greater one, and who, to top it all, poisoned my existence with the smell of his tarred boots. I recalled one day a neighbouring family of my acquaintance consisting of a retired colonel's widow and two daughters, ordered my carriage to be harnessed and went to visit them. That day must always remain fixed in my memory: six months later I was married to the widow's younger daughter!'

The speaker let his head drop and raised his arms high in the air.

'Not that,' he continued heatedly, 'I'd want to give you a poor impression of my late lamented spouse! God forbid! She was the noblest of creatures, the kindest, most loving person and capable of any kind of sacrifice, although I must, between ourselves, admit that, if I had not had the misfortune to lose her, I would probably not be in a position to talk to you today, because in my earth-floor barn you will find to this day in good shape the beam on which I had more than once intended to hang myself!'

'Some pears,' he began after a short silence, 'need to lie a while covered with earth in a cellar to enable them, as they say, to acquire their true taste; my late wife, apparently, belonged to such types of natural produce. It is only now that I can do her full justice. It is only now, for instance, that the memory of certain evenings spent in her company before our marriage not only does not arouse in me the least bitterness but, to the contrary, touches me almost to the point of tears. They were not rich people; their house, very ancient, of wooden construction, but comfortable, stood on a hill between a garden buried under weeds and an overgrown courtyard. At the foot of the hill ran a river and it was scarcely visible through the thick foliage. A large terrace led from the house into the garden, and in front of the terrace there arrayed itself in all its splendour a lengthy flower-bed covered with roses; at the end of the flower-bed grew two acacias which had been twined as young bushes into a screw shape by the late owner of the property. A little farther away, in the very depths of a neglected and wild raspberry patch, stood a summer-house, decorated with exceeding cleverness inside, but so ancient and dilapidated on the outside that it gave one the shivers to look at. From the terrace a glass door led into the drawing-room; while inside the drawing-room the following items met the curious gaze of the onlooker: tiled stoves in the corners, a flat-sounding piano on the right-hand side piled with sheets of handwritten music, a divan upholstered in a faded, pale-blue material with broad whitish patterns, a round table, two cabinets containing china and bead trinkets of the time of Catherine the Great, on the wall hung a well-known portrait of a fair-haired girl with a dove on her breast and upraised eyes, on the table stood a vase with fresh roses . . . Note in what detail I describe it all. In that drawing-room and on that terrace was enacted the entire tragic comedy of my love.

'The widow herself was a dreadful woman, with the continuous rasp of malice in her throat, a burdensome and cantankerous creature; of her daughters one of them – Vera – was in no way distinguishable from the ordinary run of provincial young ladies, the other was Sofia and it was with Sofia that I fell in love. Both sisters had another little room, their common bedroom, which contained two innocent little wooden beds, some yellow little albums, some mignonette, some portraits of friends of both sexes, drawn rather poorly in pencil (among them there stood out one gentleman with an unusually energetic expression on his face who had adorned his portrait with a still more energetic signature and had aroused in his youth unusual expectations, but had ended like all of us by doing nothing), busts of Goethe and Schiller, some German books, some withered garlands and other objects preserved for sentimental reasons. But I entered that room on few occasions and then unwillingly: somehow or other it made me gasp for breath. Besides, strange though it may be, Sofia pleased me most when I was sitting with my back to her or again, if you will, when I was thinking or, more likely, dreaming about her, particularly in the evening, out on the terrace. I would gaze then at the sunset, the trees, the tiny green leaves which, though already darkened, were still sharply outlined against the rosy sky; in the drawing-room Sofia would be seated at the piano endlessly playing over some favourite, exceedingly meditative phrase from Beethoven; the wicked old woman would be peacefully snoring on the divan; in the dining-room, illuminated by a flood of crimson light, Vera would be fussing over the tea; the samovar would be hissing fancifully to itself, as if enjoying some secret joke; pretzels would break with a happy crackling, spoons would strike resonantly against teacups; the canary, mercilessly chirping away all day long, would suddenly grow quiet and chirrup only now and then as if asking a question about something; one or two drops of rain would fall from a translucent, light cloud as it passed by ... But I would sit and sit, listening and listening and watching, and my heart would fill with emotion, and it would again seem to me that I was in love. So, under the influence of just such an evening I asked the old woman for her daughter's hand and about two months later I was married.

'I suppose that I was in love with her. Even though by now I should know, yet – my God! – I don't know even now whether I loved Sofia or not. She was a kind creature, intelligent, quiet, with a warm heart; but God knows why, whether from having lived such a long time in the country or from some other cause, she secreted at the bottom of her soul (if the soul may be said to have a bottom) a wound or, better, a festering hurt which it was impossible to cure and which neither she nor I was able to give a name to. Naturally, I did not perceive the existence of this trauma until after our marriage. What I didn't do to help her, but nothing was any good! In my boyhood I had a little finch which the cat once got her claws into; we rescued it, nursed it, but my wretched finch didn't get right again; it began to droop and ail and stopped singing. The matter ended one night when a rat got into its open cage and bit off its beak, as a result of which it finally decided to die. I don't know what cat had got its claws into my wife, but she also started to droop and ail like my luckless finch. Sometimes she herself obviously wanted to flutter her wings and frolic in the fresh air, in sunlight and freedom; she'd try it and then curl up into a ball again. Yet she certainly loved me: she assured me time and again that she had nothing more to wish for – oh, the devil take it! – and yet there she was with her eyes already fading. Is there something in her past? I wondered. I sought around for information, but there was nothing to be found. Well, then, judge for yourself: an original fellow would have given a shrug of the shoulders, perhaps, sighed once or twice and then settled down to live his life in his own way; but I, unoriginal creature that I am, began looking for suitable beams. My wife had become so profoundly imbued with all the habits of an old maid – Beethoven, nightly strolls, mignonette, writing letters to friends, keeping albums and so on – that she was quite incapable of accustoming herself to any other form of life, particularly to the life of a lady of the house; and yet it's ridiculous for a married woman to languish from some nameless heartbreak and spend her evenings singing: "Awaken her not till dawn has broken."[7]

'However, sir, in such a manner we passed a blissful three years. In the fourth year Sofia died in childbirth and – strange though it may be – I literally had a premonition that she would be in no condition to present me with a son or daughter and the earth with a new inhabitant. I remember her funeral. It happened in the spring. Our parish church is not large and it is ancient, with a blackened icon screen, bare walls and a brick floor with holes in it; each choir stall has a large antiquated icon. They brought in the coffin, set it down in the very middle of the church before the holy doors, draped it with a faded cloth and placed three candlesticks round it. The service began. A frail sexton, with a little plaited knot of hair on the nape of his neck, wearing a green girdle tied low down, made sad mumblings before the lectern; the priest, also elderly, with a small, kindly, purblind face, in a mauve cassock with yellowing patterning, officiated both for himself and for the sexton. The entire area of open windows was filled with the shimmerings and rustlings of the young, fresh leaves of weeping birches; a smell of grass wafted in from the graveyard; the red flames of the wax candles paled in the gay sunlight of the spring day; sparrows chirruped throughout the whole church and occasionally the noisy twitterings of a swallow that had flown in resounded beneath the cupola. In the golden dust of the sun's rays the auburn heads of the sparse peasant congregation rose and fell in quick obeisances as they uttered earnest prayers for the soul of the departed; incense rose from the opening in the censer in a delicate, pale-blue stream. I looked at the dead face of my wife. My God! Even death, death itself, had not freed her, not healed her wound: her face wore the same sickly, timid, dumb look, as if she literally felt awkward lying in her coffin. My blood stirred bitterly within me. Kind, kind being that you were, but you still did well for yourself in dying!'

The speaker's cheeks reddened and his eyes lost their brightness.

'Having rid myself finally,' he started to say again, 'of the weight of despondency which settled on me after my wife's death, I thought I ought to get down to work, as they say. I entered the service in the provincial centre, but the large rooms of the government building made my head ache and also had a bad effect on my eyes; other convenient reasons also came along . . . So I retired. I had wanted to go to Moscow, but, in the first place, I hadn't enough money, and in the second place . . . I have already mentioned to you that I had become reconciled. Such reconciliation came to me both suddenly and gradually. In spirit, so to say, I had long ago become reconciled, yet my head was still unwilling to bow down. I used to ascribe the humble mood of my feelings and thoughts to the influence of country life and my misfortune. On the other hand, I had long ago noticed that almost all my neighbours, both old and young, who were cowed to begin with by my show of learning, foreign travel and other perquisites of my education, not only succeeded in becoming quite used to me but even began to treat me not so much rudely as off-handedly, not bothering to hear my discourses through to the end and failing to address me in a proper manner when speaking to me. I also forgot to tell you that during the first year of my marriage I attempted out of boredom to turn my hand to writing and even sent a small piece – a short work of fiction, if I'm not wrong – to a journal; but after a certain lapse of time I received from the editor a polite letter, in which mention was made, among other things, of the fact that it was impossible to deny me intellect but it was possible to deny me talent, and talent was the one thing needed in literature. Over and above this, it came to my knowledge that a certain Moscovite who was passing through the province – the kindliest young man imaginable, by the way – had made a passing reference to me at a Governor's *soirée* as a person of no consequence who had exhausted his talents. But I still persisted in maintaining my partially voluntary blindness; I didn't feel, you know, like pulling down my ear-flaps. Eventually, one fine morning, I had my eyes opened.

'This is how it happened. The local police inspector called on me with the object of directing my attention to a broken-down bridge on my property, which I definitely had no means of repairing. Tasting a tot of vodka along with a piece of cold sturgeon, this condescending pillar of the law reproached me in a fatherly way for my lack of scruple, entered none the less into my position and advised me simply to order my peasants to spread some muck by way of repairs, lit up his little pipe and started talking about the forthcoming elections. The honourable title of provincial marshal of nobility was being sought at that time by a certain Orbassanov, an empty loudmouth and, what is more, a bribe-taker. Besides, he was distinguished neither for wealth nor lineage. I expressed my opinion about him, and even rather freely: I confess that I looked down on Mr Orbassanov. The inspector looked at me, fondly tapped me on the shoulder and declared benevolently: "Now, now, Vasily Vasilych, it's not for you and me to discuss such people, so what's it got to do with us? Every cricket should know its own hearth." "But kindly tell me," I protested in annoyance, "what difference there is between me and Mr Orbassanov?" The inspector took his pipe out of his mouth, screwed up his eyes – and burst into spluttering laughter. "Well, you're one for a joke!" he uttered eventually, through his tears. "What a thing to say, what a thing to let drop just like that! You're a one, aren't you?" – and right up to his departure he kept on making fun of me, from time to time nudging me with his elbow and adopting an extremely intimate form of address in talking to me. He left finally. His attitude was all I needed: the cup of my humiliation was full to overflowing. I walked several times about the room, stopped before the mirror, gazed for minutes on end at the look of confusion on my face and, slowly sticking out my tongue, shook my head in bitter derision. The scales had fallen from my eyes: I now saw clearly, more clearly even than I saw my own face in the mirror, what an empty, worthless, unnecessary, unoriginal person I was!'

The speaker fell silent.

'In one of Voltaire's tragedies,'[8] he continued despondently, 'some gentleman or other is overjoyed at having reached the extreme limit of unhappiness. Although there is nothing tragic in my fate, I admit that at that time I experienced something of the same kind. I learned to know the poisoned joys of chill despair; I learned to know how sweet it was, during the course of a whole morning, lying in bed and not hurrying over it, to curse the day and hour of my birth. I could not become reconciled at once. I mean, judge for yourself: lack of money tied me down in the country, which I hated; neither management of my estate, nor the service, nor literature – nothing had proved suitable; I avoided the local landowners like the plague, and books were repugnant to me; in the eyes of watery-puddingy, chronically sensitive young ladies who had a habit of shaking their curls and feverishly reiterating the word "life" (pronounced almost like "leaf") I ceased to be an object of interest once I had stopped chattering and going into raptures; I simply didn't know how to cut myself off completely and was physically incapable of it ... So I began – guess what? – I began dragging myself round from neighbour to neighbour. Literally drunk with self-disgust, I deliberately laid myself open to all sorts of petty humiliations. I was overlooked by the servants at table, greeted coldly and arrogantly, and finally, I wasn't noticed at all; I wasn't even allowed to add my bit to the general conversation, and I myself, it so happened, would deliberately nod agreement from my corner at some crass chatterbox or other who in the past, in Moscow, would have been delighted to lick the dust from my feet and kiss the hem of my overcoat ... I did not even allow myself to think that I was submitting to the bitter pleasure of irony – after all, there's no such thing as irony in isolation! So that's the sort of life I've led for several years in a row and that's how things are up to the present time ...'

'I've never heard anything like it,' the sleepy voice of Mr Kantagry-ukhin grumbled from the next room, 'who's the fool that's decided to talk away at this time of night?'

My room-mate swiftly plunged under the counterpane and, glancing out timorously, shook his finger at me.

'Tut, tut,' he whispered, and as though literally apologizing and bowing in the direction of Kantagryukhin's voice murmured respectfully: 'Of course, sir; of course, sir. Forgive me . . . His lordship must be allowed to sleep, he should sleep,' he continued again in a whisper, 'he must gather his strength, well, at least so that he can eat tomorrow with the same enjoyment as he has eaten today. We have no right to disturb him. Besides, it seems I've told you all I wanted to tell; no doubt you also want to go to sleep. I wish you good night.'

The speaker turned away in feverish haste and buried his head in his pillow.

'Permit me at least to know,' I asked, 'with whom I've had the pleasure . . .'

He swiftly raised his head.

'No, for God's sake,' he interrupted me, 'don't ask me or anyone else for my name. Let me remain for you an unknown person, a Vasily Vasilyevych who has been crippled by fate. At the same time, as an unoriginal person, I don't deserve any particular name. But if you earnestly want to give me some kind of title, then call me . . . call me Hamlet of the Shchigrovsky District. There are many such Hamlets in every district, but perhaps you haven't come across any others . . . And so farewell.'

He again buried himself in his feather-bed, and the next morning, when they came to wake me, he was no longer in the room. He had left before daybreak.

CHERTOPKHANOV AND NEDOPYUSKIN

———————— ❧ ————————

ONE time on a hot summer day I was returning in a cart from hunting while Yermolay, sitting beside me, snoozed and nodded. The sleeping dogs jumped about with each jolt under our feet as if they were dead. The driver from time to time flicked away the flies from the horses with his whip. White dust rose in a light cloud in the wake of the cart. We then drove among some bushes. The road grew bumpier and the wheels began to get tangled in branches. Yermolay sprang awake and looked around him.

'Hey!' he cried. 'There'll be grouse round here! Let's get down!'

We stopped and went into the bushy area. My dog chanced on a covey. I fired and was about to reload my gun when suddenly behind me there arose a loud crackling sound and a man on horseback rode up to me, parting the bushes with his hands.

'Parmit me to ahsk, sah,' he declared in a haughty voice, 'by what right are you a-hahnting here, sah?'

The stranger spoke unusually fast, jerkily and through the nose. I looked him in the face. In all my born days I'd never seen anyone like him. Imagine to yourself, dear readers, a small man, fair-haired, with a red turned-up little nose and the longest imaginable ginger whiskers. A conical Persian hat with an upper part covered in raspberry-coloured cloth covered his forehead right down to his eyebrows. He was dressed in a worn, tight-fitting yellow coat with black velvet cartridge pleats across the chest and frayed silver linings to the seams. He had a horn hanging over his shoulder and a dagger in his belt. A wretched, hook-nosed, ginger horse pranced about under him like one possessed and a couple of borzoi dogs, thin and bowlegged, danced around under its feet. The face, glance, voice and every movement, the very being of this strange man exuded a daredevil valour and limitless, incredible arrogance. His pale-blue, glass-like eyes darted about and squinted as if he were drunk. He had a way of throwing back his head, puffing out his cheeks, snorting and shaking his whole body as if in an excess of self-esteem exactly like a turkey-cock. He repeated his question.

'I didn't know it was forbidden to shoot here,' I answered.

'You are here, my good sah,' he continued, 'on my land.'

'I'm sorry, I'll leave.'

'Parmit me to ahsk,' he said, 'do I have the honour of speaking with a member of the nobility?'

I gave my name.

'In that case, please go on hunting. I'm also a member of the nobility and very glad to be of service to another ... My name's Cher-top-khanov, Panteley.'

He bent down, gave a whoop and tugged at his horse's neck. The horse started shaking its head, reared up on its hindlegs, flung itself to one side and crushed a dog's paw. The dog emitted a series of piercing yelps. Chertopkhanov seethed and hissed, struck the horse between the ears with his fist, jumped to the ground quicker than lightning, looked at the dog's paw, spat on the wound, gave the dog a shove in the side with his foot to stop it squealing, grabbed hold of the horse's withers and stuck his foot in the stirrup. The horse flung up its muzzle, raised its tail and dashed sideways into the bushes while he hopped along on one foot beside it before finally alighting in the saddle somehow or other. Like someone in a frenzy he twirled his whip, blew on his horn and galloped away.

I'd scarcely recovered from the unexpected appearance of Chertopkhanov when suddenly, with hardly any sound, there rode out of the bushes a stoutish man of about forty on a small black horse. He stopped, removed from his head a green-leather peaked cap and in a very delicate, soft voice asked me whether I'd seen a rider on a ginger horse. I said I had.

'In which direction did he ride off, please?' he continued in the same voice and without replacing his cap.

'That way, sir.'

'Most humble thanks, sir.'

He made a smacking sound with his lips, let his legs bounce against the sides of his little horse and set off at a steady trot – clip-clop, clip-clop – in the direction indicated. I watched until his

horned cap was hidden among the branches. This new stranger bore
no resemblance in outward appearance to his predecessor. His face,
puffy and round as a ball, expressed diffidence, warmth and meek
humility. His nose, also puffy and round and ingrained with small
blue veins, revealed him as one fond of good living. There was not a
single hair on the front of his head, while on the back there stuck up
some sparse brown tufts. His little eyes, looking just like peepholes,
blinked amiably. His small, full, red lips smiled sweetly. He was
wearing a frock-coat with a stand-up collar and brass buttons, very
worn, but clean; his short cloth trousers had ridden up high and
plump calves were visible above the yellow tops of his boots.

'Who's that?' I asked Yermolay.

'That? He's Nedopyuskin, Tikhon Ivanych. He lives with Chertopkhanov.'

'Is he a poor man, then?'

'Not a rich one. But then Chertopkhanov hasn't got a brass farthing.'

'So why's he living with him?'

'They became friends, you see. The one won't go anywhere
without the other . . . It's as they say: where the horse goes with its
hoof, so the crab goes with its claw.'

We left the bushes. Suddenly two hounds began baying beside us
and a big hare dashed through the oats which were already pretty
high. In hot pursuit dogs raced out of a nearby wood, both hounds
and borzois, and behind the dogs flew out Chertopkhanov himself.
He didn't shout, didn't urge on the dogs, didn't tell them to be at it.
He was panting and gasping and disjointed, meaningless sounds came
from his mouth. He went speeding along, his eyes screwed up,
beating his unfortunate horse frantically with his whip.

The borzois were almost on their prey . . . The hare sat down,
turned sharply backwards and flew past Yermolay towards the
bushes. The borzois rushed by.

'Go o-o-on! Go o-o-on!' the literally tongue-tied, half-dead hunter
bawled. 'Mind out, there's a good chap!'

Yermolay fired. The wounded hare spun head over heels like a top
across the smooth, dry grass, jumped up and gave a piteous cry in the
teeth of a frenzied dog. The hounds at once fell upon it.

Chertopkhanov shot down from his horse, took out his dagger, ran straddled over his dogs and with fierce oaths seized the torn hare from them and, his whole face one wild grimace, thrust his dagger into its neck right up to the hilt, thrust again and then burst into guffaws of laughter. Tikhon Ivanych appeared in the clearing.

'Ho-ho-ho-ho-ho-ho-ho-ho!' Chertopkhanov guffawed again.

'Ho-ho-ho-ho!' his friend repeated calmly.

'Surely you shouldn't be hunting for real in the summer,' I remarked, directing Chertopkhanov's attention to the trampled oats.

'It's my field,' Chertopkhanov answered, scarcely able to draw breath.

He cut the paws off the hare, fixed it to his saddle and threw the paws to the dogs.

'I owe you the cost of the shot, my good man, according to the rules of hunting,' he said, turning to Yermolay. 'And you, my good sir,' he added in the same jerky, sharp voice, 'I thank.'

He mounted his horse.

'Par-rmit me to know . . . I've forgotten . . . your name and sur-name?'

I again gave my name.

'I'm very glad to make your acquaintance. Should the occasion arise, please call on me . . . Now where's that Fomka, Tikhon Ivanych?' he went on heatedly. 'We hunted the hare without him.'

'His horse fell under him,' answered Tikhon Ivanych with a smile.

'Fell? Orbassan[1] fell? Phew, dammit! Where is he, eh?'

'There, on the other side of the wood.'

Chertopkhanov struck his horse over the muzzle with his whip and galloped off at top speed. Tikhon Ivanych bowed to me twice – for himself and for his friend – and again set off at a trot into the bushes.

These two gentlemen aroused my curiosity very keenly. What could have bound by bonds of indissoluble friendship such evidently different human beings? I began to ask around. This is what I learned.

Chertopkhanov, Panteley Yeremeich, had a reputation throughout the region as a dangerous and madcap man, an arrogant troublemaker of the first order. He served a very short time in the army and retired 'for reasons of unpleasantness' with the rank of ensign, the very rank on account of which opinion has it that a chicken's not a bird, so an ensign's not an officer. He came of a line which had at one time been wealthy. His forebears had lived sumptuously in the manner of the steppes, that is to say they'd kept open house for all comers, fed them to the limit, handed out a quarter of oats to visiting drivers for their troikas of horses, kept musicians, singers, buffoons and dogs, at time of festivals dispensed wine and ale to the peasants, in winter travelled under their own horse-power, in heavy conveyances, to Moscow and yet sometimes for months at a time they wouldn't have a penny to their name and would live off whatever livestock and provisions came to hand. Panteley Yeremeich's father inherited an estate that was already ruined. He, in his turn, had led a wild life and, dying, left his only descendant, Panteley, the little mortgaged village of Unsleepy Hollow together with thirty-five male serfs and seventy-six female and about thirty-seven acres or so of poor land in the arid Tumbledown area, for which, incidentally, no deeds could be found in the deceased's papers. The deceased, it has to be said, ruined himself in the oddest way: 'economic self-help' did for him. According to his ideas, a member of the nobility should not be dependent on merchants, townees and 'thieves of that sort', as he put it. So he set up all manner of crafts and workshops. 'Both better and cheaper,' he used to say, 'that's what economic self-help is!' Right to the end of his life he kept to this ruinous idea and it was what destroyed him.

But he had his compensations! He never denied himself a single whim. Among other projects he once built, according to his own plans, such an enormous family carriage that, despite the joint efforts of all the peasant horses in the village and their owners, it came a cropper at the first gradient and fell to pieces. Yeremey Lukich (as Panteley's father was called) ordered a monument to be set up on this gradient and, besides, was not in the least dismayed. He also took it into his head to build a church – naturally, by himself, without the help of an architect. He burned down a whole wood to fire the bricks, laid out enormous foundations as if building a provincial cathedral, raised the walls and began to erect a cupola: it fell in. He tried again and the cupola again collapsed. He tried a third time and the cupola came tumbling down a third time. This made my Yeremey Lukich think. It's a bad business, he thought. Clearly some damned witchcraft's at work. Suddenly he knew what it was and ordered all the old women in the village to be given a beating. The old women were given a beating, but still the cupola wouldn't stay up.

Then he began rearranging the structure of his peasants' houses according to a new plan, all on the grounds of 'economic self-help'. He'd set three households together in a triangle and in the middle he'd put a pole with a painted starling-house and a flag. Each day he'd think of something new, whether it was soup made from burdock or having the horses' tails docked to provide horsehair caps for his servants, replacing flax with nettles or feeding mushrooms to the pigs . . . One day he read an article in the *Moscow News* by a Kharkhov landowner, a certain Khryaka-Khrupyorsky, about the value of morality in peasant life and the very next day ordered that all the peasants should instantly learn it by heart. The peasants learned it and he asked them whether they'd understood it. His steward answered of course they'd understood it, they couldn't fail to! About the same time he ordered that all the people over whom he had authority, in the interests of order and 'economic self-help', should be given a number and each should have the number sewn into his collar. On meeting their lord and master each would instantly shout: 'Number so-and-so out walking, sir!' whereupon their lord and master would answer amiably: 'And God be with you!'

However, despite order and 'economic self-help', Yeremey Lukich gradually found himself in extreme difficulty and he began to mortgage his villages and even to start selling them. The last nest of his forebears, the village with the unfinished church, was finally sold by the state, happily not while Yeremey Lukich was still alive – he'd never have survived such a blow – but a couple of weeks after his death. He managed to die in his own home, in his own bed, surrounded by his servants and attended by his doctor. But poor Panteley inherited only Unsleepy Hollow.

Panteley learned of his father's illness while he was still in the army and at the very height of the above-mentioned 'unpleasantness'. He was just nineteen. Since boyhood he'd never been away from home and under the care of his mother, a very kind but utterly stupid woman, Vasilisa Vasilyevna, he'd grown into a spoilt brat and a little milord. She alone had concerned herself with his education. Yeremey Lukich, absorbed by his economic interests, had taken no part in it.

True, he'd once administered corporal punishment to his son for mispronouncing 'rtsy' as 'artsy', but that day Yeremey Lukich had been nursing a profound and secret grief at the fact that his best dog had been killed by running into a tree. Besides, all Vasilisa Vasilyevna's concerns for young Panteley's education had been limited to one tortuous effort. By the sweat of her brow she'd hired for him as tutor an ex-soldier from Alsace, a certain Bierkopf, and trembled before him like a leaf to the day of her death at the thought that he might refuse: 'I'd be finished! Where'd I look? Where'd I find another teacher? After all, didn't it cost me almost all my strength to entice him away from that woman neighbour of mine?' and Bierkopf, calculating chap that he was, at once made use of the uniqueness of his position to become dead drunk and asleep from morning to night. At the conclusion of his 'course of learning' Panteley went into the army. By that time Vasilisa Vasilyevna was no longer alive. She died six months before this important event, frightened to death: she'd dreamed of a man all in white riding a bear. Yeremey Lukich followed his better half shortly afterwards.

Panteley, on first learning of his illness, had galloped home at full tilt, but had not arrived in time to find his parent still among the living. Imagine the astonishment of the dutiful son when he completely unexpectedly found himself turned from a wealthy heir into a pauper! Few are capable of surviving such a sharp turn of events. Panteley became unsociable and embittered. From someone honest, generous and kind, even though spoilt and wilful, he turned into an arrogant troublemaker, ceased having any dealings with his neighbours – he felt ashamed in front of the rich ones, while disdaining the poor ones – and behaved unspeakably rudely to everyone, even to the powers-that-be, as if asserting to one and all that 'I am a true-blue aristocrat, I am.' On one occasion he almost shot dead a local constable who'd come into his room with his cap on. It goes without saying that the authorities for their part didn't give in to him and let him know how they felt whenever the occasion arose. But nevertheless people were a bit afraid of him because he had a frightful temper and at the drop of a hat would challenge you to a duel with daggers. At the slightest objection to his views Chertopkhanov's eyes would dart about and his voice would crack . . .

'Ah va-av-va-va-va!' he'd stammer. 'I may lose my head, but . . .' and he'd be off storming the walls!

Above all, though, he kept his hands clean, he didn't get involved in any dirty business. Of course, no one visited him. And yet, in spite of everything, he had a kindly soul, even a magnanimous one after his fashion. He couldn't abide any injustice or persecution and was a tower of strength in standing up for his peasants.

'What?' he'd say, tapping his own head furiously. 'Let someone get their hands on my own people, eh? Not so long as I'm a Chertopkhanov . . .'

Tikhon Ivanych Nedopyuskin couldn't, like Panteley Yeremeich, boast of his background. His father had come of modest farming stock and had only acquired nobility status after forty years in the civil service. Nedopyuskin *père* belonged to those species of person whom misfortune persecutes with untiring and unflinching bitterness, a bitterness bordering on personal animosity. In the course of sixty years, from the day of his birth to the day of his death, the poor man struggled with all the needs, handicaps and calamities common to small men. He struggled like a fish in ice, starved himself of food and sleep, fawned and fussed and groaned and despaired and trembled over every copeck earned and genuinely suffered 'for nothing' in his service career and died eventually neither exactly in an attic, nor in a cellar, but without having won either for himself or his children a true crust of daily bread. Fate was ever on his heels like a hare being coursed. He was a kind and honest man, but he took bribes 'according to rank' from ten copecks upwards to a couple of roubles inclusive. Nedopyuskin had a wife, thin and consumptive; and he had children. Luckily they all died young apart from Tikhon and a daughter Mitrodora, nicknamed the 'merchants' pin-up', who got married to a retired attorney after many sad and funny adventures. While he was still alive Nedopyuskin *père* managed to find a place for Tikhon in an office as a temporary official, but as soon as his father died Tikhon left.

The constant upsets, the tormenting struggle with cold and hunger, the dreary melancholy of his mother, the fussy desperation of his father, the crude importunings of landlords and shopkeepers, all this daily, uninterrupted misery bred in Tikhon an inexplicable shyness, so that at one glimpse of his office boss he would tremble and grow faint as a captured bird. He threw up his work. Nature, in its indifference and perhaps in a spirit of mockery, endows people with different abilities and aptitudes without taking any account of their position in society and their financial means. With its customary diligence and love it moulded out of Tikhon, the son of a poor civil servant, a person of sensitivity, lazy, soft and impressionable, a person given over exclusively to pleasure and gifted with an extraordinarily delicate sense of smell and taste, moulded him and meticulously finished him – only to leave its creation to grow up on sour cabbage and rotten fish. And so it grew up, this perfect creation, and began, as they say, 'to live'. That's when the fun began. Fate, untiring in its harassment of Nedopyuskin *père*, turned to his son, evidently having acquired a taste for them. But with Tikhon it behaved differently. It did not torment him so much as make fun of him. It never once brought him to despair and never forced him to experience the humiliating pangs of hunger, but it sent him scampering all over Russia, from Veliky Ustyug to Tsarevo-Kokshaysk, from one demeaning and laughable post to another, at one time appointing him a 'major-domo' to a shrewish and ill-tempered lady-benefactress, at another making him a hanger-on in the house of a wealthy skinflint of a merchant, yet again engaging him to be in charge of the domestic office of a pop-eyed landowner who liked to have his hair cut in the English manner, or turning him into part-butler, part-jester to a fellow who loved hounds ... In short, fate forced poor Tikhon to drink drop by drop of the bitter and poisoned cup of a servile existence. In his time he served to assuage the ponderous whims and the drowsy and malicious boredom of an idle nobility. How frequently, on his own in his own room, having been finally allowed ('And God be with you!') to go free from the host of guests who'd had their fill of fun at his expense, burning with shame, with cold tears of despair in his eyes, he'd vowed the very next day to run off and try his luck in the local town, either by finding himself a place as a copying-clerk or by dying for good and all of hunger on the street!

But in the first place God didn't give him the strength. Secondly, shyness got the better of him and, thirdly, how on earth could he find a place for himself, who could he ask? 'They won't give me one,' the unfortunate fellow'd whisper, turning over despairingly in his bed, 'they won't give me one.' And the next day he'd once more be back in harness. His position was all the more painful in that nature, caring though it was, hadn't troubled to endow him with so much as a smidgeon of those attributes and gifts without which the role of jester is impossible. For example, he didn't know how to dance until he fell, dressed up in a bearskin turned inside out, nor to play the fool and charm everyone in the immediate neighbourhood of brandished whips; flung naked out of doors in a twenty-degree frost, he sometimes caught cold and his stomach couldn't digest wine mixed with ink and other muck, no more than it could digest crumbled fly-agaric and mushroom mixed with vinegar. God knows what might have become of Tikhon if the last of his benefactors, a tax-farmer who'd grown rich, hadn't had the idea at one happy moment of including him in his will: 'I do hereby bequeath to Zozo (also known as Tikhon) Nedopyuskin, in perpetual and inherited possession, my property, the village of Besselendeevka, with all lands appertaining thereto.' A few days later, while eating fish soup, the benefactor was struck down by paralysis. A huge commotion ensued, with the law-court thunderously laying down the law and a restriction duly being placed on the property. The relatives gathered; the will was opened and read and Nedopyuskin was summoned.

Nedopyuskin put in an appearance. The majority of those present knew what role Tikhon Ivanych had played in the benefactor's lifetime and deafening exclamations and mocking congratulations greeted him.

'The landowner, there he is! There's the new landowner!' cried the other heirs.

'Here he is,' broke in one of them, a well-known joker and wit, 'here he is, the very, one might say, the very . . . your actual . . . what's called . . . the very inheritor!'

And they all burst out laughing.

Nedopyuskin took a while to believe in his good fortune. He was shown the will and went red, squeezed up his eyes, started waving it away with his hands and then broke into torrents of tears. The laughter of those present turned into a loud and continuous roar. The village of Besselendeevka consisted of no more than twenty-two peasants, so none of the other heirs felt strongly about losing it. A spot of fun, though – well, why not? Only one of the heirs from St Petersburg, a self-important gentleman with a Grecian nose and the most dignified of expressions, Rostislav Adamych Stoppel, couldn't resist the opportunity, sidled up to Nedopyuskin and glanced at him haughtily over his shoulder.

'You, my good sir, so far as I can tell,' he started saying with casual malice, 'occupied under our respected Fyodor Fyodorych the post of an entertainer-cum-lackey, so to speak, didn't you?'

The gentleman from St Petersburg expressed himself in intolerably pure, vivacious and correct Russian. Nedopyuskin, distressed and overwrought as he was, didn't catch the words of the unfamiliar gentleman, but the rest of them at once fell silent. The joker and wit smiled condescendingly. Mr Stoppel rubbed his hands together and repeated his question. Nedopyuskin raised his eyes in astonishment and opened his mouth. Rostislav Adamych screwed up his eyes wickedly.

'I congratulate you, my dear sir, I congratulate you.' Then he went on: 'True, not everyone, it might be said, would agree that it's the right way to ear-r-r-rn one's daily bread, but *de gustibus non est disputandum*, that is to say, to everyone his own taste. You agree, don't you?'

Someone at the back gave a rapid but decorous yelp of laughter in surprise and delight.

'Tell me,' continued Mr Stoppel, greatly encouraged by the smiles of the whole gathering, 'to what talent in particular are you obliged for your good fortune? No, don't be shy, tell us. We're all here, so to speak, *en famille*. It's true, gentlemen, we're all *en famille* here, aren't we?'

The heir to whom Rostislav Adamych casually turned with this question unfortunately did not know French and therefore confined himself to a slight, approving clearing of the throat. By contrast, another heir, a young man with yellow blotches on his forehead, hurriedly chimed in with '*Voui, Voui*, it goes without saying.'

'Perhaps,' Mr Stoppel resumed, 'you know how to walk on your hands with your legs raised in the air, so to speak?'

Nedopyuskin glanced miserably round him. All the faces grinned maliciously and all eyes were covered by a glaze of satisfaction.

'Or perhaps you know how to crow like a cock?'

An explosion of laughter resounded round the assembled company and instantly died in anticipation of an answer.

'Or perhaps you have on your nose . . .'

'Stop it!' a sharp, loud voice suddenly interrupted Rostislav Adamych. 'You should be ashamed of tormenting the poor man!'

All looked round. In the doorway stood Chertopkhanov. As an extremely distant relative of the deceased tax-farmer he'd also received a letter of invitation to the family gathering. In the course of the reading of the will he had, as always, kept himself at a haughty distance from the rest.

'Stop it!' he repeated, proudly throwing back his head.

Mr Stoppel turned swiftly round and, seeing a poorly dressed, unprepossessing man, asked of his neighbour in a soft voice (it pays to be cautious):

'Who's that?'

'Chertopkhanov. Small fry,' the man whispered in his ear.

Rostislav Adamych raised a haughty look.

'And who are you to issue commands?' he said through his nose and screwed up his eyes. 'What sort of a bird are you, may I ask?'

Chertopkhanov exploded like gunpowder ignited by a spark. In a frenzy he could scarcely breathe.

'Dz–dz–dz–dz,' he hissed, as if being strangled, and suddenly roared out: 'Who am I? Who am I? I'm Panteley Chertopkhanov, a true-blue aristocrat, my great-great-great-grandfather served the Tsar, and who might you be?'

Rostislav Adamych went pale and stepped backwards. He'd not anticipated such a reaction.

'Oh, I'm a bird all right, I'm a bird . . . Oh, yes, I am!'

Chertopkhanov thrust himself forward. Stoppel jumped back in great alarm and the guests rushed to restrain the angry landowner.

'Shoot, shoot, let's shoot with pistols across a handkerchief this very instant!' screamed a frantic Panteley. 'Or ask my forgiveness and his as well . . .'

'Ask his forgiveness,' the apprehensive heirs surrounding Stoppel muttered. 'You can see he's mad! He's ready to cut your throat!'

'Forgive me, please, I didn't know,' babbled Stoppel, 'I didn't know . . .'

'And ask his forgiveness too!' bellowed the incensed Panteley.

'Forgive me,' added Rostislav Adamych, turning to Nedopyuskin, who was shaking so much it was as if he had a fever.

Chertopkhanov calmed down, went up to Tikhon Ivanych, took

him by the hand, glanced boldly round him and, without encountering a single gaze directed at him, solemnly and in the midst of profound silence left the room together with the new owner of the legally acquired village of Besselendeevka.

From that day forward they were never more parted. (The village of Besselendeevka was scarcely half-a-dozen miles from Unsleepy Hollow.) The limitless gratitude of Nedopyuskin quickly grew into a fawning hero-worship. The weak, soft and not entirely spotless Tikhon prostrated himself in the dust before the fearless and unselfish Panteley.

'How astonishing!' he'd sometimes think to himself. 'He talks to the Governor and looks him straight in the eyes – just like Jesus Christ, just like that!'

He was amazed at him to the point of disbelief, to the very limits of his spiritual powers, and he regarded him as an exceptional man, clever and educated. And it has to be said that, no matter how poor Chertopkhanov's education may have been, by comparison with Tikhon's education it was brilliant. Chertopkhanov, true, read Russian little and understood French so badly that on one occasion in response to a question from a Swiss tutor: '*Vous parlez français, monsieur?*' answered: '*Je* don't ...' and after a moment's thought added: '*pas.*' But still he knew enough to remember that there'd once been Voltaire, the wittiest writer, that the French and the English had frequently fought each other and that Frederick the Great, King of Prussia, had also been an outstanding military leader. Of Russian writers he had respect for Derzhavin, but he loved Marlinsky[2] and had called his best hound Ammalat-Bek after the hero of one of his stories.

A few days after my first encounter with the two friends I set off for the village of Unsleepy Hollow to see Panteley Yeremeich. His small house was visible from some distance. It stuck out on a bare patch of land, about a quarter of a mile from the village, 'all on its own', as they say, like a hawk above ploughland. Chertopkhanov's entire estate consisted of four ancient timber-frame buildings of different sizes: his dwelling, a stables, a barn and a bath-house. Each building stood separately by itself. There was no surrounding fence and no gate. My driver stopped in bewilderment by a half-rotted well filled with rubbish. Beside the barn several thin and bedraggled borzoi pups were tearing at a dead horse, probably Orbassan. One of them raised a blood-stained muzzle, gave a quick bark and then went back to gnawing the bare ribs. Beside the horse stood a boy of about seventeen with a puffy, yellow face, dressed as a page-boy and bare-footed; he was self-importantly engaged in looking after the dogs entrusted to his care and from time to time gave the greediest of them a taste of his whip.

'Is the master home?' I asked.

'Lord knows!' answered the boy. 'Try knocking.'

I jumped down from the droshky and approached the front door.

Mr Chertopkhanov's dwelling had a very sorry appearance. The timbers had blackened and bellied out in front, one chimney had fallen down, the corners had rotted from below and were bent and the small, faded, greyish windows looked out with inexpressible sourness from beneath the shaggy rim of roof drawn down over them: they were like the eyes of elderly whores. I knocked but nobody answered. However, I could hear from the other side of the door the sound of words being sharply pronounced: 'A, B, C – well, go on, you fool!' a hoarse voice was saying. 'A, B, C, D – no, D! Then E! E! Go on, you fool!'

I knocked again.

The same voice answered: 'Come in, whoever's there . . .'

I entered a small empty hallway and through an open door saw Chertopkhanov himself. Dressed in a greasy Bokhara dressing-gown, wide trousers and a red skull-cap, he was sitting in a chair, squeezing with one hand the muzzle of a young poodle and in the other holding a piece of bread just above its nose.

'Ah!' he said with dignity and without rising. 'Very glad you've come. Please have a seat. I'm busying myself with Venzor . . . Tikhon Ivanych,' he added, raising his voice, 'come in here. We have a guest.'

'At once, at once,' Tikhon Ivanych answered from the next room. 'Masha, my cravat.'

Chertopkhanov again turned to Venzor and placed the piece of bread on his nose. I looked round. There was no furniture in the room apart from a warped expanding table on thirteen legs of uneven length and four sagging straw-bottomed chairs. The walls, whitewashed long ago, with blue spots on them in the shape of stars, were peeling in many places. Between the windows hung a broken and faded little mirror in an enormous mahogany frame. In the corners stood long-stemmed clay pipes and guns. Thick, black threads of cobweb hung from the ceiling.

'A, B, C, D,' said Chertopkhanov slowly and suddenly shrieked fiercely: 'E for eat! Eat! Eat! . . . What a stupid animal! . . . Eat!'

But the wretched poodle did no more than shake and couldn't make up its mind to open its mouth. It went on sitting there, its tail tucked painfully under it, and, drawing back its lips, blinked miserably and screwed up its eyes just as if it were saying to itself: OK, so you're the boss!

'Go on, eat! Take it!' repeated the impatient landowner.

'You've frightened it,' I remarked.

'Well, be off with it then!'

He gave the dog a shove with his foot. The wretched dog rose up calmly, let the bread drop off its nose and walked away, deeply offended, into the hallway literally on tip-toe. And with good reason: here was a stranger come to visit for the first time and look how they treated him!

The door from the next room creaked cautiously and Mr Nedopyuskin entered, bowing amiably and smiling.

I stood up and bowed.

'Don't disturb yourself, don't disturb yourself,' he muttered.

We took our seats. Chertopkhanov went into a neighbouring room.

'Have you been long here in our promised land?' Nedopyuskin began in a soft voice, cautiously coughed in his hand and, for decency's sake, kept his fingers pressed to his lips.

'Over a month now.'

'Well I never.'

We fell silent.

'Nice weather we're having now,' continued Nedopyuskin and gave me a look of gratitude as if the weather depended on me. 'The crops are looking astonishingly good, one might say.'

I bowed my head in a sign of agreement. We again fell silent.

'Panteley Yeremeich yesterday hunted two hares,' Nedopyuskin began again not without some effort, evidently wanting to enliven our conversation. 'Yes, really large hares, big ones.'

'Has Mr Chertopkhanov got good hounds?'

'Exceptionally good, sir!' exclaimed Nedopyuskin with pleasure. 'One might say they are the best in the province.' (He moved closer to me.) 'What a man, sir! Panteley Yeremeich is such a good fellow! Whatever he wants, whatever comes into his head – see, it's all ready and done, everything's literally on the boil! Panteley Yeremeich, I'll tell you . . .'

Chertopkhanov came into the room. Nedopyuskin grinned, stopped talking and directed my attention to him with his eyes as if wanting to say: see for yourself! We began talking about hunting.

'Would you like me to show you my pack of hounds?' Chertopkhanov asked me and without waiting for an answer summoned Karp.

There entered a sturdy fellow in a green nankeen caftan with a blue collar and livery buttons.

'Tell Fomka,' said Chertopkhanov sharply, 'to bring out Ammalat and Saiga and do it properly, d'you understand?'

Karp smiled broadly, emitted an indefinable sound and went out. Fomka then put in an appearance, with his hair brushed, his buttons done up, wearing boots and accompanying the hounds. Out of politeness I expressed my admiration for the stupid animals (all borzoi hounds are extraordinarily stupid). Chertopkhanov spat into Ammalat's nostrils, which quite obviously didn't please the hound in the least. Nedopyuskin also patted Ammalat from behind. We once more started chatting. Little by little Chertopkhanov became completely mollified and stopped showing off and snorting. The expression of his face changed. He gave both me and Nedopyuskin a look.

'Hey!' he exclaimed suddenly. 'Why should she go on sitting there by herself? Masha! Masha! Come in here!'

Someone made a movement in the next room, but there was no answer.

'Ma-a-sha,' Chertopkhanov repeated softly, 'come in here. Don't be frightened.'

The door opened quietly and I saw a woman of about twenty, tall and well-built, with a dark gypsy face, yellowish-brown eyes and plaited hair as black as tar. Large white teeth literally glittered between full red lips. She wore a white dress; a sky-blue shawl, fastened at her neck with a gold pin, stretched down to cover half of her fine, well-bred arms. She took a couple of steps forward with the shy ungainliness of a wild girl, stopped still and lowered her head.

'Let me introduce you,' said Panteley Yeremeich, 'a wife who's not a wife but should be treated as one.'

Masha blushed slightly and smiled in confusion. I gave her an unusually low bow. She was very attractive. The delicate aquiline nose with open, semi-transparent nostrils, the bold line of her high eyebrows and the pale, very slightly sunken cheeks, all the features of her face expressed a uniquely passionate nature and an uncaring audacity. Below her plaited hair at the back of her neck ran two lines of small shiny hairs, signs of blood and strength.

She went to the window and sat down. I didn't want to increase her confusion and struck up a conversation with Chertopkhanov. Masha slightly turned her head and began glancing at me from under her brows in a covert, rapid and untutored way. Her glances just flashed at me like a snake's tongue. Nedopyuskin sat down beside her and whispered something in her ear. She smiled once again. In smiling she would slightly wrinkle up her nose and raise her upper lip, which gave her face not so much a cat-like as a leonine expression.

'Ah, I see. You're one of the "hands-off" kind,' I thought, glancing covertly in my turn at her sinuous waist, flat bosom and angular, rapid movements.

'What d'you say, Masha,' asked Chertopkhanov, 'isn't it right to give our guest something to eat?'

'We've got jam,' she answered.

'Well, then, let's have some jam and some vodka as well. Listen, Masha,' he shouted after her, 'bring the guitar, too.'

'Why should I bring the guitar? I'm not going to sing.'

'Why not?'

'Don't want to.'

'Hey, that's nonsense. You'll want to if . . .'

'If what?' Masha asked, knitting her brows quickly.

'If I ask you,' said Chertopkhanov not without some embarrassment.

'Ah!'

She went out and returned soon with the jam and the vodka and again sat by the window. Her brow still wore a frown and both her eyebrows rose and fell like the antennae of a wasp. Have you noticed, dear reader, what malicious faces wasps have? Well, I thought, a storm's brewing. The conversation faltered. Nedopyuskin fell completely silent and smiled tensely. Chertopkhanov huffed and puffed, his face grew red and his eyes bulged, and I was just on the point of going.

Masha suddenly jumped up, in a flash opened the window, stuck out her head and cried out the name 'Aksinya!' sharply at a woman who was passing by. The woman gave a jump, tried to turn round, slipped and fell heavily on the ground. Masha sprang back and burst into loud laughter. Chertopkhanov also burst out laughing. Nedopyuskin squealed with laughter. We were all stirred out of our gloom. The storm had passed with only one flash of lightning and the air had cleared.

Half an hour later no one would have recognized us, because we were chatting and fooling about like children. Masha was in the highest of spirits and Chertopkhanov simply devoured her with his eyes. Her face had gone pale, her nostrils flared and her eyes flashed and darkened at one and the same time. The wild girl had really let her hair down. Nedopyuskin hobbled about after her on his fat, short legs like a drake after a duck. Even Venzor crept out from under his bench in the hall, stood in the doorway, looked at us and suddenly took to jumping about and barking. Masha dashed into another room, brought back a guitar, threw her shawl off her shoulders, swiftly sat down, raised her head and started singing a gypsy song. Her voice rang and quivered like a cracked glass bell, rising up and then dying away . . . One's heart was both moved and appalled by it. 'Hey, light up my heart and speak,' she sang and Chertopkhanov set about dancing to it. Nedopyuskin stamped and minced. Masha was alight from head to toe like a birch log on a fire and her fine fingers ran briskly over the guitar and her dark neck gradually rose higher and higher above her double-stranded amber necklace. Sometimes she would suddenly grow quiet and sink into exhaustion, as if she were even unwilling to finger the strings, and Chertopkhanov would stop, merely shrugging a shoulder and shuffling his feet, while Nedopyuskin did no more than nod his head like a porcelain Chinaman; and then again she'd pour the words and start singing crazily, straightening her waist and thrusting out her chest, and Chertopkhanov'd again squat down in a Cossack dance and leap almost to the ceiling, crying:

'Eez*ee*!'

'Easy, easy, easy, easy!' chimed in Nedopyuskin in a rush.

It was late in the evening when I left Unsleepy Hollow.

THE END OF CHERTOPKHANOV

---❦---

A COUPLE of years after my visit to Panteley Yeremeich his misfortunes began – and I mean misfortunes. Dissatisfactions, failures and even accidents had happened to him before, but he'd paid no attention to them and reigned supreme in his world as usual. The first misfortune that befell him was for him the most sensitive: Masha left him.

It's hard to say what made her leave his place, to which, it seemed, she'd become so accustomed. To the end of his days Chertopkhanov was of the opinion that the cause of Masha's betrayal was a certain young neighbour, a retired cavalry captain known as Jaffe who, according to Panteley Yeremeich, had his way by ceaselessly twiddling his moustaches, plastering his hair with lotion and frequently going 'Ahem!' But it has to be supposed that a more important role was played by the wild gypsy blood that flowed in Masha's veins. Whatever it was, one fine summer evening Masha tied up her few bits and pieces in a small bundle and walked out of Chertopkhanov's house.

She'd previously spent three days sitting in a corner, bent double and pressed to the wall, like a wounded vixen. It would've been all right if she'd said something, but she simply moved her eyes about and was consumed by her thoughts and twitched her eyebrows and slightly bared her teeth and moved her arms about as if trying to wrap herself up. She'd had such moods before but they'd never lasted long.

Chertopkhanov knew this and therefore hadn't been disturbed and hadn't disturbed her. But when, returning from the kennels, where, in the words of his whipper-in, his last two hounds 'were stiff as boards', he'd been met by a maid who informed him in a trembling voice that Mariya Akinfievna'd said she'd wanted him to have her regards and be told that she wished him all the best but wasn't coming back, Chertopkhanov had spun round once or twice on his heels, emitted a hoarse whine and at once set out after the runaway, taking a pistol with him.

He caught up with her a little over a mile from home, close to a small birch wood on the main road to the local town. The sun was low on the skyline and everything round suddenly became purple – trees, grass and earth.

'You're off to Jaffe! You're going to Jaffe!' groaned Chertopkhanov the moment he saw Masha. 'It's Jaffe!' he went on, rushing up to her and almost stumbling at every step.

Masha stood still and turned to face him. She had her back to the light and seemed all black, as if carved from dark wood. Only the whites of her eyes shone like silver almonds while the eyes themselves, the pupils, were darker than ever.

She threw her bundle to one side and crossed her arms.

'You're off to Jaffe, you good-for-nothing!' Chertopkhanov went on and was about to seize her by the shoulder, but, encountering her look, was taken aback and stopped short.

'I wasn't on my way to Mr Jaffe, Pantaley Yeremeich,' Masha answered evenly and calmly, 'but I simply cannot live with you any more.'

'Why can't you? Why not? Have I done something to offend you?' Masha shook her head.

'You haven't done anything to offend me, Pantaley Yeremeich. It's simply that I've got bored living with you . . . Thank you for past times, but I can't stay – No!'

Chertopkhanov was astonished. He even slapped his hands against his thighs and gave a little jump.

'What d'you mean? You've lived with me, there's been nothing but happiness and peace of mind and now suddenly it's – Oh, I'm bored! I've had enough of him! I'll get my things, put my kerchief on and be off! You received every respect, as much as any lady . . .'

'That I'm not needing,' Masha interrupted.

'How – not needing? To be turned from a wandering gypsy girl into a lady – you don't need that? What d'you mean, you lowdown bitch? D'you really expect me to believe that? It's disloyalty, that's what's behind it, disloyalty!'

He again hissed.

'I'm not disloyal in my thoughts and I never have been,' said Masha in her clear and ringing voice, 'but I've already told you – I've got bored.'

'Masha!' cried Chertopkhanov and struck himself on his chest with his fist. 'Look, stop, it's enough! You've made your point . . . That's enough! By God, just think what Tisha'll say! At least have pity on him!'

'Give Tikhon Ivanych my regards and tell him . . .'

Chertopkhanov waved his arms.

'No, you're lying! You mustn't go! Your Jaffe'll not have you!'

'Mr Jaffe . . .' Masha started saying.

'What sort of a *Mis-ter* Jaffe is he?' Chertopkhanov teased. 'He's just a skinflint and a scoundrel, that's all he is – an' he's got a face like a monkey!'

For a whole half-hour Chertopkhanov tried to persuade Masha. He'd go up close to her, then jump back, or he'd shake his fist at her or bow low to her, and cry and swear.

'I can't,' Masha kept on repeating, 'sad though I am . . . I've got this longing.' Gradually her face acquired such an indifferent, almost sleepy expression that Chertopkhanov asked her if she'd been given something to drink.

'It's the longing,' she said for the tenth time.

'Well, what if I kill you then?' he shouted suddenly and whipped his pistol out of his pocket.

Masha smiled and her face grew lively.

'So what? Kill me, Panteley Yeremeich! It's up to you! But I'm not going to come back.'

'So you won't come back?' Chertopkhanov cocked the pistol.

'I won't come back, my dear. Never in all my life. That's my final word.'

Chertopkhanov suddenly thrust the pistol into her hand and sat down on the ground.

'Well, then, you kill *me*! Without you I don't want to go on living. If I've grown boring for you, then everything's grown boring for me.'

Masha bent down and picked up her bundle, laid the pistol down on the grass with the barrel pointing away from Chertopkhanov and then went up close to him.

'Oh, my darling, why're you doing this to yourself? Is it 'cos you don't understand what we gypsy girls are like? We're like this, it's our way. If the longing to be off comes on us, if something calls us to be off into far-distant lands, then what's the point of staying? You'll always remember your Masha – you'll never find another like me – and I'll never forget you, my bold falcon. But our life together's finished!'

'I loved you, Masha,' Chertopkhanov muttered into the fingers which covered his face.

'And I loved you, my darling Panteley Yeremeich!'

'I've loved you, I've loved you past all thinking, past all forgetting – and when I think about you now, how you're just up and going without so much as a farewell and leavin' me and going wandering off round the world, well, then, it seems to me if I weren't such a miserable pauper you wouldn't have given me up!'

Masha simply laughed at these words.

'And you used to call me "the girl without a silver bit"!' she cried and struck Chertopkhanov hard on the shoulder.

He jumped to his feet.

'Well, at least take some money from me! You can't go off without a farthing, can you? But best of all – just kill me! I mean what I say: kill me and be done with it!'

Masha again shook her head.

'I've got to kill you, eh? Don't they send people to Siberia for that, my darling?'

Chertopkhanov shuddered.

'So you won't do it 'cos of that, 'cos of fear of forced labour . . .'

Once more he collapsed on the grass.

Masha stood for a while silently above him.

'I'm sorry for you, Panteley Yeremeich,' she said with a sigh. 'You're a good man . . . But it's no use! Goodbye!'

She turned round that instant and took a couple of steps. It was already night and murky shadows rose around them on all sides. Chertopkhanov jumped up quickly and seized Masha from behind by her elbows.

'So you're off, you snake! You're going to Jaffe!'

'Goodbye!' Masha repeated expressively and sharply, tearing herself away from him and walking off.

Chertopkhanov watched her go, dashed to where the pistol was lying, picked it up, aimed and fired. But before pressing the trigger he jerked his hand upwards and the bullet went whistling over Masha's head. As she went she glanced at him over her shoulder and then continued on her way, giving a little sway of her hips as if to taunt him.

He covered his face and hurled himself forwards at a run . . .

But he'd scarcely run fifty paces when he suddenly stopped as if rooted to the ground. A familiar, all-too-familiar voice reached him. Masha was singing. She sang 'Time of youth, time so lovely . . .'[1] and each sound receded into the evening air in plangent, torrid strains. Chertopkhanov listened intently. The voice went further and further away, continuously dying down and then returning again barely audibly but still in a molten stream of sound . . .

'She's just doing this to me out of pique,' Chertopkhanov thought, but then he gave a great groan: 'Oh, no, it's not that! It's because she's leaving me forever!' and he burst into tears.

The next day he put in an appearance at the apartment of the said Mr Jaffe who, as a true man of the world, sparing no favours for isolation in the country, had settled in the local town 'to be closer to the ladies', as he put it. Chertopkhanov did not find Jaffe at home. He'd left the previous day for Moscow, so the footman said.

'So that's it!' exclaimed Chertopkhanov fiercely. 'They were in it together! She's run off with him! In that case . . .'

He forced his way into the young cavalry captain's study, notwithstanding the footman's resistance. In the study above a divan hung an oil portrait of the owner in his Uhlan uniform.

'So there you are, you tail-less monkey!' thundered Chertopkhanov, jumped up on the divan and, striking at the stretched canvas with his fist, tore a huge hole in it.

'Tell your layabout master . . .' he turned to the footman '. . . that in the absence of his own foul face the honourable nobleman Chertopkhanov has disfigured his painted one. And if he wants satisfaction from me he knows where to find the honourable nobleman Chertopkhanov! Otherwise I'll find him! I'll seek out the bloody monkey even if it's at the bottom of the sea!'

Having said these words, Chertopkhanov jumped off the divan and solemnly departed.

But cavalry captain Jaffe did not demand any satisfaction from him — he didn't even meet him anywhere — and Chertopkhanov didn't bother about seeking out his enemy and so nothing came of the matter. Masha herself soon afterwards disappeared without trace. Chertopkhanov took to drink, but then came to his senses. At which point a second misfortune struck.

II

The second misfortune was that his bosom friend Tikhon Ivanovich Nedopyuskin died. A couple of years before his death his health had begun to fail him. He'd begun to suffer from shortness of breath, continuously dropped off to sleep and on waking couldn't come to himself again quickly. The local doctor assured him that he was suffering a series of small strokes. During the three days preceding Masha's departure, during the days when she was growing aware of her 'longing', Nedopyuskin was lying on his own in Besselendeevka where he'd caught a serious cold. Masha's behaviour was that much more shocking to him for being so unexpected and it shocked him almost more profoundly than it shocked Chertopkhanov. Due to the gentleness and shyness of his nature, apart from expressing the most sincere regrets to his friend and an anguished bewilderment, he said nothing at all, but inside him everything had burst and collapsed. 'She's gone off with my soul,' he would whisper to himself as he sat on his favourite oilskin-covered divan and twiddled his fingers. Even when Chertopkhanov recovered from the shock, he, Nedopyuskin, didn't and continued to feel an emptiness inside him. 'Here,' he'd say, pointing to the middle of his chest, just above his stomach.

In this state he remained until the beginning of winter. His shortness of breath was improved by the first frosts, but then he suffered not so much one of the small strokes as a real stroke. He didn't lose consciousness at once. He was still able to recognize Chertopkhanov and in response to the desperate cry of his friend: 'How can you, Tisha, without my permission, abandon me? You're no better than Masha . . .' answered with a tongue that was already growing stiff: 'But I P. . .a. . .ley Ye. . .e. . .eich, I've a. . .ways o. . .bey. . .ed you.' However, that didn't prevent him from dying the very same day, without even waiting for the arrival of the local doctor who, at the sight of his barely cold corpse, could do no more in tearful acknowledgement of the transitoriness of all earthly things than order himself 'a glass of vodka and some salted fish'. Tikhon Ivanovich willed his estate, as could have been expected, to his most honoured benefactor and magnanimous patron 'Pantaley Yeremeich Chertopkhanov'. But it brought no great benefit to the most honoured benefactor because it was quickly sold by public auction – partly in order to cover the costs of a monument over the grave, a statue which Chertopkhanov (evidently his father's blood still ran in his veins!) wanted to erect over the ashes of his friend. He ordered the statue, which should have been that of an angel in prayer, from Moscow, but the man recommended to him to commission it, aware that in the provinces there are few sculpture experts, sent instead of an angel a goddess Flora which had for many years decorated one of the overgrown suburban parks of Catherine the Great's time. This statue, exceedingly elegant, certainly, in rococo style, with chubby little hands, fluffy curls, a garland of roses on her naked bosom and a noticeably curved waist, was obtained by the commissioner for nothing. So it is that to this very day there stands above Tikhon Ivanovich's grave a mythological goddess with one foot graciously raised who looks with truly aristocratic disdain at the calves and sheep strolling round about her, those devoted visitors to our country graveyards.

III

After being deprived of his faithful friend Chertopkhanov again took to drink, but on this occasion much more seriously. His affairs generally went downhill. There was no point in going hunting, his last money had gone and the last of his servants ran away. Complete isolation ensued for Pantaley Yeremeich, leaving him no one to talk to, no one to open his heart to. Only his arrogance remained undiminished. On the contrary, the worse his circumstances became, the more haughty, overbearing and unapproachable he became himself. At last he grew quite wild. One pleasure, one joy only remained to him: an astonishing horse, a grey, of Don breed and named by him Malek Adel,[2] a really remarkable animal.

He came by the horse in the following way.

Riding on horseback on one occasion through a neighbouring village, Chertopkhanov heard a noisy hubbub of peasant voices from a crowd round the tavern. In the midst of this crowd, at one point, sturdy hands were constantly being raised and lowered.

'What's going on there?' he asked in his usual commanding tone, addressing an old woman standing by the doorstep of her hut.

Leaning on a lintel and seeming half-asleep, the old woman glanced several times in the direction of the tavern. A fair-haired little boy in a cotton shirt, with a small cypress-wood crucifix on his bare chest was sitting, his feet outspread and his little fists clenched, between her own bast shoes, while a chick pecked at a wood-hard crust of rye bread.

'The Lord knows, sir,' the old woman answered and, leaning forward, placed her dark wrinkled hand on the little boy's head. 'It sounds like our lads are beatin' up a Jew.'

'What d'you mean – a Jew? What Jew?'

'The Lord knows, sir. Some Jew's dropped in here. Who knows where he's come from. Vasya, to Mum now, there's a good boy. Shoo, shoo, you bad thing!'

The old woman shooed away the chick and Vasya seized hold of her skirt.

'So there they are beatin' him up, my good sir.'

'Why? What for?'

'I dunno, sir. Probably it's over some business. An' why shouldn't he be beaten? Didn't he crucify Christ, sir?'

Chertopkhanov emitted a shout, gave his horse a touch of the whip on the neck and dashed straight at the crowd. On bursting into it, he began thrashing about to right and left indiscriminately at the peasants with the same whip, ordering in a breaking voice: 'Arb-it-ra-ry justice! Arb-it-ra-ry justice! The law must punish, not pri-vate per-sons! The law!! The law!! The la-a-aw!'

Within a couple of minutes the entire crowd had dispersed in various directions, leaving lying on the ground in front of the tavern door a small, emaciated, dark-skinned creature in a nankeen caftan, dishevelled and bleeding. The white face, rolled-up eyes and wide-open mouth – what could it mean? Was it being frightened to death or death itself?

'Why've you killed the Jew?' cried Chertopkhanov thunderously, threatening them with his whip.

The crowd gave a feeble murmur in response. One peasant held his shoulder, another his side, yet another his nose.

''E's one for a fight!' somebody said from the back.

'With 'is whip, see! Anyone can!' said another voice.

'Why've you killed the Jew? I'm asking you, you blasted crowd of Asians!' repeated Chertopkhanov.

But at that point the creature lying on the ground quickly jumped to his feet and, dashing towards Chertopkhanov, frantically seized hold of the edge of his saddle. Loud laughter broke out among the crowd.

''E's alive!' voices shouted from the back. 'A bloody cat, that's what 'e is!'

'Your Ever-so-high Highness, help me, save me!' babbled the unfortunate Jew, pressing his chest hard up against Chertopkhanov's leg. 'They're going to kill me, kill me, your Ever-so-high Highness!'

'Why?' asked Chertopkhanov.

'In God's name I can't say! Their cattle's begun to die . . . they think I . . .'

'All right, we'll talk about it afterwards,' interrupted Chertopkhanov. 'But now you grab hold of the saddle and come along with me. As for you,' he added, turning to the crowd, 'you know me, don't you? I'm landowner Panteley Chertopkhanov and I live in the little village of Unsleepy Hollow. That means you can lay a complaint against me if you like and the Jew as well!'

'Why would we do that?' asked a grey-bearded, dignified peasant who looked exactly like some patriarch of old, bowing low as he spoke. (He'd been beating the Jew in any case with the best of them.) 'We, Panteley Yeremeich, your honour, know well how kind you are. We're very grateful to you for teaching us such a lesson!'

'Why would we do that?' other voices chimed in. 'But we'll get even with that 'eathen! 'E won't escape! We'll be after 'im like a rabbit . . .'

Chertopkhanov twitched his whiskers, gave a snort and set off at a walking pace towards his village accompanied by the Jew whom he'd liberated from his oppressors much as he'd once liberated Tikhon Nedopyuskin.

IV

A few days later the sole servant-boy remaining with him informed Chertopkhanov that someone had arrived on horseback and wished to talk to him. Chertopkhanov went out on to his porch and saw his friend the little Jew sitting on a beautiful Don horse which stood proud and motionless in the middle of the yard. The little Jew wasn't wearing his hat. He was holding it under his arm. He'd put his feet not in the stirrups themselves but in the straps. The torn fringes of his caftan hung over both sides of the saddle. On seeing Chertopkhanov, he smacked his lips, jerked his elbows and let his legs hang free. But Chertopkhanov not only didn't reply to his greeting, he even grew angry and suddenly flew into a temper at the thought that a wretched Jew should dare sit on such a beautiful horse ... Completely improper!

'Hey, you, you blasted Ethiopian!' he shouted. 'Get off at once, unless you want to be pulled off into the mud!'

The Jew obeyed instantly, fell out of the saddle like a sack and, still holding a rein in one hand, smiling and bowing, came towards Chertopkhanov.

'What d'you want?' asked Panteley Yeremeich with dignity.

'Your 'onour, sir, be good enough to see what a fine horse, eh?' said the Jew, continuing to bow.

'Sure ... it's a good horse. Where'd you get it? Stole it, did you?'

'O-o-o, your 'onour, how can you! I'm an 'onest Yid, sir, an' I didn't steal it, but I got it special for your 'onour, sir, I did! I looked all over for it, all over! An' 'ere's the horse at last! You won't find a finer horse on the whole Don river. Just see, your 'onour, what a horse he is! Come 'ere, sir, please! There, there ... turn a bit, stand sideways to 'im! We'll take the saddle off ... There! See, your 'onour?'

'It's a good horse,' Chertopkhanov repeated with feigned indifference while his heart literally started hammering in his breast. He was a passionate devotee of horse-flesh and knew a good horse when he saw one.

'Go on, your 'onour, stroke 'im! Stroke 'im on 'is neck, hi-hi-hi, like this!'

Chertopkhanov barely willingly placed his hand on the horse's neck, patted it a couple of times, then ran his fingers from the withers along the back and, on reaching the well-known spot above the kidneys, lightly pressed it in the manner of an expert rider. The horse instantly arched his back and, glancing sideways at Chertopkhanov with his haughty black eye, snorted and stamped his front hoofs.

The Jew laughed and lightly clapped his hands together.

''E recognizes 'is master, your 'onour, 'e really does!'

'O, don't talk rubbish!' Chertopkhanov interrupted in annoyance. 'I've got nothing with which to buy this horse from you, and I've never accepted gifts from a Jew, nor from the Lord God either!'

'An' I wouldn't be so bold as to give you anything, for heaven's sake!' exclaimed the Jew. 'You buy it, your 'onour . . . an' as for the monies, I'll wait for 'em.'

Chertopkhanov grew thoughtful.

'What'll you take for him?' he asked finally through his teeth.

'What I paid. Two hundred roubles.'

The horse actually cost twice and perhaps three times more than this.

Chertopkhanov turned away and yawned feverishly.

'When would you like it – the money?' he asked, forcibly knitting his brows and not looking at the Jew.

'Whenever's convenient to your 'onour.'

Chertopkhanov threw back his head but didn't raise his eyes.

'That's not an answer. Talk sense, you child of Herod! Shall I owe it you, eh?'

'Well, let's say,' the Jew said hurriedly, 'in six months . . . agreed?'

Chertopkhanov didn't answer.

The Jew tried to glance into his eyes.

'Agreed? Shall I have him put in the stable?'

'I don't need the saddle,' Chertopkhanov jerked out. 'Take your saddle, d'you hear?'

''Course, 'course, I'll take it,' babbled the delighted Jew and heaved the saddle on to his shoulder.

'The money,' Chertopkhanov went on, 'it'll be paid in six months. And not 200 but 250 . Don't say a word! Two hundred and fifty, I tell you! That's my promise.'

Chertopkhanov still couldn't make up his mind to raise his eyes.

His pride had never been made to suffer in this way before. 'It's obviously a present,' he thought. 'He's brought it out of gratitude, the devil!' He couldn't make up his mind whether to embrace the Jew or thrash him.

'Your 'onour,' the Jew began, growing bold and grinning, 'we should do it the Russian way, my palm on your palm . . .'

'What'll you think of next? A Jew talking about the Russian way! Hey, is there anybody there? Take the horse, put him in the stable! And give him some oats. I'll come and take a look at him in a moment. And know this – his name's Malek Adel!'

Chertopkhanov was on the point of going back indoors when he turned sharply on his heel and, rushing up to the Jew, seized him firmly by the hand. The other bowed and extended his lips ready to offer a kiss, but Chertopkhanov skipped backwards and with the words: 'Don't tell a soul!' spoken under his breath disappeared through his front door.

V

From that day onwards Malek Adel became the chief concern and joy in Chertopkhanov's life. He fell in love with him as he'd never fallen in love with Masha and grew more attached to him than he had been to Nedopyuskin. And what a horse he was! As fiery as fire itself and sharp as gunpowder, and yet as stately and lordly as a boyar! Indefatigable, ready to endure anything, turn him where you might, and always compliant, he cost nothing to feed and would eat the soil itself if there was nothing else to be had. Going at a walking pace it was as if he held you in his arms, at a trot it was like being rocked in a cradle and at a gallop he went so fast even the wind couldn't catch him! He never got winded because he had so many air-vents. He had legs of steel and, as for stumbling, that was unheard of! Jumping a ditch or a fence meant nothing to him. And how intelligent he was! He'd come running at the sound of a voice, craning his neck. If you ordered him to stand still and then went away, he wouldn't budge; only as soon as you started coming back he'd neigh slightly as if to say: 'See, here I am.' And he was never frightened of a thing. In the dark, even in a snowstorm, he'd find his way. And he never let a stranger near him – he'd sink his teeth into him if he did! Should a dog get in his way he'd immediately strike it on the forehead with a front hoof – crack! and that'd be the dog done for. He was a horse with ambitions of his own – you could flourish a whip over him, but God help you if you touched him! Still, there's no point in going on about him. He was a treasure, not a horse!

When Chertopkhanov took it upon himself to describe his Malek Adel, it was amazing how eloquent he waxed! And the way he used to groom and look after him! His coat used to fairly glow with silver – not old silver, mind you, but new, with that dark gloss to it, and if you smoothed it with the palm of your hand it was like velvet! Saddle, saddle-cloth and bridle, the whole harness was so perfectly fixed and clean as a new pin and in perfect order that it just required an artist to come along with his pencil and draw it! Chertopkhanov himself – who else? – with his own hands plaited his favourite's forelocks, and washed his mane and tail in beer, and even oiled his hoofs on more than one occasion.

He'd mount Malek Adel and go riding – not on visits to his neighbours, because he still wouldn't have anything to do with them, but across their fields and past their houses, as if he were saying to them: 'Just you eat your hearts out, you fools, from a distance!' Or as soon as he heard that a hunt was in the offing, with some wealthy landowner preparing to set out, he'd be off there at once and prance away in the distance, on the horizon, astonishing all the spectators by the beauty and speed of his horse and never allowing anyone near him. On one occasion a hunter even dashed after him with his entire retinue. Seeing that Chertopkhanov was getting away from him, he started shouting at him with all his strength, going at full tilt:

'Hey, you there! Listen! Take whatever you like for your horse! I don't mind if it's a thousand roubles! I'll give you my wife and children! Take the last thing I've got!'

Chertopkhanov suddenly reined back Malek Adel. The hunter raced up to him.

'My good sir,' he shouted, 'just tell me what it is you want, eh? My father, my own flesh and blood!'

'Even if you were a king,' declared Chertopkhanov, pausing between each word (and, mind you, he'd never heard of Shakespeare[3] in his life), 'and you gave me your whole kingdom for my horse, I wouldn't take it!'

So saying, he gave a roar of laughter, made Malek Adel rear up on his hind legs and spun him round like a top or a child's plaything on only his hind legs – and then he was off like a flash, literally flashing through the field of stubble. But the hunter (he was rumoured to be a very wealthy prince) flung his hat to the ground and then flung himself face downwards on to his hat! And that's where he stayed for up to half an hour.

And why shouldn't Chertopkhanov have treasured his horse? Wasn't it on his account that he'd once again acquired an undoubted and ultimate superiority over his neighbours?

VI

Meanwhile time passed and the date for payment approached, but Chertopkhanov not only didn't have 250 roubles, he didn't even have fifty. He wondered what to do and how he could help himself. 'Well,' he decided finally, 'if the Jew won't be merciful and doesn't want to wait, I'll give him my house and land and I'll jump on my horse and simply follow my nose! Even if I die of hunger, I'll never give up Malek Adel!'

He grew very worried and even thoughtful, but at this point fate – for the first and last time – took pity on him and smiled on him. Some distant aunt, whose very name was unknown to Chertopkhanov, left him in her will a sum that was enormous in his eyes – a whole 2,000 roubles! And he received the money just in time, a day before the Jew's arrival. Chertopkhanov was out of his mind with joy – but he never gave a thought to vodka. From the very day that Malek Adel had arrived he'd never taken a drop into his mouth. He dashed to the stables and gave his friend several kisses on either side of his mouth above the nostrils where a horse's skin is particularly tender. 'Now we'll never be parted!' he exclaimed, slapping Malek Adel on the shoulder below his well-combed mane. On going back into the house he counted out 250 roubles and sealed them in a packet. Then he started dreaming, lying on his back and smoking his pipe, contemplating how he'd dispose of the rest of the money and, more especially, what kind of hounds he'd get – proper Kostroma hounds, for sure, and with red and white spots! He even had a chat with Perfishka, to whom he'd promised a new knee-length caftan with yellow braid at the seams, and then went to sleep in the most blessed contentment of spirit.

He had a bad dream. He'd gone hunting, only not on Malek Adel but on some strange animal like a camel. A white vixen, white as snow, ran towards him and he tried to wave his whip to encourage the hounds to go after her, but instead of a whip he found a washing-up mop in his hand and the vixen ran right in front of him sticking out her tongue. He jumped down from his camel, stumbled and fell – fell right into the arms of a gendarme who took him off to the Governor-General in whom he recognized Jaffe . . .

Chertopkhanov woke up. It was dark in the room and already time for second cockcrow.

Somewhere very far off a horse neighed.

Chertopkhanov raised his head. Once more he heard that very faint neighing.

'It's Malek Adel,' he thought. 'It's his neighing! But why so far away? Oh, my God, it can't be . . .'

Chertopkhanov suddenly went all cold, jumped instantly from his bed, felt around for his boots and clothes, dressed, and, having taken the stable key from under his pillow, rushed out into the yard.

VII

The stables were at the far end of the yard with one wall facing on to the fields. Chertopkhanov took his time to insert the key into the lock, because his hands were shaking so much, and didn't immediately turn the key. He stood there motionless, holding his breath in the hope that there might be some kind of movement on the other side of the door.

'Malek, my dear! Malek!' he cried in a soft voice. There was dead silence!

Chertopkhanov jerked the key despite himself and the door creaked and opened. It turned out it wasn't locked. He stepped across the doorstep and again called out to his horse, this time using the full name:

'Malek Adel!'

But his friend didn't answer. Only a mouse rustled in the straw. Then Chertopkhanov flung himself towards the one of the three stalls in which Malek Adel was usually kept. He lighted on it at once even though all around was so dark you couldn't see a thing . . . It was empty! Chertopkhanov's head began to spin just as if a bell had begun to toll in his skull. He tried to speak but could do no more than hiss and, running his hands up and down and along the sides, gasping as his knees began to give way under him, he felt his way from one stall to another until, in the third, almost filled to the top with hay, he struck against one wall, then another, fell, turned head over heels, lifted himself up and suddenly dashed headlong through the half-open door into the yard . . .

'He's been stolen! Perfishka! Perfishka! He's been stolen!' he yelled at the top of his voice.

The servant-boy Perfishka came flying like a top out of the cupboard in which he slept, in nothing but his shirt. Just as if they were both drunk the two of them – the master and his only servant – collided in the middle of the yard. Like mad things they spun round each other. Neither the master nor the servant had the faintest idea what was going on.

'It's a catastrophe! Catastrophe!' muttered Chertopkhanov.

'Catastrophe! Catastrophe!' repeated the servant-boy.

'Get a lantern! Go and light a lantern! Light! Light!' were the cries finally torn from Chertopkhanov's constricted chest. Perfishka dashed into the house.

But it was no easy matter to light the lantern and create light. Sulphur matches were considered a rarity in Russia at that time and the last coals in the kitchen had died long ago. The tinder and flint took a long time to find and didn't work well. Grinding his teeth, Chertopkhanov seized the tinder from the hands of the amazed Perfishka and started trying to strike a light himself. Sparks flew about abundantly and even more abundantly oaths and even groans, but the tinder either didn't catch or simply smouldered despite the joint efforts of four puffed-out cheeks and both their lips! At last, after five minutes and no sooner, the tallow candle-end at the bottom of the broken lantern was kindled into life and Chertopkhanov, in the company of Perfishka, burst into the stable, raised the lantern above his head and looked round . . .

Everything was empty!

He jumped out into the yard, dashed round it in all directions and could find no horse anywhere. The wattle fencing surrounding Panteley Yeremeich's estate had long since fallen into decay and in many places was leaning over or flat on the ground. Next to the stables it was completely down for about three feet or so. Perfishka pointed this out to Chertopkhanov.

'Master, sir, look! It wasn't like this yesterday! Look, there are stakes sticking up! Someone must've pulled 'em up!'

Chertopkhanov rushed up with the lantern and moved it around over the ground.

'Hoofmarks, hoofmarks, traces of horseshoe, fresh traces!' he cried all in a rush. 'That's where they led him through! There, right there!'

He instantly jumped over the fence and with a cry of 'Malek Adel! Malek Adel!' ran straight out into the fields.

Perfishka remained standing in bewilderment by the fence. The bright circle of light from the lantern quickly vanished before his eyes, swallowed up in the dense darkness of the starless and moonless night.

Ever weaker and weaker grew Chertopkhanov's desperate shouts.

VIII

Dawn had already broken when he returned home. He'd lost all human semblance and there was mud all over his clothing, his face had acquired a wild and terrible appearance and his eyes looked morose and dismal. In a husky whisper he drove Perfishka from him and locked himself in his own room. He could scarcely keep on his feet from tiredness but he didn't go back to bed, he sat in a chair by the door and clutched hold of his head.

'Stolen! Stolen!'

But how could a thief have contrived to steal Malek Adel at night from a locked stable? Malek Adel, who wouldn't let anyone strange near him even in broad daylight – so how could he be stolen without a single sound, just like that? And how could one explain that none of the yard dogs barked? True, there were only two of them, two young puppies, and they'd burrowed in the earth from hunger and cold – still!

'And what on earth will I do,' thought Chertopkhanov, 'without Malek Adel? I've been deprived of my last joy, so it's time I died.

Why should I buy another horse, even though I've got the money? And where'd I find another horse like him?'

'Panteley Yeremeich! Panteley Yeremeich!' came a timid cry from the other side of the door.

Chertopkhanov jumped to his feet.

'Who is it?' he shouted in a voice that wasn't his own.

'It's me, your servant, Perfishka.'

'Whaddya want? Or has he been found, has he come home?'

'Not at all, sir, Panteley Yeremeich, but that Jew, what sold 'im . . .'

'Well?'

''E's come.'

'Ho-ho-ho-ho-ho!' roared Chertopkhanov and instantly flung open the door. 'Bring him here! Bring him! Bring him!'

At the sight of the dishevelled, wild-eyed figure of his 'saviour' who had put in such a sudden appearance the Jew, standing behind Perfishka's back, was on the point of making a dash for it when Chertopkhanov sprang at him with a couple of leaps and, like a tiger, had him fast by the neck.

'Ah! So you've come for the money! It's the money you're after!' he cried hoarsely, as if it wasn't *he* doing the strangling but someone strangling *him*. 'You steal him at night and then in the daylight you come for the money? Eh? Eh?'

'Ple-e-eze, yo-o-our 'onour, sir,' groaned the Jew.

'Tell me where my horse is, eh? Where've you taken him, eh? Who's got him now? Go on, tell, tell, tell me!'

The Jew wasn't even capable of groaning. Even a look of fear had vanished from his face as it turned blue. His arms had dropped and hung loose. His whole body, in Chertopkhanov's fierce shaking of it, swayed backwards and forwards like a reed.

'I'll pay you your money, I'll pay you in full, down to the last copeck!' screamed Chertopkhanov. 'But I'll simply wring your neck like the merest chick if you don't tell me here and now . . .'

'But, sir, you've already throttled him,' remarked Perfishka the servant-boy calmly.

At that point Chertopkhanov realized what he'd done. He released the Jew's neck and the man instantly collapsed on the ground. Chertopkhanov lifted him up, sat him down on a bench, poured a glass of vodka into his mouth and brought him to his senses. And, having brought him to his senses, began discussing things with him.

It turned out that the Jew didn't know a thing about the theft of Malek Adel. And what would be the point of his stealing the horse which he had himself obtained for 'your most 'onoured self, Panteley Yeremeich'?

Then Chertopkhanov led him into the stables. The two of them scrutinized the stalls, troughs and doorlock, rooted about in the hay and straw and then came out into the yard. Chertopkhanov pointed out to the Jew the hoofmarks by the wattle fence. Suddenly he struck himself on his thighs.

'Stop!' he exclaimed. 'Where'd you buy the horse?'

'In Maloarkhangelsk county, at the Verkhosensk fair,' the Jew answered.

'From whom?'

'From a Cossack.'

'One moment! Was he young or old, this Cossack?'

'Middle-aged, well set-up . . .'

'But what sort was he? What did he look like? Was he a right crook?'

'Likely 'e was a crook, your 'onour!'

'And what did he say to you, this crook – did he say he'd had the horse a long time?'

'I remember he said he'd had it a long time.'

'Well, then, if it's anyone stolen it, it's him! Judge for yourself! Listen, come here . . . What's your name?'

The Jew quivered and fluttered his black little eyes at Chertopkhanov.

'What's *my* name?'

'Yes, what d'they call you?'

'Moshel Leiba.'

'Well, judge for yourself, Leiba, my friend, you're an intelligent man – to whom if not to his old master would Malek Adel have surrendered? After all, he'd have saddled him and put on the bridle and taken off his cloth – there it is, lying in the hay! . . . He'd have gone about things just as if he were at home! Anyone else apart from his master Malek Adel would have trampled under his hoofs! He'd have set up such a racket he'd have woken up the whole village! D'you agree with me?'

'Agree, I do agree, your 'onour, sir!'

'Well, it means the first thing we must do is seek out that Cossack!'

'But how can we seek 'im out, your 'onour? I only saw 'im that one time, sir, an' where he is now and what 'is name is, oy vay, oy vay!' added the Jew, miserably shaking his short locks.

'Leiba!' screamed Chertopkhanov suddenly. 'Leiba, look at me! Look, I've lost my reason, I'm not myself! I'll lay hands on myself if you don't help me!'

'But how can I?'

'Come with me and we'll start looking for that thief!'

'But where'll we go?'

'To fairs, along roads big and small, to known horse thieves, to the towns, the villages, to the farms – everywhere! And as for money, don't you worry – I've come into an inheritance, my dear fellow! I'll spend every last penny of it until I get my friend back! And our Cossack what done us wrong, he won't get away! Wherever he goes we'll go too! If he goes into the ground, we'll go there too! If he goes to the devil, we'll go to Satan himself!'

'Why be goin' to Satan?' remarked the Jew. 'Him we can be doing without!'

'Leiba!' broke in Chertopkhanov. 'Leiba, you may be a Jew and have a heathen religion, but your soul's better than any Christian's! You've taken pity on me! There's no point in my going by myself, I couldn't do it all by myself. I'm a hothead, but your head's good as gold! Your people're like that – you know it all without having to learn it! Maybe you're doubtful where I got that money from? Let's go into my room and I'll show you all the money. Take it, take the very cross from round my neck, only give me back Malek Adel, give him back!'

Chertopkhanov was shivering as if in a fever and the sweat poured down his face in torrents and, mixing with his tears, got lost in his whiskers. He was continuously pumping Leiba's hands, beseeching him, nearly kissing him. He was in a frenzy. The Jew made every effort to object and assure him that there was no way he could absent himself, that he had business matters to attend to ... So what! Chertopkhanov didn't want to hear anything about it! There was no way out: poor Leiba had to acquiesce.

The next day Chertopkhanov and Leiba rode out of Unsleepy Hollow on a peasant cart. The Jew had a somewhat confused look and held on to the side of the cart with one hand while his whole frail body jumped up and down on the shaking seat. His other hand was pressed to his stomach where the wad of banknotes lay wrapped in newspaper. Chertopkhanov sat still as a statue, only his eyes roving about and breath being drawn fully into his lungs. There was a dagger sticking out of his belt.

'Well, you thieving bastard, just you watch out now!' he muttered as they drove out on to the high road.

He'd entrusted his house to the servant-boy Perfishka and the cook, an old, deaf woman whom he'd taken in out of compassion.

'I'll return to you on Malek Adel,' he'd shouted to them in farewell, 'or I won't return at all!'

'You'd be better off getting married to me!' joked Perfishka, sticking his elbow in the old woman's ribs. 'There'll be no point hanging around just for the master, otherwise we'll die of boredom!'

IX

A year passed – a whole year, and no news came of Panteley Yeremeich. The old woman cook died. Perfishka himself was on the point of giving up the house and going into the town, to which his cousin, who lived as an assistant at a hairdresser's, was enticing him, when suddenly news spread that the master was returning! The parish deacon received a letter from Panteley Yeremeich himself in which he informed him of his intention to return to Unsleepy Hollow and asking him to inform his servants, so that appropriate arrangements could be made for his arrival. Perfishka interpreted these words to mean that he ought to try and get rid of some of the dust, although he placed no great faith in the correctness of the information. However, he was forced to accept that the deacon had been speaking the truth when, a few days later, Panteley Yeremeich himself, as ever was, appeared in the yard of his estate seated on Malek Adel.

Perfishka dashed to his master and, holding on to the stirrup, was about to help him alight from the horse, but he jumped down himself and, glancing round triumphantly, declared loudly: 'I said I'd find Malek Adel and I found him in spite of enemies and Fate itself!'

Perfishka tried to kiss his hand, but Chertopkhanov paid no attention to his servant's zeal. Leading Malek Adel behind him by the rein, he strode towards the stables. Perfishka looked more intently at his master and quailed at the way he'd grown thinner and older in the course of the year – 'and how stern and severe his face is!' And Panteley Yeremeich should've been overjoyed that he'd achieved what he set out for, and he was overjoyed, true . . . Still, Perfishka quailed at what he saw, and he even began to feel frightened.

Chertopkhanov placed the horse in his old stall, lightly slapped him on the hindquarters and muttered: 'Well, you're home again now! Just you watch out!'

That very day he hired a reliable watchguard from among the untaxed, homeless peasantry, settled once again into his rooms and started living as before . . .

Not, however, exactly as before . . . But about that later.

On the day after his return Panteley Yeremeich summoned Perfishka to him and for want of another person to talk to set about telling him – without losing, of course, his sense of personal dignity and in a deep voice – how he had succeeded in finding Malek Adel. In the course of his tale Chertopkhanov sat facing the window smoking his long-stemmed pipe. Perfishka stood behind him in the doorway, his arms behind his back, and, gazing respectfully at the nape of his master's neck, listened to the story of how, after many false trails and unnecessary journeys, Panteley Yeremeich finally landed up at the horse-fair in Romny, now by himself, without the Jew Leiba, who, out of weakness of character, hadn't been able to endure it and had run away; how on the fifth day, already on the point of leaving, he'd made a last tour of the lines of carts and suddenly seen, between three other horses and tied to a feeding-bag, none other than Malek Adel! He'd recognized him at once and Malek Adel had recognized him and begun neighing and trying to break free and scoring the earth with his hoof.

'And he wasn't with any Cossack,' Chertopkhanov continued, still not turning his head and in the same deep voice, 'but with a gypsy horse-dealer. I naturally set about getting hold of my horse at once and wanted to take him back by force, but that beast of a gypsy started yelling his head off like he'd been scalded, yelling all over the place and swearing to God he'd bought the horse off another gypsy and wanting to call on witnesses . . . I spat at that, but I paid up, devil take him and all his works! For me the chief thing was that I'd found my friend and achieved peace of mind. Otherwise it'd be like when I was in Karachevsky County and, on the word of the Jew Leiba, got my hands on a Cossack whom I took to be the thief and beat his face to a pulp. But he turned out to be the son of a priest and skinned me of 120 roubles for the dishonour I'd done him. Well, money's all to do with profit, but the main thing is that Malek Adel's back with me! Now I'm happy – and I'm going to enjoy my peace of mind. And I've got one instruction for you, Porfiry – the moment, which God defend us may not be, the moment you see a Cossack anywhere near us, that very second, without saying a word, run and bring me my gun and I'll know then what I've got to do!'

That is what Panteley Yeremeich told Perfishka. That's what his lips said. But in his heart he was not as calm as he claimed.

Alas, in the depths of his heart he was not entirely sure that the horse he'd brought with him was really Malek Adel!

X

For Panteley Yeremeich hard times began. It was precisely peace of mind that he enjoyed least of all. True, there were good days when the doubt aroused in him seemed so much nonsense. He drove away the foolish thought like a persistent fly and even laughed at himself. But there were also bad days when the irrepressible thought once again started covertly gnawing and scratching at his heart like a mouse under the floorboards and he was tormented bitterly and secretly. In the course of the memorable day when he'd found Malek Adel Chertopkhanov had felt nothing save a blissful joy, but the next day when, under the low overhanging roof of the little wayside inn, he'd begun saddling his find, close to whom he'd spent the whole night, he was first riven by doubt. He merely gave a shake of the head, but the seed had been implanted. During the journey home (it lasted a week) doubts were rarely stirred in him. They became stronger and more open as soon as he'd returned to his Unsleepy Hollow and found himself in the very place where the former, undoubted Malek Adel had lived . . .

On the journey he'd ridden mostly at a walk, jogging along, and gazed about him and smoked tobacco in a short-stemmed pipe and not given a thought to anything in particular – except he'd now and then thought to himself: 'We Chertopkhanovs, when we want something, we get it! You won't fool us!' and grinned to himself at that. Well, now he was home the situation was different. Of course, he kept all his doubts to himself. Sheer pride prevented him from displaying any of his inner turmoil. He'd have 'broken in half' anyone who so much as intimated that the new Malek Adel didn't seem to be quite like the old one. He accepted congratulations on his 'happy find' from the few people he happened to meet, but he did not solicit congratulations and avoided meeting people even more than before – which was a bad sign! He almost constantly, if one may put it this way, subjected Malek Adel to examination, riding off a great distance and then testing him, or, creeping into the stable, locking the door behind him and standing right in front of the horse's head, he'd start looking him in the eyes and asking in a whisper: 'Are you he? Is it you? Is it you?' and then he'd either study him, intently, hour after hour, or, in an access of joy, he'd mutter: 'Yes, it's him! Of course it's him!' or then again he'd be doubtful and even be covered in confusion.

And it wasn't so much that Chertopkhanov was confused by the physical differences between *this* Malek Adel and *that* one – besides, there weren't so many of them: *that* one's tail and mane had been more paltry, the ears sharper, the pasterns shorter and the eyes brighter, but all these could only have seemed so – no, it was that Chertopkhanov was confused by the moral differences, so to speak. *That* one's habits had been different, his whole behaviour hadn't been the same. For example, *that* Malek Adel had always looked round and neighed slightly each time Chertopkhanov had entered the stables, but *this* one always went on munching his hay as if nothing'd happened or went on snoozing with his head lowered. Both of them used to stand still when he jumped out of the saddle, but *that* would come the instant he called him while *this* one would remain standing there like a stump. *That* one galloped just as quickly but jumped higher and further; *this* one had an easier way of going at a walking pace but was much rougher at a trot and sometimes 'clashed' his hoofs, meaning he struck his back hoofs against his front ones, something *that* one would've been ashamed to do, God preserve us! *This* one, so Chertopkhanov thought, was forever twitching his ears and looking foolish, while *that* one, by contrast, always had one ear laid back and kept it there – so as to keep an eye on his master! *That* one, as soon as he saw there was mess around him, would instantly kick a hind hoof against the wall of his stall, but *this* one couldn't care less if he was up to his belly in horse shit. *That* one, if he'd been facing into the wind, for instance, would immediately fill his lungs with air and give himself a shake, but *this* one'd simply snort; *that* one'd be disturbed by the smell of rain damp, *this* one couldn't care less . . . This one was cruder, much cruder! And he didn't have any of the other's niceness and would tug at the reins . . . No use going on and on! That horse was nice, whereas this was . . .

Such were the thoughts that sometimes occurred to Chertopkhanov, and these thoughts were resonant with bitterness for him. Despite them at other times he'd set his horse going at full tilt across recently ploughed land or make him jump down into the very bottom of a dried-out ravine and jump out again by the steepest part and his heart'd literally stop within him from excitement, a loud halloo-ing would burst from his lips and he'd know, know for certain, that beneath him was the real, the undoubted, Malek Adel, because what other horse would be capable of doing what he did?

However, even here things were not without sin and misery. The prolonged search for Malek Adel had cost Chertopkhanov a lot of money and he no longer had plans for Kostroma hounds, and rode about the neighbourhood on his own as he'd done before. One fine morning Chertopkhanov was some three or so miles from Unsleepy Hollow when he chanced upon the very same princely hunt before whom he'd pranced about and shown off only eighteen months before. And the very same thing was just bound to happen – on that day as on this a hare came and jumped out of a boundary fence on some sloping ground right in front of the hounds! 'At him! At him!' The whole hunt literally took off and Chertopkhanov as well, save that he didn't go with them but some two hundred paces to one side, just as he'd done the first time. A large water-course wound its way down the slope and, in the course of the ascent, growing progressively narrower, cut across Chertopkhanov's path. At the point where he had to jump it – and where he'd actually jumped it a year and a half before – it was about eight paces wide and more than twelve feet deep. In anticipation of a triumph, such a wondrously repeated triumph, Chertopkhanov started yelling victoriously and waving his whip – the members of the hunt were all going at a gallop but not taking their eyes off the daredevil rider – his horse flew like an arrow, and the water-course was there right in front of him, and in a moment, well, it'd be just as it was then!

But Malek Adel dug his hoofs in sharply, veered to the left and galloped *along* the gully no matter how strongly Chertopkhanov pulled his head to the side, towards the water-course.

It meant he'd lost his nerve, he didn't trust himself!

Then Chertopkhanov, burning with shame and fury, almost in tears, let go of the reins and drove the horse straight uphill right away from the hunters so that he couldn't hear how they made fun of him and to get away as fast as possible from their accursed eyes!

With weals on his flanks and all covered in soapy lather Malek Adel galloped home and Chertopkhanov immediately shut himself up in his room.

'No, it's not him, it's not my friend! He'd've risked his neck, but he wouldn't have let me down!'

XI

The following circumstance was, as they say, 'the last straw' for Chertopkhanov. One day while out on Malek Adel he rode through the back gardens of the priest's holding surrounding the church, in the parish of which the little village of Unsleepy Hollow resided. His fur cap pulled down over his eyes, crouched down, with both hands resting on the pommel of his saddle, he was going slowly along, his heart and soul joyless and full of worries. Suddenly someone called to him.

He brought his horse to a halt, raised his head and saw it was his correspondent, the deacon. In a brown cap with ear flaps and a back flap which was set on brown hair plaited into a pigtail, clad in a yellowish nankeen caftan tied below the waist with some bluish material, this altar server had come out to take a look at his 'patch' and, having set eyes on Panteley Yeremeich, considered it a duty to convey him his respects and, besides, to see if he could drum up any offerings from him. Without hindsight of that kind, as is well known, gentlemen of the cloth do not engage in conversation with the laity.

But Chertopkhanov was in no mood for the deacon. He'd scarcely responded to his bow and, muttering something through his teeth, already had his whip waving about . . .

'What a most sumptuous horse you have!' the deacon added in a hurry. 'It can be said in all truth it does you credit! Verily you are a man of wondrous mind, like unto a very lion!' Father deacon was renowned for his eloquence, which was a source of great annoyance to his reverence, the priest, who had no gift of speech and even vodka couldn't loosen his tongue. 'One animal, through the design of wicked men, you've been deprived of,' the deacon went on, 'and, in no way despairing, but, on the contrary, nay, more, trusting in divine providence, you've acquired another, in no way worse, and one might even say better . . . so . . .'

'What're you blathering about?' Chertopkhanov interrupted him morosely. 'What other horse? It's the very same one, it's Malek Adel . . . I sought him out, I did! It's nonsense, your talk . . .'

'Aye-aye-aye-aye!' exclaimed the deacon, pausing between each sigh almost deliberately as he fingered his beard and studied Chertopkhanov with his bright, greedy eyes. 'How can that be so, my dear sir? Your very horse, if memory serves me right, was stolen last year two short weeks after the Feast of the Protection, while right now we're almost through November.'

'Well, so what of it?'

The deacon went on fingering his beard.

'It means a year and a bit's flowed by since then, but your horse, which was then a dappled grey, is like he is now. He's even got darker still. How's that come about? Grey horses usually get much lighter in the space of a year.'

Chertopkhanov shuddered. It was as if someone had literally speared him in the heart. And in fact the grey coats of horses do change! How was it that such a simple thought hadn't entered his head until this moment?

'You bloody bundle of lies! Out of my way!' he shrieked suddenly, his eyes glittering wildly, and instantly vanished from the astonished deacon's sight.

'Well, now! It's all over!'

That's when it really was all over, the bubble was burst and his final card had lost! Everything had come tumbling down as a result of 'get much lighter'!

Grey horses get much lighter!

Gallop, gallop, you wretch! You'll never gallop away from that!

Chertopkhanov rushed home and again locked himself in.

XII

That this wretched animal wasn't Malek Adel, that there wasn't the least resemblance between it and Malek Adel, that anyone with the least know-how should've seen it at the first glance and that he, Panteley Chertopkhanov, had been deceived in the grossest possible way – no! he'd deliberately, intentionally fooled himself and let such confusion come upon him – about all of this now there couldn't be the slightest doubt! Chertopkhanov walked to and fro in his room, turning on his heels at each wall in exactly the same way like an animal in a cage. His self-esteem suffered unendurably. But it wasn't only the pain of wounded pride that tore at him, a kind of desperation possessed him, malice choked him and a thirst for vengeance sprang up within him. But against whom? Who should be avenged? The Jew, Jaffe, Masha, the deacon, the thieving Cossack, all his neighbours, the entire world, finally himself? He was out of his mind. His final card had lost! (He liked that comparison.) And he was once again the most worthless, the most despised of men, a general laughing-stock, a right hayseed, an out-and-out fool and an object of derision – and of all people for that deacon! He imagined, he clearly imagined to himself how that bloody bundle of lies'd start telling stories about how there was this grey horse and this silly old land-owner . . . Oh, hell and damnation! Vainly Chertopkhanov tried to staunch his outflow of bitter anger. He tried vainly to assure himself that this so-called horse, even though it wasn't Malek Adel, was anyhow not too bad and could go on serving him for many years yet . . . He then and there rejected such a thought ferociously, as if it contained yet a further slight to *that* Malek Adel before which, in any case, he felt guilty . . . And with good reason! Like a blind fool, like a real oaf, he'd compared this shitty creature, this wretched horse of his to him, to Malek Adel! And as for the service this wretched animal might still give him, would he ever deign to ride it again? No way! Never! Fit for a Tartar, for dog food – that's all it was worth! Yes, that'd be the best thing!

Chertopkhanov tramped to and fro in his room for a couple of hours and more.

'Perfishka!' he commanded suddenly. 'In here this minute! Bring me half a bucket of vodka! D'you hear? Half a bucket and quick about it! I want the vodka standing here on my table this minute.'

The vodka wasn't long in appearing on Panteley Yeremeich's table, and he began drinking.

XIII

Had someone seen Chertopkhanov then, had someone been witness to the gloomy moroseness with which he emptied glass after glass, that person would certainly have felt fear despite himself. Night came on. A small tallow candle burned faintly on the table. Chertopkhanov stopped scuttling from corner to corner and sat all red in the face with glazed eyes which he would continually lower to the floor or raise in stubborn stares at the dark window. He'd get up, pour himself more vodka, drink it, again sit down, again fix his eyes on one point and not move an inch, except that his breathing became more frequent and his face got even redder. It was as if he were gradually reaching a decision which appalled even him, but to which he was gradually growing used. One and the same thought inevitably and remorselessly grew closer and closer, one and the same image appeared ever clearer and clearer ahead, while in his heart, under the molten pressure of heavy drunkenness, the aggravation produced by anger was already yielding to a feeling of cruelty and an evil grin played on his lips . . .

'Well, the time's come!' he declared in a kind of business-like, almost bored tone of voice. 'I must cool it now!'

He drank back a last glass of vodka, got a pistol out from under his bed (the very pistol with which he'd shot at Masha), loaded it, placed several caps in his pocket 'just in case' and set off for the stables.

The nightwatchman was just about to rush at him when he started opening the door, but he shouted at him: 'It's me! Can't you see? Be off!' The man retreated a little to one side. 'Go back to sleep!'

Chertopkhanov shouted at him again. 'There's nothing here for you to guard! Such a wonderful sight, such a treasure indeed!' He went into the stables. Malek Adel, the false Malek Adel, was lying in the straw. Chertopkhanov nudged him with his foot, announcing: 'Get up, you old crow, you!' Then he untied the halter from the manger, took off the blanket and threw it on the ground and, rudely turning the obedient horse in its stall, led it out into the yard and from the yard into the field, to the extreme astonishment of the nightwatchman who couldn't for the life of him understand where the master was setting off for at night with an unbridled horse. It goes without saying that he was too frightened to ask him and simply followed him with his eyes until he disappeared beyond a turn in the road leading to a neighbouring forest.

XIV

Chertopkhanov strode along with big steps without stopping and without looking round. Malek Adel (we'll call him that right to the end) followed obediently behind him. The night was fairly bright. Chertopkhanov could make out the jagged outline of the forest which was as black ahead of him as a solid splodge. In the grip of the night's chill he'd certainly have grown drunker as a result of all the vodka if it hadn't been for a different and much stronger intoxication that had possession of him. His head was heavy and the blood boomed loudly in his throat and ears, but he strode on firmly and knew where he was going.

He'd decided to kill Malek Adel. All day he'd spent thinking about that and nothing else. Now he'd decided!

He strode on this business not so much calmly as with self-assurance, irreversibly, like a man submitting to a sense of duty. To him this 'matter' seemed extremely 'simple': in destroying the imposter he'd at one stroke be calling it quits with 'the lot' – he'd be punishing himself for his stupidity and justifying himself before his real friend and demonstrating to the whole world (Chertopkhanov was very much concerned about 'the whole world') that you couldn't play jokes on him. But chiefly: he'd destroy himself along with this imposter, because what would there be left to live for? How all this came to be in his head and why it seemed to him so simple would be hard to explain, although not completely impossible: humiliated, alone, without any human soul close to him, without a brass farthing, and, what's more, with his blood ignited by drink, he was in a state close to madness, and there's no doubt that in the silliest acts of deranged people there is, in their eyes, their own kind of logic and even authority. Of his own authority Chertopkhanov was in any case completely certain. He did not waver but hurried to carry out the sentence on the guilty party without having any clear idea who he was calling guilty. Truth to tell, he gave little thought to what he was intending to do. 'I've got to finish it, got to,' he repeated to himself, bluntly and sternly, 'I've just got to finish it!'

And the guiltless guilty party jogged along behind his back at a servile trot . . . But there was no pity in Chertopkhanov's heart.

XV

Not far from the edge of the forest where he led his horse there was a small ravine half overgrown with oak trees. Chertopkhanov descended into it. Malek Adel stumbled and nearly fell on him.

'So you want to crush me, you damned animal!' shrieked Chertopkhanov and, literally as if he were defending himself, whipped the pistol out of his pocket.

He felt no bitterness but only that particular wooden feeling which, so they say, seizes hold of a man before the commission of a crime. But the sound of his own voice frightened him because it sounded so wild under the canopy of dark branches, in the rotten and fetid rawness of the wooded ravine. What's more, in response to his shriek some large bird suddenly started fluttering in a tree-top above his head. Chertopkhanov shuddered. It was just as if he'd alerted a witness to his deed – but where exactly? In, of all places, this back-of-beyond where he shouldn't have come across a single living soul . . .

'Be off, you devil, to all four corners of the earth!' he muttered through his teeth and, letting go Malek Adel's halter, struck him hard on the shoulder with the butt of his pistol. Malek Adel immediately turned back, scrambled up out of the ravine and ran off. But the sound of his hoofs couldn't be heard for long. A wind that had sprung up blurred and smoothed out every sound.

In his turn Chertopkhanov slowly climbed out of the ravine, came to the edge of the forest and set off on the road home. He was dissatisfied with himself. The heaviness which he'd felt in his head and heart was spreading to all his limbs. He walked along angry, gloomy, dissatisfied and hungry just as if someone had done him an injury or seized his catch from him, taken away his food . . .

A suicide who has been prevented from committing suicide knows such feelings.

Suddenly something struck him from behind, between the shoulders. He glanced round and saw Malek Adel standing in the middle of the road. He'd followed behind his master and he'd touched him with his muzzle. He'd let it be known that he was there . . .

'Ah!' shouted Chertopkhanov. 'It's you, you've come for your own death! So be it!'

In the twinkling of an eye he whipped out his pistol, cocked it, pressed the barrel to Malek Adel's forehead and fired.

The poor horse shied away to one side, reared up on its hind legs, jumped ten or so paces back and suddenly collapsed heavily and started wheezing, going into convulsions on the ground.

Chertopkhanov covered both ears with his hands and ran off. His knees were bending under him. The drunkenness and the anger and the unquestioning self-assurance – all had vanished at a stroke. There remained only a feeling of shame and outrage – and an awareness, a clear awareness, that on this occasion he'd done for himself as well.

XVI

About six weeks later the servant-boy Perfishka considered it his duty to stop the local constable as he rode past the Unsleepy Hollow estate.

'Whaddya want?' asked the guardian of the law.

'Please, your 'onour, come an' see us,' answered the servant-boy with a low bow. 'It seems like Panteley Yeremeich's gettin' ready to die. That's what I'm 'fraid it is.'

'What's that? Ready to die?' cross-examined the constable.

'Yes, sir. First he was all day drinkin' vodka, an' now he's laid down in 'is bed, an' very thin he is. I don't think he's able to understand anything now. Not a word from 'im.'

The constable got down from his cart.

'Leastways, have you been to fetch the priest? Has your master made his confession? Has he received communion?'

'No, sir.'

The constable frowned.

'How can that be, boy? Surely that can't be right, eh? Or perhaps you're not knowing that for that ... there's a grave responsibility, isn't there?'

'Yes, I asked 'im the day before yesterday and yesterday I asked,' agreed the chastened servant-boy, 'wouldn't he want me, I asked, Panteley Yeremeich, wouldn't he want me to go for the priest. "Shut up, you fool," he said. "Don't stick your nose in where it's not wanted!" An' today, as soon as I started tellin' 'im something he just looked at me an' twitched his whiskers.'

'And did he drink a lot of vodka?'

'Gallons! Your 'onour, please be good enough to go an' see 'im in 'is room.'

'Well, lead the way!' exclaimed the constable and followed behind Perfishka.

An astonishing sight greeted him.

In the back room of the house, dank and dark, lying on a threadbare bed covered with a horse cloth and with a tattered old felt cloak for a pillow was Chertopkhanov, no longer looking pale but yellowish-green like a corpse, with sunken eyes under lustrous eyelids and a sharpened but still reddish nose over dishevelled whiskers. He lay there dressed in his invariable old-fashioned caftan with the cartridge pleats on the chest and in wide blue Circassian trousers. The conical Persian hat with the upper part covered in raspberry-coloured cloth covered his forehead right down to his eyebrows. In one hand Chertopkhanov held his hunting crop, in the other an embroidered tobacco pouch, Masha's last gift to him. On a table next to the bed stood an empty vodka bottle. But at the head of the bed, fastened to the wall with large pins, could be seen two water-colours. One, so far as one could tell, depicted a stout man with a guitar in his hands – presumably Nedopyuskin. The other depicted a galloping horseman ... The horse resembled those fairy-tale animals which children draw on walls and fences, but the assiduously shaded dapplings on the horse's coat and the cartridges on the rider's chest, the sharp toes to his boots and the enormous whiskers left no room for doubt: it was a picture that strove to show Panteley Yeremeich riding Malek Adel.

The astonished constable didn't know what to do. A deathly silence reigned in the room. 'Yes, he's already dead,' he thought and in a loud voice he said:

'Panteley Yeremeich! Eh, Panteley Yeremeich!'

Something quite unusual happened at that moment. Chertopkhanov's eyes slowly opened, the lightless pupils moved first from right to left, then from left to right and fixed on the visitor and saw him. Something flared momentarily in their murky pallor, the semblance of a gaze appeared in them, the already blue lips gradually parted and there emerged a husky voice, literally a voice from the grave:

'The hereditary nobleman Panteley Chertopkhanov is dying. Who can stand in his way? He owes no one anything and asks for nothing . . . Leave him be, good people! Go away!'

The hand holding the riding crop made an attempt to raise itself, but in vain. The lips again came together and the eyes closed. And once again Chertopkhanov lay on his hard bed, flat on his back with his heels together.

'Let me know when he dies,' whispered the constable to Perfishka as he went out of the room, 'and I suggest it's the right time now to send for the priest. One's got to observe the right procedures and see he receives the last rites.'

Perfishka went for the priest that very day. And the next morning it fell to his lot to let the constable know that Panteley Yeremeich had died that night.

When he was buried, his coffin was accompanied by two mourners, the servant-boy Perfishka and Moshel Leiba. News of Chertopkhanov's death had reached the Jew somehow or other and he did not let pass the need to acknowledge his last debt to his benefactor.

LIVING RELIC

❧

Homeland of longsuffering –
Thou art the land of Russia![1]
F. Tyutchev

THERE is a French saying which runs: 'A dry fisherman and a wet hunter have the same sad look.' Never having had a fondness for catching fish, I am unable to judge what a fisherman must experience at a time of fine, clear weather and to what extent, when the weather is bad, the pleasure afforded him by an excellent catch outweighs the unpleasantness of being wet. But for a hunter rainy weather is a veritable calamity. It was precisely to such a calamity that Yermolay and I were subjected during one of our expeditions after grouse in Belev county. The rain did not let up from dawn onwards. The things we did to be free of it! We almost covered our heads completely with our rubber capes and took to standing under trees in order to catch fewer drips – yet the waterproof capes, not to mention the way they interfered with our shooting, let the water through in a quite shameless fashion; and as for standing under trees – true, at first it did seem that there were no drips, but a little later the moisture which had gathered in the foliage suddenly broke its way through and every branch doused us with water as if it were a rainpipe, cold dribbles gathered under my collar and ran down the small of my back . . . That was the last straw, as Yermolay was fond of saying.

'No, Pyotr Petrovich,' he exclaimed eventually, 'we can't go on with this! We can't hunt today. All the scent's being washed out for the dogs and the guns are misfiring . . . Phew! What a life!'

'What do we do, then?' I asked.

'This is what. We'll drive to Alekseyevka. Perhaps you don't know it, but there's a small farm of that name belonging to your mother, about five miles away. We can spend the night there, and then tomorrow . . .'

'We'll come back here?'

'No, not here . . . I know some places on the other side of Alekseyevka. They're a lot better than this for grouse!'

I refrained from asking my trusty companion why he had not taken me straightaway to those places, and that very same day we reached the farm belonging to my mother, the very existence of which, I admit, I had not suspected until that moment. The farm-house had an adjacent cottage of considerable antiquity, but not lived-in and therefore clean; here I spent a reasonably quiet night.

The next day I awoke pretty early. The sun had only just risen and the sky was cloudless. All around glistened with a strong, two-fold brilliance: the brilliance of the youthful rays of morning light and of yesterday's downpour. While a little cart was being got ready for me, I set off to wander a little way through the small, once fruit-bearing but now wild, orchard, which pressed up on all sides against the cottage with its richly scented, luxuriantly fresh undergrowth. Oh, how delightful it was to be in the open air, under a clear sky in which larks fluttered, whence poured the silver beads of their resonant song! On their wings they probably carried drops of dew, and their singing seemed to be dew-sprinkled in its sweetness. I even removed my cap from my head and breathed in joyfully, lungfuls at a time . . . On the side of a shallow ravine, close by the wattle fencing, a bee-garden could be seen; a small path led to it, winding like a snake between thick walls of weeds and nettles, above which projected – God knows where they had come from – sharp-tipped stalks of dark-green hemp.

I set off along this path and reached the bee-garden. Next to it there stood a little wattle shed, a so-called *amshanik*, where the hives are put in winter. I glanced in through the half-open door: it was dark, silent and dry inside, smelling of mint and melissa. In a corner boards had been fixed up and on them, covered by a quilt, a small figure was lying. I turned to go out at once.

'Master, but master! Pyotr Petrovich!' I heard a voice say, as faintly, slowly and hoarsely as the rustling of marsh sedge.

I stopped.

'Pyotr Petrovich! Please come here!' the voice repeated. It came to me from the corner, from those very boards which I had noticed.

I drew close and froze in astonishment. In front of me there lay a live human being, but what kind of human being was it?

The head was completely withered, of a uniform shade of bronze, exactly resembling the colour of an ancient icon painting; the nose was as thin as a knife-blade; the lips had almost disappeared – only the teeth and eyes gave any gleam of light, and from beneath the kerchief wispy clusters of yellow hair protruded on to the temples. At the chin, where the quilt was folded back, two tiny hands of the same bronze colour slowly moved their fingers up and down like little sticks. I looked more closely and I noticed that not only was the face far from ugly, it was even endowed with beauty, but it seemed awesome none the less and incredible. And the face seemed all the more awesome to me because I could see that a smile was striving to appear on it, to cross its metallic cheeks – was striving and yet could not spread.

'Master, don't you recognize me?' the voice whispered again: it was just like condensation rising from the scarcely quivering lips. 'But how would you recognize me here! I'm Lukeria . . . Remember how I used to lead the dancing at your mother's, at Spasskoye . . . and how I used to be the leader of the chorus, remember?'

'Lukeria!' I cried. 'Is it you? Is it possible?'

'It's me, master – yes, it's me, Lukeria.'

I had no notion what to say, and in a state of shock I gazed at this dark, still face with its bright, seemingly lifeless eyes fixed upon me. Was it possible? This mummy was Lukeria, the greatest beauty among all the maid servants in our house, tall, buxom, white-skinned and rosy-cheeked, who used to laugh and sing and dance! Lukeria, talented Lukeria, who was sought after by all our young men, after whom I myself used to sigh in secret, I – a sixteen-year-old boy!

'Forgive me, Lukeria,' I said at last, 'but what's happened to you?'

'Such a calamity overtook me! Don't feel squeamish, master, don't turn your back on my misfortune – sit down on that little barrel, bring it closer, so as you'll be able to hear me . . . See how talkative I've become! . . . Well, it's glad I am I've seen you! How ever did you come to be in Alekseyevka?'

Lukeria spoke very quietly and faintly, but without pausing.

'Yermolay the hunter brought me here. But go on with what you were saying . . .'

'About my misfortune, is it? If that's what you wish, master. It happened to me long, long ago, six or seven years ago. I'd just then been engaged to Vasily Polyakov – remember him, such a fine upstanding man he was, with curly hair, and in service as wine butler at your mother's house. But by that time you weren't here in the country any longer – you'd gone off to Moscow for your schooling. We were very much in love, Vasily and I. I couldn't get him out of my mind; it all happened in the springtime. One night – it wasn't long to go till dawn – I couldn't sleep, and there was a nightingale singing in the garden so wonderfully sweetly! I couldn't bear it, and I got up and went out on to the porch to listen to it. He was pouring out his song, pouring it out . . . and suddenly I imagined I could hear someone calling me in Vasya's voice, all quiet like: "Loosha! . . ." I glanced away to one side and, you know, not awake properly, I slipped right off the porch step and flew down – bang! – on to the ground. And, likely, I hadn't hurt myself so bad, because – soon I was up and back in my own room. Only it was just like something inside – in my stomach – had broken . . . Let me get my breath back . . . Just a moment, master.'

Lukeria fell silent, and I gazed at her with astonishment. What amazed me was the almost gay manner in which she was telling her story, without groans or sighs, never for a moment complaining or inviting sympathy.

'Ever since that happened,' Lukeria continued, 'I began to wither and sicken, and a blackness came over me, and it grew difficult for me to walk, and then I even began to lose control of my legs – I couldn't stand or sit, I only wanted to lie down all the time. And I didn't feel like eating or drinking: I just got worse and worse. Your mother, out of the goodness of her heart, had medical people to look at me and sent me to hospital. But no relief for me came of it all. And not a single one of the medicals could even say what kind of an illness it was I had. The things they didn't do to me, burning my spine with red-hot irons and sitting me in chopped-up ice – and all for nothing. In the end I got completely stiff . . . So the masters decided there was no good in trying to cure me any more, and because there wasn't room for a cripple in their house . . . well, they sent me here – because I have relations here. So here I'm living, as you see.'

Lukeria again fell silent and again endeavoured to smile.

'But this is horrible, this condition you're in!' I exclaimed, and not knowing what to add, I asked: 'What about Vasily Polyakov?' It was a very stupid question.

Lukeria turned her eyes a little to one side.

'About Polyakov? He grieved, he grieved – and then he married someone else, a girl from Glinnoye. Do you know Glinnoye? It's not far from us. She was called Agrafena. He loved me very much, but he was a young man – he couldn't be expected to remain a bachelor all his life. And what sort of a companion could I be to him? He's found himself a good wife, who's a kind woman, and they've got children now. He's steward on the estate of one of the neighbours: your mother released him with a passport, and things are going very well for him, praise be to God.'

'And you can't do anything except lie here?' I again inquired.

'This is the seventh year, master, that I've been lying like this. When it's summer I lie here, in this wattle hut, and when it begins to get cold – then they move me into a room next to the bath-house. So I lie there, too.'

'Who comes to see you? Who looks after you?'

'There are kind people here as well. They don't leave me by myself. But I don't need much looking after. So far as feeding goes, I don't eat anything, and I have water – there it is in that mug: it always stands by me full of pure spring water. I can stretch out to the mug myself, because I've still got the use of one arm. Then there's a little girl here, an orphan; now and then she drops by, and I'm grateful to her. She's just this minute gone . . . Did you meet her? She's so pretty, so fair-skinned. She brings me flowers – I'm a great one for them, flowers, I mean. We haven't any garden flowers. There used to be some here, but they've all disappeared. But field flowers are pretty too, and they have more scent than the garden flowers. Lilies-of-the-valley now – there's nothing lovelier!'

'Aren't you bored, my poor Lukeria, don't you feel frightened?'

'What's a person to do? I don't want to pretend – at first, yes, I felt very low, but afterwards I grew used to it, I learnt to be patient – now it's nothing. Others are much worse off.'

'How do you mean?'

'Some haven't even got a home! And others are blind or dumb! I can see perfectly, praise be to God, and I can hear everything, every little thing. If there's a mole digging underground, I can hear it. And I can smell every scent, it doesn't matter how faint it is! If the buckwheat is just beginning to flower in the field or a lime tree is just blossoming in the garden, I don't have to be told: I'm the first to smell the scent, if the wind's coming from that direction. No, why should I make God angry with my complaints? Many are worse off than I am. Look at it this way: a healthy person can sin very easily, but my sin has gone out of me. Not long ago Father Aleksey, the priest, was beginning to give me communion and he said: "There can't be any need to hear your confession, for how can you sin in your condition?" But I answered him: "What about a sin of the mind, father?" "Well," he said and laughed, "that kind of sin's not very serious."

'And, it's true, I'm not really sinful even with sins of the mind,' Lukeria went on, 'because I've learned myself not to think and, what's more, not even to remember. Time passes quicker that way.'

This surprised me, I must admit.

'You are so much by yourself, Lukeria, so how can you prevent thoughts from entering your head? Or do you sleep all the time?'

'Oh, no, master! Sleep's not always easy for me. I may not have big pains, but something's always gnawing at me, right there inside me, and in my bones as well. It doesn't let me sleep as I should. No . . . I just lie like this and go on lying here, not thinking. I sense that I'm alive, I breathe — and that's all there is of me. I look and I smell scents. Bees in the apiary hum and buzz, then a dove comes and sits on the roof and starts cooing, and a little brood-hen brings her chick in to peck crumbs; then a sparrow'll fly in or a butterfly — I enjoy it all very much. The year before last swallows made a nest over there in the corner and brought up their young. Oh, how interesting that was! One of them would fly in, alight on the little nest, feed the young ones — and then off again. I'd take another look and there'd be another swallow there in place of the first. Sometimes it wouldn't fly in but just go past the open door, and then the baby birds'd start chirping and opening their little beaks . . . The next year I waited for them, but they say a hunter in these parts shot them with his gun.

Now what good could he have got from doing that? After all, a swallow's no more harm than a beetle. What wicked men you are, you hunters!'

'I don't shoot swallows,' I hastened to point out.

'And one time,' Lukeria started to say again, 'there was a real laugh! A hare ran in here! Yes, really! Whether dogs were chasing him or not, I don't know, only he came running straight in through the door! He sat down quite close and spent a long time sniffing the air and twitching his whiskers – a regular little officer he was! And he took a look at me and realized that I couldn't do him any harm. Eventually he upped and jumped to the door and looked all round him on the doorstep – he was a one, he was! Such a comic!'

Lukeria glanced up at me, as if to say: wasn't that amusing? To please her, I gave a laugh. She bit her dried-up lips.

'In the winter, of course, things are worse for me. I'm left in the dark, you see – it's a pity to light a candle and anyhow what'd be the good of it? I know how to read and was always real keen on reading, but what's there to read here? There are no books here, and even if there were, how would I be able to hold it, the book, I mean? Father Aleksey brought me a church calendar so as to distract me, but he saw it wasn't any use and picked it up and took it away again. But even though it's dark, I've always got something to listen to – maybe a cricket'll start chirruping or a mouse'll begin scratching somewhere. That's when it's good not to be thinking at all!'

After a short rest, Lukeria continued: 'Or else I say prayers. Only I don't know many of them, of those prayers. And why should I start boring the Lord God with my prayers? What can I ask him for? He knows better than I do what's good for me. He sent me a cross to carry, which means he loves me. That's how we're ordained to understand our suffering. I say Our Father, and the prayer to the Blessed Virgin, and I sing hymns for all who sorrow – and then I lie still without a single thought in my mind. Life's no bother to me!'

Two minutes went by. I did not break the silence and I did not stir on the narrow barrel which served as a place for me to sit. The cruel, stony immobility of the unfortunate living being who lay before me affected me also, and I became literally rigid.

'Listen, Lukeria,' I began finally. 'Listen to what I want to propose to you. Would you like it if I arranged for you to be taken to a hospital, a good town hospital? Who knows, but maybe they can still cure you? At least you won't be by yourself . . .'

Lukeria raised her brows ever so slightly.

'Oh, no, master,' she said in an agitated whisper, 'don't send me to a hospital, let me alone. I'll only have to endure more agony there. There's no good in trying to cure me! Once a doctor came here and wanted to have a look at me. I said to him, begging him: "Don't disturb me for Christ's sake!" What good was it! He started turning me this way and that, straightening and bending my legs and arms and telling me: "I'm doing this for learning, that's why. I'm one who serves, a scientist! And don't you try to stop me, because they've pinned a medal on me for my contributions to science and it's for you, you dolts, that I'm working so hard." He pulled me about and pulled me about, named what was wrong with me – and a fine name it was! – and with that he left. But for a whole week afterwards my poor bones were aching. You say I'm alone, all the time by myself. No, not all the time. People come to see me. I'm quiet and I'm not a nuisance to anyone. The peasant girls come sometimes for a chat. Or a holy woman will call in on her wanderings and start telling me about Jerusalem and Kiev and the holy cities. I'm not frightened of being by myself. Truly it's better, truly it is! Let me alone, master, don't move me to hospital. Thank you, you're a good man, only leave me alone, my dear.'

'Just as you wish, as you wish, Lukeria. I was only suggesting it for your own good . . .'

'I know, master, it was for my own good. But, master, my dear one, who is there that can help another person? Who can enter into another's soul? People must help themselves! You won't believe it, but sometimes I lie by myself like I am now – and it's just as if there was no one on the whole earth except me. And I'm the only living person! And a wondrous feeling comes over me, as if I'd been visited by some thought that seizes hold of me – something wonderful it is.'

'What do you think about at such times, Lukeria?'

'It's quite impossible to say, master – you can't make it out. And afterwards I forget. It comes out like a cloud and pours its rain through me, making everything so fresh and good, but what the thought was really you can never understand! Only it seems to me that if there were people round me – none of that would have happened and I'd never feel anything except my own misfortune.'

Lukeria sighed with difficulty. Like the other parts of her body, her breast would not obey her wishes.

'As I look at you now, master,' she began again, 'you feel very sorry for me. But don't you pity me too much, don't you do that! See, I'll tell you something: sometimes even now I ... You remember, don't you, what a gay one I was in my time? One of the girls! ... D'you know something? I sing songs even now.'

'Songs? You really sing?'

'Yes, I sing songs, the old songs, roundelays, feast songs, holy songs, all kinds! I used to know many of them, after all, and I haven't forgotten them. Only I don't sing the dancing songs. In my present state that wouldn't be right.'

'How do you sing them – to yourself?'

'To myself and out loud. I can't sing them loudly, but they can still be understood. I was telling you that a little girl comes to visit me. An orphan, that's what she is, but she understands. So I've been teaching her and she's picked up four songs already. Don't you believe me? Wait a moment, I'll show you ...'

Lukeria drew upon all her reserves of energy. The idea that this half-dead being was preparing to sing aroused in me a spontaneous feeling of horror. But before I could utter a word, a long-drawn, scarcely audible, though clear sound, pitched on the right note, began to quiver in my ears, followed by another, then a third. Lukeria was singing 'I walked in the meadows of green grieving for my life'. She sang without altering the expression on her petrified face, even gazing fixedly with her eyes. But so touchingly did this poor, forced, wavering little voice of hers resound, rising like a wisp of smoke, that I ceased to feel horror: an indescribable piteousness compressed my heart.

'Oh, I can't any more!' she uttered suddenly. 'I've no strength left ... I've rejoiced so very much already at seeing you.'

She closed her eyes.

I placed my hands on her tiny cold fingers. She looked up at me and her dark eyelids, furred with golden lashes like the lids of ancient statuary, closed again. An instant later they began to glisten in the semi-darkness. Tears moistened them.

As before, I did not stir.

'Silly of me!' Lukeria uttered suddenly with unexpected strength and, opening her eyes wide, attempted to blink away the tears. 'Shouldn't I be ashamed? What's wrong with me? This hasn't happened to me for a long time – not since the day Vasya Polyakov visited me last spring. While he was sitting with me and talking it was all right. But when he'd gone – how I cried then all by myself! Where could so many tears come from! For sure a woman's tears cost nothing. Master,' Lukeria added, 'if you have a handkerchief, don't be finicky, wipe my eyes.'

I hastened to do what she asked, and left the handkerchief with her. She tried to refuse at first, as if she were asking why she should be given such a present. The handkerchief was very simple, but clean and white. Afterwards she seized it in her feeble fingers and did not open them again. Having grown accustomed to the darkness which surrounded us both, I could clearly distinguish her features and could even discern the delicate flush which rose through the bronze of her face and could make out in her face – or so at least it seemed to me – traces of her past beauty.

'Just now you were asking me, master,' Lukeria started saying again, 'whether I sleep. I certainly don't sleep often, but every time I have dreams – wonderful dreams! I never dream that I'm ill. In my dreams I'm always so young and healthy . . . I've only one complaint: when I wake up, I want to have a good stretch and yet here I am, just as if I were bound in fetters. Once I had such a marvellous dream! Would you like me to tell it to you? Well, listen. I dreamt of myself standing in a field, and all around me there was rye, so tall and ripe, like gold . . . And there was a little rust-red dog with me, wickedly vicious it was, all the time trying to bite me. And I had a sickle in my hand, and it wasn't a simple sickle, but it was the moon when the moon has the shape of a sickle. And with the moon itself I had to reap the rye until it was all cut. Only I grew very tired from the heat, and the moon blinded me, and a languor settled on me; and all around me cornflowers were growing – such big ones! And they all turned their little heads towards me. And I thought I would pick these cornflowers, because Vasya had promised to come, so I'd make myself a garland first of all and then still have time to do the reaping. I began to pluck the cornflowers, but they started to melt away through my fingers, to melt and melt, no matter what I did! And I couldn't weave myself a garland. And then I heard someone coming

towards me, coming close up to me and calling: "Loosha! Loosha!"
Oh dear, I thought, I'm too late! It doesn't matter, though, I
thought, because I can put the moon on my head instead of the
cornflowers. So I put the moon on my head, and it was just like
putting on one of those tall bonnets – at once I glowed with light
from head to foot and lit up all the field around me. I looked, and
there, through the very tips of the heads of rye, someone was
smoothly approaching ever so quickly – only it wasn't Vasya, it
was Christ Himself! And why I knew it was Christ I can't say – He's
never depicted as I saw Him – but it was Him! He was beardless, tall,
young, clad all in white, except for a belt of gold, and He put out a
hand to me and said: "Fear not, for thou art My chosen bride, come
with Me. In My heavenly kingdom thou shalt lead the singing and
play the songs of paradise." And how firmly I pressed my lips to His
hand. Then my little dog seized me by the legs, but at once we
ascended up into the heavens, He leading me, and His wings stretched
out to fill the heavens, as long as the wings of a gull – and I followed
after Him! And the little dog had to leave go of me. It was only then
that I understood that the little dog was my affliction and that there
was no place for my affliction in the Kingdom of Heaven.'

Lukeria fell silent for a minute.

'But I also had another dream,' she began again, 'or perhaps it was
a vision I had – I don't know which. It seemed that I was lying in this
very wattle hut and my dead parents – my mother and my father –
came to me and bowed low to me, but without saying anything.
And I asked them: "Why do you, my mother and father, bow down
to me?" And they answered and said: "Because thou hast suffered so
greatly in this world, thou hast lightened not only thine own soul
but hast also lifted a great weight from ours. And for us in our world
the way has been made easier. Thou hast already done with thine own
sins and art now conquering ours." And, having said this, my parents
again bowed low to me – and then I couldn't see them any longer:
all I could see were the walls. Afterwards I was very full of doubt
whether such a thing had happened to me. I told the priest of it, only
he said it couldn't have been a vision, because visions are vouchsafed
only to those of ecclesiastical rank.

'Then there was yet another dream I had,' Lukeria continued. 'I
saw myself sitting beside a big road under a willow, holding a

whittled stick, with a bag over my shoulders and my head wrapped in a kerchief, just like a holy wanderer! And I had to go somewhere far, far away on a pilgrimage, offering prayers to God. And the holy wanderers, the pilgrims, were continually going past me; they were walking quietly past me, as if unwillingly, all the time going in the same direction; and their faces were all sad and very much alike. And I saw that weaving and hurrying among them was one woman, a whole head taller than all the others, and she wore a special kind of dress, not our kind, not like a Russian dress. And her face was also of a special kind, stern and severe, like the face of one used to fasting. And it seemed that all the others made way for her; and then she suddenly turned and came straight towards me. She stopped and looked at me. Her eyes were like the eyes of a falcon, yellow and big and bright as could be. And I asked her: "Who are you?" And she said to me: "I am your death." I should've been frightened, but instead I was happy as a child, I swear to God I was! And this woman, my death, said to me: "I am sorry for you, Lukeria, but I cannot take you with me. Farewell!" O Lord, what sorrow there was for me then! "Take me," I cried, "beloved mother, dear one, take me!" And my death turned to face me and began to speak . . . And I understood that she was appointing the hour when I should die, but I couldn't quite grasp it, it wasn't clear, except that it would be some time after Saint Peter's Day . . . Then I woke up. Such surprising dreams I've been having!'

Lukeria raised her eyes to the ceiling and grew reflective.

'Only I have this one trouble, that a whole week may pass and I never once go to sleep. Last year there was a lady who came by, saw me and gave me a little bottle with some medicine to make me sleep. She told me to take ten drops each time. That was a great help to me, and I slept. Only now that little bottle's long ago finished. Do you know what that medicine was and how to get it?'

The lady who came by obviously gave Lukeria opium. I promised to procure such a little bottle for her and again could not restrain myself from remarking aloud at her patience.

'Oh, master!' she protested. 'What d'you mean by that? What sort of patience? Now Simon Stilites' patience was really great: he spent thirty years on a pillar! And there was another of God's servants who ordered himself to be buried in the ground up to his chest, and the ants ate his face . . . And here's something else that an avid reader of the Bible told me: there was a certain country, and that country was conquered by the Hagarenes, and they tortured and killed all who lived therein; and no matter what those who lived there did, they could in no way free themselves. And there appeared among those who dwelt in that country a holy virgin; she took a mighty sword and arrayed herself in heavy armour and went out against the Hagarenes and did drive them all across the sea. But when she had driven them away, she said to them: "Now it is time that you should burn me, for such was my promise, that I should suffer a fiery death for my people." And the Hagarenes seized her and burned her, but from that time forward her people were freed for ever! Now that's a really great feat of suffering! Mine's not like that!'

I wondered to myself in astonishment at the distance the legend of Joan of Arc had travelled and the form it had taken, and after a brief silence I asked Lukeria how old she was.

'Twenty-eight . . . or twenty-nine. I'm not thirty yet. What's the good of counting them, the years, I mean! I'll tell you something else . . .'

Lukeria suddenly coughed huskily and gave a groan.

'You are talking a great deal,' I remarked to her, 'and it could be bad for you.'

'That's true,' she whispered, hardly audible. 'Our little talk's got to end, no matter what happens! Now that you'll be going I'll be quiet as long as I wish. I've unburdened my heart to the full . . .'

I began to take leave of her, repeating my promise to send her the medicine and imploring her again to give careful thought to my question whether there was anything that she needed.

'I don't need anything, I'm quite content, praise God,' she uttered with the greatest of effort, but moved by my concern. 'God grant everyone good health! And you, master, tell your mother that, because the peasants here are poor, she should take a little less in rent from them! They haven't enough land, there isn't an abundance of anything . . . They'd give thanks to God for you if you did that . . . But I don't need a thing – I'm quite content.'

I gave Lukeria my word that I would fulfil her request and was already on the way to the door when she called to me again.

'Remember, master,' she said, and something wondrous glimmered in her eyes and on her lips, 'what long tresses I had? Remember, they reached right down to my knees! For a long time I couldn't make up my mind ... Such long hair! ... But how could I comb it out? In my state, after all! ... So I cut it all off ... Yes, that's what I did ... Well, master, forgive me! I can't go on any more ...'

That very day, before setting out for the hunt, I had a talk about Lukeria with the farm overseer. I learned from him that she was known in the village as the 'Living Relic' and that, in this regard, there had never been any trouble from her; never a murmur was to be heard from her, never a word of complaint. 'She herself asks for nothing, but, quite to the contrary, is thankful for everything; a quiet one, if ever there was a quiet one, that's for sure. Struck down by God, most likely for her sins,' the overseer concluded, 'but we don't go into that. And as, for instance, for passing judgement on her – no, we don't pass judgement. Let her alone!'

A few weeks later I learned that Lukeria had died. Her death had come for her, as she thought – 'after Saint Peter's Day'. There were rumours that on the day of her death she heard a bell ringing all the time, although from Alekseyevka to the church is a matter of three miles or more and it was not a Sunday. Lukeria, however, said that the ringing did not come from the church, but 'from above'. Probably she did not dare to say that it came from heaven.

CLATTER OF WHEELS

❦

'WHAT I want to tell you,' said Yermolay, coming into the hut – while I, for my part, had only just had dinner and stretched myself on a little travelling bed to rest for a short while after a fairly successful, but tiring, grouse shoot (it was some time in mid-July and the prevailing heat was awful) – 'What I want to tell you is that all our shot's used up.'

I jumped up from the bed.

'The shot's all used up! That's impossible! Surely we brought with us from the village by any reckoning about thirty pounds of it! We had a whole sackful!'

'Right. And it was a large sack, enough for two weeks. Who knows what's happened to it! Maybe the sack got a hole in it, but whatever it was, the fact is there's no shot left – ten more charges and that'll be it.'

'Well, what on earth are we going to do now? The best places are ahead – they've promised us six coveys for tomorrow . . .'

'Send me into Tula. It's not far from here – only about thirty miles. I'll fly like the wind and bring you back, if you like, a whole ton of shot.'

'All right, but when'll you be able to go?'

'Right now. Why delay? 'Cept there's only one thing – we'll have to hire some horses.'

'Hire some horses! What's wrong with our own?'

'We can't use ours. The shaft-horse's gone lame . . . Something awful.'

'When did this happen?'

'Just the other day. The driver took him off to be shod. So he was shod. But the blacksmith must've been poor at his job. Now the horse can't even stand on his leg. It's a front leg. He carries it lifted up, like he was a dog.'

'What's been done about it? At least he's been unshod, hasn't he?'

'No, he's still the same, but it's high time he was unshod. I reckon a nail's been driven into the fleshy part.'

I ordered the driver to be brought to me. It transpired that Yermolay had been telling the truth: the shaft-horse could not in fact stand on its leg. I at once arranged for the horse to be unshod and placed on damp clay.

'What about it now? Will you order horses to be hired for going to Tula?' Yermolay badgered me.

'Do you really think it's possible to hire horses in this back of beyond?' I cried out in a fit of vexation.

The village where we had found ourselves was out of the way and dead; all its inhabitants seemed to be poverty-stricken and it was only with difficulty that we had come across even so much as a hut with a chimney, let alone one that was in the least spacious.

'It's possible,' Yermolay answered with his usual imperturbability. 'It's true what you've said about this village, and yet in this very place there was once a peasant living – the cleverest man, he was! Rich, too! He had nine horses. He himself is dead and it's now his eldest son who looks after everything. As a person he's a real fool, but still he hasn't yet managed to get rid of all his father's property. From him we'll be able to fit ourselves out with horses. You give the order and I'll bring him along. They say his brothers are real bright lads, but he's still their boss.'

'Why so?'

'Because he's the eldest! That means the younger ones've got to kowtow!' At this point Yermolay expressed himself strongly and unprintably about younger brothers in general. 'I'll bring him along. He's a bit simple. You should be able to make a deal with a man like that, eh?'

While Yermolay was fetching this 'simple' man, the thought occurred to me: wouldn't it be better if I went into Tula myself? Firstly, schooled by experience, I had learnt to put little faith in Yermolay: I had sent him into town once to make some purchases, he promising to do everything he was told in the course of a single day – and he had disappeared for a whole week, drunk away all the money and returned on foot, whereas he had gone there in a racing buggy. Secondly, there was a horse-dealer I knew in Tula, and I could buy a horse from him in place of the lame shaft-horse.

'That's decided then,' I thought. 'I'll go myself and I can sleep on the way – which is the blessing of having a comfortable carriage.'

'I've brought him!' Yermolay exclaimed a quarter of an hour later as he tumbled into the hut. He was followed by a tall peasant in a white shirt, blue trousers and blue bast shoes, with a head of tousled fair hair and a myopic look, a light-coloured and wedge-shaped little beard, a long puffy nose and a gapingly open mouth. He looked exactly like a simpleton.

'Here he is,' Yermolay said. 'He's got horses and he's agreed to help.'

'It's like this, see, I . . .' the peasant stammered in a hoarse voice shaking his wispy locks and running his fingers along the band of the hat which he held in his hand. 'I, you see . . .'

'What is your name?' I asked.

The peasant lowered his head and literally started to ponder the question.

'What's my name?'

'Yes, what name have you?'

'My name will be Filofey.'

'Well, that's it, then, my good friend Filofey – I've heard that you have horses. Bring along three of them, if you would, and we'll harness them to my carriage – it's a light one – and you can take me into Tula. It's a moonlit night tonight, bright and fresh for travelling. What's the road like in your parts?'

'The road? Not bad. It'll be about fifteen mile to the main road – no more'n that. There's one little part where it's bad, but that's nothing really.'

'What's this bad part?'

'It's where we'll be needin' to cross a river.'

'Does this mean you yourself'll be going into Tula?' inquired Yermolay.

'Yes, I'll be going myself.'

'Well!' declared my trusty servant, and gave a shake of the head. 'Well, well, well!' he repeated, spat and left the hut.

A journey into Tula obviously no longer offered any attractions for him; it had become an empty matter of no interest.

'Do you know the road well?' I asked, addressing myself to Filofey.

'For sure I know the road! Only I, you see, beggin' your pardon, I can't go . . . seein' as it's so sudden-like . . .'

It transpired that Yermolay, in hiring Filofey, had declared to him that he had no doubt that he, the fool, would be paid – and that would be all! Filofey, although a fool, in Yermolay's estimation, had not been satisfied by this declaration in itself. He began by demanding from me fifty roubles in notes – an enormous sum; I offered him ten roubles – a small sum. We set about bargaining; Filofey was stubborn to start with, then he began to give way, albeit slowly. Yermolay, who had come in for a moment, began to assure me that 'This fool' ('See how fond he is of that word!' Filofey remarked under his breath) 'this fool has no idea of the value of money,' and incidentally reminded me how twenty years ago a coaching inn which had been established by my mother at a busy point at the intersection of two main roads had proved a complete failure because the ancient house-serf who had been put in charge of it literally did not know the value of money, but valued the coins according to number – that is to say, he would, for instance, give a silver quarter for half a dozen five-copeck coppers and swear strongly into the bargain.

'Damn you, Filofey, you're a right Filofey, you are!' Yermolay exclaimed finally and, going out, slammed the door angrily behind him.

Filofey did not answer him, as if acknowledging that it was certainly no easy matter to be called Filofey, that a man could even be held blameworthy for having such a name, although the real blame lay with the priest at his christening who had not been properly paid for his services.

Eventually, however, we agreed on twenty roubles. He went off to get the horses and an hour later brought five of them for me to choose from. The horses turned out to be suitable, although they had tangled manes and tails and large bellies stretched tight as drums. Filofey was accompanied by two of his brothers, who were quite unlike him. Small of stature, dark-eyed and sharp-nosed, they did indeed produce the impression of being 'bright lads', talking a great deal and at great speed – 'Shooting their mouths off', as Yermolay expressed it – but they still deferred to the eldest.

They pulled the carriage out from under the lean-to and for a whole hour and a half fussed round it with the horses. At one moment they would loosen the shaft fastenings, at the next they would do them up as tight as could be! Both the brothers insisted on harnessing a roan as shaft-horse because 'that un'd run mighty fine downhill', but Filofey decided on a shaggy horse and that was the horse they finally harnessed in the shafts.

The carriage was stuffed with hay and the collar from the lame shaft-horse was pushed under the seat – in case it became necessary to drive the horse into Tula in exchange for a newly purchased one. Filofey, having managed to dash home and return dressed up in his father's long, white, loose-fitting coat, tall hat and blackened boots, climbed solemnly up on to the box. I sat down, noting that my watch showed the time as a quarter to eleven. Yermolay did not even say goodbye to me, but took it upon himself to beat his dog Valetka. Filofey gave a jerk of the reins, called out: 'Gee up, there, my pretties!' in the most high-pitched of voices – his brothers jumped up on either side of us and lashed the underbellies of the outer horses – and the carriage started away, turning through the gate into the street. The shaggy horse would have turned back into the courtyard if left to its own devices, but Filofey admonished it with a few blows of the whip; and soon we had sped briskly out of the village and were travelling along a fairly smooth road between thick lines of nut trees.

The night was quiet and splendid, perfect for a journey. A wind would rustle occasionally in the bushes, set the branches quivering and then die away. Motionless, silvery clouds were visible here and there in the sky. The moon floated high up and bathed the country-side in its clear rays. I stretched myself out on the hay and was on the point of dozing when I suddenly remembered the 'bad part' and roused myself.

'Hey there, Filofey. Is it far to the ford?'

'To the ford? It'll be about five miles.'

'Five miles,' I thought. 'In that case it'll be an hour before we get there and I can have a sleep in the meantime.'

'D'you know the road well, Filofey?' I asked again.

'And why shouldn't I know her well – the road, I mean? It's not the first time I've been along here . . .'

He added something else, but I had already stopped listening. I was asleep.

I was awakened not by my own intention of waking up in an hour's time, but by some kind of unfamiliar, though faint, splishings and sploshings right beside my very ear. I raised my head.

What on earth had happened? I was lying in the carriage as before, but all around it, and barely more than a foot below its edge, a flat area of water, illuminated by the moon, was fragmented and criss-crossed by tiny, distinct ripples. I looked toward the front and there was Filofey sitting on the box, his head fallen forward, his back bent, solemn as an idol, and further ahead still, above gurgling water, I could see the bent line of the shaft and the horses' heads and backs. And everything was so still, so soundless, as if it were in an enchanted kingdom, a dream, a fairy-tale sleep. Fantastic! Then I looked towards the back from under the hood of the carriage. We were indeed in the very middle of a river, with the bank a good thirty paces from us!

'Filofey!' I exclaimed.

'What d'you want?' he answered.

'How can you say "What d'you want?" For heaven's sake, where are we?'

'In the river.'

'I can see we're in the river. And any minute now we'll drown. So you're crossing by the ford, are you? Eh? Filofey, you're sleeping. Answer me!'

'I made a wee mistake,' my driver announced, 'and went a little to one side, you know, took the wrong way, sad to tell, but we'll have to do some waiting now.'

'Why've we got to do some waiting? What're we going to wait for?'

'Let the shaggy horse look around 'isself, 'cause where 'e turns is where we'll be going.'

I raised myself on the hay. The head of the shaft-horse was motionless above the water. All that could be seen by the bright light of the moon was one of his ears moving slightly backwards and forwards.

'And he's asleep as well, that shaggy horse of yours!'

'No,' answered Filofey. 'What he's doing now is sniffing the water.'

And everything again fell quiet, with only the water giving faint splashings. I also froze into immobility. The moonlight, the night, the river and ourselves in the middle of it . . .

'What's that hissing?' I asked Filofey.

'That? It's ducklings in the reeds . . . or maybe it's snakes.'

Suddenly, the shaft-horse began shaking its head, pricked up its ears, started snorting and fussing.

'Gee up, gee-gee-gee!' Filofey unexpectedly howled at the top of his voice, rose up and began wielding his whip. The carriage at once jolted from the place where it had been standing and thrust itself forward against the flow of the river. It went a short way, jerking and wobbling. To start with, it seemed to me that we were sinking, going in deeper, but after two or three jolts and slips, the surface of the water appeared suddenly to grow lower. It went farther and farther down and the carriage rose out of it. Then the wheels appeared and the horses' tails and then, raising large, powerful splashes of water that exploded in the moon's dull white brilliance like flashing sheaves of diamonds – no, not of diamonds but of sapphires – the horses all pulling happily together drew us out on to the muddy bank and followed the road uphill, stepping out in irregular strides on their glittering, wet legs.

'What,' it occurred to me, 'will Filofey say now: You see, I was right! or something on those lines?' But he said nothing. For that reason I did not consider it necessary to blame him for carelessness and, bedding down in the hay, attempted once again to go to sleep.

But I couldn't sleep – not because I wasn't tired from hunting, not because the alarm which I had experienced had driven away my sleepiness – simply due to the extremely beautiful regions through which our route took us. These were free-ranging, expansive, well-watered grassy meadowlands with a host of small pastures, miniature lakes, streams and large ponds overgrown at each end with willows, absolutely Russian, places dear to the heart of the Russian people, like the places to which the legendary warriors of our old folk sagas used to travel to shoot white swans and grey-hued ducks. The smooth road unwound behind us like a yellowish ribbon, the horses were going at an easy pace and I couldn't close my eyes for joy at my surroundings. And everything flowed past so softly and surely under the friendly moon. Even Filofey was affected by the scene.

'Them there meadows are named after Saint Yegor,' he said, turning to me. 'And beyond 'em there'll be the Grand Duke's. You'll not see any other meadows the likes of these in the whole of Russia. There's real beauty for you!' The shaft-horse snorted and shook its mane. 'The Lord be with you!' Filofey declared gravely in a low voice. 'There's real beauty for you!' he repeated and sighed, but went on to make a protracted clearing of his throat. 'Soon the haymaking'll be beginning, and they'll rake in a whole heap of hay from them meadows. And there's a whole lot of fish in them ponds. Such bream you've never seen,' he added in a singsong. 'That's what life's worth living for!'

Suddenly he raised his hand.

'Hey, look over there! On the other side of the lake, isn't that a heron standing there? Can that be a heron catching fish at night? Blast it, it's a bough of a tree, sticking up, not a heron! I made a muck of that one! It's the moon fools you.'

So we travelled on and on. Then the meadowlands came to an end, and woodlands and ploughed fields appeared; to one side there twinkled two or three lights of a village. There still remained about two miles to the main road, and I drifted off to sleep.

Again, I did not wake of my own accord. On this occasion I was roused by the voice of Filofey.

'Master . . . Hey, master!'

I raised myself up. The carriage was standing on a level place in the very centre of the main road. His face turned to me from the box with wide open eyes (I was astonished, because I had not imagined that he had such big eyes), Filofey was whispering meaningfully and mysteriously:

'There's a clattering! . . . A clattering!'

'What are you talking about!'

'I say there's a clattering. Lean outside and listen. Do you hear it?'

I stuck my head out of the carriage and held my breath – I did, in fact, hear somewhere very far off behind us a faint, intermittent clattering, as of turning wheels.

'D'you hear it?' Filofey repeated.

'Yes, I do,' I answered. 'It sounds like a carriage on the road.'

'But don't you hear it! Listen . . . there! The bells . . . and also a whistling . . . Hear it? Take your cap off and you'll be able to hear it better.'

I did not take my cap off, but bent my ear to the sound.

'Well, yes . . . perhaps so. What about it?'

Filofey turned to face the horses.

'It's a cart on its way, travelling light, with iron-shod wheels,' he said and took up the reins. 'There's bad people travelling in it, master. Hereabouts, around Tula, there's many people up to no good.'

'What nonsense! What makes you suppose they're bound to be bad people?'

'I am telling you the truth. With bells on 'em . . . and in an empty cart . . . Who else would it be?'

'Well, then, is it far yet to go to Tula?'

'It'll still be 'bout 'leven miles and there's none living round these parts.'

'Well, let's get a move on. There's no need to loiter about.'

Filofey gave a wave of his whip and the carriage once more rolled on its way.

Although I gave no credence to Filofey, I was still not able to get to sleep. And what if he was, indeed, telling the truth? An unpleasant feeling stirred within me. I sat up in the carriage – for until this time I had been lying down – and began looking about on either side of me. While I had been sleeping a light mist had gathered – not a ground mist but one that obscured the sky. It stood high up in the sky and the moon hung in it like a whitish blur, as if surrounded by smoke. Everything up in the sky had grown blurred and confused, but closer to the earth, it was clearer. All around there was a flat, despondent landscape: all fields and more fields with here and there a bush or a ravine – and then more fields, chiefly lying fallow and dotted with patches of weed. It was empty and dead. I only wished that a quail would cry.

We drove for about half an hour. Filofey all the while waved his whip and smacked his lips, but neither he nor I exchanged a single

word. Then we ascended a slight rise in the terrain, Filofey stopped
the three horses and announced at once:

'There's the clattering . . . it's clattering, master!'

I again stuck my head out of the carriage, but it would have been
just as well if I had stayed under the hood of the carriage so clearly
now, although still far off, could be heard the clatter of the cart-
wheels, people whistling, the jingling of harness bells and even the
thud of horses' hoofs. I even thought I could hear singing and
laughter. The wind, it is true, was coming from that direction, but
there was no doubt that these strange travellers had grown a mile or
more closer to us.

Filofey and I exchanged looks. All he did was to tilt his hat from
the back of his head on to his brow and at once, crouching over the
reins, started whipping up the horses. They broke into a gallop, but
they were unable to gallop for long and settled once again into a trot.
Filofey continued to lash at them. For we simply had to get away!

I could not explain to myself why, this time, after having at first
rejected Filofey's suspicions, I now suddenly felt convinced that those
travelling in our wake were in fact bad people. There was nothing
new to be heard: the same jingling bells, the same clatter of an
unladen cart, the same whistling, the same vague clamour . . . But
now, I was no longer ready to doubt. Filofey couldn't be wrong!

About another twenty minutes went by. Towards the end of these
twenty minutes there grew audible above the clatter and rumble of
our own carriage another clattering and another rumbling.

'Stop, Filofey!' I said. 'It doesn't matter – it'll have to come to an
end some time!'

Filofey called a cowardly halt. The horses stopped instantly, as if
glad of the opportunity of resting.

Good heavens! By this time the harness bells were simply thundering at our very backs, the cart was roaring and rattling, the people
whistling and shouting and singing, the horses snorting and beating
the earth with their hoofs . . . They'd caught up with us!

'Glo-o-ory be!' Filofey uttered in a soft voice, elongating the
syllables, and after clicking his tongue irresolutely, started urging on
the horses. But at that instant there was a loud tearing sound, a
roaring and thundering – and an outsized rickety cart, pulled by
three wiry horses, overtook us like a whirlwind, swerving sharply,

galloped on beyond us and at once slowed down to a walking pace, blocking the road.

'That's the way robbers do it,' Filofey whispered.

I confess that a chill tremor seized my heart. I started peering tensely into the semi-darkness of the mist-veiled light of the moon. The cart in front of us contained – not exactly lying, not exactly in sitting positions – six men in peasant shirts and open cloth coats; two of them were hatless; huge, booted legs hung dangling between the cart's side supports, arms flopped up and down, bodies shaken against each other. It was clearly a case of a cart-load of drunks. Some were bellowing the first thing that came into their heads at the tops of their voices; one of them was whistling very piercingly and clearly; another was using foul language; and a giant of a man in a sheepskin coat was sitting on the box and driving. They went along at walking pace as though paying no attention to us.

What could we do? We drove along behind them also at walking pace, despite ourselves. For about a quarter of a mile we travelled in this fashion. The waiting was sheer torment. There was no way of saving or defending ourselves, in such a situation. There were six of them, and I didn't even have a stick! Turn the shafts round? They'd catch up with us at once. I recalled the line from Zhukovsky (where he is speaking about the murder of Field Marshal Kamensky):

The robber's axe, despiséd thing . . .[1]

Or if they didn't use an axe, then they'd throttle you with a dirty piece of rope and hurl you into a ditch to croak and beat about like a hare caught in a snare . . . The whole thing was foul!

All the while they continued to travel at walking pace and paid no attention to us.

'Filofey,' I whispered, 'try going to the right and see if you can get past them.'

Filofey tried. He went to the right, but they at once went to the right as well and it was impossible to pass them. Filofey tried again, going to the left this time, but here again they wouldn't let him pass the cart. They even laughed. So they were not going to let us pass.

'Exactly like robbers,' Filofey muttered to me over his shoulder.

'What are they waiting for?' I asked, also in a whisper.

'Up there ahead of us, in a hollow, there's a little bridge over a stream – that's where they'll do for us! That's where they always do it – close to bridges. We're in for it, master, plain as anything!' he added with a sigh. 'They'll surely not let us get away alive. 'Cos the main thing for 'em's to have water to hide the remains in. What's worrying me, master, is that my three horses'll be lost and won't be passed on to my brothers.'

I should have been amazed at the way Filofey could be worried about his horses at such a time, but I must confess that I didn't have much thought for him. 'Surely they're not going to kill us?' I went on repeating to myself. 'What for? I'll give them everything I've got with me.'

Meanwhile, the little bridge continued to grow closer, becoming all the while more clearly visible.

Suddenly there were piercing shouts and the trio of horses drawing the cart literally wound themselves up, dashed forwards and, having galloped to the little bridge, stopped dead as if rooted to the spot a little to one side of the road. My heart quite simply sank within me.

'Oh, Filofey, my good fellow,' I declared, 'you and I're going to our deaths. Forgive me if I've been the cause of it all.'

'What fault is it of yours, master! One can't escape one's fate! Hey there, shaggy one, faithful horse o' mine,' said Filofey, addressing the shaft-horse, 'move on, there's a good chap! Perform a final service for me! It's all the same . . . O Lord! Bless us!'

And he sent his three horses off at a trot.

We began to approach the little bridge, began to approach the motionless, threatening cart . . . As if intentionally, everyone in it had grown quiet. Not so much as a whisper! In just the same way a pike, a hawk, any predator becomes quite still as its prey draws close. We drew level with the cart. Suddenly the giant in the sheepskin coat jumped down from it and came straight towards us!

He said not a word to Filofey, but Filofey at once reined in the horses. Our carriage came to a stop.

The giant placed both hands on the doors of the carriage and, leaning his tousled head forward and screwing up his mouth in a grin, uttered in a soft, level voice and factory dialect the following speech:

'Guv'nor, sir, we're on our way from a real good party, a wedding party. We've married off one of our mates, see. Put him to bed, real and proper. They're all young lads 'ere, a bit wild – we've downed a lot, but haven't got nuthin' for the hair of the dog, see. So maybe it'll be your pleasure you'll let us have just a little bit o' small change, so as there'll be a round for each of us? We'd drink your health, sir, and raise a toast to your highness. But if it isn't to your liking – don't get mad at us!'

'What's this?' I asked myself. 'A joke? Is he putting one over?'

The giant continued to stand there, his head lowered. At that moment the moon broke through the mist and lit up his face. It wore a grin, the face did, a grin of the eyes and lips. But there was nothing threatening to be discerned in it, except that it seemed to be literally on its guard, and the man's teeth were so large and white . . .

'With pleasure I'll . . . here, take this,' I said in a hurry and, having extracted my purse from my pocket, took out two silver roubles; at that time silver coins were still in circulation in Russia. 'Here it is, if that'll be enough.'

'Mighty thankful!' the giant barked out in military fashion and his large fingers instantly seized from my hands – not the whole purse, but only the two roubles. 'Mighty thankful!' He shook back his hair and ran to the cart.

'Lads!' he shouted. 'The guv'nor in the carriage's given us two roubles!' The rest of them at once made a fine uproar. The giant tumbled on to his box.

'The best o' luck to you!'

And that was all we saw of them! The horses started away, the cart thundered off uphill – it flashed into sight once more against the dark line of horizon dividing the earth from the sky, sank from view and disappeared. Soon even the clattering and shouting and jingling bells were no longer audible.

Deathly silence reigned.

Filofey and I did not come to our senses immediately.

'You're a right joker, you are!' he said eventually and, removing his hat, began to make the sign of the cross. 'A right joker, that's for sure,' he added and turned to me, radiant with joy. 'But he must've been a good chap, that's for sure. Gee-up, gee-up, my pretties! Get wheeling! You'll be whole! We'll all be whole! He didn't let us pass, you see, 'cos he was driving the horses. A right joker that lad was! Gee-up, gee-up, get along there! God's speed to you!'

I did not say anything, but I began to feel much happier. 'We'll be whole!' I repeated to myself and spread myself out in the hay. 'We got off cheaply!' I was even a little ashamed of having recalled the line from Zhukovsky.

Suddenly, a thought occurred to me:

'Filofey!'

'What is it?'

'Are you married?'

'I am.'

'And have you children?'

'I have.'

'How is it you didn't think of them? You worried about the horses, but what about your wife and children?'

'What would've been the good of worrying about them? After all, they wouldn't have fallen into the hands of thieves. Still I had them in mind all the time, and I still do . . . sure I do.' Filofey paused. 'It may be, 'cos of them, the good Lord had mercy on the two of us.'

'And what if they turned out to be robbers after all?'

'How's that to be known? D'you think it's possible to get inside another's soul, eh? Another's soul sure is a mystery. It's always best to be on God's side. No . . . I keep my family always . . . Gee-up, gee-up, my pretties! God's speed!'

It was almost quite light by the time we began to approach Tula. I lay in the oblivion of a half sleep.

'Master,' Filofey said to me suddenly, 'take a look over there! That's them standing by the tavern – and there's their cart.'

I raised my head – true enough, it was them; and their cart and horses. All of a sudden the familiar giant in the sheepskin coat appeared on the threshold of the drinking house.

'Guv'nor!' he exclaimed, waving his cap. 'It's your money we're drinking! But as for the driver,' he added, giving a nod of the head towards Filofey, 'you most likely had a fright, eh?'

'Highly divertin' fellow,' remarked Filofey, driving a good fifty yards on beyond the tavern.

Finally we reached Tula. I purchased some shot, also some tea and spirits, and I even procured a horse from the dealer friend of mine. At midday we set off on our return journey. Travelling past the place where we had first heard the clattering of the cart behind us,

Filofey, who, having had a drink in Tula, turned out to be a man of extremely garrulous disposition (he even regaled me with fairy-tales) – travelling past that place, Filofey suddenly burst out laughing.

'Remember, master how I kept on saying to you: There's a clattering . . . a clattering, hear it, clatter-clatter?'

He made several sweeping, dismissive gestures with his hand. The word 'clattering' seemed to be a source of special amusement to him.

That evening we got back to his village.

I informed Yermolay of what had occurred to us. Being in a sober condition, he expressed no sympathy, simply grunted – whether approvingly or scornfully he did not know himself, or so I believe. But a couple of days later he took pleasure in letting me know that on the very same night Filofey and I had been travelling to Tula, and on the very same road, some merchant or other had been robbed and killed. At first I did not believe this news. But later I had occasion to change my mind, the truth of it being confirmed for me by the local police-officer who had galloped up to attend the investigations. Was it not perhaps from this 'wedding' that our 'wild ones' had been returning, and was this not the 'mate' that, as the jocular giant expressed it, they had been putting to bed real and proper? I remained in Filofey's village another five days or so. It happened that each time I met him I would ask him:

'There's a clattering, eh, a clattering?'

'A divertin' fellow,' he would answer me each time and burst out laughing.

FOREST AND STEPPE

———————— ❦ ————————

... Little by little he felt his desire harden,
Drawing him back to the village and shady garden,
Where lindens stood in stately dark magnificence,
And lilies of the valley spread their virgin fragrance,
Where round-shouldered willows by the weir,
Bend in a row above the water clear,
Where a stout oak grows above the fat-eared wheat,
Where hemp and nettles make the air smell sweet ...
He was drawn back to those broad fields so lush,
Where the earth like velvet is so black and plush,
So that, no matter where you may direct your eye,
Everywhere is a rustling of soft waves of rye,
And through transparent clouds, so round and white,
Fall heavy beams of sunshine's golden light;
There is it good ...

(From a poem consigned to the flames)

THE reader, perhaps, has already had enough of my
Sketches, but I hasten to allay his fears with the promise that
they are to be limited to these printed extracts; and yet, in making
my farewell, I must say a few words about the sport of hunting.

Hunting with a gun and a dog is a delight in itself, *für sich*, as they
used to say in the past. But let us suppose that you are not a born
hunter, though you still love nature; in that case, you can hardly fail
to envy the lot of your brother hunters ... Pray listen a while.

Do you know, for instance, how delightful it is to drive out before a
spring dawn? You walk out on the porch and here and there on the
dark grey sky stars wink at you, light waves of a moist breeze

occasionally stir the air about you, the muffled, indistinct murmurs of the night can be heard and the trees rustle softly, immersed in shadow. A cover is drawn over the cart and a box with a samovar is placed at your feet. The trace-horses fret, snort and affectedly stamp their hoofs; a pair of newly awakened white geese make their way slowly and silently across the road. In the garden, on the other side of the fencing, the night-watchman snores peacefully from time to time. Every sound hangs as if frozen upon the still air – hangs there frozen and motionless. Then you take your seat; the horses start away at once and the cart clatters off on its journey . . . You drive past a church, downhill and to the right across a dam; a mist is just beginning to rise from a pond. The air chills you slightly and you cover your face with your coat collar; you are pleasantly drowsy. The horses' hoofs squelch in the puddles and the driver whistles to himself. By the time you've travelled two miles or so the rim of the sky is beginning to crimson; in the birches jackdaws are awakening and clumsily fluttering from branch to branch; sparrows twitter about the dark hayricks. The air grows brighter, the road clearer, the sky lightens, suffusing the clouds with whiteness and the fields with green. Lights burn red in the cottages and sleepy voices can be heard beyond the gates. In the meantime dawn has burst into flame; stripes of gold have risen across the sky and wreaths of mist form in the ravines; to the loud singing of skylarks and the soughing of the wind before dawn the sun rises, silent and purple, above the horizon. Light floods over the world and your heart trembles within you like a bird. Everything is so fresh, gay and lovely! You can see for miles. Here a village glimmers beyond the woodland; there, farther away, is another village with a white church and then a hill with a birchwood; beyond it is the marsh to which you are driving . . . Step lively there, horses! Forward at a brisk trot! . . . No more than two miles to go now. The sun is rising quickly, the sky is clear . . . The weather will be perfect. You meet a herd of cattle coming in a long line from the village. Then you ascend the hill . . . What a view! The river winds away for seven miles or more, a faint blue glimmer through the mist; beyond it are the water-green meadows: beyond them, low-lying hills; in the distance lapwings veer and cry above the marsh; through the gleaming moisture which pervades the air the distance emerges clearly . . . there is no summer haze. How freely one breathes the air into one's lungs, how buoyant are one's limbs, how strong one feels in the grip of this fresh springtime atmosphere!

And a summer morning in July! Has anyone save a hunter ever experienced the delight of wandering through bushes at dawn? Your feet leave green imprints in grass that is heavy and white with dew. You push aside wet bushes – the warm scent accumulated in the night almost smothers you; the air is impregnated with the fresh bitter-sweet fragrance of wormwood, the honeyed scent of buckwheat and clover; far off an oak forest rises like a wall, shining purple in the sunshine; the air is still fresh, but the coming heat can already be felt. Your head becomes slightly dizzy from such an excess of sweet scents. And there's no end to the bushes ... Away in the distance ripening rye glows yellow and there are narrow strips of rust-red buckwheat. Then there's the sound of a cart; a peasant drives by at walking pace, leaving his horse in the shade before the sun gets hot. You greet him, pass on, and after a while the metallic rasping of a scythe can be heard behind you. The sun is rising higher and higher, and the grass quickly dries out. It's already hot. First one hour, then another passes. The sky darkens at the edges and the motionless air is aflame with the prickly heat.

'Where can I get a drink, friend?' you ask the peasant.

'There's a spring down there in the ravine.'

You make your way down to the floor of the ravine through thick bushes of nut which are entwined with bindweed. There it is; at the very bottom of the ravine hides the spring; a small oak has greedily spread its webbed branches over the water; large silver bubbles rise in clusters from the spring's bottom nestling in a thin, velvety moss. You fling yourself to the ground and drink your fill, but have no wish to rise again. You are in a shady place, breathing in the pungent dampness; you're glad to be here while beyond you the branches burn with heat and literally turn yellow in the sun. But what's that? A breeze has suddenly risen and scurried by you; the surrounding air shudders. You leave the ravine ... What's that lead-grey strip running along the horizon? And the heat's thicker, isn't it? Is there a cloud forming? ... Then comes a faint lightning flash – yes, it's a storm all right! Yet the sun is still shining brightly and hunting's still possible. But the cloud grows: its nearest edge is stretched out like a sleeve and looms like an arch. Bushes, grass, everything suddenly darkens ... Quick, quick! There's a hay barn over there. Quick ... You reach it, go in and come rain, come lightning, it makes no difference ... Here and there water drips through the straw roof into the fragrant hay; soon the sun's out again. The storm passes and you step outside. Oh, how gaily everything glitters around you, how fresh and liquid is the air, how sweet the scent of mushroom and wild strawberry!

But now evening is approaching. The sunset has burst into flame and covered half the sky with fire. The sun sinks. The air near by is somehow particularly lucid, exactly as if made of glass; in the distance a soft haze is settling, warm as heat-haze in appearance; along with the dew a crimson glow is descending on the open fields which were so recently inundated by torrents of liquid gold; from trees, from bushes, from tall hayricks have run long shadows ... The sun has set; a star ignites and twinkles in the fiery sea of the sun's sinking ... Now the sun pales: the sky grows blue; separate shadows vanish away and the air fills with dusk. It is time to go home, to the village, to the hut where you are spending the night. Slinging your gun over your shoulder, you walk at a brisk pace despite your tiredness. And in the meantime night descends; you can hardly see twenty paces ahead of you; your dogs are barely visible in the murk. Over there, above the blackness of the bushes, the rim of the sky shines dimly ... What's that? Is it a fire? No, it's the rising of the moon and there below you, to your right, the lights of the village are already glimmering. Finally, you reach your hut. Through the little window you see a table covered with a white cloth, a lighted candle and supper ...

Or you order the racing buggy to be harnessed and off you go into the forest after grouse. It is a happy feeling to be making your way along a narrow track between two high walls of rye. The heads of grain gently strike you across the face, while cornflowers catch at your feet, and quail cry in the vicinity and the horse goes at a lazy trot. Then comes the forest. Shade and silence. Stately aspens murmur high above you; the long hanging branches of the birches hardly stir; a powerful oak stands like a warrior beside a gracious linden. You travel along a green track that is dappled with shadows; large yellow flies hang motionless in the gold-dust air and suddenly fly away. Gnats weave in spirals, glittering in the shade, darkening in the sunlight; birds sing peacefully. The small golden voice of the robin makes a sound of innocent prattling gaiety: it accords with the scent of lilies of the valley. You go farther and farther, deeper into the forest. The forest thickens. An inexplicable quietude begins to descend on your soul; and all around it is so dream-like and still. But now a breeze has sprung up and the tips of the trees have begun to rustle like tumbling waves. Through last year's rust-brown fallen leaves tall grass grows here and there; mushrooms stand individually under their little hats. A white hare jumps suddenly into view and the dog races after it with loud barks . . .

And how fine that very same forest looks in late autumn, when the snipe fly in! They do not frequent the forest depths, but must be sought along its outskirts. There is no wind, nor is there any sun, any brightness, any shade, any movement, any noise; the soft air is saturated with an autumnal fragrance, like the bouquet of wine; a thin mist hangs in the distance over the yellow fields. Through the naked, dark-brown branches of the trees the still sky peacefully shines; here and there on the lindens hang the last golden leaves. The damp earth is springy under your feet; the tall dry blades of grass are perfectly still; long threads gleam in the pale-hued grass. Your breathing is calm, though a strange anxiety invades your soul. You walk along the edge of the forest, keeping your eyes on the dog, but in the meantime there come to mind beloved images, beloved faces, the living and the dead, and long-since dormant impressions unexpectedly awaken; the imagination soars and dwells on the air like a bird, and everything springs into movement with such clarity and stands before the eyes. Your heart either suddenly quivers and starts beating fast, passionately racing forward, or drowns irretrievably in recollections. The whole of life unrolls easily and swiftly like a scroll; a man has possession of his whole past, all his feelings, all his powers, his entire soul. And nothing in his surroundings can disturb him – there is no sun, no wind, no noise . . .

And a clear, autumnal, slightly cold day with frost in the morning, when the birch, literally a tree out of a fairy-tale arrayed all in gold, stands out in beautiful outline against a pale-blue sky, when the sun, low on the horizon, has no more power to heat, but shines more brightly than the sun of summer, when the small aspen wood glows through and through as if it were delighted and happy to stand there naked, when the hoar-frost still whitens the floors of the valleys, but a fresh breeze ever so quietly rustles and drives before it the fallen twisted leaves, when blue waves race gaily along the river, making geese and ducks scattered on its surface bob evenly up and down; when in the distance a watermill, half hidden by willows, makes a clattering sound and, colourfully flickering in the bright air, pigeons circle swiftly above it . . .

Wonderful also are hazy summer days, although hunters dislike them. It is impossible to do any shooting on such days: a bird, though it rises from beneath your very feet, immediately disappears into the whitish murk of the motionless haze. But how quiet, how unimaginably quiet is everything around you! Everything is awake and everything is silent. You walk past a tree – it does not even so much as stir: it simply swoons in the stillness. Through the fine mistiness with which the air is evenly suffused a long strip of something black emerges in front of you. You take it for a nearby forest; you approach – and the forest turns into a high bank of wormwood on the boundary of a field. Above you and all about you, everywhere there is haze. But then a breeze stirs faintly – and a patch of pale-blue sky vaguely emerges through the thinning mist, which has literally begun to rise like smoke; a golden-yellow ray breaks through suddenly, streams out in a long flood, strikes across the fields, runs up against a wood – and then once more everything clouds over. This struggle continues for a long while; but how indescribably magnificent and lucid is the day itself, when the sunlight finally triumphs and the last waves of sun-warmed haze either roll away and spread themselves out smooth as tablecloths, or spiral upwards and vanish in the deep, gently gleaming atmosphere . . .

But now you've set off into the distant fields and the steppeland. You've made your way for six or seven miles along country roads and now, at last, you've reached the main road. Past endless lines of carts, past little wayside inns with samovars hissing under the lean-to out front, with their wide-open gates and well-holes for water, from one village to another, through endless expanses of fields, beside plantations of green hemp, you travel for hour after hour. Magpies flit from one clump of broom to another; women with long rakes wander in the fields; a traveller on foot wearing a worn nankeen coat, with a small bundle over his shoulder, plods on his way at a tired pace; a bulky landowner's carriage, harnessed with six full-grown and jaded horses, trundles towards you. The corner of a cushion is sticking out of a window, but on the rear step, on a mat, holding on by a rope, a lackey in an overcoat sits sideways, spattered with mud up to his eyebrows. Then there is a little county town with small lop-sided wooden houses, endless fences, vacant merchants' dwellings built of stone and an ancient bridge over a deep ravine . . . Farther, farther! The steppelands are approaching. You look down from a hill – what a view! Round, low hillocks, ploughed and sown right up to their tips, billow in all directions like broad waves; ravines overgrown with bushes weave among them; small woods are scattered here and there like elongated islands; from village to village run narrow tracks; churches gleam white; between thickets of willow glitters a small river, its flow staunched in four places by dams; far off in the field wild cranes stick out as they waddle in file; an antiquated landowner's mansion with its outbuildings, orchard and threshing floor is settled comfortably beside a small pond. But you go on travelling, farther and farther. The hillocks grow shallower and shallower and there is hardly a tree to be seen. Finally, there it is – the limitless, enormous steppe no eye can encompass!

And on a wintry day to go walking through the high snowdrifts in search of hares, to breathe in the frosty, sharp-edged air, to crinkle one's eyes unwillingly against the dazzling, finely speckled glitter of the soft snow, to wonder at the green hue of the sky above a reddening forest! . . . And then there are the first spring days, when all around everything gleams and crashes down, and the smell of the warmer earth begins to rise through the heavy steam of melting snow, and skylarks sing trustingly under the sun's oblique rays on patches where the snow has thawed, and, with a gay noise, a gay roaring, the torrents go whirling from ravine to ravine . . .

★

It is time, however, to finish. Appropriately I have mentioned the spring; in springtime it is easy to say goodbye, in the spring even the happy are enticed to far-off places ... Farewell, my reader; I wish you lasting happiness and well-being.

THE RUSSIAN GERMAN

❧

ONCE I followed my dog into a field of buckwheat which did not belong to me at all. In our obliging Fatherland anyone is free to shoot where he likes, on his own land or on his neighbour's. Apart from a few elderly and shrewish ladies, and landowners who have perfected themselves on the English pattern, no one so much as thinks of forbidding strangers from hunting on their lands. I had barely succeeded in taking a few steps when I heard loud shouts from behind me. It did not occur to me that I was being shouted at in person, and I continued very calmly, with all the thorough conscientiousness of a hunter, walking backwards and forwards across the field, until I finally heard quite clearly:

'What're you doing, master, trampling down the buckwheat? You mustn't, it's not allowed . . .'

I turned round and saw a peasant in a cloth coat, with an unusually picturesque and wavy beard, who was walking directly towards me and waving his arms wildly. I stopped.

'T'ain't right for you to be walking through the buckwheat. Stop, or I'll take you to the bailiff. A fine's laid down for this and there's an order issued about it,' the peasant said as he walked, shaking his head.

Eventually he came up to me. I apologized. He made a grumbling sound. But the prohibition against walking through the buckwheat seemed to me so strange in our beautiful Russia, the more so since it was a steppe province, that I could not refrain from asking the peasant who had given him such an order.

'Who?' the peasant retorted with displeasure. 'Who? The master himself.'

'And who's your master?'

The peasant did not answer at once and played with his belt. 'Makarat Ivanych Shvokhtel . . .'

'Who on earth . . .?'

The peasant repeated his master's name. 'But maybe,' he added, 'you'd be having some snuff?'

'No, I don't, but take this to buy some with.'

The peasant thanked me, took off his cap and became much happier.

'So it's not allowed, is it?' I asked him.

''S not allowed,' he replied smiling, like a man who, though he is doing what his master orders, feels for his own part that the orders are in fact ridiculous. ''Course,' he continued, 'buckwheat's not peas; no point in having someone to guard it, seein' as someone might start eatin' it raw . . . But that's the sort of master we have. He'd grind rye in a thimble, he would, the Lord forgive us.'

That same week it happened that I became acquainted with the very man. Mr Leberecht Fochtlender was born, so rumour had it, in the glorious German township of Guzbach. In his twenty-fifth year he entered the Russian civil service, occupied various posts for a period of thirty-two and a half years, retiring with the seventh-grade rank of aulic councillor and the Order of St Anne. He had married at forty. He was small in stature and on the thin side; he used to sport a brown frock-coat of old-style cut, grey trousers, a small silver watch attached by a string of blue beads and a high white cravat which gathered in folds right up to his ears. He held himself very straight and walked about with a prim haughtiness, now and then turning his small head. He had a small, smooth face, light-blue eyes, a sharp little nose, semicircular sideburns, a forehead covered with tiny wrinkles and thin tightly closed lips.

THE REFORMER AND THE RUSSIAN
GERMAN

————————— ❧ —————————

I WAS sitting in the so-called 'clean' room of a wayside inn on the main Kursk road and asking the innkeeper, a stout man with wavy grey hair, bulging eyes and sagging stomach, about the number of hunters who had recently visited the Telegin marsh, when the door was suddenly flung wide open and a traveller entered the room, a tall, graceful gentleman in a stylish travelling coat. He removed his cap.

'Yevgeny Alexandrych!' I cried. 'What luck, eh?'

'Ah, ★★★!' he exclaimed in his turn.

We shook each other's hands. 'How pleased I am, how pleased,' we both babbled, not without a certain tenseness.

'Where in God's name are you going?' I asked at last.

'To Kursk . . . I've come into an inheritance.'

'Has your aunt died?' I asked with a modest show of sympathy.

'She's died,' he answered with a faint sigh. 'Innkeeper!' he added in a loud voice, 'the samovar – and quick about it! Yes,' he continued, turning to me again, 'she's died. I'm just now on my way to receive what she's left me.'

Yevgeny Alexandrych's servant came in, a young man with reddish-coloured hair and dressed in the manner of a *chasseur*.

'Hans!' my acquaintance declared. '*Geben Sie mir eine Pfeife.*'

Hans went out.

'Is your valet a German?' I asked.

'No, he's – er – a Finn,' answered Yevgeny Alexandrych, leaving intervals between the words. 'But he understands German.'

'And he speaks Russian?'

Yevgeny Alexandrych paused briefly before saying: 'Oh, yes, he speaks it!'

Hans returned, respectfully set the pipe directly between his master's lips, placed a square-shaped scrap of white paper on the bowl and touched a match to it. His master began to smoke, taking the pipe with the side of his mouth, and contorting his lips over the amber stem like a dog seizing a hedgehog. The innkeeper brought in a hissing and bubbling samovar. I took a seat beside Yevgeny Alexandrych and struck up a conversation with him.

I had known Yevgeny Alexandrych Ladygin in St Petersburg. He was a tall, personable man with large bright eyes, an aquiline nose and a resolute expression of the face. All who knew him, and many who did not, spoke of him as a 'practical' man. He expressed himself without grandiloquence, but powerfully; while listening to others, he used to clench his jaws in impatience and let his cheek twitch; he was self-assured in his speeches and he would walk about the streets at a brisk pace without moving either his arms or his head, darting his eyes rapidly from side to side. Seeing him, more than one passer-by no doubt exclaimed despite himself: 'Phew, there's a man for you, by God! Where's that fellow off to?' But Yevgeny Alexandrych was simply on his way to dinner.

Rising from the table, he used to button his coat right up to the neck with such chill and concentrated resoluteness that he might have been setting off at that very moment to fight a duel, having just put his signature to his will. And yet, despite this, there was not a trace of boastfulness to be discerned in him: he was a stubborn man, one-sided and insistent in his opinions, but no fool, not malicious, looking everyone straight in the eye and fond of justice ... True, he would have found it much pleasanter to punish oppressors than alleviate the lot of the oppressed, but there can be no accounting for people's tastes. He did four years or so of service in a guards regiment, and the remainder of his life was fearfully busy – with what? you may ask ... With nothing save various futile matters, which he always set about in a fever of activity and with systematic stubbornness. He was a type of Russian pedant – Russian, take note, not Little Russian. There is an enormous difference between the two, to which attention should be paid more than ever now that, since Gogol's time,[1] these two related, but opposed, nationalities have often been confused.

'Are you going to spend a long time in the country?' I asked Ladygin.

'I don't know – perhaps it'll be a long time,' he answered me with concentrated energy and glanced away indifferently, like a man of strong character who has taken an irrevocable decision but is ready, notwithstanding, to take account of that fact.

'You must have a host of plans in mind?' I remarked.

'Plans? It depends what you call plans. You don't think, do you,' he added with a grin, 'that I belong to the school of young landowners who find difficulty in telling the difference between oats and buck-wheat and dream of English winnowing machines, threshing machines, rotation of crops, sugar-beet factories and brick huts with little gardens facing on to the street? I can assure you that I have nothing in common with those gentlemen. I'm a practical man. But I do have a number of ideas in mind . . . I don't know whether I'll succeed in doing everything I intend doing,' he added with modest arrogance, 'but, in any case, I'll try.'

'It's like this, you see,' he continued, transferring his pipe with dignity from his right hand to his left and grandly emitting smoke through his whiskers, 'it's time for us landowners to start using our brains. It's time to look into the way our peasants live and, having once understood what their needs are, to lead them firmly along a new road towards a chosen aim . . .' He fell into a reverential silence in the presence of his own phrase. 'That's my basic idea for you,' he started up again. 'Russia in general must have – and consequently the way of life of the Russian peasant must have – its own indigenous, characteristic, so to speak, aim for the future. Isn't that true? It must, mustn't it? In that case you must strive to perceive it and then act in accordance with its spirit. It's a difficult task, but nothing is given us for nothing. I will gladly devote myself to it . . . I'm free to do it and I sense in myself a certain firmness of character. I have no pre-conceived system: I'm not a Slavophil and I'm not a devotee of the West . . . I, though I say it again, I am a practical man – and I know . . . I know how to get things done!'

'That's all very fine,' I protested. 'You – if I may be so bold as to say so – you want to be a little Peter the Great of your own village.'

'You're laughing at me!' Yevgeny Alexandrych said animatedly. 'Though,' he added after a short pause, 'what you've said has an element of truth in it.'

'I wish you every possible success,' I remarked.

'Thank you for wishing . . .'

Yevgeny Alexandrych's servant entered the room.

'*Sind die Pferde angespannt, Hans?*' my acquaintance asked.

'*Ja . . . Sie sind*. They're ready, sir,' Hans answered.

Yevgeny Alexandrych hastily finished his tea, rose and drew on his overcoat.

'I don't dare to invite you to stay with me,' he declared. 'It's more than seventy miles to my village. However, if it should occur to you to . . .'

I thanked him. We said goodbye. He drove off.

For the space of a whole year I heard nothing of my St Petersburg friend. Once only, I recall, at a dinner given by the Marshal of Nobility a certain eloquent landowner, a retired chief of the fire brigade called Sheptunovich, referred in my presence (between swigs of madeira) to Yevgeny Alexandrych as a member of the nobility given to daydreaming and a man readily carried away by his own ideas. The majority of the guests at once expressed agreement with the fire-brigade chief, but one of them, a stout man with a purplish face and unusually wide teeth, who vaguely reminded one of some sort of healthy root vegetable, added for his own part that he, Ladygin, had something wrong with him up there (indicating his temples) – and gave regretful shakes of his own remarkable head. Apart from this instance, no one even so much as uttered Yevgeny Alexandrych's name in my presence. But on one occasion, in the autumn, it happened to me, while travelling from marsh to marsh, to land up a long way from home. A fearful thunderstorm caught me out on the open road. Happily, a village could be seen not far off. With difficulty we reached the outskirts of the village. My driver turned towards the gates of the nearest hut and shouted for the hut's owner. The man, an upstanding peasant of about forty, let us in. His hut was not remarkable for its neatness, but it was warm inside and not smoky. In the entrance-way a woman was frantically chopping up cabbage.

I seated myself on a bench and asked for a jug of milk and some bread. The woman set off to get the milk.

'Who is your master?' I asked the peasant.

'Ladygin, Yevgeny Alexandrych.'

'Ladygin? Are we already in Kursk Province here?'

'Kursk, of course. From Khudyshkin it's all Kursk.'

The woman entered with a jug, produced a wooden spoon that was new and had a strong smell of lamp-oil attaching to it, and pronounced:

'Eat, my dear sir, to your heart's content,' and went out, clattering in her bast shoes. The peasant was on the point of going out behind her, but I stopped him. Little by little we started talking. Peasants for the most part are not too willing to chat with their lords and masters, particularly when things are not right with them; but I have noticed that some peasants, when things are going really badly, speak out unusually calmly and coldly to every passing 'master' on the subject that is close to their heart, just as if they were talking about someone else's problem – save that they may occasionally shrug a shoulder or suddenly drop their eyes. From the second word the peasant uttered I guessed that Yevgeny Alexandrych's wretched peasants made a poor living.

'So you're not satisfied with your master?' I asked.

'We're not satisfied,' the peasant answered resolutely.

'How so? Does he oppress you, is that it?'

'Fagged us right out, worked us to the bone, that's what he's done.'

'How's he done it?'

'This is how. The Lord knows what sort of a master he is! Not even the old men in the village can remember such a master. It isn't that he's ruined the peasants; he's even reduced the quit-rent of those who pay it. But things don't go no better, God forbid. He came to us last autumn, at the Feast of the Saviour – arrived at night, he did. The next morning, just as soon as the sun'd started to show, he'd jumped out of bed and – dressed, he had, real lively – and he came running from house to house. He's a one for dashing here and there; dreadful fluttery he is, like he's got a fever shaking him. And so he went from house to house. "Fellow," he says, "all your family is here!" An' he stands there in the very middle of the hut, not shifting at all and holding a little book in his hands, and looks all round him, he does, like a hawk. Fine eyes he's got, bright ones. An' he asks the man o' the house: "What's your name? How old are you?" Well, the peasant answers, of course, and he notes it down in his book. "And what's your wife's name? Children's names? How many horses have you? Sheep? Pigs?

Sucking-pigs? Chickens? Geese? Carts? Ploughs and harrows? Are the oats in? The rye? How much flour? Give me some of your *kvas* to try! Show me your horse-collars! Have you got boots? How many jugs? Basins? Spoons? How many sheepskin coats? How many shirts?" By God, yes, he even asked about shirts! An' he notes everything down, just like he was making an investigation. "What d'you trade in?" he asks. "D'you go into town? Often? Precisely how many times each month? Are you fond of drinking? D'you beat your wife? D'you also beat your children? What's your heart set on?" Yes, twice, by God, he asked that,' the peasant added, in response to my involuntary smile.

'And he went round all the yards, all the huts, he did. He quite wore out Tit, the elder, and Tit even fell on to his knees in front of him and said: "Good master, have mercy on me! If I've done something wrong in your eyes, then I'd rather you ordered me to be flogged!" The next day, again before it was light, he got up and ordered all the peasants there are here to come to an assembly. So we all came. It was in the yard of his house. He came out on to the porch, greeted us and started talking. Talk, he did, talk and talk. The strange thing was we didn't understand what he was saying though he seemed to be talking Russian. "Everything," he said, "is wrong, you're doing everything the wrong way. I'm going to lead," he said, "in a different way, though I don't want at all to have to force you. But," he said, "you're my peasants. You fulfil all your obligations," he added. "If you fulfil them, fine; if you don't, I shan't leave a stone unturned." But God knows what he wanted done!

'"Well," he said, "now you've understood me. Go back to your homes. My way's going to start from tomorrow." So we went home. We walked back to the village. We looked at each other and looked at each other – and wandered back to our huts.'

NOTES

Apart from the two fragments in the Appendix, the source for these translations is I. S. Turgenev, *Polnoe sobranie sochinenii i pisem*. izd. Akad. nauk (M.-L., 1963), Vol. IV. The ensuing notes are taken largely from this source. Also consulted for this translation has been the second edition of the *Polnoe sobranie sochinenii (v tridtsati tomakh)*, izd. 'Nauka' (M., 1979). The fragments in the Appendix are taken from *Literaturnoe nasledstvo: iz parizhskogo arkhiva I. S. Turgeneva*, izd. 'Nauka' (M., 1964), Kn. I, pp. 26–33.

KHOR AND KALINYCH

1. *Zhizdra*: a region of Kaluga Province (in pre-Revolutionary Russia), in which Turgenev owned seven villages containing a peasant population of more than 450 'souls'.
2. corvée: unpaid labour which serfs were obligated to perform for their masters.
3. *Akim Nakhimov*: (1783–1815), a second-rate satirist, versifier and prose-writer.
4. Pinna: a sentimental romance by M. A. Markel (1810–76), first published in 1843.
5. kvas: a kind of cider made from rye-bread.

RASPBERRY WATER

1. *Raspberry Water*: The name of the spring remains the same to this day: *Malinovaya voda*, Raspberry Water. It flows into the river Ista in the Arsenyev region of Tula *oblast*.
2. *Saints Cosmas and Damian*: patron saints of medicine, martyred under Diocletian in AD 303.

MY NEIGHBOUR RADILOV

1. *Victory, thy trumpets sound!*: a polonaise for orchestra and choir by the composer I. A. Kozlovsky (1757–1831) to words by Derzhavin. It acquired the popularity of a national anthem in its time.
2. *as Voltaire . . . hurriedly*: The words are those of Dr Pangloss in Voltaire's *Candide* (1759).
3. *once in Turkey . . . half dead*: Radilov is presumably referring to the Russo-Turkish War of 1828–9 in which the Russian army suffered considerable losses from epidemics.

FARMER OVSYANIKOV

1. *Krylov*: I. A. Krylov (1769–1844), Russia's only renowned writer of fables.
2. *pre-Petrine times*: a reference to Muscovite Russia, before Peter I created St Petersburg at the beginning of the eighteenth century.
3. *homesteading farmers like him*: odnodvorets, the description given to Ovsyanikov, was a designation given to a special group of state peasants who owned a single dwelling on a smallholding. Their social position was midway between the land-owning, serf-owning nobility and the enserfed peasantry.
4. *Orlov-Chesmensky*: Count A. G. Orlov (1737–1807), military leader and statesman, responsible for the defeat of the Turkish fleet in Chesmen Bay (1770), for which he received the honorary title of Chesmensky (of Chesmen).
5. *coachman's caftan*: a reference to the fondness of those who were 'Slavophile' or ultra-patriotic for wearing supposedly national costume. Turgenev always parodied such affectation, even though he was on friendly terms with some of the leading Slavophiles.

LGOV

1. gris de lin *or* bleu d'amour: a colour combination presumably involving shades of pale red and pale blue–grey.

KASYAN FROM THE BEAUTIFUL LANDS

1. *Beautiful Lands*: Krasivaya mech, a tributary of the river Don and regarded as one of the most beautiful regions in European Russia.
2. *Gamayun*: a legendary bird associated with falconry.

BAILIFF

1. The Wandering Jew: *Le Juif errant*, a novel by Eugène Sue, popular in the mid 1840s.
2. Lucia: a reference to the opera of 1835 by Donizetti, in which Pauline Viardot sang the leading role during her first visit to St Petersburg in the 1843–4 season.
3. Les Somnambules: an opera (1831) by Bellini, in which Pauline Viardot also sang.
4. *Carême*: Marie-Antoine Carême (1784–1833), famous French cook, who worked for Talleyrand and later at the Russian and Austrian imperial courts.

THE OFFICE

1. *The Temple of Contentment*: There was a picture of two old men eating a melon at Spasskoye, Turgenev's home.
2. *Oy be offter . . .(and so on)*: The opening lines of a folksong first published in 1798.
3. *two little grey 'uns . . . self*: a reference to grey banknotes of fifty-rouble value and white banknotes of twenty-five-rouble value.

LONER

1. *like a boat on the waves*: a quotation from the poem 'The Three Palms' (1839) by M. Yu. Lermontov (1814–41).

TWO LANDOWNERS

1. *Saadi*: (?1215–91) the Persian poet, referred to by Pushkin in the last stanza of Chapter VIII of *Eugene Onegin*.

LEBEDYAN

1. *Pechora*: major river in the north-east of European Russia which flows over 1,000 miles from the Urals to the Barents Sea.
2. *Pan Tvardovsky*: an opera by A. N. Verstovsky (1828), libretto by M. N. Zagoskin (1789–1852). The reference is probably to separate gypsy episodes from the opera, which enjoyed widespread popularity.
3. *Aeneas . . . past misfortune*: a reference to the opening lines of Virgil's *Aeneid*, Book II.

TATYANA BORISOVNA AND HER NEPHEW

1. *Viotti*: J.-B. Viotti (1753–1824), Italian violinist and composer.
2. *Bettina von Arnim*: (1785–1859), a German authoress, whom Turgenev knew during his student days in Berlin, 1838–40.
3. *in the bosom of rural tranquillity*: a quotation from Pushkin's *Eugene Onegin*, Chapter VIII, Stanza 2.
4. *Giacobo Sannazaros*: (1834) a dramatic fantasy by N. V. Kukolnik (1809–68) which for Turgenev epitomized the worst excesses of Romanticism.
5. *And races fast . . . troika*: a popular song, with words by F. N. Glinka (1786–1880), a cousin of the famous composer. The composer of this song, however, is unknown.
6. *Varlamov . . . more*: A. E. Varlamov (1801–51) was the composer of the second of the songs, to words by F. N. Glinka. The first was composed by N. A. Titov (1800–75) to words by M. A. Ofrosimov (1797–1868).
7. *Be gone, you restless passions*: a song by M. I. Glinka (1803–57) entitled 'Doubt' (1838), to words by N. V. Kukolnik.
8. *Come, come . . . dearest friend*: Although author and composer are unknown, this song was popular from the 1820s onwards.

DEATH

1. *Zusha*: a tributary of the river Oka, situated about three miles from Spasskoye.
2. *Johanna Schopenhauer*: a German novelist and the mother of Arthur Schopenhauer, the philosopher.
3. *had supplanted them but not replaced them*: a paraphrase of a line from Chapter I, Stanza 19 of Pushkin's *Eugene Onegin*.

4. *Koltsov*: A. V. Koltsov (1809–42), a Russian poet, many of whose poems, written in the manner of the folk-song, have been set to music. The lines are from his poem 'The Forest' of 1838.
5. *What if a falcon's . . . denied*: quoted from the third stanza of Koltsov's 'Dream of a Falcon' (1842).

PYOTR PETROVICH KARATAEV

1. *hunting dogs*: the dogs hunted in pairs, linked together by short chains.
2. *Moscow coffee-house*: probably Bazhanov's coffee-house, situated on Resurrection Square, now the Square of the Revolution.
3. *Polezhaev . . . Mochalov*: A. I. Polezhaev (1804–38), poet of civil and political protest (with whom, by implication, Karataev identifies himself) who was persecuted by the Tsarist authorities and forced into the life of an army conscript. P. S. Mochalov (1800–48), famous actor, of serf origin, who achieved his greatest success in playing Hamlet at the height of Romanticism in Russia, during the 1830s.
4. *To die, to sleep*: Hamlet, III.1; other – slightly garbled – quotations are from Hamlet's soliloquies in *Hamlet* I.2 and II.2.

HAMLET OF THE SHCHIGROVSKY DISTRICT

1. *sideburn-ites*: by a decree of April 1837 Tsar Nicholas I forbade the wearing of beards and whiskers by officials in the civil service. The interdiction also extended to students. This explains the reference to 'the distant past', since *Hamlet of the Shchigrovsky District* is known to have been written in 1848, and it also explains the 'ravening hunger' of disapproval with which the dignitary later glances at Prince Kozelsky's beard. It must be assumed that the prince was not in the civil service.
2. *With my fate is no one very much concerned*: from 'Testament' (1840), a poem by M. Yu. Lermontov.
3. Mon verre n'est pas grand, mais je bois dans mon verre: from a dramatic poem, 'Coupe et les livres' (1832), by A. de Musset (1810–57).
4. *encyclopedia of Hegel*: a reference to Hegel's *Enzyklopädie der philosophischen Wissenschaften im Grundrisse* (1817). Turgenev possessed a copy of this work in its third edition (Heidelberg, 1830).
5. *Moscow sages*: a reference to the Slavophiles.
6. Gefährlich ist's den Leu zu wecken: a slightly inaccurate quotation from Schiller's *Das Lied von der Glocke*.
7. *Awaken her not till dawn has broken*: from a lyric by A. A. Fet (1820–92), supposed to have been set to music by A. E. Varlamov.
8. *In one of Voltaire's tragedies*: the reference is possibly to Act II of Voltaire's *Mérope* (1743).

CHERTOPKHANOV AND NEDOPYUSKIN

1. *Orbassan*: a character in Voltaire's tragedy *Tancrède*, translated into Russian in 1816.
2. *Marlinsky*: A. A. Bestuzhev-Marlinsky (1797–1837), popular writer of romantic tales, whose 'Ammalat-Bek' dates from 1832.

THE END OF CHERTOPKHANOV

1. *Time of youth, time so lovely*: a Moscow gypsy song, composed by A. L. Gurilev (1802–56) to words by N. M. Konshin (1793–1859).
2. *Malek Adel*: hero of the novel by the French authoress Sophie Cottin (1770–1807), *Mathilde, ou Mémoires tirés de l'histoire des Croisades* (1805).
3. *Shakespeare*: the reference is presumably to Richard III's cry 'A horse! A horse! My kingdom for a horse!' from *Richard III*, V. 4.

LIVING RELIC

1. *Homeland of longsuffering ... Russia*: from the first stanza of a short poem of 1855 entitled 'These wretched hamlets'. F. Tyutchev (1803–73), a remarkable philosophical and nature poet, was first brought to the notice of a wide reading public through a collection of his lyrics that Turgenev prepared for publication in *The Contemporary* in 1854.

CLATTER OF WHEELS

1. *The robber's axe, despiséd thing*: a line from a poem on the death of Field-Marshal Count Kamensky by V. A. Zhukovsky (1783–1852), leading exponent of Russian Romanticism and well-known for his translations of German and English Romantic poetry.

THE REFORMER AND THE RUSSIAN GERMAN

1. *Since Gogol's time*: a reference presumably to the Little Russian (Ukrainian) extraction of Nikolay Gogol (1809–52), whose first successful work *Evenings on a Farm near Dikanka* (1831) was devoted to stories about life in Little Russia. Gogol's descriptions of life in Little Russia have been compared with – or, more aptly, contrasted with – Turgenev's description of life in the Russian countryside in his *Sketches*.

READ MORE IN PENGUIN

In every corner of the world, on every subject under the sun, Penguin represents quality and variety – the very best in publishing today.

For complete information about books available from Penguin – including Puffins, Penguin Classics and Arkana – and how to order them, write to us at the appropriate address below. Please note that for copyright reasons the selection of books varies from country to country.

In the United Kingdom: Please write to *Dept. EP, Penguin Books Ltd, Bath Road, Harmondsworth, West Drayton, Middlesex UB7 0DA*

In the United States: Please write to *Consumer Services, Penguin Putnam Inc., 405 Murray Hill Parkway, East Rutherford, New Jersey 07073-2136.* VISA and MasterCard holders call 1-800-631-8571 to order Penguin titles

In Canada: Please write to *Penguin Books Canada Ltd, 10 Alcorn Avenue, Suite 300, Toronto, Ontario M4V 3B2*

In Australia: Please write to *Penguin Books Australia Ltd, 487 Maroondah Highway, Ringwood, Victoria 3134*

In New Zealand: Please write to *Penguin Books (NZ) Ltd, Private Bag 102902, North Shore Mail Centre, Auckland 10*

In India: Please write to *Penguin Books India Pvt Ltd, 11 Community Centre, Panchsheel Park, New Delhi 110017*

In the Netherlands: Please write to *Penguin Books Netherlands bv, Postbus 3507, NL-1001 AH Amsterdam*

In Germany: Please write to *Penguin Books Deutschland GmbH, Metzlerstrasse 26, 60594 Frankfurt am Main*

In Spain: Please write to *Penguin Books S. A., Bravo Murillo 19, 1°B, 28015 Madrid*

In Italy: Please write to *Penguin Italia s.r.l., Via Vittorio Emanuele 45/a, 20094 Corsico, Milano*

In France: Please write to *Penguin France, 12, Rue Prosper Ferradou, 31700 Blagnac*

In Japan: Please write to *Penguin Books Japan Ltd, Iidabashi KM-Bldg, 2-23-9 Koraku, Bunkyo-Ku, Tokyo 112-0004*

In South Africa: Please write to *Penguin Books South Africa (Pty) Ltd, P.O. Box 751093, Gardenview, 2047 Johannesburg*